THE AVENGER OF BLOOD

by MIGUEL BATISTA

Translated by DIANE STOCKWELL

© Copyright 2006 Miguel Batista

Note for Librarians: A cataloguing record for this book is available from Library and Archives
Canada at www.collectionscanada.ca/amicus/index-e.html
ISBN 1-4251-0363-4

English translation:	Diane Stockwell
Page design:	Marta Lucia Gomez Z.
	Modesto Cuesta
Graphics and maps:	Jerilee Martinez Anillo
Cover art:	Devonna Nelly
	Domingo Quiñones
Photo:	Yerry Batista
Author's representative:	Elizabeth Martinez

Printed on paper with minimum 30% recycled fibre.
Trafford's print shop runs on "green energy" from solar, wind and other environmentally-friendly
power sources.

TRAFFORD
PUBLISHING™

Offices in Canada, USA, Ireland and UK

Book sales for North America and international:
Trafford Publishing, 6E–2333 Government St.,
Victoria, BC V8T 4P4 CANADA
phone 250 383 6864 (toll-free 1 888 232 4444)
fax 250 383 6804; email to orders@trafford.com
Book sales in Europe:
Trafford Publishing (UK) Limited, 9 Park End Street, 2nd Floor
Oxford, UK OX1 1HH UNITED KINGDOM
phone +44 (0)1865 722 113 (local rate 0845 230 9601)
facsimile +44 (0)1865 722 868; info.uk@trafford.com
Order online at:
trafford.com/06-2120

10 9 8 7 6 5 4 3 2 1

There are many things that cannot be proven in the eyes of the law; they are the law in the eyes of humanity...

Dedicated to the greatest defense attorney for all mankind: Jesus of Nazareth

Acknowledgements

A heartfelt thanks to everyone who helped make this book possible, in one way or another: Detective James Coking and Monique Rodriquez, for providing information on the city of Phoenix; Judge Edgar Campoi; Judge Gregory Martin; the journalist Jude la Cava; Dr. Rosa Llopis; Dr. Heather "The Doc" Smith; Dr. Philip Keen, Head of the Maricopa County Medical Examiners Office; Sergeant Steve Lowe, Arizona Department of Corrections; Martin J. Arburua, Attorney; Paul V. Godfrey, Attorney; Pastor Sergio Sabino, Cecilia Maria Rodriguez; Warden Bennie Rollins, Director of the Arizona State Prison in Florence, and to the administrative staff. And to Eli, thank you for teaching me that truly having faith means believing more than you should, trying even harder than some thought possible. It's healing with a word, giving life with a look. Without you, The Avenger of Blood would never have come to us...

PHOENIX, ARIZONA

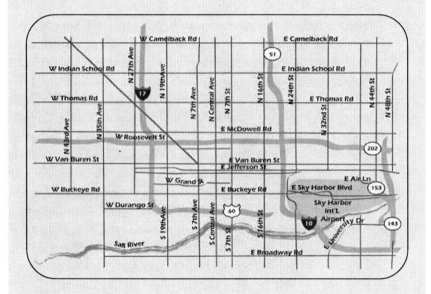

1

MARICOPA COUNTY SUPERIOR COURT
201 WEST JEFFERSON STREET
PHOENIX, ARIZONA

Caught up in the restless crowd that had gathered outside the courthouse, the young reporter tried to find a place to stand that would best highlight the stately building's impressive facade.

"Ready, Molly?" the cameraman called out, while he held the camera steady, standing beside the network news station's white van.

"Yes," she replied, as she snapped shut her compact and put it back in her purse; her touched-up makeup made her pretty blue eyes look even more beautiful.

"We're on the air in twenty seconds..."

"Make sure you get the crowd and their signs in the shot," she instructed as she tucked a windswept lock of hair behind her ear.

"Ten seconds!" the cameraman shouted, putting on his headset and preparing for the shoot.

"Sound check... testing one, two... one, two..." she repeated, speaking directly into the microphone she held. Then she seemed to talk to herself quietly between clenched teeth as she paced back and forth in a tight circle, rehearsing what she would say at the beginning of the segment.

The cameraman pointed at her with his right hand as he balanced the camera on his left shoulder:

"On the air in three, two, one!"

The young reporter took a few deep breaths, trying to calm her nerves. The red light on the camera lit up: they were on the air.

"Molly, can you hear us?" she heard the voice from the station resonate in her earpiece. "What can you tell us about what's happened?"

With all the confidence and poise she could muster, she began her report:

"Right now we are waiting for Judge Edgar Fieldmore to arrive here at the courthouse; as he will preside over the Thomas Santiago case. Thomas Santiago is a fourteen year old boy accused of having committed a series of bizarre murders all over the state of Arizona over the past two-and-a-half years. The crimes include the murder of former city councilman Dan Howard, of Phoenix, and the shocking murder of Father Fabian Campbell in his church in Gilbert, this past January the 31st. The most recent killing took place just two weeks ago, in the city of Glendale, at the gas station on the corner of Cactus Street and 59th Avenue..."

In the studio, the news anchorwoman clasped her hands together on the desk and leaned forward as she asked:

"Who are the lawyers that will be handling this case?"

"The state will be represented by Morgan Stanley, one of the most respected District Attorneys in the country, and the defense will be handled by Samuel Escobar, considered one of the strongest defense attorneys in the area. A long, difficult battle is widely anticipated between these two pillars of the criminal justice system."

The reporter nodded toward the crowd over her left shoulder and continued:

"As you can see, many people from across the state, especially Native Americans from the reservations of Ship Rock and Kayenta, have gathered here today to find out what direction this story will go in, a story that over the past thirty-six months has held the entire state in a grip of terror."

Back in the studio, the anchor leaned back in her seat, crossed her arms and commented,

"I think Arizona hasn't seen a case that has captivated the community to this extent since Jonathan Doody and The Temple Murders back in 1991, right?"

Molly blinked rapidly, trying to recall the few details that she knew about that malevolent mass murder.

On August 1991, nine monks were killed in a Buddhist temple on the west side of Phoenix. The case was regarded as the most shocking murder ever committed in Arizona. Jonathan Doody, a young boy who was only seventeen years old at the time, and a few of his friends killed the Buddhist Monks in military execution style, under circumstances which were still very murky to most people.

To this day, that had been the harshest blow ever dealt to the Buddhist religion in all of its two thousand, five hundred year history.

"I think you're right: this has got to be only the second time where the entire state has become so intently focused on one trial. Many people who came here today are carrying posters and signs demanding justice and that Thomas Santiago receive the death penalty," Molly observed.

The commentator in the studio hesitated for a moment, looking pensive before going on,

"It's understood that, according to the laws of the state of Arizona, he could be tried as an adult, but could he actually receive the death penalty? And if not, can you tell us what outcome we can most likely expect?"

Molly gripped her microphone tightly in both hands, gazing closely into the camera as she replied,

"As you said, he will in fact be tried as an adult, and if he is found guilty, he could receive the maximum prison sentence possible, but not the death penalty. We have to remember that the new law 13-703 F-9 prohibits minors, fifteen years of age and under, from facing execution. What we could see here is a sentence of two hundred to three hundred and fifty years in prison, as in Jonathan Doody's case, if he is found guilty of all the charges against him."

Then the news anchor glanced down at the sheets of paper on her desk, and with a look of surprise asked,

"The question on everyone's minds, Molly, is how could he possibly have escaped from the Glendale police station?"

"That is certainly the most puzzling aspect of this case" the reporter agreed. "No one has been able to explain it; the very same night that he was arrested, he managed to escape from custody and commit another heinous murder. According to our sources, the police officers who arrested him are being questioned, but as of this moment no one has the faintest idea of how it happened."

Molly read from a sheet of paper she was handed: "The body of another victim he is accused of killing was found last night, near the Ship Rock reservation. According to the police report, the name of the victim is Andrew Seahawk, twenty-four years of age, and a member of a gang on the reservation known as The Headhunters."

She continued, "According to reports, Thomas Santiago has been transferred to the Arizona State Hospital, in Maricopa County, on Twenty-Fourth Street and Van Buren. The decision was made by the governor in response to several protests that broke out across the city in response to news reports that Thomas Santiago had escaped, and news of the latest homicide. We also have been informed that a special area in the hospital has been outfitted with sophisticated security equipment to prevent him from escaping again. The suspect is currently in FBI custody. Several marines have been assigned to stand guard at the psychiatric hospital."

"Is it true that the boy's grandmother and his defense attorney are not satisfied with how the authorities have been treating Thomas?" the anchor asked, folding her hands on the desk.

"Yes, that is true. They have both alleged that the excessive security measures constitute inhumane treatment, rumors have begun circulating that they have resorted to chaining the boy to the wall."

The reporter looked at the paper she held again and added "We just found out that Thomas's older brother, Juan Manuel, has been granted a leave of absence from the Arc of Our Lord Seminary in Los Angeles, where he is studying to be a priest. Juan Manuel arrived here yesterday to be with his younger brother during this time of devastating family crisis..."

Just then, the crowd surged towards the entrance of the courthouse; all the reporters and cameramen tried to shove their way through the crowd to get as close as possible, to catch the first glimpse of what many experts agreed would surely be the most important news story of the year.

"It looks like the judge has just entered the courthouse," the reporter said, as the cameraman followed the action with his lens and they both scrambled through the multitude, trying to make their way inside.

"We'll give you an update with all the latest developments at the top of every hour..."

"From the studio, the anchorwoman" concluded "That was Molly Fernandez, reporting from the Maricopa County Superior Court, with the most recent on the case of the "Devil Child", Thomas Santiago. We will give you all the latest information as this story develops, here on RNN, where news always comes first. We will be right back after this quick commercial break."

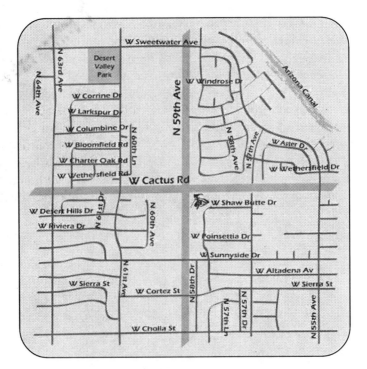

2

Gas Station
5881 West Cactus Road,
Glendale, Arizona
(Two weeks earlier)

The police tried to control the huge crowd of curious onlookers milling around the gas station at the intersection of 59th Avenue and Cactus Road. A line of yellow police tape ringed the establishment to prevent anyone from interfering with the investigation.

A warm breeze was blowing from the northeast: it was a typical night in Arizona, like so many others. The dry heat in the air and rising up from the pavement in the early evening served to confirm the state climate's well-known reputation.

A navy-blue Crown Victoria with a police light on top pulled up and parked right in front of the gas station's glass door.

A man who seemed to be about thirty, with dark hair and light brown eyes, dressed in a suit and tie, got out of the car. In the door of the station, a uniformed police officer handed him a pair of rubber gloves, and the detective put them on as he slowly trained his expert gaze around the whole place. Another detective, who had been examining a man's body on the floor, lying in a pool of blood, stood and approached him.

The detective gestured silently to one police officer who was busily taking photos of the crime scene, and wordlessly signaled to him to take some pictures of the victim from the doorway's vantage point. Finally he asked,

"What have we got here?"

He quickly got his answer:

"Patrick McKinney, forty-five years old, approximate time of death 10:43 P. M." the other detective responded as he wiped the sweat from his forehead with his wrist, carefully avoiding any contact of the rubber gloves against his skin.

"According to the forensic examiner, the cause of death was strangulation and a series of powerful blows to the back of the skull" he continued, handing the detective the victim's identification while leaning over as he carefully examined the body.

"Any witnesses?"

"The woman who works here," answered another police officer who had just arrived, reading from what he had written down in his small notebook.

"Very good. Do we have a description of the killer this time?"

The other officers gave the detective a strange look without replying.

"What's going on?" the detective demanded.

Sighing, the officer lowered his notebook, looked the detective in the eye and said, "You'll have to read for yourself the statement the witness gave..."

The detective looked around for the witness, but there was no sign of her.

"The paramedics took her to the hospital," the officer said, anticipating the detective's question.

"But, was she hurt?"

"No, sir, she's in a state of shock..."

The detective looked around again and noticed something written on the wall in what appeared to be blood. He turned to the detective by his side and asked, "What do you think?"

He had just finished examining the body. He removed his rubber gloves, and letting out a deep breath, he looked down again at the victim lying rigid on the floor in his own blood, and murmured, "the only thing I know for sure is that McKoskie is going to be furious if we don't have a suspect soon."

S 1st Avenue

S 3rd Avenue

W. Jefferson St.

3

MARICOPA COUNTY SUPERIOR COURT
201 WEST JEFFERSON STREET
PHOENIX, ARIZONA
(PRESENT TIME)

The Superior Court is comprised of the East, West, and Central buildings. Their combined 395,000 square feet take up about six city blocks, and require twenty-five thousand fluorescent lights to illuminate all the facilities. This is where the most critical trials in the state of Arizona take place; there are seventy-two courtrooms presided over by eighty-seven judges, including thirty-two judges assigned to juvenile cases.

A persistent murmuring rose from the crowded courtroom. Everyone anxiously awaited the arrival of the judge, and the defendant, who was being held in a small cell directly behind the courtroom under heavy guard.

The District Attorney representing the State, Morgan Stanley, was respectfully known to his colleagues as "the Bulldog" because of his cruel style of cross-examination. Seated next to him at the prosecution's table was his assistant, Nicole Bach, an attractive young blonde with brown eyes. Her beauty and natural elegance had drawn stares from everyone in the courtroom when she walked in.

On the other side of the room the defense attorney, Samuel Escobar, spoke in a low voice to his assistants, two women and a man, as they discussed their strategy. Escobar, a proud graduate of Stanford University Law School, was widely considered the best defense lawyer in the whole country. His university thesis on human rights had made a tremendous impact. It was on exhibit at the Stanford University library, next to a copy of the Constitution.

Suddenly, the door at the far left corner of the room opened with a high-pitched creak that seemed to cast a magic spell, and in an instant a hushed silence fell over the courtroom. Two uniformed police officers stepped through the doorway and took their places on either side. The atmosphere crackled with tension, as if the whole world had come to a stop, suspended in time. The faint clinking sound of chains rattling could be heard, growing gradually louder.

An adolescent boy with a dark complexion, black round eyes, prominent cheekbones and shoulder-length, straight black hair, shuffled into the courtroom. The bright orange prison jumpsuit he wore obscured his lanky frame. He was tall for his age, at fourteen he was already six feet. The chains at his ankles made it almost impossible for him to walk.

Two more police officers followed closely behind him, so there would be no doubt in anyone's mind as to the extreme level of tightened security around him.

The handcuffs around his wrists were connected by a chain running down to the restraints around his ankles, and looped through a thin chain circumventing his waist. He walked like a penguin, waddling from side to side, as he slowly approached the defense's table. When he sat down next to his lawyer, Escobar put a reassuring hand on the boy's shoulder and whispered, "Don't worry. Everything's going to be okay."

The boy's grandmother, Mariela, sat directly behind him in the first row. As she watched him enter the courtroom, her eyes filled with tears and she couldn't stifle a sob. Thomas's older brother, Juan Manuel, put his arms around her and hugged her tightly, as they both wordlessly contemplated the horrifying scene that was unfolding before them.

The looming silence seemed to grow heavier. All eyes were on the accused, like a swarm of enraged wasps. Just then, a man's booming voice rang out, harshly breaking the silence as if shattering a sheet of glass with a rock: "All rise for the Honorable Judge Edgar Fieldmore!"

A man who seemed to be around sixty years old with a stern demeanor, wearing a black robe entered the courtroom; his serious expression, slightly balding head of gray hair and small stature all lent him a certain air of respectability.

Judge Edgar Fieldmore was, without doubt, the most well-known and most feared judge in the whole state of Arizona. In spite of his unimposing physical stature, his incisive mind and broad legal knowledge had brought him to lead the Judges Committee, and put him at the forefront of legal reformers. After the Jonathan Doody case, he and his colleagues had exerted a great deal of pressure on the state's Congress to successfully convince them to pass the new law 13-703 F-9, which stipulated that anyone over eight years of age could be tried as an adult, and in the state of Arizona, anyone fifteen years of age and older could receive the death penalty.

Seated at his podium, the judge put on his reading glasses and opened the folder he had carried in with him. Then he looked up and briefly studied the defendant, his lawyer, and finally the district attorney before saying, "Good morning, Counsels."

Then he trained his gaze on the boy again, who rose to his feet along with Escobar.

"Thomas Santiago, the state of Arizona accuses you of eighteen counts of murder in the first degree. How do you plea?" the judge pronounced gravely.

Thomas looked at the judge, terrified. Escobar answered for him in an assured, calm tone, in spite of the light sweat that had broken out across his forehead.

"Your honor, the defense needs time to have a complete psychiatric evaluation performed on the defendant before responding to any charges against him."

The District Attorney quickly broke in, "Your Honor, the state has sufficient evidence demonstrating that the accused is in control of all his mental faculties and is fully capable of understanding the charges that have been brought against him."

The judge thought for a moment before responding, "I am in agreement with the District Attorney, Mr. Escobar; motion denied."

Escobar picked a photograph up from the table, quickly walked up to the bench and showed it to the judge as he explained, "Your Honor, the State has based its case around this photograph, taken from a video surveillance camera. It is impossible to accurately discern the killer's face. And the image has been manipulated by the police department, to the point that the Defense considers it simply impossible to believe that the person in this picture is the defendant."

"Your Honor," the DA countered, jumping to his feet, "please allow me to remind the court that the victim's blood was found on Thomas Santiago's pajamas the morning after the video was taken, and that fact is sufficient evidence to proceed with the charges," he shot Escobar a defiant look.

The judge addressed Thomas directly, "Mr. Santiago, do you understand the seriousness of the charges pressed against you?"

Escobar put his hand lightly against the boy's chest, signaling that he would answer for him, "Your Honor, I have instructed my client to refrain from answering this question, since his response could be incriminating."

The judge crossed his arms and leaned back in his chair. He asked deliberately, "The accused will invoke the Fifth Amendment when asked if he understands the charges or not?"

"Yes, Your Honor..."

A wave of commotion rippled through the courtroom in response to this unexpected announcement.

Two loud strokes from the judge's mallet against the podium and his demand that the spectators come to order or they would be ejected quickly returned the courtroom to an expectant silence.

"Until a thorough psychiatric evaluation has been conducted, my client will plead the Fifth Amendment in response to all questions. It is clear that, aside from the fact that my client is a minor, his uncertain mental state qualifies him for protection under the law," his lawyer reiterated after the room had gone quiet.

He approached the bench again, handing the judge a form, and giving a copy to the DA before continuing, "There have been several legal precedents in similar cases, as you can see on that summary..."

The judge carefully studied the sheet of paper for a moment. He addressed the defense attorney sternly: "Counselor, are you trying to suggest that your client is innocent by reason of temporary insanity?"

"Your honor, the defense will refrain from making any declaration until the accused has undergone a complete psychiatric evaluation."

A new wave of murmuring broke out; rising in volume until the judge angrily ordered everyone to be silent.

The DA stood, straightened his tie quickly and said tersely, "Your Honor, in response to the defense's request, the State asks that the accused be examined by a doctor appointed by the State."

"Granted," the Judge replied immediately.

Thomas turned to look at his grandmother and brother. They both saw terror in his eyes and tried to console him, but his grandmother couldn't stop her tears from flowing again. Juan Manuel bit his lip and held back a sob, determined not to let his little brother see him cry.

"Your Honor, the defense would like to make a request for bail. The defendant has no criminal records and the state should not consider him a flight risk," Escobar argued, closing a folder on the table and standing.

"Request denied," the judge said flatly, removing his glasses. "Because of the serious nature of the charges, I am compelled to deny that any bail be set, even though the defense has every right to request it. Under the circumstances, I do not believe that it would be a wise thing to do."

He put on his glasses again and looked at the defendant as he continued, "The trial is scheduled to begin on the nineteenth, next month; any motions should be received by Monday at ten A.M. at the latest."

The judge looked at both attorneys and asked, "Anything else?"

"Yes, Your Honor," Escobar stood, "the Defense requests a change of venue."

The judge crossed his arms skeptically and frowned. He looked over his glasses at the attorney and asked, "And what is this request based on, Mr. Escobar?"

"Your Honor, the Defense wishes to ensure that the members of the jury will be chosen very carefully, since my client is an American citizen, but he was born in another country..."

"Mr. Escobar, Arizona does not have a reputation as being a particularly racist state," the judge shot back, leaning over the podium. He made no attempt to hide his anger. An assistant for the defense passed Escobar a piece of paper, which he hastily brought up to the bench:

"Your Honor, it is my obligation to point out to the court that in 1985, in two similar cases in the state of Mississippi vs. Palacios and Hernandez, the fact that a change of venue had not been considered was the main basis for overturning the verdicts on appeals to the Supreme Court."

The judge gave the defense lawyer a stony look and said, "I will wait for your formal, written request to arrive in my office no later than Monday at 10 A.M., understood?" Then he addressed Thomas:

"Mr. Santiago, I order you to remain under state custody until your trial... This court will reconvene on the nineteenth of next month at eleven o'clock in the morning, at which time opening arguments for the defense and prosecution will be heard. Court is adjourned."

The judge picked up the folder in front of him and stood to leave.

"All rise!" the court officer announced.

The police officers who had accompanied Thomas into the courtroom approached him; Escobar put a hand on his shoulder again and said, "Everything's going to be alright; your grandmother, your brother and I will see you very soon."

The chilling sound of clanking chains could be clearly heard as the boy left with the officers, and grew faint as he disappeared through the door and shuffled down the hall. Everyone in the courtroom watched him go with a mix of fear and bewilderment, and their quiet murmurings grew louder.

The reporters and cameramen rushed to get out of there as fast as possible to file their reports to the stations. Then everyone else filed out of the room, talking excitedly in rising voices.

"Let's go, in an hour they'll take him to the state hospital and we can talk to him there," Escobar said to Thomas's grandmother and brother, as he quickly gathered up his papers scattered on the table.

"They had him chained like an animal!" his grandmother wailed, as she dabbed at the tears that still flowed copiously from her eyes.

"Samuel, you have to do something; Thomas is just a kid, the way they're treating him-it's so cruel," Juan Manuel added.

Samuel studied them and felt his chest tighten; he understood their pain, but he knew that he had to think like a lawyer first and foremost.

His mind suddenly flooded with memories, images of the most treasured moments from his youth popped up one after the other. He remembered how he used to play hide-and-seek with Thomas and Juan Manuel, when he was home on breaks from the university. He remembered how Thomas, just barely a toddler, had run chasing after him around the house, his little face lit up with a beautiful smile.

"I know, but right now there's nothing we can do; we just have to wait," he answered, turning to pick up his briefcase.

"Wait? What for? Didn't you see how they had him chained? That is no way to treat any human being, much less a fourteen-year-old boy!" Mariela shouted, on the verge of hysterics.

Samuel looked into her eyes, bloodshot from crying and exhaustion. He put his hand softly on her shoulder as he said, "Nana, we have to accept that this is necessary; Thomas has escaped from jail and no one knows how. The state will go to great lengths to make sure that it doesn't happen again..."

Samuel leaned down toward her, wiping at her tears with his handkerchief, and sensing the depth of her sorrow, he said, "Alright, I'll talk with the judge and see what can be done. Okay?"

She nodded almost imperceptibly and stood to go.

4

MARICOPA COUNTY PSYCHIATRIC HOSPITAL
2500 EAST VAN BUREN STREET
PHOENIX, ARIZONA

In 1887, the Arizona State Hospital opened its doors as the "Insane Asylum of Arizona." It is located on the corner of 25th and Van Buren streets.

Its grounds cover ninety-three acres, twenty-three of which are reserved for patients with the severest forms of mental disorders, adolescents as well as adults who are ordered by the court to remain under ongoing treatment and observation.

When Samuel arrived, he found a small crowd of people assembled in front of the facility, carrying hand-made signs and shouting, "We want justice! Death to the killer!"

As Samuel pulled into the driveway, one of the soldiers standing guard at the entrance ordered him to stop his car. Samuel lowered his window.

"I'm sorry but we're not letting anyone in right now," the soldier said as he tightened his grip on his M-16 rifle.

"We have an order from a judge," Samuel explained, offering him the piece of paper.

The soldier examined the paper very carefully. The look he gave Samuel plainly revealed his distrust, and even more, his disrespect.

"Go ahead," he sneered, as he alerted his superiors of the visitors' arrival by radio.

A Marine soldier and a doctor were already waiting for them at the entrance to the building. As they went inside and walked down a short hallway, Mariela's eyes opened wide in astonishment: there were no windows along the twenty-foot hall, but there were nine security cameras bolted to the ceiling on either side. The white walls made the light emanating from the fixtures in the ceiling seem even brighter.

The doctor led the way, walking briskly, his long white coat undulating with each step. The Marine holding a machine gun brought up the rear, making sure that no one made any unexpected detours.

They came to a spiral staircase that descended down to a basement level. The typical hospital odor of chloroform and antiseptic changed as they went down; it was as if a palpable feeling of suffering had permeated the very air, making it hard to breathe. An eerie silence reinforced the impression that there was absolutely nothing good about the place.

"I didn't know that the hospital had this kind of facility in it," Samuel commented.

The doctor responded in a voice that seemed unexpectedly deep, "Almost all state-run institutions of this size have some areas that the public is not made aware of..."

At the bottom of the stairs, they found a huge steel door with a small window at eye-level. The doctor knocked on the door and the small window opened. A set of blue eyes appeared and studied the doctor; then the heavy door slowly swung open; the groaning hinges made a piercing, squealing sound that echoed ominously.

The cell was an oversized metal box with reinforced bulletproof glass on one side. There were security cameras hanging from each corner.

Thomas was sitting on a little bed that was barely big enough for his long, gangly frame. Bracelets around his wrists were attached to long metal chains bolted into the wall, and he still had shackles fastened around his ankles.

A bright lamp hanging from the ceiling illuminated every square inch of the cell. The thick bulletproof glass prevented him from having any kind of human contact.

When he saw his grandmother who had raised him, Thomas jumped up and shuffled over to the glass. With all his strength, struggling against the chains that held him, he managed to put his palms flat against the glass as he yelled, "Mom!"

Mariela tried to get as close as possible, even as one of the guards held her back. She placed her hand against his on the other side of the glass.

"My baby!" she said through tears.

"Open this cell!" Samuel ordered the soldier who stood next to him. But they were under strict orders not to let anyone inside with the prisoner.

"Damn it! We're his family, and we have every right. Besides, we have a court order!" Juan Manuel shouted angrily.

Samuel tried to maintain his composure. He said quietly to the soldier,

"Come on, Sergeant, have a heart, you can see how this poor woman is suffering..."

The Sergeant turned to look at Mariela through his clear blue eyes and considered her for a moment, absently stroking his thick black mustache. Crying, Mariela desperately touched her hands against the glass, trying in vain to make contact with Thomas.

The Sergeant observed the soldier restraining Mariela, and with a curt gesture he signaled to let her go. The soldier freed her and took some keys from his pocket; he put them in the lock, turned it to the right and heard the lock release. He pulled the cell door toward him to open it.

Mariela practically stepped right over the soldier as she bounded into the cell and threw her arms around Thomas. They both cried openly, as Juan Manuel stepped inside, his eyes shining with fury.

Juan Manuel had always been extremely patient, even as a young child. His sweet smile and gentle personality were clearly evident ever since kindergarten. His athletic physique and charming charisma had made him very popular with the girls, but his great love for all humankind had compelled him to enter the world of religion.

Samuel was the last to enter the cell; he leaned against the steel wall as he took a deep breath, and shaking his head said to himself, "My God, this is cruel!"

Then he addressed the doctor and the sergeant who had followed him inside, "Can you leave us alone for a minute, please? There are four surveillance cameras in here and two out there, you can watch us through the glass... I just want a word alone with my client and his family..."

The sergeant turned to the soldier and gestured for him to leave the cell with a quick nod. The soldier hesitated, his stunned expression clearly indicating that he didn't agree with the order at all.

"I can't believe you're going to leave them alone," he said quietly to his superior as they both stepped out of the cell. "You know that we're under strict orders not to leave him alone for a second."

Out in the hall, the sergeant put his hands in his pockets and studied Thomas intently through the thick glass; he had a glint in his eye as he said to the soldier, "Can you believe that little piece of shit escaped from the police station, under watch..."

The soldier took a step closer to the glass and replied, "I don't know, Benny, but when I look at the kid... there's something really creepy about him, you know? We saw that video, of when he killed that guy...I don't get how a skinny little bastard like that, he can't be more than, what, a hundred forty pounds, could pick up a man of two hundred fifty pounds with just one hand and pound him against the wall over and over, like it was nothing..."

Not taking his eyes off of Thomas, the Sergeant quickly answered. "Did you see that weird light that was glowing around him? And did you hear that crazy language he was speaking when he was killing that guy?"

They both stared at Thomas as he rested his head on his grandmother's shoulder while she rubbed his back tenderly.

"You know what, Benny? I've seen a lot of stuff in all my years in the Marines that scared the shit out of me, but that damn kid gives me the creeps..."

The Sergeant took his hands out of his pockets and crossed his arms over his chest, standing in a typical military "at ease" stance. He took a deep breath and after a brief pause added, "But this isn't some rinky-dink little police station like Glendale, now he's under military guard. I'd like to see him try to get outta here..."

5

Mariela sat down on the right side of the little bed, while Juan Manuel, wearing his long, black seminary vestment, sat down on the floor. As Samuel opened up his briefcase, he asked Thomas if he wouldn't mind answering a few questions.

Nestled on the bed next to his grandmother with his head resting on her lap, he said okay.

Samuel took out a pad of paper and a pen: as he had learned in law school, it never hurts to have a written record of what a witness says, no matter how good you think your memory is.

Then he took a small digital recorder out of the briefcase and put it on the bed. "I'd like to record our conversation, if you don't mind."

Thomas nodded, and Samuel asked him to try and tell him everything he remembered, down to the most inconsequential detail.

Thomas sat up on the bed and then got to his feet. His mind started to churn. He blinked rapidly as he recalled the disturbing events of that terrible morning.

"That day, I woke up covered in blood, just like so many times before. Nana called the doctor, and he told her about a specialist I should see... Two days later the police came to my school and they arrested me right in the middle of basketball practice..."

"When did you start waking up covered in blood?"

Thomas looked at Mariela, and she quickly answered, "The first time was two years ago on September 30th."

"But, how many times has this happened?"

"Totally covered in a lot of blood, I think just five times..." she added.

Samuel couldn't dissimulate his surprise, "What do you mean by totally?"

Thomas took a step back and sat down next to his grandmother again. "A lot of times, there was just a little blood on my hands..."

"The first time it happened, I thought he must have had a nose bleed," Mariela remembered, as she ran a hand softly over the boy's hair and gave him a reassuring smile. "When it happened again, I decided to take him to the doctor, but he said he couldn't find any cause for the blood since there was no sign of any internal bleeding, or any external injury, and the physical exam, they did, showed that he was in perfect health. They recommended some other tests, but everything just indicated that he was fine."

"They never did a blood analysis to prove that the blood was actually Thomas's own?"

"The blood test concluded that it was type A-positive, just like his, so that's why we didn't think anything really bad. Then the doctor said I should take him to see a psychiatrist."

Puzzled, Samuel frowned. Something just didn't add up. "Can you give me that doctor's name?"

"His name is Josh Raymond," Mariela answered, rubbing Thomas back soothingly just as she had done when he was a little boy.

Samuel continued questioning, "What happened next?"

"The next time that happened, the psychiatrist recommended more tests, and that was when we figured out something really weird was going on, since the lab found that the blood on Thomas's pajamas wasn't his own. The psychiatrist had promised me that they would call me so we could talk about what the next step should be... but two days later, the police came and arrested him..."

"The last time that he woke up with blood on him, was that when he escaped from the jail?" he pressed.

Mariela nodded.

"How did you escape, Thomas?"

The boy tried to stand up again, but he wobbled for a moment because of the shackles at his feet. Mariela reached up and put a hand on his arm to steady him.

"All I remember is that I fell asleep at around eleven that night, and when I woke up later I was at home, in my own bed, all covered in blood again..."

Samuel turned and looked out through the glass: the two soldiers were watching everything. Sighing heavily, he paced around the cell and said, "Thomas, the State has requested that a psychiatrist examine you, it's a legal requirement and they are within their rights to solicit it. The exam will determine whether you are mentally capable of understanding the charges against you and if you were consciously aware of what you were doing when all of this happened..."

Alarmed, Thomas said, "But I already told them I don't remember anything! I don't know why they're accusing me of something like that!"

Perplexed, Samuel looked at Mariela and Juan Manuel. "He doesn't know about the video?"

Mariela stood and took a step toward Samuel, quietly replying, "No, we thought it would be best for him if he didn't see it..."

Thomas looked at each of them, with mounting confusion and frustration. He asked, "What are you talking about? What video?"

No one said anything, but Thomas waited expectantly for some kind of response. Finally, Samuel explained that the police suspected him because at the gas station on 59th and Cactus Street someone was murdered and the security camera videotaped the killer; and even though they couldn't be completely sure, the person in the video bore a striking resemblance to him... and the blood of the victim was on his pajamas the next day after the murder. Since he had escaped from the jail, and another victim had been found the following morning after that, things looked even worse for him.

Thomas felt as though he had been punched in the stomach. His face grew pale, and he was speechless. He tried to take a few steps around the cell, as he scratched his head, his chains clinking. Crying, Mariela fell to her knees in front of him. She grabbed his hands and wailed,

"Thomas, listen to me, you didn't know what you were doing. It wasn't your fault!"

Juan Manuel tried to shed some light on the situation, "Thomas, when the judge asked you if you were going to plead 'innocent' by reason of temporary insanity, what he was really asking was if you suffered from some kind of mental illness, and because of that you would be innocent... But that doesn't mean that they don't think that you were the person who committed the murders. Do you understand?"

The boy's eyes welled with tears, until one slowly ran down his cheek. Mariela stood and gently wiped it away, but he stood completely still, looking down at Juan Manuel.

"All this time," Thomas said, "I thought that this all must be a big mistake, and they would figure that out any minute, and they would let me go home..."

He bowed his head and stared down at the handcuffs and chains that bound him. He clenched his fists tightly and when he looked up again, everyone was unsettled by his expression, for they saw something in his eyes they had never seen there before. It was a bright, seething anger that seemed to transform him into a completely different person. Thomas fists were still clenched as he looked at Samuel straight in the eye and said,

"What can you do?"

Stunned for a brief moment, Samuel composed himself and answered, "First I have to go through all the evidence against you and closely examine all the possibilities, we only have a month before the trial begins. There are several witnesses that I want to interview, since there are several troubling inconsistencies in the police report... So, if there's anything else you remember, anything at all, no matter how unimportant it may seem, I'll need you to tell me, alright?"

Thomas nodded.

"This is going to be a long, very difficult process," Samuel added as he put the recorder and notebook back in his briefcase, "so I ask you all to please be patient..." he hugged Thomas, and stepped out of the cell.

Juan Manuel stood and ruffled his little brother's hair as he always did, and asked, "Are you going to be okay?"

"Uh-huh," Thomas murmured without much conviction.

Mariela touched Thomas cheek and said tearfully, "Don't worry, sweetheart, I would never, ever let anyone hurt you..."

6

Santiago Family Residence
6610 North 61ST Avenue
Glendale, Arizona

At their front doorstep, Samuel shook Juan Manuel's hand firmly, and then he gave Mariela a hug and said, "Don't worry, Nana, I promise I'll do absolutely everything in my power."

"I know you will," she answered, but the tears started to spill down her cheeks again. She brusquely wiped them away. Just thinking about where she had just left her grandson broke her heart.

Mariela closed her eyes and remembered the promise she had made her daughter just before she had passed away at the hospital in San Juan, Puerto Rico. Ana

Isabel had been admitted because of complications with her pregnancy. She was only in her seventh month but she was already dilating, she had lost a great deal of blood and the doctors had decided to perform an emergency cesarean to save the baby. Mariela had held her daughter's hand as they wheeled her gurney down to the operating room:

"Promise me, mom, that you'll take care of Juan Manuel and the baby if anything happens to me," Ana Isabel had pleaded.

"Of course, sweetheart, your children are like my own; but you'll see, you're going to be just fine." Mariela had stroked her daughter's hair and Ana Isabel had kissed her mother's hand and released it as she disappeared behind the glass doors.

Mariela sighed deeply, trying to calm down. Samuel offered her his handkerchief to dry her tears.

She thanked him, and added, "You know full well that Thomas couldn't hurt a fly, you've known him ever since he was a little baby."

"Yes, Nana, I know. I can't believe this is happening either."

"There is one thing I know for sure: it was not my Thomas who killed all those people."

Samuel took her hands in his and looked intently into her eyes: "Nana, you've seen the video from the gas station. Then there's the blood they found on his pajamas...it all suggests that it was Thomas."

Mariela violently jerked her hands out of his, and waving her index finger at him she scolded, "I don't care what that video shows, I know that... that thing is not my grandson! I raised my children right, the same way I raised you and a real mother knows her boys better than anyone..."

Juan Manuel hugged her; she sobbed as she buried her face against his shoulder. He embraced her tenderly as he silently gestured to Samuel that he should leave.

7

M. J. A. Attorneys at Law
Bank of America Tower
201 East Washington Street
Phoenix, Arizona

The Bank of America Tower is one of the tallest buildings in downtown Phoenix. It is part of the Collier Center. Of its eighteen stories, ten are occupied by the bank, while the rest are taken up by private offices.

"Good morning, Samuel."

"Good morning, Celia." He had barely replied when Celia immediately started summarizing what had transpired so far that day. The DA's office had called to coordinate dates for jury selection. As she handed him some files he needed to look over, Celia kept talking hurriedly, her rushed monologue providing a perfect rhythmic counterpoint to Samuel's hurried footsteps as he rushed to his office.

"And your mother called!" she yelled as he closed the glass door behind him.

The large, gleaming mahogany table was at the center of the room; there were two women and three men already seated around it, awaiting Samuel's arrival: from the head of the table, the men were on the right, and the women were on the left. Samuel was convinced that having all the women on his left somehow helped him to think more clearly.

A small-scale reproduction of Michelangelo's "The David" statue was displayed in a corner atop a Romanesque column. Sunlight softly lit up the room through the large windows, illuminating a bronze statue of Temis, the goddess of Justice. She held her sword high in the air, while, blindfolded, she balanced a scale from her other hand. With the sunlight directly landing on her, she looked dazzling.

In typical fashion, Samuel got right to the point. He wanted to know what they had found out so far. One of the women responded quickly,

"The Court has already sent over a list for jury selection."

One of the men, Marcos, cut in to explain that the police had sent over a copy of the complete video from the gas station security camera. He took it out of his briefcase and stood to put it into the VCR.

"Samuel, I've already looked at the final police report and it looks like there was only one witness, Amanda Leroy, the woman who worked at the gas station, she quit her job the next day," the other woman elaborated. "I called the police to see if they had a number where I could reach her, but all I got was an address..."

"Find out if she still lives there, and try to set up a time when we could talk to her."

The video was ready, and everyone turned to look at the flat plasma television screen on the wall. At the beginning, a woman was clearly visible behind the counter; five seconds later a man came in and appeared to be buying a pack of cigarettes. Suddenly, a brilliant white light seemed to pass right through the glass door. The video showed how the woman fell backwards, while the man, stunned, just stared at that unearthly light, as it moved closer and closer to him. The light suddenly materialized into the shape of a person, with an intense glow around him.

"What the hell is that?!" Marcos blurted out, his eyes wide with terror.

Then, the glowing figure grabbed the shorter man by the neck and lifted him up to his own eye level.

The expressions of everyone around the table revealed growing amazement and horror at what they were seeing.

Without even realizing it, Samuel stood up, his gaze fixed on the screen. His heart started to pound, and his hands trembled slightly.

In the video, the man's feet were dangling about three feet above the floor. The glowing being held him in the air as it strangled him, although the man fought futilely to free himself. The woman behind the counter stared numbly at the unbelievable scene unfolding in front of her. Suddenly, the bright figure started to speak in a strange dialect, as he furiously crushed the man's skull against the wall over and over.

Blood gushed from the victim's head and spattered all around, as his feet kicked frantically in the air, as if he were trying to detect something to stand on.

But the glowing figure didn't stop bashing the man's head against the wall until his body had gone completely limp. There was no doubt that the man was dead.

The killer slowly relaxed his grip and let the body fall to the ground. He looked down at his victim, his shoulders rising and falling heavily with each breath. Then he looked up at the large splotch of his victim's blood on the wall, and tracing a finger through it, he wrote ﲒﱪﺱ .

Then he turned and looked directly to the eyes of the woman hidden behind the counter, who appeared to be frozen with fear. The camera focused on the killer's face: flames seemed to dance in his eyes, and maybe because of that, the features of his face seemed to glow. But his face was clearly human. The figure turned and, like a ray of light, seemed to penetrate right through the glass door. He was gone. The screen went black: the video was over.

Everyone was silent for several minutes, shocked and horrified by what they had just seen. Finally, Samuel straightened his tie and slowly sat down at the head of the table. No one knew what to say.

At Samuel's signal, Marcos turned off the television.

Samuel seemed nervous. He lifted his hands off the table and, to his surprise; he noticed that his palm imprints were clearly visible on the table's smooth surface because he had been sweating so profusely. His head was swimming. The odd shine in his eyes confirmed that what he had just seen had rocked him to his very core.

The room seemed to grow increasingly tense. Samuel was still quiet. It was the first time his staff had ever seen him truly speechless. Finally he managed to stutter,

"That's... that's all, for now... Please... please leave me alone."

Everyone gathered their things and slowly left his office.

Samuel stood and put his hands in his pockets. He stepped over to the window and looked out over the city streets below, until, far off in the distance, he could make out the cross atop St. Mary's Church.

"God help us!" he whispered.

8

Maricopa County Psychiatric Hospital
2500 East Van Buren Street
Phoenix, Arizona

Suddenly awakened by the abrupt sound of the key turning in the lock to his cell, Thomas peeked out from the threadbare blanket that he used to shield his eyes from the bright light that was always on, day and night. He blinked sleepily and said,

"Samuel?"

He knew that it had to be really early. He sat up in bed and rubbed his eyes, trying to wake up.

"Hi, Thomas, I just came by to see if you had remembered anything..."

There was something strange in his voice. Samuel looked at Thomas closely, suspiciously, as if he were studying his features and gestures. An unnatural smile played across his lips. There was definitely something wrong...

"Are you sure that's the only reason you're here?" Thomas asked seriously, as Samuel sat down on the bed next too him.

"Why don't you just ask me what you really want to know? You wanna know if I killed all those people, right?"

Samuel tried to stay quiet. His heart was racing, and he still seemed to study every movement that Thomas made, no matter how slight. It was obvious Samuel was terrified, no matter how cool and calm he tried to look.

Thomas stood and shuffled over to the other side of the cell:

"Ever since I've been locked up in this place, I've been trying to answer that question myself..."

Samuel discreetly eyed the handcuffs around the boy's wrists and the manacles at his feet, and the long chains that ran from each attached to a bolt in the wall, as if to reassure he was securely restrained. Thomas could see the fear in Samuel's eyes. Sadly, he asked,

"I don't know what kind of monster they think I am? There have been protesters outside in front of the hospital, day and night, demanding that I get executed," the boy's eyes were red from crying. "All my friends are ashamed of me! And look at you, Samuel; you're so scared, like you were standing in the same room with the devil himself!"

Samuel let out a long breath and looked down at the floor, embarrassed.

"I'm so sorry, Thomas, there are so many things running through my mind right now, I don't know what to think... I can't believe this is happening to you; I've known you ever since you were a little baby and I can't understand how you've gotten mixed up in something like this..."

They were both quiet, and the creepy hushed silence of the hospital settled over them. Thomas looked out through the thick glass at the guards, who didn't take their eyes off him. He went back to sit on the bed, and placing his hands on his knees, he asked,

"What's going to happen?"

Samuel sighed heavily. He stood and paced back and forth before answering. "I don't know. Like I said, I have to study all the evidence very carefully and see what can be done, but I can promise you one thing, I will not let them convict you for a crime that you did not commit."

Thomas stood and took a step towards Samuel, and holding out his hand to him, he waited for his reaction. Samuel firmly shook his hand, and pulled the boy to him to embrace him.

Thomas' eyes filled with tears again, and with a lump rising in his throat, his head resting on Samuel's shoulder, he said,

"I'm scared, I'm so scared!"

Then he pulled back and with a faint smile he added, "My family and I are sure that nobody could defend me any better than you."

"I appreciate the vote of confidence, but I have to warn you this is a very, very difficult case..."

Thomas smiled a little more brightly, "That doesn't scare me, we've heard all about the impossible cases you've won in your career..."

Samuel let out a loud laugh, "But that's not enough! When it comes to the law, you have to have evidence."

Thomas' expression grew serious, and raising his eyebrows, he asked, "Counselor, are you suggesting to your own client that he shouldn't have faith in your defense strategy?"

Samuel straightened his shoulders and replied playfully, "No, your honor, the defense drops the charges."

9

M. J. A. ATTORNEYS AT LAW
BANK OF AMERICA TOWER
201 EAST WASHINGTON STREET
PHOENIX, ARIZONA

Samuel asked to speak to Dr. Rusvel, and while he was put on hold, he looked up to see who had just knocked on his open door. A young Hispanic woman was standing politely just outside his office,

"Mr. Escobar, everyone's waiting for you in the conference room. They all cancelled their other appointments for the day, as you requested."

Samuel covered the phone with his hand and said, "Thanks, Celia, tell them that I'm on the phone and I'll be there in just a minute."

Celia quickly let him know that one of his clients, Mrs. Medrano had called to see if there had been any news...

Samuel told her to call her back and say that he would be calling her soon himself. Then he put the receiver to his ear again and said, "Rusvel?"

They chatted politely for a minute, exchanging news about their families. Then Samuel explained the reason for his call: the Thomas Santiago case.

"The Devil Boy, of course," the doctor replied.

"Where did you get that from?" Samuel asked, uncomfortable with his friend's response, although he knew full well that all the news media referred to the case with that sensationalistic phrase, the same phrase that was being loudly broadcast on news reports all across the whole country.

"Are you familiar with the case?" he asked the doctor.

Rusvel only knew what had been reported in the press. But he did know the boy's defense lawyer very well.

"He's the youngest grandson of the woman who took care of me when I was little, she was my nanny," Samuel explained.

"You're kidding!" Rusvel exclaimed, incredulous. He considered this for a minute and remembered having heard his old friend mentioning a Nana Mariela many times, the woman who had been like a second mother to him.

"I need your help with this. There is a video taken from a security camera at a gas station that allegedly shows Thomas killing someone. I'd like you to take a look at it, study it very carefully, and tell me if you notice anything strange about it."

They agreed that a copy would be sent over to the doctor's office as soon as possible, and before hanging up, Rusvel asked,

"But, how could he have escaped from the Glendale police station?"

"It's something very bizarre, not even Thomas himself can explain it."

"But, that's just not possible..."

"I'd rather not discuss it over the phone. You'll understand after you see the video. You can't even imagine the kind of strict security he's under now. Remember the movie "The Silence of the Lambs," how they had Hannibal Lecter locked up? Well, this is even worse..."

"It's as bad as that?"

Samuel ran a hand through his hair and switched the phone to his other ear before replying,

"I didn't know such extreme facilities even existed anywhere in Arizona before this...

A lot of government institutions have special secret units that the public doesn't even know about, apparently..."

"I can imagine..."

"I don't know, Rusvel, this is honestly the strangest case I've ever seen..."

"Why?"

"I just have a feeling that there is more to this than meets the eye. It seems like something out of a horror movie."

"I don't really know what you're talking about, but I'm sure you have good reason to feel that way."

"You'll understand as soon as you watch the video..."

10

MARICOPA COUNTY PSYCHIATRIC HOSPITAL
2500 EAST VAN BUREN STREET
PHOENIX, ARIZONA

"Hey, champ! How are you holding up?" Juan Manuel said, his arms raised in the air as the guard finished patting him down.

"Juan!" Thomas shouted happily, even as he worried that the visit would be all too short.

Juan Manuel sat down on a chair next to Thomas and asked him how he was doing, although he knew the answer. He explained that Mariela was working, so she hadn't been able to come visit.

"Poor Mom, she works so hard, sometimes I wonder where she finds the energy to even get out of bed every day. Hey, how are Samuel's parents? He was here yesterday, and I forgot to ask about them..."

"They're fine, they said "hello" to you and they asked me to tell you that you are in their prayers, every night."

Thomas put his hand on Juan Manuel's shoulder, but as the chains attached to his wrist brushed against his brother's back, Juan Manuel visibly flinched. Embarrassed, Thomas lowered his hand again.

"Sorry, I didn't mean to..."

Juan Manuel cut him off and held his brother's face in both hands:

"Thomas, you're my brother, don't you ever forget that!"

Then he pulled his little brother to him and hugged him as tight as he could.

"I love you, no matter what you're going through right now or how it's going to turn out. I will always love you, and I could never, ever be ashamed of you..."

He felt the tears running down his cheeks. Putting his hands firmly on Thomas' shoulders, he said, "Did you hear what I said?"

He brushed his tears away as his younger brother smiled weakly.

"You don't know how bad I feel about you leaving the seminary because of me."

"Don't worry about it, the bishop gave me permission to take off all the time I needed."

"But that's going to delay your ordination."

"That doesn't matter, you're my brother, and I'm not going to abandon you at a time like this."

Thomas turned and walked over to the bed. He tried to untangle the chains that ran from the cuffs at his wrists to the bolt in the wall. Juan Manuel saw how hard it was for his brother to simply try and move around, and a wave of sadness washed over him. His voice was full of anguish when he said, "You don't know how painful it is for me to see you like this."

"Don't worry, I'm practically an expert. At first it really bothered me, but I've learned how to manage."

Thomas saw the pity in his brother's eyes and tried to smile. "Who could have ever thought that after we last saw each other at the seminary, the next time we'd meet would be here."

Juan Manuel smiled back and shook his head, "Even if the Pope himself had told me, I wouldn't have believed it... This is like a nightmare I can't wake up from, no matter how hard I try."

Thomas tried to lighten the situation and changed the subject, "So how are your friends doing, the ones I met at the seminary when I visited?"

"You remember Kevin, the Australian? He said to say 'hello,' and Alberto had to go back to his country, since his father passed away..."

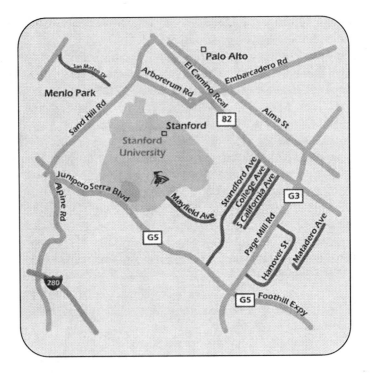

11

STANFORD UNIVERSITY LAW SCHOOL
CROWN QUADRANGLE
559 NATHAN ABBOTT WAY
STANFORD, CALIFORNIA

The professor picked up a piece of chalk and wrote the word "evidence" on the blackboard. He turned to address his students, "The most important part is the collection of evidence, no matter what the..."

He was interrupted by a light knock at the door. A man smartly dressed in a dark pinstriped suit stepped into the classroom. "Excuse me, professor," he said.

"Samuel!" the professor cried, and rushed over to give the man a hearty embrace. He turned to his students and said, "Ladies and gentlemen, you have here before you a true star of the criminal litigation world, Samuel Escobar..."

Samuel waved to the students and raised an eyebrow at his old teacher. "Don't exaggerate, I learned everything I know from you, the best law professor in the whole country."

The teacher announced to the students, "That will be all for today. Read Chapter 16 for next Tuesday." The students gathered their things and started to file out, while the professor put an arm around Samuel's shoulder and they slowly walked out of the classroom and headed towards his office.

A very pretty young woman came up to them in the hall, and after offering Samuel a flirtatious smile, she said, "Professor, I'm really sorry, but I haven't been able to finish the report on the new law 1509 yet..."

The professor tried to look stern, but her wide-eyed angelic expression won him over. "Alright, Tania, but if you don't hand it in by tomorrow, you are going to be in serious trouble."

Both of the men watched as she turned and walked away. "She's very pretty," Samuel said with a smile. "How do you deal with it?"

"Oh, you have no idea what I have to put up with here," the professor joked.

Samuel grew serious. "Oliver, I've come to see you today because I need your help."

"You need my help? But you know the law just as well as I do, if not better." With a hand on Samuel's shoulder, they continued walking down the hallway, and toward a large window that looked out on to the law school's quadrangle. It was inconceivable to the professor that such a brilliant talent as Samuel would actually require his assistance. Oliver opened a door at the end of the hall and held it open for Samuel.

"Is this about the Devil Boy case?"

"Oh come on, Oliver, not you with the name, too," Samuel sighed, closing the office door after them.

"I've been following the news reports, and it seems as if there's not much that can be done..."

Samuel sat on the edge of the desk, while Oliver picked a book up off a table, closing it and carefully returning it to its place in a large antique wooden bookshelf, the finish dark and partly worn away from age.

Oliver was not a typical law professor. His passionate teaching style and tireless pursuit of justice had earned him quite a reputation among his colleagues and the students. His powerful, lean physique, with broad shoulders and well-toned arms, and his penetrating blue eyes seemed to sharply contrast with his gentle demeanor. His Romanesque nose and well-trimmed goatee only enhanced his distinctive, careful appearance.

"What do you think?" Oliver asked.

"I don't know. I've talked with him several times, I'm examining the evidence, and everything seems to lead to a dead-end, but I just have this feeling that there's something here that isn't right."

"Like what?" Oliver asked, stroking his beard.

Samuel crossed his arms, as he tended to do reflexively when he was thinking hard, and lowered his gaze, "Do you remember when you told us in class that if our instinct as lawyers was telling us that something was wrong, even if on the surface everything seemed to be in order, then we would have to go through everything again?"

Oliver nodded.

Samuel walked over to the window, and watched the students walking in all directions across the courtyard, carrying their books and talking with one another.

"I have a feeling that he's innocent..."

"Are you sure? Everything seems to indicate that he is guilty..."

Samuel talked about Thomas, explaining his personal connection to his family, and looked Oliver straight in the eye and said, "I've known this boy ever since he was a baby. His grandmother was my nanny, since I was ten years old. He could be many things, but he could never, ever be a serial killer... that's why I'd like you to study this case with me."

Oliver sat behind his desk and leaned back in his chair, "I'd be happy to help you however I can, but you know that I'm never going to enter a courtroom again. You know the law as well as I do, or better..."

"But you're the best cross-examiner that the courts in this country have ever seen; you know how to trick anybody into confessing. You know when a person is lying, as soon as they open their mouth..."

Samuel took a step towards Oliver, and looking at him intently, he went on, "I know the law, but I don't have enough experience to manage a case like this."

"What's so difficult about this case that makes you think you can't handle it on your own?"

"You'd have to see for yourself: the state's charges are largely based on a video taken from a surveillance camera, where you can see the killer murdering one of the victims. It looks a little like Thomas, but it's impossible to tell for sure..."

"Why?"

"It's hard to explain. Come to the office on Monday and watch the video; if after seeing it you still think there's nothing you can do, then I'll leave you alone..."

Oliver was quiet. Samuel asked, "How long has it been?"

Surprised by the question, the professor's eyes turned dark, as if a thick cloud of sadness had suddenly descended over him. In a deeper tone, he answered, "Eighteen years, three months, and nine days..."

"And from what I can tell, you still haven't gotten over it," Samuel murmured, sitting down in a chair in front of the desk. He asked, "Remember the time you told me that one of the greatest things about being a lawyer was that it gave you the chance, not always a clear chance, but nevertheless, a chance to play a part in another human being's destiny?" Samuel took a deep breath and looked at Oliver directly before continuing, "Well, now you have a chance to play a part in another person's destiny; help me to save this boy."

Oliver was still quiet, his eyes locked with Samuel's, while his mind revisited the shadows of his past.

"You can't change what happened back then; your retirement from the courts will not give those two boys their lives back..." Samuel stood and put a hand on Oliver's shoulder.

Oliver's expression was contorted with pain and anger.

"I'm still not ready," he responded, looking away, avoiding Samuel's eyes.

"Oliver, it's been almost twenty years!"

"I know, but I am never going to set foot in a courtroom ever again..."

N 25th Street

E Van Buren St

12

MARICOPA COUNTY PSYCHIATRIC HOSPITAL
2500 EAST VAN BUREN STREET
PHOENIX, ARIZONA

The Marine officers arrived precisely at noon, as usual, for the changing of the guard and to deliver the prisoner his meal. After exchanging military salutes, one of the guards opened the cell door and ordered Thomas to stand against the wall with his hands in plain view behind his head. The other soldier had his M-16 rifle aimed directly at Thomas, until the first soldier had placed the tray on the floor next to the prisoner and stepped backwards out of the cell to take up his position just outside of it. Thomas obeyed the orders without objection, since he had grown accustomed to the routine.

A half hour later, one of the guards stepped away, and Thomas looked closely at the soldier that had stayed to watch him. He noticed that he wore a small cross on a chain around his neck.

"Are you a Christian?" Thomas asked politely, trying to start a conversation.

The soldier was silent, not taking his eyes off the prisoner for even a second. Sitting on his bed, Thomas persisted, "Where are you from? I know you're Latin American, I've seen how you look at me, and how you look at my family when they come to visit...It's bad manners to ignore somebody when they ask you a question..." he added, after another minute of silence. He stood and took a step towards the guard, but in reaction he quickly raised his rifle and pointed it at the boy, shouting, "Don't come any closer!"

Thomas held his hands out so the soldier could see them. "I'm chained to the wall, my feet are shackled, and I'm behind bars and a thick sheet of bullet-proof glass... How could I possibly hurt you?"

The soldier studied him doubtfully; his erratic breathing revealed how terrified he was. Thomas didn't move, continuing to hold his hands out. "I just want to talk to someone, I'm so tired of the silence all the time," he sighed, slowly lowering his hands.

He has a point, the soldier reasoned, as he lowered his rifle and replied, "My name is Casey Mendez, I'm Mexican-American." Thomas asked where he had been born and where his parents were from, and told him that he was Puerto Rican. He sat down on the floor, in front of the soldier.

Casey nodded, still watching his every move very closely... And just then, the other guard returned. Seeing them talking, he shouted, "Mendez! What the hell are you doing? You know we're not allowed to talk to the prisoner."

Casey quickly stood at attention and answered, "I'm sorry, sir."

Thomas turned and sat down on his bed. He looked out at Casey with a deeply pained expression, and mumbled "I'm sorry..."

13

ESCOBAR FAMILY RESIDENCE
6889 EAST TURQUOISE AVENUE
SCOTTSDALE, ARIZONA

Catherine came into the study, cradling their sleeping baby daughter in her arms. She was about to go to bed herself, after putting the baby down in her crib.

Samuel put down the papers he was holding, and stood to kiss both of them. He would finish up looking over the papers and follow her to bed.

"Is this about Mariela's boy?" she asked, gently stroking the baby's hair.

Samuel nodded. To Catherine, it seemed completely beyond comprehension how that boy could have gotten involved in such a horrible situation. "What do you think's going to happen to him?" she asked.

"I don't know, baby... it's a very complicated case, and there's so much evidence against him..."

"I hope you can help him."

"I hope so too, but I can't promise anything. I'll do everything I can for him..."

Catherine shifted the baby's weight on her shoulder and rubbed her back. She kissed her husband and left him alone to finish his work.

Samuel sat down at his desk again and continued reading the Mesa city police report on one of the victims.

Several lines that had been highlighted in yellow grabbed his attention. One of them was particularly disquieting: "A strange smell of flowers was detected at the crime scene, although no sign of flowers was found anywhere.

He picked up another report, and on the second page, he found underlined in red pen a paragraph that also mentioned a persistent smell of flowers at the scene.

"What the hell is that?" he asked himself. He looked through three other police reports, and found that each one of them made mention of the same phenomenon.

Samuel hunched over his desk with his forehead in his hands and studied the photo of the victim that had been included as part of the report. He turned the page and read the medical examiner's report, and highlighted: "The cause of death was suffocation due to strangulation of the windpipe. The imprint of a single hand was visible on her neck. There were no indications of sexual abuse, no broken bones, or any other wounds on the body."

Samuel turned back a few pages to reread the police report. A photograph of that indecipherable word, written on the wall using the victim's own blood, was included also. Samuel thought aloud, "What in God's name does this mean?"

Leafing through yet another report, Samuel let out a long sigh. He quickly discovered that something there did not add up: the victim had been murdered at five-thirty in the morning on Wednesday the 27th, in the reservation of Kayenta.

He suddenly remembered a conversation he had had with one of the teachers at Thomas' school. He rifled through the pile of files on his desk to find a copy of the school's attendance record, which he had requested to show what a responsible student Thomas had been over the last five years. He opened a manila envelope from the school and read, "Thomas has not missed a single day of school over the past three years." He looked up: the clock on the wall indicated it was almost one in the morning. It didn't matter. He picked up the phone and called Marcos. He listened as the phone rang once, twice, three times...

"Hello..."

"Marcos, it's Samuel."

"What's up? How come you're calling so late?"

"I need you to go to Thomas' school tomorrow and get a list of all the school bus drivers... I think I've found something that could help us."

"What is it?" Marcos asked, sounding wide awake now.

"I'll tell you all about it tomorrow, set up a staff meeting in the conference room first thing in the morning. We have a lot of work to do..."

14

M. J. A. ATTORNEYS AT LAW
BANK OF AMERICA TOWER
201 EAST WASHINGTON STREET
PHOENIX, ARIZONA

"Good morning, sir," the lovely young woman greeted him, folding the paper she had been reading.

"Good morning, Celia," Samuel gathered the telephone messages that were on top of her desk. He read them quickly as he listened to her.

"Remember that you have a doctor's appointment today, at ten o'clock." She handed him a newspaper and a hot mug of coffee.

The coffee mug had a very special significance to him, it had been a gift from his grandmother. An old Indian saying was inscribed on it, along with a picture of a man pointing his spear towards the sky as he watched an eagle fly high above near a mountain's peak. The saying read, "Take time to listen to the wind and look to the sky, for in them you will see what will come to pass on Earth."

When he asked Celia to change the doctor's appointment to Thursday, the young woman's eyes filled with concern. This would be the third time that she would reschedule it. "If you keep this up, no one in the whole county will give you an appointment, and besides you shouldn't take risks with your health."

Samuel accepted the rebuke, taking a sip of coffee as he walked away. Raising his mug, he added, "I promise I'll really go on Thursday, alright?"

"If you keep this up I'm going to tell Catherine..."

"Ouch! That's playing dirty," Samuel frowned.

He went into the conference room, sat down at the head of the table and asked everyone in turn if they had any good news to report. Smiling mischievously at her boss, Marta said, "Tell me how much you love me?"

Samuel took a sip of coffee and replied with mock sincerity, "More than you can possibly imagine..."

"Remember that you asked me to find out what had happened to that woman Leroy? I found out she moved and has a new job. But, guess what? I talked with her sister, who also worked at the gas station, and still works there. She told me about this guy, Maglio Contie..."

"Who's 'Maglio Contie'?"

"He's a transient, he lives in the streets, a young guy, and he would come by the gas station at night. He helped Ms. Leroy take out the trash and sweep the floor, in exchange for cigarettes. According to the sister, ever since that night, he stopped coming around, and she said she saw him the other day by chance, but he wouldn't talk to her, as soon as he saw her he took off. The sister believes that he was there that night, and that he saw everything."

"How did you find out all of this?"

The young woman smiled modestly while turning to look at her finger nails. "It's amazing what a hundred dollars cash and a good conversation about makeup will get you these days..."

Samuel chuckled as he took his favorite pen out of his inside jacket pocket. It was aqua blue, with his initials engraved in gold. His father had given it to him as a high school graduation gift. Now it was his habit to absently turn it over and over with his fingers when he was lost in intense concentration.

"We only have three weeks, and we don't have a single witness who can help our case."

Everyone around the table stared expectantly at their boss, since they well knew his talent for coming up with the perfect solution under high-pressure situations. Then Samuel suddenly stood and started barking out orders: he instructed Sabrina to investigate each member of the jury: he wanted to know everything about them, if they had kids, what church they attended, what they had for dinner on Sundays, what did they talk about with their neighbors. He made sure she understood her assignment completely.

Then he turned to Marcos and reiterated how important it was for him to obtain information on the school bus drivers from Thomas' route.

"There's something here that doesn't make sense... Last night, I was studying several of the police reports," Samuel opened his briefcase and took a folder from it, placing it on the conference table. "In this report, it says that, according to the medical examiner, Billy Black Horse was killed at approximately 5:30 in the morning of Wednesday, October 27th in Kayenta, the Indian reservation..."

"What's so strange about that?" Marta asked.

"Well, according to the school's administration office, Thomas didn't miss a single day of school, and, according to his grandmother, the school bus picked him up that day at seven-thirty in the morning, like it did every day, just fifty yards away from their house..." With a puzzled expression, he added, "How could it have been possible for Thomas to kill that man in Kayenta, and then return to Phoenix, in less than two hours? Kayenta is more than five hours away from here..."

Everyone exchanged nervous looks.

"I want you all to study these police reports with me, and see if there's anything else we can find."

Samuel pressed the intercom on the phone, and asked Celia to gather all the information she could about mental disturbances, split personality disorders, paranoia, catatonia, and cases of patients who exhibited supernatural powers...

"As soon as possible, please," he urged.

Then Samuel gathered the papers that were strewn over the table. He noticed that everyone was looking at him. "What are you waiting for? Get to work, that's what I'm paying you for," he joked.

As Sabrina stood to go, she smiled ironically and said, "I'm going to need a little time on this."

Samuel patted her shoulder and replied with a broad smile, "That's why I pay you the big bucks: for you to make miracles."

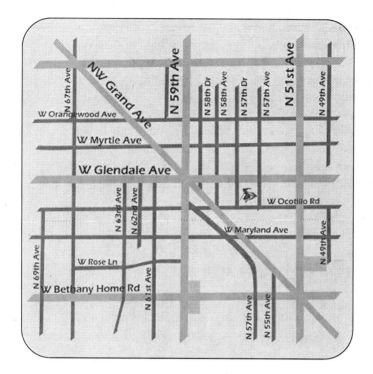

15

GLENDALE POLICE HEADQUARTERS
6835 NORTH 57TH AVENUE
GLENDALE, ARIZONA

Samuel pulled the glass door open and went into the building. Behind the counter, a uniformed officer was talking to another officer who had brought in a young man in handcuffs. He ordered the suspect to take a seat next to a desk, and he sat down and started typing his report into the computer.

"Ten-four," said another officer rushing down the hallway, speaking into his walkie-talkie. The constant commotion and nervous energy was just another typical day at the Glendale police station.

Samuel walked up to the counter and asked the dark-skinned, corpulent desk officer where he could find a Detective McKoskie.

"He's in Homicide, at the end of the hall, taking a left, it's the second door on the right," the officer replied, barely looking up, pointing down the hall.

Samuel walked down to the Homicide Department, knocked politely at the door and stepped inside. An attractive young woman in uniform, wearing sunglasses, her blonde hair tied back in a ponytail, was just finishing putting on a bullet-proof vest.

"Can I help you?" she said with a smile.

"I'm looking for McKoskie."

She yelled out his name, asked Samuel to wait there, and then walked quickly out into the hallway.

Samuel looked around, and a wall filled with photos caught his eye. He stepped over to get a closer look, and he was drawn to a picture of a young woman, covered in blood. Her body was lying on the ground face-up, she had a wound at her throat, and another at her chest...

"Horrific," Samuel thought, just as he heard a man's voice behind him,

"Lovely pictures, aren't they?"

The man looked to be around forty, with dark hair and brown eyes that had an unusual glint, reflecting a strong spirit. He held out his hand to Samuel: "I'm McKoskie. How can I help you?"

Samuel shook his hand, and turned to look at the photos again. He pointed to the picture of the young woman and asked who she was.

"She was found stabbed in her apartment two weeks ago."

Samuel glanced at the photo one more time and then turned to the Detective to properly introduce himself, "I'm Samuel Escobar, Thomas Santiago's ..."

"Attorney, I know who you are, I saw you on TV the other day," the detective interrupted. "So, how can I help you?"

Samuel explained that he had read the detective's report on Nathaniel Brown, and that he needed to ask him a few questions.

"What do you want to know?" McKoskie asked.

"Anything, any piece of information, no matter how small, that could help me."

The detective gestured for Samuel to sit, as he sat down on the edge of the desk and crossed his arms. "If you read the report carefully, you know that there isn't much to say; there weren't any clues... What really surprised us was that whoever the killer was, he was able to strangle the victim using just one hand... Nathaniel was a big, strong guy."

Samuel asked about the smell of flowers that had been mentioned in the report.

"That struck me as very strange too; we figured that it was somehow part of this killer's personal signature."

McKoskie paused for a moment, uncrossing his arms and resting his hands on his knees. He went on, "We searched the whole apartment and couldn't find any sign of any actual flowers. Our experts examined the walls and the floor to detect any perfume or other substance that the killer may have sprayed in the room, but they couldn't find anything. When I got in touch with Detective Sanchez in Gilbert, I found out that they had found the same thing at the crime scenes of their three victims."

"So what do you think about all this?"

The detective looked squarely at Samuel with an ironic expression and replied, "If you're asking if I think your client is guilty or innocent, I'd say that it's not for me to say, that's something for the courts to decide. My job is to find them, bring them in, and get them out of circulation..." he stood and took a few steps around the desk. After a short pause, he added, "Now, if you want my honest opinion, I'd say that your client did me a favor..."

Samuel was shocked by the detective's response. He blinked several times, as if he were trying to convince himself that he must not have heard correctly, and looking closely at McKoskie, he waited for him to finish.

"Nathaniel Brown had a very long criminal history: robbery, homicide, drug-dealing, just about anything you could think of..."

Samuel thought that the detective looked genuinely relieved, as if he really was happy about what had happened. He shook the detective's hand again and stood to leave. He paused, and turned to ask, "Detective, do you know what the strange symbol on the wall means?"

"According to a language expert who we contacted at Harvard University, it's a word from the Syrian Aramaic language, an ancient Biblical dialect over two thousand years old. What was scrawled on the wall was a single word, and it means "demon.""

Samuel remembered having heard of the dialect when he was a student. He knew that it was considered one of the most ancient languages in the world, and that just a few small sects in Israel still spoke it.

E Turquoise Av

16

Escobar family residence
6889 East Turquoise Avenue
Scottsdale, Arizona

"Sweetheart, dinner's ready," Catherine called as she finished setting the table.

Samuel was playing with his baby daughter on the rug in the living room, when the phone rang. He got up to answer it, leaving the baby among her toys.

It was Rusvel calling. He had just watched the video... Samuel switched the receiver to his other ear to have a better view of his daughter, who was happily playing with a little stuffed animal.

Samuel could hardly wait to hear what the doctor had found.

"You were right when you said there were some things in the video that were just beyond imagination..."

Catherine came out of the kitchen and seeing her husband on the phone; she picked the baby up and quietly told him that they would wait for him in the dining room.

Samuel nodded to her, but all of his attention was on Rusvel's voice and what it was about to tell him: "The video is the original; it has not been altered in any way..."

Samuel was still quiet.

"Look, that damned thing actually passed right through the glass door, as if it were a ghost. We did every kind of test we could think of to try and find some kind of sign that the video wasn't completely authentic, but everything that is seen on that tape is what actually happened..."

"Are you totally sure?"

"As sure as I'm talking to you right now."

Samuel lowered his head and took in a deep breath. But Rusvel's revelations weren't over. He continued, "Remember the light that was shining around the figure? Well, the only plausible explanation we could come up with is that it's his own aura. According to a psychoanalyst and other experts I consulted on this, it's the first time that a human aura has been registered with such intensity..."

"But what about the eyes? What can you tell me about its eyes? How can the eyes actually look like two little flames?"

Rusvel sighed. "I don't know, buddy. I have no idea how to explain that. But there's one thing I'm sure of, and it's that whatever's going on with that boy is absolutely unbelievable..."

Then neither man spoke. Finally, sounding very tense, Rusvel went on, "I also took the liberty of asking B. J. Wilson, one of our professors of psychiatry, to watch the video with me. We're both sure that this is a totally unique case without precedent. There is no medical explanation for how a person could pass through a glass door as if it were a cloud of smoke, much less for an aura that shines as brightly as a thousand megawatts, Samuel. Those are superhuman powers, and they aren't caused by any mental disturbance. I can assure you that he escaped from the police station the same way he passed through that glass door, that's how..."

They were both silent again, until Rusvel continued, "And as for that strange language that you can hear him speaking as he's strangling the victim... Well, I talked to some expert linguists, and they are certain that it's a Biblical dialect, over six thousand years old, but they couldn't decipher what he was saying exactly. But they are sure about what he wrote on the wall, and that the language he was speaking was Syrian Aramaic."

Samuel thought about his conversation with Detective McKoskie as he listened to his friend say, "Aramaic is one of the oldest languages in the world, it seems that only a few very small sects in Israel still speak it today. How do you think he learned it?"

Although he was desperately searching for answers and rational explanations for all of it, Samuel hadn't found them.

"I don't know, Rusvel, but I promise I'm going to find out. I paid a visit to one of the detectives in Glendale today, and he told me that according to experts, what was written on the wall in blood is a single word, and it's in an ancient language, that predates Christ; and it means "demon.""

"What?"

"You heard me."

"And what about what he's saying in the video—he didn't say anything about that?"

Samuel said no, and Rusvel added, "I have a friend who's a linguist in Boston, he might be able to help me with a translation, what do you think..."

"Of course that would be great, find out all you can, and let me know."

17

MARICOPA COUNTY PSYCHIATRIC HOSPITAL
2500 EAST VAN BUREN STREET
PHOENIX, ARIZONA

Later that night, Samuel went to visit Thomas.

He took a photo out of his jacket pocket and showed it to him. "Do you know what this is?"

Thomas studied the picture carefully. Samuel had taken it from one of the police reports, and it clearly showed the word written in blood on the wall, which had been found at every one of the crime scenes.

"I don't have any idea," Thomas said, handing the photo back.

Samuel explained where it had been found. Thomas' eyes opened wide, he wanted to know what it meant.

"I was hoping you could tell me," the lawyer said, disappointed.

Thomas took the photo again, and after examining it for a few more minutes, he gave it back. He really didn't know anything about it.

Sitting beside each other, Samuel explained that they knew what language it was, and he asked if he had ever heard anyone speaking in Syrian Aramaic.

Thomas shook his head and said, "No... But what does that word mean?"

"It means 'demon.'" Samuel got up and paced back and forth, and then leaned heavily against the bars.

Thomas looked down at the floor, trying to understand what all of this could mean.

"I'm sorry, Samuel. I wish I could help, but I really don't have the slightest idea of what's behind all this. It's the truth, I just don't know..."

Samuel signaled to the guard to let him out. Before he left, he asked, "Do you like flowers, Thomas?"

Thomas looked up, clearly puzzled. Where had that question come from, so out of the blue? "They are nice to look at, but I don't really like them all that much... What does that matter, anyway?"

Samuel waved goodbye and, turning to leave, his back to the boy, he replied, "It's nothing, I was just curious..."

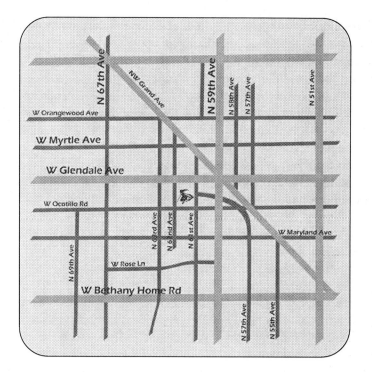

18

Ms. Leroy residence
6821 North 62ND Avenue
Glendale, Arizona

Samuel and Marta got out of the car and looked around. The waves of heat reflecting off the road's blacktop made the temperature rise to an almost unbearable level. Samuel peeled off his jacket, exclaiming, "Jesus Christ, this heat is killing me!"

"Come on, Samuel, it's barely June. Just wait 'til July and August, then you'll really have something to complain about," Marta replied with a wry smile, wiping her damp forehead with the back of her hand.

Samuel noted that the street was practically deserted. But they were definitely at the right address.

A small ranch house painted brown clearly showed the number "6821" in gold numbers displayed on the front door. The grass on the postage-stamp front lawn was dried and yellow; a feeble row of withered wildflowers ran along the front of the house.

Marta knocked on the door, and a woman quickly opened it. She looked to be about thirty-five, with dyed blonde hair and dark roots, round blue eyes, a sharp nose and prominent cheek bones. She wore a tank top and faded jeans, ripped at the knees.

"Amanda Leroy?" Marta asked.

Irritated, the woman slowly looked Marta and Samuel over from head to toe, and then asked coarsely who they were.

"I'm Samuel Escobar, and this is my assistant, Marta Lumier. We're looking for Amanda Leroy," Samuel offered the woman his business card.

"You're not cops?"

"We're from the M.J.A. Law firm."

The woman glanced quickly at the business card and handed it back to Samuel. She sighed impatiently and demanded, "Whaddaya want?"

When she heard the reply, her expression hardened even more.

"I already told the police everything and I don't wanna talk about it anymore."

She moved to shut the door, but Marta held it open, pressing against it with her hand: "Your sister Lena talked to us, and she told us that she's really worried about you. She said you haven't been able to get a good night's sleep since that night, and that you're very nervous all the time."

The woman's face slackened, as if she had just suffered a horrible tragedy. Then she lowered her head, seemingly embarrassed, and murmured, "Lena told you all that?"

She looked up again, and saw them both nod. She opened the door wider and let them come in.

Once inside, she gestured for them to take a seat on the couch in the small living room, and she sat down across from them. She picked up a pack of cigarettes from the coffee table and lit one. Her hands shook. Marta and Samuel noticed the large ashtray was overflowing with cigarette butts.

They got right to the point: they wanted to know exactly what she had seen that night.

Amanda took a deep drag from her cigarette and brushed her stringy hair back from her face. "I'm not even sure myself... I just remember that

I was giving the customer his change, when out of the corner of my eye; I saw a really bright light, coming closer. Then all of a sudden I saw it go right through the door, and it changed into this...this weird thing..."

Amanda paused, took another drag and exhaled a long stream of smoke. She shook her head, as if trying to shake off the pain that remembering that horrible night brought to the surface, a night she wanted to erase from her memory completely.

"That... that thing grabbed the man by the throat, and started to strangle him, and bang his head against the wall, over and over again." Her eyes welled with tears, although she tilted her head back and blinked rapidly, trying to hold them in.

"Why didn't you call 911, or leave to get help?" Marta asked quietly.

Amanda puffed nervously on her cigarette, a long trail of ash balancing precariously from its end, and her eyes grew red with new tears. "I tried to yell, but I couldn't, nothing came out. My knees were shaking. Just then, at that moment, that strange feeling came over me..."

"What do you mean?" Samuel pressed.

Amanda crushed the cigarette out and wiped at her bloodshot eyes. She breathed deeply, trying to calm her nerves, and clasped her hands tightly, hunching forward.

"I was totally terrified, but something inside me said that nothing was going to happen to me, that I had nothing to fear. It was so weird... Then everything smelled like flowers... I didn't know what to do... Then after it let go of the man, it started to go back towards the door, and then it looked at me. Its eyes... Oh God!" Amanda sobbed. "I felt like its eyes could see right into my soul, it was like I was naked in front of him..."

Marta stood beside Amanda, and put her hand lightly on her back to console her.

"Who is Maglio Contie?" Samuel asked.

"Maglio?" Amanda sounded surprised.

"Your sister told us that, ever since that night, Maglio still hangs around the gas station sometimes, but he hasn't wanted to talk to her," Marta explained.

"Maglio is a homeless guy, he used to help me take out the trash, and I'd give him something to eat, a cup of coffee, once in a while..."

"And was he at the gas station that night?" Samuel insisted.

Amanda didn't remember having seen him.

"Why did you quit your job the very next day?"

Amanda sighed heavily. She bit her lip, and then finally responded, "Ever since that night, I haven't been able to sleep. I just remember those shiny eyes, and that horrible moment, when I saw him killing that man..."

Samuel looked at Marta: that was enough.

They thanked her and left.

Once they were in the car, sounding unsure, Samuel asked, "What do you think, Marta?"

Marta fastened her seat belt, and thought for a moment. "It's an incredible story, but what she said wasn't anything more than what we could see for ourselves in the video..."

"The problem is that everything just leads us back to the same conclusion..."

"What conclusion?"

"That this is more than a series of senseless murders, committed by a fourteen-year-old boy."

Samuel was quiet while he stared unseeing into the distance. Finally he said, "It seems more like the beginning of the Apocalypse."

He had no idea how prophetic those words would prove to be.

19

M. J. A. ATTORNEYS AT LAW
BANK OF AMERICA TOWER
201 EAST WASHINGTON STREET
PHOENIX, ARIZONA

Samuel called a staff meeting for first thing that Monday morning. The fact that he arrived eating a chocolate donut was a clear indication of the matter's urgency. He only had donuts on days when he had to go to court, because the glucose seemed to calm his nerves.

The meeting was to announce the arrival of Dr. Oliver Donnells, who had been his law professor and mentor at Stanford University, and who he had asked to help on this case.

Samuel glanced at his watch. "His flight was supposed to land over twenty minutes ago, so he should be here any minute."

"Who's Oliver Donnells?" Marta asked wanting to know why there was so much chaos.

"Oliver Donnells was one of the best criminal litigators in the whole country," Marcos chimed in, recalling some of the newspaper headlines he had seen when he was only around twelve years old, and just beginning to fantasize about being a lawyer himself one day.

Because of his stellar reputation throughout the criminal law community, Oliver Donnells' resignation had taken everyone completely by surprise. Many had been sure that, eventually, he would doubtlessly wind up as a judge on the Supreme Court. But, one day out of the blue, he resigned. Then he seemed to disappear off the map for several years, until he applied for a professorship at Stanford University Law School, a position that the University was, of course, eager to give to him.

Samuel took his seat, and looked around at his staff. He calmly explained, "Eighteen years ago, Oliver won a case against two boys who had been accused of the brutal rape and murder of a twelve-year-old girl. It was an especially difficult case, but Oliver convinced the jury and the boys were sentenced to death. Two years after they were both executed, the police discovered who the real killers had been. Oliver couldn't get over his feelings of guilt, and he quit practicing. I am telling you all about this so that you will all be careful to not bring up that subject, understood?"

Just then the phone in the conference room rang, announcing Oliver's arrival.

Oliver walked into the conference room, elegantly dressed in a dark suit. After greeting everyone, he sat next to Samuel.

"Let's dive right in, Oliver. Like I told you, the strongest piece of evidence is the video taken from the gas station's security camera."

"Can we take a look at it?"

"Of course, Marcos, please..."

The video started. Even though everyone else had already seen it, they all watched with rapt attention just the same.

Oliver was clearly perplexed, but he remained sitting with his arms crossed, calm in the face of the shocking seen that unfolded on the screen. He stroked his chin, a gesture he had inherited from his father, which tended to emerge in moments of deepest thought.

He picked the remote control up off the table and hit 'rewind.'

"What is that written on the wall?" Oliver asked.

Samuel explained everything they had found out, what the experts that had been consulted had concluded, and what the police reports had to say about it.

"What is he saying while he's killing the victim?" Oliver asked evenly.

Picking up one of the folders on the table, Samuel read from a sheet of paper inside: "The Lord rebukes you, sinner, son of your father Satan..."

He slowly lowered the paper and put the folder back on the table. Looking at Oliver, he said simply, "That's what he's saying..."

All around the table, everyone's eyes opened wide in wonder, and stared intently at Samuel. Until that moment, none of the staff members had known what the litany on the video meant, and they were clearly shocked by what they had just heard.

Oliver stood and slowly walked over to the window. The others tried to conceal how deeply disturbed they were by this latest revelation.

Oliver looked down at the people casually walking on Washington and Third Streets far below. Several miles off in the distance, the colossal Camelback Mountain was clearly visible, the sun reflecting brightly off its red rock surface. Oliver let his gaze wander off to the horizon.

Around the table, the staffers started to quietly murmur among themselves, but Samuel closely observed his mentor's unusual reaction.

"That boy is possessed."

Oliver's voice abruptly silenced everyone else.

Samuel wasn't quite sure he had heard right.

"That boy is possessed," Oliver repeated plainly.

Samuel felt all of his strength drain from him, as if he had suddenly been stabbed in the chest by a razor-sharp sword. Oliver had confirmed his darkest fear.

"Why do you think that, sir?" Marcos asked with his voice cracking.

"Because one of the main indications of possession is an ability to speak in tongues."

Oliver walked back towards the table, and stood in front of a small blackboard on the far wall. He picked up a piece of chalk and wrote as he spoke: "The Zodiac Killer, David Berkowitz, the "Son of Sam;" Ted Bundy; Anatoli Onoprienko of the Soviet Union, Richard Ramirez, the "Night Stalker;" Albert Fish... of all the deadliest serial killers, even those who claimed to kill for religious motivations, none of them ever exhibited supernatural powers..."

Then he wrote Thomas's name in parentheses: "But this boy does..."

Samuel leaned back in his chair and read all of the names that were written on the board. He knew that Oliver was right: Onoprienko, Ramirez and Berkowitz had all testified in court that they had been inspired to kill by supernatural forces.

Oliver continued, "In concordance with the tenets of psychology and logic, and as suggested by history, a human being can acquire supernatural powers in only one of two ways: through faith, or through possession. Anyone can believe that they have been sent by God, or the Devil, and start killing people; but that belief won't give them supernatural powers. They would only be diagnosed as having some sort of mental illness."

He looked around the table at each of them before going on, "According to the few studies that have been conducted on this subject, only people who have allegedly been possessed, or have some sort of divine power are capable of doing something like what we have just seen... But that doesn't make them serial killers. Obviously, in this case, we can see that his motive is religious: the message on the wall, and his damning words addressed to the victim clearly indicate the reason for the crime."

It was clear why Samuel had sought out his help; Oliver was the best.

"In the eyes of the law, this boy is innocent, because he is not aware of his own actions," he added, stroking his chin thoughtfully. "The problem isn't whether he is innocent or not, but rather, how to prove it?"

"Why? You just demonstrated that according to the law, he is innocent," Samuel leaned forward, alarmed.

"He is innocent according to a strict interpretation of various statutes, since a person who exhibits signs of possession is not mentally competent; he is unaware of what he is doing while he is possessed..." Oliver shrugged, "But how can you prove it? That's the challenge. For example, a defendant who has a multiple personality disorder could be pressured during an interrogation, to the point that he totally withdraws, and another personality emerges, right there. But with possession, as the word would suggest, it is completely against one's own will."

He shrugged again, and opening his arms, he asked, "Are you going to have some sort of séance in the courtroom, to try and invoke the possessing spirit? According to the law, possession does not exist, only multiple personality disorder, schizophrenia or hallucinations, which are mental illnesses that can be clearly demonstrated. But possession cannot be demonstrated in legal terms. What are you going to argue to the jury, that God, or the Devil, has taken over your client?"

Oliver sensed the fear and discomfort that gripped everyone in the room. He looked directly at Samuel, "This case is even more difficult than you can even imagine. The boy is innocent according to the law, but he is guilty of having killed those people. If it can be proven that he is the person in that video, he is the killer. And what's worse, his ability to escape from jail makes him a clear and present danger to society."

Samuel slumped back in his chair again, taking a deep breath. He rubbed the back of his neck, and asked the question on everyone's minds: "What do you think's going to happen?"

"Honestly, I don't know. It would be foolish to try and predict the outcome so prematurely. I only know that Morgan, that son of a bitch, is going to do all he can to get that boy convicted..."

"So...?" Samuel asked.

Oliver thought for a minute, pacing back and forth. Finally he went back to the blackboard and wrote quickly, as he talked excitedly, "We have to very carefully study each possible step, every possible strategy; first of all we need to determine what all of the victims have in common. Aside from his supernatural powers, the fact is that we're dealing with a serial killer, and all of the victims must have something in common... Second, we need to find someone who can give us more information about that strange language that he is speaking on the tape, because I would venture that we will find many more answers once we know more about what he's saying."

Oliver wiped at his hands to get rid of the chalk dust, and took a few steps toward his seat. "Finally, we need to carefully study each case, since I'm sure that, just as this is an extraordinary case, the degree of detail required to solve it will also be extraordinary."

He sat down again and added, "If there's anything that seems peculiar, bring it up. We can't overlook even the most seemingly inconsequential things. The insignificant details tend to be the keys that unlock the greatest hypotheses."

After a heavy silence, Samuel was the first to speak, "There's something in the police report for the Luisa Mcbell case, one of the victims that caught my attention. She was found under a tree, on some very muddy ground, but according to the police, only one set of footprints were detected: her own. No one can explain how the killer could have left the scene of the crime without leaving any sign that he was there; and there was no sign that any attempt was made to cover his tracks."

He searched through one of the files in front of him on the table, and finding the note he was looking for, he added, "According to the forensic report, Billy Black Horse was killed on the morning of Wednesday, October 27, on the Kayenta Indian reservation."

Samuel picked up another sheet of paper and handed it to Oliver: it was a copy of the attendance report from Thomas' school, and revealed a troubling discrepancy in the time transpired between the homicide and the time that he boarded the school bus...

Oliver just smiled wanly, "Like I said, we are dealing with one of the most difficult and interesting cases ever tried in a courtroom..."

20

SAINT MARY'S BASILICA
231 NORTH THIRD STREET
PHOENIX, ARIZONA

Samuel left the office to take a walk, trying to briefly distract his mind from all that was going on. Once outside the building, he took a right on Washington Avenue, and then a left on Second Street. When he came to Monroe Street he took a right. Many people were returning to their offices after lunch. The strong midday heat made walking uncomfortable. When he saw Saint Mary's Church, he crossed the street and went inside.

Saint Mary's Basilica is the oldest church in the whole valley, founded in 1881. Construction concluded in 1914, it was dedicated in 1915, and it was declared a

National Historic Monument in 1978. In 1985, it was designated a Basilica by Pope John Paul the Second, who visited there two years later while passing through Phoenix.

Samuel slowly sat down in a pew towards the back of the church. He looked at the crucified Jesus behind the altar, at the front of the sanctuary. The charged silence and faint flickering from the candles illuminating the statues of the saints inspired a vaguely unsettling feeling in him.

"What is it, my son, why so pensive?" a voice behind him asked.

Samuel visibly jumped, since he had assumed that the church was completely deserted when he had walked in. He turned abruptly, but his eyes met with those of an old man with white hair, dressed in a long black robe, whose calm gaze radiated palpable warmth. He offered his hand with a smile, "I'm Father Steven, the priest of this church..."

Samuel introduced himself, still impressed by the brilliant intensity visible in the priest's eyes. "I haven't seen you around here before," Father Steven remarked.

"I haven't been inside a church in years, Father, but today I went out for a walk, and when I passed by here, I decided to come inside..."

The priest sat down in the pew across the aisle. "That happens to a lot of people... There are some days when the spirit is restless, and it seeks the peace and tranquility of a place where there is no need for words. For many of us, the church is that place..."

Father Steven crossed his legs and smoothed his robe. He was about to ask if he would like to confess, as was his habit, but Samuel said first, "Maybe you can help me... Look: I'm a lawyer, and I'm working on a very special case. Several people have suggested to me that my client is possessed, but I don't know what to think..."

"Possessed?" the priest smiled indulgently. "What reason do they have to think such a thing?"

"My client has supernatural powers, and no one can explain where they came from..."

Suddenly Father Steven's eyes opened wide as he exclaimed, "Oh, my heavens! Now I know why your name sounded familiar. The Thomas Santiago case, of course... But, what kind of powers are you talking about exactly?"

"The kind of powers you only see in horror movies... He can speak in an ancient Biblical language, and he has superhuman strength..."

The priest blinked rapidly. "What language?"

Then Samuel told him everything, including how the experts that had been consulted concluded that the language was Syrian Aramaic. He reached into his pocket and pulled out a photo, the same one he had shown Thomas in his cell, and held it out to the priest:

"This is Aramaic, right, Father?"

The priest's reaction scared him. Concerned, Samuel stood and put a hand on his shoulder.

Father Steven didn't take his eyes off the picture. His legs trembled. Samuel was disconcerted.

"Where was this picture taken?" Father Steven finally asked, wiping his brow.

"It's from one of the crime scenes. Why?"

"They found this word at all of the crime scenes, didn't they?"

The priest suddenly stood and raced towards the back of the church.

Jogging after him, Samuel asked what was going on. But Father Steven didn't even look behind him, he ignored Samuel's questioning. They went through a door and then behind a heavy white curtain with a gold border and a purple cross embroidered in the middle. The father went into what seemed to be a little office, and picked up an address book on the desk. He searched for a number, but his hands shook so badly it took a while to find it. Finally he found the page he was looking for, picked up the phone and started punching in the number.

Frozen in place, Samuel contemplated the surreal scene. The voices sounded far, far away, echoing in the distance. Father Steven spoke in a deep voice, his tone conveying enormous agitation and emotional anguish. He seemed not to even notice that Samuel was there. The phone was on speaker.

"Damian, It's Steven..."

"Well, what a surprise! How are you?"

"I think it's starting..."

"What do you mean?"

"Your prophecy, Damian, about The Blood Avenger... it started..."

"Where?"

"Right here, in Phoenix."

"Are you completely sure?"

"I'm holding a photograph of the word in my hands, right at this very moment..."

"And is it written in blood?"

The priest assented and placed the photo in a fax machine, and pressed the 'send' button. Samuel reacted immediately and tried to stop him. "No, you can't do that! It's police evidence!"

Father Steven forcefully knocked Samuel backward, and sat down in front of the phone again. Shocked, Samuel got to his feet, and heard the voice at the other end of the line:

"Oh dear God!"

"What are we going to do?" then he let out a long, weary sigh.

Father Steven slowly hung up. He seemed to be terrified: his jagged breathing and suddenly pale complexion made it clear to Samuel just how serious the situation was. The priest collapsed into a chair of oak with a cross carved into the back. He extracted a handkerchief from his pocket and mopped his face.

Samuel stood in front of him, asking him to please explain what was going on.

The priest almost sobbed as he stared out the window and began to speak:

"Thirty-five years ago, I was studying in Rio de Janeiro, and there I met a young man named Damian Santos. He wasn't a typical youth, his unusual devotion and faith made him different from the rest. In all of my sixty years, I've never known anyone like him. In these times, while the Catholic Church is rocked by scandals of rape and sexual abuse, he is the only person that I would swear is completely without sin... Ten years ago, he called me to tell me about a vision he had had. In that vision, he saw God's punishment for the world, something he called "The Blood Avenger," who would rise up to defend the oppressed..."

The priest stood and with his hands clasped behind his back, he began to pace back and forth across the floor. "At first, I thought it must have just been a dream, until two years later, he told me that an angel of the Lord had manifested itself to him to tell him that there would be a sign that would let us know that the Avenger had arrived: it would be a word written in blood, in the sacred language..."

"The 'sacred language'?"

"According to certain legends, which still have not been proven, Aramaic was the language that Adam and Eve spoke in paradise. It was the language that Jesus spoke with his disciples, and it was even the language of the angels. That is why it is considered a sacred language."

"What else did the message say?"

"That what God would send would mean the destruction of faith for some, and the beginning of faith for others..."

Both men were quiet. Finally Samuel couldn't help but ask, "Why didn't he tell the Pope or a bishop about this vision?"

Father Steven let out a bitter laugh: "Come on, Mr. Escobar. Do you have any idea how many believers go to their superiors with stories about the end of the world or saying that God spoke to them directly? Thousands. All the bishops do is laugh right in their faces. I'm his friend and I didn't even believe him... until today."

"Why not?"

"I don't know, I thought it was just his fanatical devotion..."

Samuel wanted to know more, but the priest interrupted, "Damian will tell us all about it when he gets here... He's already on his way..."

E Turquoise Av

21

ESCOBAR FAMILY RESIDENCE
6889 EAST TURQUOISE AVENUE
SCOTTSDALE, ARIZONA

The telephone rang, breaking the night's peaceful silence and abruptly waking Samuel. He searched around the bedroom in the dark until he found it, and in a groggy voice he answered,

"Hello..."

"Samuel, it's Marcos, I think you'd better get up..."

The alarm clock showed a ridiculously early hour, and Samuel asked why he was calling before dawn. Marcos added, "Thomas escaped again, and he killed somebody in Mesa... I'm at Mariela's house, and let's just say things don't look too good..."

Samuel turned on the light. Catherine was awake by then too.

"When did it happen?"

"At around eleven o'clock last night..."

Samuel sat on the edge of the bed and rubbed his face, trying to come fully awake.

"Where's Thomas?"

"No one knows, the whole house here is surrounded by people already, some of them are carrying torches, and they want to burn it down. The police are trying to hold them back."

"Make sure Mariela and Juan Manuel are okay, I'll be there as soon as I can."

When Samuel hung up, he was already up out of bed and starting to get dressed. While he put his shirt on, he tried to explain what was going on to Catherine, who seemed to be having a hard time understanding what could possibly be so urgent at that hour.

"Thomas escaped again..."

"Oh my God! Oh my God!" she wailed.

Samuel hurriedly put on his jacket and kissing his wife's forehead, he promised he would keep her informed about everything as it happened.

22

SANTIAGO FAMILY RESIDENCE
6610 NORTH 61ST AVENUE
GLENDALE, ARIZONA

When Samuel turned on the corner of Maryland and 61st Avenue, he was met with the shocking sight of a huge throng of people gathered in the street, carrying torches and jugs of gasoline, trying to set the house on fire, while armed police in riot gear tried to keep the angry mob at bay.

Samuel parked his car and struggled to make his way through the crowd.

Finally he caught up to Marcos who was waiting for him, and the police let them through. Inside the house, he found Mariela in the living room, sitting on the couch, her head bowed, while Juan Manuel sat beside her and gently rubbed her back. When she looked up and saw Samuel, she sprang to her feet and threw herself into his arms, crying bitter tears.

He embraced her tenderly.

"What are we going to do? What are we going to do now?" she moaned.

"We'll see, Nana... No one knows where Thomas is?" Samuel looked at Juan Manuel.

"No one knows his exact whereabouts, but the FBI and the police in Glendale and Mesa are on the lookout for him," a man with a dark complexion, all dressed in black had answered. He looked like a classic homicide detective. His almost totally gray hair was cut short, and he had a big bushy mustache over his thick lips, that contrasted with the sharply intelligent gleam in his eyes.

Observing Samuel's questioning look, he offered him his hand, "I'm Special agent Quincy Morrison, FBI, and this is Detective Dan McKoskie, from Glendale..."

Samuel spotted McKoskie in a corner of the room, and as he shook Morrison's hand he explained, "He and I have already had the pleasure..."

Then Samuel immediately asked to know all the details.

"Your boy escaped and killed somebody in Mesa..."

"But, how could he have escaped?"

The FBI agent explained that they still knew very little about what had happened, but the security cameras had filmed the whole thing, so they would have to wait until they could see those.

Samuel blinked nervously and asked about the two marines who had been guarding him.

"One of them is in a state of shock, and the other is completely terrified. As soon as the doctor has taken a look at them, they can be questioned," said McKoskie.

Samuel sat down on the couch next to Juan Manuel and ran a hand through his hair.

"Who was the victim this time?" Samuel asked, looking up at the detective.

"It was a ten-year-old boy," Morrison replied.

Juan Manuel simply exclaimed "Oh my God!" and hugged his grandmother, who buried her face in his shoulder, trying to hide her tears.

"A ten-year-old? But this is extraordinary... none of the victims before were minors," Samuel observed.

"We were talking about that with McKoskie before you got here," Morrison said, pacing around the room. "His modus operandi is not predictable. All serial killers have a specific type of victim, but these wide variations are very unusual..."

"Who found the child?" Samuel asked.

"His mother," Morrison answered quickly. Taking a small notebook from his coat's pocket, he read, "According to her statement, she discovered the body at around twelve-thirty. She said she heard a loud noise coming from her son's room, and when she opened the door, she found him dead, lying on the bed. There was blood everywhere, and something was written on one of the walls. She tried to see if her son was still alive, and after not finding a pulse, she called 911..."

23

Everyone waited in silence for some news to come, anything that could help them locate Thomas.

Over two hours had passed since Samuel had arrived; the sun was starting to rise, and soon chaos would break out across the whole city as the news hit.

At that early hour, all of the television news programs made an announcement every few minutes about Thomas Santiago's latest escape, and how he was still at large.

Samuel had a cup of coffee, hoping it might calm his nerves. There was nothing he could do, and his state of paralysis drove him crazy. He looked out the window and watched as McKoskie and Morrison seemed to be giving some instructions to the police protecting the house.

Most of the people who had gathered outside had left, now only a few curious onlookers remained. Marcos and Jan Manuel had fallen asleep on the couch, while Mariela, completely exhausted from crying so much, now seemed to be resting quietly in a chair near the kitchen, her head leaning against the wall.

"Poor woman," Samuel thought. "This agony is just eating her up... Why is all of this happening to her? Why couldn't it happen to someone else? There are so many bad people out there, who deserve something like this and a lot worse, but no, it has to happen to this poor, good woman..."

A bloodcurdling shriek ripped through the quiet of the house: "Mommy!"

Mariela's eyes shot open while she reflexively stood up and shouted back, "Thomas!"

She knew the voice had come from the second floor so she bolted up the stairs, with Samuel, Juan Manuel and Marcos following close behind.

Mariela burst into his room. Thomas was sitting on his bed, surrounded by a sphere of glowing light, wearing the orange prison uniform, covered in blood. He was crying inconsolably, horrified by the sight of all the blood. When he saw his grandmother, he held his hands out to her: "Mommy, what's happening to me?"

She fell to her knees before him.

When the others came into the bedroom, Juan Manuel hugged his grandmother and tried to lift her to her feet.

But when he saw Thomas he started to cry, and as he made the sign of the cross, he prayed, "May the Lord have mercy on you, Father, have mercy..."

Samuel leaned against the wall, painfully contemplating the horrifying scene.

Morrison and McKoskie crowded into the room, their weapons drawn, shouting, "Ma'am, step away from him! Thomas, put your hands where we can see them!"

Thomas was shaking with fear and kept crying helplessly. His grandmother stood and hugged him, imploring the detectives not to shoot.

Juan Manuel stood between the bed and the detectives, and opened his arms wide to shield his grandmother and his brother. His face had hardened, and he screamed at the detectives, "Don't you dare shoot!"

Morrison trained his gun on Juan Manuel and ordered him to step aside. Then Samuel intervened, "Is all this really necessary?"

The detectives looked at each other. What they had here was a crying boy holding on to his grandmother for dear life.

The detectives lowered their guns, and McKoskie went over to Thomas and slowly handcuffed him.

Mariela clung to Juan Manuel and wept. Detective Morrison took out his radio transmitter and advised the police outside that they had the fugitive, and were preparing to remove him from the house.

They put a bulletproof vest on Thomas, and covered his head with a blanket.

Now the sun had begun to rise in earnest.

A black jeep with tinted windows pulled up in front of the house. Morrison and McKoskie led Thomas outside and helped him get inside the vehicle, as quickly as possible. The people that were still gathered outside shouted angrily and threw things at the jeep as it drove away.

The early-morning sun seemed to bathe everything in a strange orange light. A few white clouds far away in the sky accented the beauty of the sun rise, with that wonderfully distinctive light that can only be seen from the desert.

Thomas raised his head and looked out the window, contemplating the sky, and for the first time in a long time, he smiled.

24

M. J. A. ATTORNEYS AT LAW
BANK OF AMERICA TOWER
201 EAST WASHINGTON STREET
PHOENIX, ARIZONA

Samuel got to his office at around nine o'clock in the morning, his eyes bloodshot from worry and lack of sleep. Celia urged him to go home and get some rest, he obviously really needed it. But she could have predicted his response:

"I'll rest later... Is Oliver here?"

While he looked through his phone messages, Celia let him know that Oliver was on his way. She also told him that Judge Fieldmore had called and urgently needed to see him in his office.

Samuel glanced at the clock on the wall. "Call him and tell him that I'll be there in twenty minutes."

He eagerly took his favorite mug filled with fresh coffee from her. As he walked into the conference room, he was met with an expectant silence from his staff.

"I need somebody here to tell me, please, that we have at least one credible witness. We are only one week away from trial, and we haven't found anyone that can testify in our favor... Marta, what happened with that man that Ms. Leroy's sister told us about? He's a homeless guy who hangs out on the streets at night. I'm sure there's got to be some place around the gas station where he goes that we could find him..."

Just then Oliver breezed in, carrying a briefcase and several psychology books. He put everything on top of the table and said breathlessly, "Sorry I'm late, but I think I've found everything that we were lacking..."

Samuel took out a notebook and asked if anyone had anything to report.

Sabrina opened the folder in front of her. "Javier and I spent the whole weekend trying to find out anything that would help us figure out the commonalities of all of the homicides. We got some very interesting information from a friend who works in the police department. Listen to this: Mark Hailey, charged with rape of a minor on two occasions, one in '97, and the other in 2000; he was never convicted for lack of evidence. Bryan Woodsong, a police officer who had been suspended, under investigation as an accomplice to a robbery and murder; Nathaniel Brown, ex-convict, ten charges of drug dealing, assault with a deadly weapon, gang violence, wanted for murder in the first degree; Lisa Anderson, twice charged with child abuse, alcoholic and drug addict; A.D. White, fourteen years old, gang member, accused of raping a classmate at school, got out on probation..."

Sabrina turned and addressed Samuel, "Do you want me to go on?"

Not hiding his surprise, Samuel looked to Oliver, who held his hand out to Sabrina for her to pass him the folder. He looked through each of the cases, and removed his glasses with a sober expression.

"Most of the victims have been formally accused or convicted of some kind of crime."

"How can we use this in court without it hurting us?" Samuel asked.

Oliver folded his arms over his chest. "We'll have to find a way..."

The telephone rang, cutting the meeting short. It was father Steven, from St. Mary's church...

Samuel sprang to his feet and pulled Oliver toward the door. "Let's go, you've gotta hear this. I'll tell you what it's about on the way..."

25

Saint Mary's Basilica
231 North Third Street
Phoenix, Arizona

They went inside St. Mary's Basilica. Oliver looked around him, and felt strangely uncomfortable. "It's been so long since I've been inside a church, I feel funny..."

Samuel smiled, remembering how he had felt when he was first there.

In the middle of the church were Father Steven and another man, sitting beside each other in silence. They walked over and Samuel shook Father Steven's hand.

"This is my friend, Oliver Donnells." Father Steven greeted him politely and introduced the man beside him. He was around sixty, his dark brown eyes looked small behind his thick glasses. Thin and fragile-looking, he seemed completely harmless. His fair skin and the wrinkles around his eyes made his gaze look even more penetrating.

To the Vatican, and Pope John Paul II in particular, Father Damian Santos was their most trusted authority in the world when it came to translations, proving the authenticity of certain documents, and interpreting archeological findings.

According to the Catholic Church, Damian Santos was, in no uncertain terms, "a Godsend."

One cold morning in February 1944, in a small church in Sesuntepeque, El Salvador, the Father Ismael Santos heard the faint sound of a baby crying. He got out of bed and searched through the whole church. There he found a baby who was only a few months old, abandoned in one of the pews, with a note pinned to his blanket that said, "God forgive me."

The priest took the child in, and raised him.

The boy grew up in the church, under Father Ismael's watchful eye, instilling in him an abiding belief in the importance of religion and the Christian faith.

By the time he was sixteen, the young Damian Santos could already speak and write in seven languages. Because of his excellent qualifications, he received scholarship offers from many universities around the world.

The sacraments and a search for truth were always his strongest sources of inspiration. By the age of twenty-one, he had earned a graduate degree in Theology, and had learned to speak five more languages. Two years later, he was selected by the Vatican to be a part of an elite group of translators and document and archeological researchers. But it wasn't until after 1980, when access to the Dead Sea Scrolls was more widely granted, and when a powerful scandal rocked the world in 1992, that Father Damian Santos became famous. At that time, he confronted the director of the Qumran Institute and head of the Bible Studies Department at Groningen University in the Netherlands, who also oversaw the international commission in charge of publishing the scrolls.

In 1992, the press asked the director of the Institute about the polemic unleashed by Damian's reports to the Vatican, which suggested that Rome and Jerusalem were concealing some secrets contained in the scrolls that had yet to be published. Damian claimed no one could gain access to the scrolls to consult them, either. The director flatly denied Father Damian's charges, and assured him that neither the Vatican nor the Rabbinical leaders had imposed any form of secrecy on the commission or had forbid them to grant access to the controversial texts which could prove potentially harmful to both religions.

Father Damian Santos greeted them in a serene tone, with a slight nod of his head.

"Father Damian, Father Steven told me about your vision…" Samuel began.

"I know that it must sound crazy to you, but I can assure you that it is real. Let me ask you something, Mr. Escobar. At all of the crime scenes, the same word was found written in blood, correct?"

Samuel nodded.

"And it was written in Aramaic? And they have confirmed that the significance of the word translates to "Demon"?"

It was all very hard for Oliver and Samuel to believe. Still, it was clear that Father Damian knew much more about what was happening to Thomas than they did. So Samuel ventured to ask, "What is happening to my client? What is that strange power that comes over him, and changes him into that demonic thing?"

"I must talk to him myself, to analyze his symptoms, before I can come to any definite conclusions. Can I see the boy?"

"Yes, of course, but first I have to get permission from the judge… I'll let you know."

Father Damian gestured for them to sit down.

"What I can tell you is probably what you already know. Thirty years ago, I had a vision. The angel of Jehovah appeared before me, and told me that God would demand atonement for the blood of the innocent, and he would send the Avenger. As a sign that it was a divine act, we would see a word in the sacred language, written in blood…"

E Butte Av.

26

Arizona State Prison
1305 East Butte Avenue
Florence, Arizona

Mariela and Juan Manuel went to visit Thomas at the new prison he had been taken to.

The high-security prison in Florence had two large buildings, which the prison guards referred to as "The Pocket" and "Weed Row."

Since 1900, the most dangerous criminals in the state had been held there. It is the only prison in the state where executions are carried out. They were told that their newest arrival was being held in the TB section, known by the old-timers as "Snakes," because in the desert, those sly creatures always found somewhere to hide.

It was an underground cell area in the basement, used to isolate inmates who were highly dangerous or as punishment.

Mariela and Juan Manuel were taken to the director's office. A man wearing a suit with a thin black mustache, with gray hair and bright blue eyes opened his office door to greet them. His strong, broad shoulders complimented his tall stature. Two other men were seated at the far side of the office.

"Good morning, ma'am. I'm Mr. Whitefield, the institution's director," he said politely.

Mariela shook his hand warily. He gestured towards the other men, "That is Dr. Michael Leech, and Dr. Dempster Thompson." They both stood and approached the visitors.

"This is my grandson, Juan Manuel, he's Thomas' older brother. But, to what do we owe the honor of this invitation, Mr. Whitefield? Somehow I doubt it's to let us know how proud you are to have Thomas here," she said hurriedly, a feeling of foreboding rising in her.

Whitefield glanced at the doctors, and clasping his hands, he said, "The reason we wanted to meet with you is because Dr. Leech, a scientist, and Dr. Thompson, a medical psychiatrist from Boston, would like to talk to you about Thomas..."

Impatience hardened Mariela's expression. Dr. Thompson asked if she had seen the two videos which showed the boy's transformation.

"Just the one from the gas station, why?"

Dr. Leech stepped in, "Ma'am, what's happening with your grandson is a very unique case, because he has demonstrated the ability to walk through walls, as if he were a ghost. The government has given us authorization to perform any studies that may help us determine what is happening to him... but Thomas is a minor, and we need to have your permission..."

"What kind of studies are you talking about?" Juan Manuel asked, clearly concerned.

The doctors exchanged a look. Dr. Thompson answered, "Well, I don't know how much you know about medical psychiatry... But, to put it simply, we would start by taking some electromagnetic readings, which would give us an idea of what's happening when he's asleep, since it seems as if the problem originates when he's sleeping..."

Dr. Leech leaned forward slightly, adding, "We know that everything happens when he's asleep. That's why we have had a special cell constructed for Thomas. We have placed special lights inside of the cell, which function much as an X-ray does, and will allow us to observe what kind of physical transformation his body goes through when he is in a trance state. There are some other studies we would like to perform, if we are able to attach sensors to his head. Those would give us an indication of brain functioning, providing a better understanding of what's going on in his mind at the very moment of transformation..."

Anger danced in Juan Manuel's eyes. He said sarcastically, "Let's see if I have this straight... You want us to give you permission to take Thomas and put things in his head, filling it up with some kind of sensors, to find out what's going on in his brain when he's sleeping, so that he won't even be able to have a moment's peace while he's asleep..."

"But the problem surfaces when he's asleep," Dr. Leech rationalized.

Mariela gave him a scornful look. "My grandson is not a lab rat, Dr. Leech. And if you dare to do anything to Thomas that is unnecessary, I will sue you..." she stopped abruptly.

Mariela grabbed Juan Manuel's arm and led him out the door. She turned and concluded, "Now, if you'll excuse me, I have to go see my grandson."

27

JUDGE FIELDMORE'S OFFICE
MARICOPA COUNTY SUPERIOR COURT
201 WEST JEFFERSON STREET
PHOENIX, ARIZONA

Samuel arrived at Judge Fieldmore's office at ten-thirty in the morning. The office was filled with books, neatly shelved in a large bookcase that ran diagonally from the left side of the room to behind the desk where the judge now sat. The floor was of light-brown marble. The front wall of the office was dominated by an engraving of Plato, who was depicted stroking his beard pensively as he walked across a plaza. It was the judge's favorite image of Plato. In all of his lectures on criminal law, he would paraphrase one of the great philosopher's sayings: *"We will never have a perfect society until our rulers truly become philosophers, and our philosophers become rulers."*

The judge was accompanied by the District Attorney Morgan Stanley. To Samuel, his presence there was not a good sign.

The judge invited Samuel to sit down, but he preferred to remain standing.

"Counselor, the District Attorney and I agree that the situation with your client is out of control, and something must be done about it..."

There seemed to be a touch of sarcasm in his tone. Samuel nervously put his hands in his pockets and asked, "What do you suggest, Your Honor? He's already chained to the wall like an animal, he has a military guard watching him every second of the day, there are about fourteen security cameras installed in the cell he has just been transferred to today... The cell has a wall of bullet-proof glass, on top of the iron bars..."

The judge shot Samuel an angry look. Sensing an argument was about to break out, he explained, "The reason we called you here today is to make you an offer. If Thomas pleads guilty and puts himself at the mercy of the court, he will get one hundred and fifty years. With good conduct, he could get parole in ninety..."

"No thank you, I'd rather take my chances in front of a jury," Samuel cut him off.

Stanley shifted his weight in his chair. "You have to understand, Samuel; we have to find some kind of solution here, because soon this is going to turn into a security issue..."

"What do you want to do, then? Rewrite the law and sentence him without a trial?" Samuel turned to the judge, "Your Honor, I know that if it were up to the DA, he would have asked that my client get the death penalty, even though the law protects him because he is only a boy..."

"A boy who's already killed nineteen people, Your Honor!" Stanley shouted furiously.

"But according to the law he is innocent and you know that perfectly well!" Samuel shot back.

"*Innocent?!* Aren't you forgetting that he was caught in the act on video, killing one of the victims?" Stanley's voice dripped with sarcasm.

"But if you've both seen the video, then you know very well that what is happening to Thomas is not normal..."

"Gentlemen, please, calm down!" the judge intervened.

There was a brief, heavy silence, until Samuel added, "I know that this situation is driving us to our wit's end, but you have to understand that what is happening to that boy is something that has never been seen before; something that may be even more disturbing than anything we are capable of imagining, but we cannot forget that our responsibility as legal people is to act according to the law..."

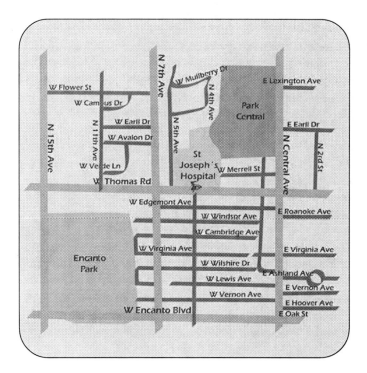

28

St. Joseph's Hospital
350 West Thomas Road
Phoenix, Arizona

Samuel parked his car at the corner of Third Avenue and Thomas Road. He got out and looked up at the enormous building that housed St. Joseph's Hospital. He took a deep breath and buttoned his suit jacket.

The large glass doors opened automatically. A woman passed in front of him, aided by a nurse: she walked with great difficulty, connected to a machine by two plastic tubes that ran from her nostrils. Samuel felt his chest tighten; just observing the obvious pain the woman was in provoked a feeling of tremendous anguish in him.

At the reception desk, a young nurse wearing a light-blue uniform smiled sweetly and asked how she could help him.

"I'm looking for two Marines who were admitted here yesterday."

Just then, he heard someone call his name in a loud voice. Samuel turned and saw Special Agent Morrison.

"You got here just in time; the doctor just gave us permission to question one of them," he shook Samuel's hand firmly.

"What about the other one?" he asked as they stepped inside an elevator.

"He's still under heavy sedation. We could only observe him through a window."

"Which one can we talk to?" Samuel wanted to know.

"His name is Jasey Martinez."

As they stepped out of the elevator, Samuel followed the agent down a hallway, until they reached Room 320. Two Marines were stationed just outside the door. As they walked up to the soldiers, Morrison showed them his FBI badge and they let them both enter the room.

Jasey was standing by the window looking out, but as he heard people coming into the room he turned to face the door.

"Martinez, I'm Special Agent Quincy Morrison, FBI, and this is Mr. Samuel Escobar, he's Thomas Santiago's lawyer."

The young man shook both of their hands and seemed perfectly willing to answer their questions about what had happened the night before. He sat down on the edge of the bed and, staring down at the floor, asked them what exactly they wanted to know.

Morrison, who had taken his notepad out of his pocket, spoke first: "Why don't you tell us what you saw?"

Jasey put his hands on the bed and looked out the window. He drew a deep breath, and began, "It was about ten o'clock at night. I remember it very well because Johnny had gone to get a coffee, and I looked at my watch to see how long he would take, since he always snuck out for a smoke too. Thomas was asleep, and I was sitting in front of him. Suddenly, a bright flash of light blinded me... I tried to cover my eyes, to see what was going on... Then I saw that thing..."

The soldier's eyes grew moist, and he started breathing rapidly. Morrison stepped over to him and put a hand on his shoulder, in an effort to reassure him.

"Thomas... Thomas was floating in the air, he was in this bright ball of light," he went on, still visibly upset. "His face was glowing; really bright... His handcuffs just fell onto the floor..."

He took another deep breath and brushed away a tear. He stood, crossing his arms before continuing, "I fell to my knees. This really weird feeling came over me, I know that I was crying, and my legs couldn't hold me up. He looked right at me. Just then, the cell door opened, and he came toward me. I didn't know what to do... I was so scared. His eyes looked like two little flames..."

Morrison looked at Samuel. What they were hearing was beyond belief. He lowered his notepad and asked, "Why were you crying?"

"I don't know, I felt so weird, the tears were just streaming out of my eyes, I couldn't help it..."

The soldier rubbed his face with both hands and looked at the floor again. "Just then Johnny came back... he dropped his cup of coffee and he fired his rifle at Thomas over and over again..."

He walked over to a little white table and poured himself a glass of water. His hands were shaking.

"Then what happened?" Samuel prompted.

Jasey took a sip of water and set the glass back down on the table.

"That thing raised its right hand, and the bullets fell at its feet. Then he looked at Johnny and pointed at him with his finger, until he fell to his knees, and brought his hands to his head, he started screaming, like he was in really bad pain... then he turned to me, I couldn't move... then, it was just like in a movie, going really fast, he just went right through the wall and disappeared. Then I don't know how long I just stayed there, I couldn't stop crying, it was like a nightmare... the only thing I remember after that is waking up in the hospital."

"You said that he went through the wall and disappeared? As if he were a ghost?"

Martinez drank the rest of the glass of water and slammed the glass down on the table. Angry, he said to Morrison, "You think I'm lying?"

Morrison put his notepad back in his pocket and sighed, "Soldier, you must be aware that what you're telling us here is pretty out of the ordinary; you're talking about people floating in mid-air, and passing through walls like they're ghosts..."

"I know it sounds crazy. I wouldn't believe it myself, if I hadn't seen it with my own eyes," he admitted sheepishly.

"Morrison, have you watched the video from the security camera at the gas station?" Samuel asked. "I think you need to take a look at that as soon as possible."

Morrison was already heading out the door, while Samuel said goodbye to Jasey, "Thanks for talking to us. Would you be willing to testify in court about what you saw?"

The soldier nodded silently.

"Here's my card, my office will call you. If you remember anything else, please let me know..."

29

M. J. A. Attorneys at Law
Bank of America Tower
201 East Washington Street
Phoenix, Arizona

Samuel was watching the news in his office at the end of the day. He was reclining in his oversized leather chair, which Catherine had given to him as a gift when he had opened his law firm. He remembered that day as if it were yesterday...

Catherine had gotten there two hours before she had said she would. She came in with two men carrying a huge box, with a red ribbon tied around it. She told them to put it down and they left.

"What's that?" Samuel asked, surprised.

"It's a little present I got for you..."

Samuel looked at her, not knowing what to say. Catherine pretended to be angry:

"I would think that right about now you'd be overwhelmed with happiness, jumping up to kiss me, ripping open your present..."

Still stunned, Samuel kissed her warmly on the lips, and started to open up the box, as his wife watched closely:

"You told me once that there were two things in life that you loved with all your heart: justice, and... me. And now that you'll be spending a lot of time here, I wanted you to have somewhere to relax whenever you wanted, when you can't be with me..."

Samuel stood up, put his arms around her waist and gently pulled her to him, whispering in her ear,

"You know that, really, you're what I love the most?"

Catherine murmured, "Even more than justice?"

Catherine's beautiful, moist lips trembled with desire, very close to his. Samuel nodded, but she prodded playfully, "Are you sure?"

"Beyond a shadow of a doubt, my love..."

Catherine started to unbutton his shirt.

"And now what do you think you're doing?" Samuel asked devilishly.

"Well, exactly what it looks like I'm doing..."

Samuel ran his hand lightly over her back. "Are you crazy? People are going to start coming in soon..."

Catherine looked at the clock, bit his lip and finished unbuttoning his shirt...

"We have just over an hour..."

Samuel gently touched the arm of the leather chair, thinking how hard it was to believe that ten years had gone by since that day.

But the images on the television screen pulled him out of his reverie: the Chief of Police and the governor were making statements at a press conference about the latest developments in the Thomas Santiago case.

"We have moved him to the Prison in Florence to ensure not only his own security, but the security of the entire community. He will be under strict surveillance twenty-four hours a day, in a special cell equipped with all the latest technology. We are sure that he will not escape again."

On the intercom, Celia informed him, "Father Steven and Father Damian are here."

Samuel had started to put the papers on his desk in order when both men walked into his office. After the routine pleasantries were out of the way, he explained to them that he wanted them to watch the video of Thomas escaping from the prison together. He needed to find out what they thought about it. He talked to them as he set up the video.

Thomas appeared on the screen, lying in his prison bed, a blanket covering him. The Marine Martinez was in front of him, just outside the cell, his head down. Suddenly, Thomas started to shake violently, and he moaned loudly, it looked as if he were having a seizure. But then his body started to slowly levitate. Suddenly, there was a bright flash of dazzling light. Thomas was no longer moving, and he appeared to have lost consciousness. He was floating about four feet above the ground, enveloped within a sphere of brilliant light. His body was curved in on itself, in the fetal position. The camera showed how Martinez suddenly dropped to his knees...

"Oh God in heaven!" Father Steven cried, as he tightly gripped the arms of the chair. Father Damian was completely motionless, his eyes glued to the screen.

Then the chains around Thomas' wrists and feet fell to the ground, and the cell door inexplicably opened. As the other soldier who had just returned fired at him, Thomas held out his hand, as if he were stopping traffic, and deflected the bullets, while the soldier screamed, clutched his head and fell in a heap at Thomas' feet.

Father Damian took a few steps towards the television, his eyes still fixed on the screen, unblinking.

Suddenly, as if pulled by a powerful suction force, Thomas disappeared, right through the wall...

Samuel stopped the tape. The video had corroborated Martinez' account, from beginning to end.

"Let me tell you what I think. I've watched this video countless times, just like the gas station video, and... my eyes just can't believe what they're actually seeing."

Both priests were very still, and had grown dramatically pale. Clearly, the scene they had just watched had deeply disturbed them.

Father Damian staggered over to the window and looked out, letting out a long breath.

Samuel looked at both men, waiting in vain for some kind of answer, until finally he asked simply, "How could a human being possibly be capable of something like that?"

Father Damian responded, "You're forgetting something, Mr. Escobar: the force that takes control of that child changes him into something much more powerful than a mere human being... According to scripture, Jesus was one hundred percent man, and one hundred percent God..."

Samuel didn't understand, but Father Steven seemed equally puzzled by Damian's words, who continued after a brief pause, "Jesus had all of the characteristics of a flesh-and-blood man: he felt hunger, and thirst, he experienced fear, he cried, and died just like everyone else. But he was also God, since he walked on water, he could heal the sick with a word or simply a touch of his hand, he could calm a storm, he conquered death... There are many things in this world that are only possible through faith and spirituality..." his voice trailed off.

"I see your point, Father Damian, but I need proof, something that will help me prove in court that Thomas is innocent. I can't go to trial with nothing more than religious beliefs and Bible verses, I need evidence." Samuel observed that his strong words and exasperated tone had had an effect on the priest.

Father Steven didn't look up as he remarked to no one in particular that maybe telling Samuel about Father Damian had been a mistake.

Samuel sighed and joined Damian at the window, lightly putting his hand on his shoulder. "Forgive me, Father, it's just that this whole thing is really doing a number on me... We're just a few days from going to trial, and we don't have a single credible witness, somebody that could really bolster our case and show that he's innocent..."

"I'm only telling you what I know, Mr. Escobar... I know that whatever takes hold of that boy changes him into something beyond human, it's some kind of demon, or angel of death..."

Samuel just looked at him. He could tell by the steely glint in his eye that his faith was unshakeable. Then, resigned, he said, "I'm going to go see Thomas this afternoon. If you want, you can come with me. But, please, don't say anything to Thomas about your vision, or the dream with the angel. At least not yet..."

Damian nodded his agreement. "How many people has he killed so far?" he asked, while Father Steven unsteadily rose to his feet.

"Nineteen, counting the one yesterday," Samuel replied bitterly.

Father Damian was quiet as he stroked his chin pensively.

"Is there anything else that you haven't told me yet? Are you sure you're not leaving anything out? Something else that seems very strange? Something else that all of the crime scenes had in common?"

Samuel remembered the intense flower smell, and as soon as he mentioned it, Father Damian's eyes lit up. With a slight smile, he affirmed, "But they never found the slightest sign of any actual flowers at all, did they?"

Samuel was startled by his insight. Then Father Damian turned to face Father Steven and said, "Let's go... I need to call Rome."

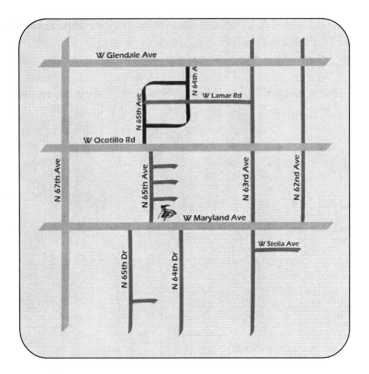

30

NATHANIEL BROWN'S APARTMENT
6478 WEST MARYLAND
GLENDALE, ARIZONA

Samuel and Marcos pulled up in front of 6478 West Maryland, in the city of Glendale. They were in front of a low-rise, red brick apartment complex.

"What are we doing here?" Marcos asked, as they got out of the car.

"They found one of the victims here, a Nathaniel Brown..."

"So who are we going to question?" Marcos was still constantly surprised by his boss' methods.

"No one; we're just going to study the scene of the crime..." they went up the walk to one of the apartments; they each had a separate street-level entrance.

Samuel took a key ring out of his pants pocket, and raising an eyebrow, he showed it to Marcos.

"Where did you get that?"

"Morrison let me borrow it," Samuel answered, as he put the key in the lock and pushed the door open. He felt around on the wall and turned on the light switch, illuminating the still-undisturbed crime scene. The small apartment's kitchen sink overflowed with dirty dishes, and several beer cans were scattered on the floor.

Samuel looked around, carefully studying every detail. He walked toward the rear of the apartment, and on the left he saw a bedroom, its door ajar. He opened it, and from the doorway he could see how one of the walls was spattered with blood and in the middle of the wall on the right, the word in Aramaic appeared. There was an outline in white chalk drawn on the floor, indicating where they had found Nathaniel Brown's body.

A subtle smell of flowers could still be detected in the air.

The left wall had several bullet holes, which Marcos studied closely.

"This creeps me out," he said, but his remark didn't interrupt Samuel's painstaking inspection, as his eyes traveled over every corner of the room.

"Oliver told me once that crime scenes are three-dimensional, that every scene has things to say that you can only hear when you're actually there," Samuel said, staring at the word written in blood on the wall.

"Every scene has something in it that tells the beginning, the middle, and, often, the conclusion of the crime... it all depends on how good the investigator is at interpreting the clues."

He bent down to run his fingers over a stain on the carpet, and continued, "Each scene illustrates how the perpetrator behaved with his victim, and these indicators let us know how the killer attacks, reacts, and kills..."

Suddenly they heard a noise coming from the front of the apartment. Rattled, Samuel and Marcos looked out the window, spotting someone trying to desperately run away. The window had no screen, so Marcos pushed it open and jumped out, chasing after the fleeing figure, while Samuel followed him out the window and headed around the other side of the building to cut the man off.

Marcos caught up to the guy and grabbed him, pushing him up against a chain-link fence. Samuel ran up to them, out of breath. He was a black teenager, wearing jeans, a baseball cap and a Los Angeles Lakers t-shirt.

They asked his name several times, but the boy just looked at them, not saying a word. He seemed terrified. Marcos didn't loosen his grip, still holding him against the fence.

"Are you cops?" he finally asked.

"No, we're lawyers... what's your name?" Samuel asked again, indicating to Marcos to let go of him.

"I'm TJ."

"So why did you take off running when we saw you?" Marcos asked.

"I thought you were cops..."

"What were you doing in that apartment?"

"I was walkin' by and the door was open, I thought one of the guys must've come back..."

"What guys?"

"Charlie, or Mike...they worked for Nathy... And I was afraid that maybe that thing was comin' back..."

Marcos and Samuel exchanged incredulous looks.

"What 'thing,' what are you talking about?" Samuel asked, knowing full well what he was talking about.

The boy lowered his head: "That ET, that killed Nathaniel..."

Samuel glanced at Marcos and then back at the boy: "Were you here when it happened?"

The boy slowly shook his head yes.

He was quiet for a minute, trying to search through his mind for the right words to explain. Still not looking up, his voice breaking, he started to tell them.

"We were all there, in the livin' room, Mike and Charlie was gettin' ready to go out and sell the weed they had left, Nathy went to get his pistol, it was in the bedroom. Then we heard two shots, and Nathy was screamin', we ran back there to see what was goin' on, and then we saw that thing was stranglin' Nathaniel. Mike and Charlie shot at it, over and over, but the bullets didn't do nothin'. Then it turned and looked at us, and we all fell down on the floor, we were scared..."

The boy started to sweat, his hands shook, and his eyes welled with tears.

"I don't care what nobody says! That thing that killed Nathy, it was an ET. Its eyes was all shiny like fire, its face was all bright, like lookin' right at the sun...that wasn't no person..."

Samuel looked at Marcos again, and then asked the boy to go on.

"That martian started sayin' all this crazy stuff, and it wrote on the wall with Nathaniel's blood, and then it just disappeared right through the window. I ran outta there and called 911."

"Why didn't you tell any of this to the police?" Samuel asked.

"You *crazy?!* The police never woulda believed me, they woulda said me and the other guys was the ones who killed him..."

He pushed his baseball cap back, adding, "I'm not a criminal. I just help them out sometimes, baggin' the weed, and they give me a few joints for free, but that's it... Yeah, I've smoked dope, but I've never sold it, and I've never killed anybody." He looked down at the ground again, his expression deeply pained.

Samuel reached out and gently raised the boy's chin, to look him in the eye:

"Would you be willing to testify in court, telling the same story you just told to us?"

"Look, man, you gotta be beyond crazy if you think I'm gonna ever mention this ever again, I've seen lotsa times on TV what happens to people who say bad things about the space aliens..." the boy looked at both of them, and pointing at them with his finger, he explained, "You know, the martians come and kidnap the people up to their space ships and brainwash them. I'm not gonna get involved with nothin' about no extraterrestrials."

Marcos lightly swatted the back of his head, knocking his cap to the ground.

"How can you believe such crazy stories? And anyway, letting everybody know you're a Lakers fan is much worse, if you live around here..."

TJ bent down to pick up his cap, brushing it off against his leg. Standing up straight, he said proudly, "You don't know anything about basketball, Los Angeles has the best player in the whole NBA, and that's Shaquille O'Neal."

Marcos put his arm around the boy's shoulder, replying, "Only a team like the Lakers would dare to pay so much money to somebody who can't even sink a free throw."

E Butte Av.

31

ARIZONA STATE PRISON
1305 EAST BUTTE AVENUE
FLORENCE, ARIZONA

Samuel arrived at the prison to visit Thomas, accompanied by Father Damian and Father Steven.

Both priests were fascinated by all of the facility's tight security measures, but when they saw Thomas chained to the wall, they couldn't help feeling a stab of pain in their hearts.

Father Damian was immediately reminded of the ancient texts he had read so many times when he had first begun translating documents for the Vatican: that was the same method the Romans used to immobilize prisoners in their jails; but he had believed that the practice had ended long ago.

Infrared lights hung from the ceiling of the cell. Six heavily-armed soldiers wore masks and dark sunglasses that would enable them to see clearly in very bright light. They didn't take their eyes off the prisoner.

While one of the soldiers patted him down, Father Damian observed that the motion-activated security cameras followed every move.

Thomas was sitting on the bed, with a totally bereft expression. His red-rimmed eyes and the dark circles under them implied that he had been up all night.

Samuel embraced him, and introduced the priests, but Thomas barely even looked up.

Father Damian went over to him and held out his hand. Thomas looked up at Samuel in disbelief: he couldn't understand how he dared to stand so close to him, knowing that he had just killed somebody a few hours earlier. But with an encouraging gesture from Samuel, Thomas adjusted the chains attached to his wrists and raised his hand to shake the priest's. Father Damian's sharp gaze revealed a quick intelligence, and his warm smile made Thomas feel confused, it seemed like he was proud to meet him.

Samuel explained that Father Steven and father Damian were working with him on his case, and he asked Thomas if he was holding up alright. But he seemed not to be paying any attention to what was being said.

Damian sat down on the bed next to the boy. He began a strange line of questioning, which Thomas felt compelled to answer, prompted by the warm, inviting tone of the priest's voice.

"Are you a Catholic, Thomas? How long have you been going to mass?"

He hesitated for a moment, thinking. He really didn't know where this was headed, and he looked to Samuel with a puzzled expression before replying, "Ever since I was little. I was an alter boy for a few years, until I started junior high..."

"His older brother is a seminary student at the Arc of Our Lord in Los Angeles," Samuel added.

With a quick look Father Damian indicated that he would like to hear more about that later, but for the moment his attention quickly returned to Thomas. He wanted to know if he had had dreams relating to his faith, if he had ever talked to God in any of his dreams...

"Not that I remember... Why do you ask?"

"These are just certain things that I need to know, my son..."

"Do you have an altar in your home?" Father Steven joined in.

"My grandmother has a picture of the Virgin of Charity in her bedroom, and there's a crucifix in the living room..."

The priests exchanged looks, as if turning to each other for some kind of answer.

Thomas turned to Samuel and asked, "Who did I kill this time?"

The three men were moved by the blunt question, making them suddenly feel small and confused.

"A ten-year-old boy," Samuel couldn't keep his voice from breaking.

Tears welled in Thomas' eyes, and he was wracked with sobs.

Father Damian kneeled in front of the boy, placing his warm, firm hand on his forehead: "Don't suffer so, my child; we will do everything possible and more to stop what is happening to you..."

32

Saint Mary's Basilica
231 North Third Street
Phoenix, Arizona

Morning finally came, and when Father Steven walked into the office at the little church, he found Father Damian there, reading.

"You're still up?"

It was clear that neither man had been in any condition to fall asleep.

Father Damian took off his glasses and rubbed his eyes, trying to alleviate his fatigue. He was searching for answers for something that still had no plausible explanation.

Father Steven plugged in an electric coffee maker and started heating up the water. He took two coffee cups and a box of tea out of a cabinet and asked, "What do you believe is going on with that boy?"

"I don't know what to say...there are so many things that just don't add up..."

Father Steven poured hot water into the cups over the teabags, he offered one to Damian. "Sugar?"

"Two, please..."

Father Steven took a sip of tea. "What things do you mean?"

They were both sitting down in the office, facing each other. Father Damian leaned back in his chair, stretching, and put his hands behind his head. "As men of faith, we know that there are only two ways to possess supernatural powers of that magnitude: through good, or through evil. I know that his powers come from good, because I have seen it in my dreams. What I can't understand is why he in particular was chosen to be God's messenger..."

Father Damian took another sip of tea, and set the cup down on the desk, crossing his arms over his chest: "You heard it for yourself: his religious beliefs are nothing extraordinary, he is not devoted to religion, and that's the part I just can't understand..."

"But, what did you hope to find?"

Damian recited, "Abraham, David, Solomon, Noah, and Isaiah, all the great men of the Bible...God chose them because of their strong faith..."

Pointing with his index finger, Father Steven countered, "But don't forget that Paul wasn't a man of faith, and neither was Moses. Not until God chose them..."

Father Damian stood and paced around the desk. "They were different: Moses saw the burning bush and heard the voice of God talking to him. Paul was changed after Jesus appeared to him and blinded him, just like Saint Francis of Assisi, who dreamed of a vast, dark hall hung with armor all bearing the mark of the cross. They were chosen by God to teach the world that when a man discovers the truth, and, humbled, he changes his ways, he becomes a saint, through his devotion and the sacrifice that the Christian faith demands."

Father Steven persisted, "But, what about all this strikes you as the strangest?"

"Finding out how it happened, what triggered it... Everything in the universe has a reason for being, even if we cannot understand it."

Father Steven took the last sip of his tea. "We have to remember that many of God's reasons are beyond human comprehension."

"And that is why our limited human capacity keeps us from true understanding. I am sure that there is a reason why that boy has become possessed in that manner. But in order to help him, of course, first we have to know how it began..."

N 61st Avenue

W Maryland Av

33

SANTIAGO FAMILY RESIDENCE
6610 NORTH 61ST AVENUE
GLENDALE, ARIZONA

Juan Manuel opened the door and greeted Samuel with a hug.

"Where's Nana?" Samuel asked right away.

"She's in the kitchen... Did something happen?" the unexpected visit worried Juan Manuel.

But Samuel really just wanted to see them, and have a chance to talk with them before the trial began. They both went into the living room and sat down on a gently curved, beige sofa.

The lawyer told him about the latest developments: they now had four reliable witnesses from Thomas' school, two teachers and two students, who would testify in his favor. And he talked briefly about the priest from St. Mary's Church and his friend from Brazil. They were helping with the case, and would like to have a word with him.

"They want to talk to me? About what?" Juan Manuel was intrigued.

"I don't know, but can you go down there?"

"Of course. Who should I ask for?"

"Ask for Father Steven; his friend is named Damian."

Just then Mariela came out of the kitchen, drying her hands in her apron.

"How are you, dear? How are Catherine and the baby?"

Samuel stood and kissed her on the cheek. "They're fine, the baby's growing a little more every day..."

"And, what's this visit all about?" Mariela asked directly, taking off her apron and sitting beside Juan Manuel on the couch.

"I wanted to let you know about what's going on with the case, before we go to trial. I was just telling Juan Manuel we have several people who will testify in favor of Thomas: his teacher Mrs. Thompson, another teacher and two classmates."

"Do you think it's going to turn out alright?" Mariela asked.

Samuel looked at Juan Manuel, as if asking for his help, he seemed caught off guard by Mariela's need for reassurance.

"Nana, you have to understand how hard this case is. The District Attorney has some very strong evidence, at least for the case at the gas station."

Finally, he folded his hands together over his knees, and plunged ahead, "The District Attorney made me an offer..."

"What kind of offer?" Juan Manuel and Mariela were clearly surprised.

"If Thomas pleads guilty and puts himself at the mercy of the court, they will reduce the sentence to one hundred and fifty years...and with good behavior, he could be eligible for parole at ninety..."

Frightened, Mariela looked at Juan Manuel, who bowed his head, terribly disappointed.

"I told them no, we'll go to trial..."

Juan Manuel looked up. His eyes were red and welled with tears, his voice said: "What are the chances that Thomas will be free, if we go to trial?"

"I'm not going to lie, the chances are very slim. We're doing all we can, but the evidence against him is very strong..."

Samuel looked Mariela straight in the eyes and took her hands in his: "Nana, I promise that I will do everything possible and even more if I have to, but we must be prepared for the worst..."

E Turquoise Av

34

ESCOBAR FAMILY RESIDENCE
6889 EAST TURQUOISE AVENUE
SCOTTSDALE, ARIZONA

That night, Samuel was having dinner with Catherine when the phone rang. She got up to answer it with a smile, even though she knew it would be for him.

It was Father Damian.

"I watched the video from the gas station again... There's something you have to see..."

Samuel felt his heart speed up; a wave of anxiety coursed through him. For some inexplicable reason, he had a feeling that what he was about to hear would go beyond even his wildest imaginings.

"I think I may know what is taking possession of Thomas."

Samuel leaned against the wall, his heart beating even faster. His knees buckled. He replied in a shaky voice, "Are you sure, Father?"

"At least I know where we should begin to look..."

Samuel took off like a shot into the bedroom and hurriedly pulled a shirt out of his closet, put it on and grabbed his car keys off of the dresser.

"Baby, I have to go out for just a minute to see Father Damian."

Catherine gave him a quick hug, and looking into his eyes, she said, "When I married you I knew that, even though your heart would belong to me, your soul would always be dedicated to your work..." She kissed him on the lips and, with her hands on his shoulders, she whispered, "Don't worry, my love, go do what you have to do; we'll be fine..."

35

Saint Mary's Basilica
231 North Third Street
Phoenix, Arizona

Samuel got to St. Mary's as quickly as he possibly could. As he stepped out of the car, he felt vaguely disquieted as he noted how completely deserted the streets were. There wasn't a sound to be heard, as if the entire city were fast asleep.

He dashed up the stairs in front of the church and knocked on the door. Father Damian opened it right away: he had in his right hand a candelabrum with four lit candles, which he held high as they walked through the dark church.

"Why don't you turn the lights on?" Samuel asked, unsettled by the shadowy darkness.

"It's one of the things I like most about churches," the priest replied, a hint of pride in his voice. "I love seeing how the statues and other images look so different under the constant flickering light of the candles, like a mysterious halo..."

The church did look very different in the dark of night. The angel in one of the stained-glass windows seemed to come to life in the tenuous light from the street. Samuel felt a strange foreboding rise in him again and tried to ignore the phantasmal images, looking away.

When they went inside the little office in the back of the church, Father Damian turned on the light and blew out the candles, placing the candelabrum down on the desk. He offered Samuel a cup of tea.

"Where's Father Steven?"

"He already went to bed, we had so much to do today and he was completely exhausted..."

As he got the VCR ready, he explained that he had translated what was being said on the video. He picked up a sheet of paper from the desk and handed it to Samuel, "This is the translation."

Samuel read every line with intense concentration. But when he finished, his eyes hinted at a sense of disappointment.

"This is the same as the translation we already have..."

Father Damian started to play the video, and repeated the words in Aramaic that they heard:

"The Lord rebukes you, the Lord rebukes you sinner, son of your father Satan..."

Father Damian paused the video and took off his glasses. "That's why he writes the word "*Demon*" after he kills the victims..."

"What are you talking about, Father?"

"The reason is he considers these people, his victims, to be demons..."

Samuel sat down across from the priest, rubbing his face, trying to ward off fatigue and a troubling sensation of not being able to understand completely, and waited for him to continue.

Father Damian picked up a Bible and opened it to the letter of St. Jude chapter 1. He passed the book to Samuel so that he could read a verse that had been underlined: "*Verse 9: But when the archangel Michael, contending with the devil, disputed about the body of Moses, he did not presume to pronounce a reviling judgment upon him, but said, The Lord rebukes you.*"

Samuel lowered the Bible and looked up at Father Damian with an even more confused expression. He didn't understand what that text had to do with Thomas...

"Those are the first words that Thomas says in the video..."

The priest stepped around the desk: "If the vision in my dream is true, Mr. Escobar, we know that his powers come from good; what we don't know is what, exactly, takes possession of him."

Father Damian took the Bible from Samuel and began leafing through it, searching for another passage. "Perhaps what I am about to say to you, Mr. Escobar, will seem unreal to you since you are not a man of faith; but the only explanation that I have been able to find for Thomas's actions is this."

He handed the Bible back to Samuel, this time opened to the book of Acts, where Chapter 12, Verse 7 had been highlighted: "*And behold, an angel of the Lord appeared, and a light shone in the cell; and he struck Peter on the side and woke him, saying, "Get up quickly." And the chains fell off his hands.*"

The look in Samuel's eyes revealed shock and wonder; his mouth open, the Bible in his hands, he found the priest's enigmatic smile.

"Are you implying that..."

Father Damian interrupted, "It's the same that happened at the prison when Thomas escaped! Right?"

"And... yes," Samuel stammered. "But that doesn't mean that..."

Father Damian took the Bible again and opened to the book of Acts, Chapter 5, Verse 19, and returned it to Samuel's hands:

"There's no use trying to deny it, Mr. Escobar, they are the same displays of power that the boy has shown."

Samuel read: "*But at night an angel of the Lord opened the prison doors and brought them out and said...*"

Silent, he shut the Bible. His legal mind refused to accept it, but he had to admit that Father Damian had scored some points in his favor.

"But, in the story, Paul is freed by an angel..." Samuel ventured.

The priest nodded, stepping over to the window.

"Of all the men of God that lived before Christ, the only ones who exhibited great supernatural powers were Moses and Elijah..."

"Elijah?"

"I don't know how familiar you are with The Scripture, Mr. Escobar, but according to the Bible, Elijah brought a child back to life, a widow's son, in Jerusalem..." he leaned against the wall and after a brief pause, he stroked his chin and continued, "There are two things that I still don't understand. The first is, how could this power come to him, without being devoutly religious or a mystic. And the second, why did he think these particular people were so evil that he would write the word "demon" next to them."

Samuel suddenly thought of the meeting with his staff and Oliver:

"Oh my God! The reports..."

Samuel looked frightened. A sweat broke out on his brow, his eyes shone. Father Damian noticed his hands were shaking.

"Is there something I don't know about? Which reports? What's going on, Mr. Escobar?"

"Two weeks ago, we were trying to figure out what all of the victims had in common. We were looking for clues, something that would lead us to a motive for the crimes, since the District Attorney didn't seem to have one. Then we figured out that most of the victims had a criminal record, or had been accused of some sort of serious crime..."

"But, what about the ten-year-old boy?" the priest asked in an anguished tone.

"He had violently attacked other children in his school on seven different occasions. He had been expelled for hitting a six-year-old girl with a baseball bat..."

"That confirms my theory. So it seems that I am right..."

They were both quiet. In light of everything they had seen, the smallest doubt they may have harbored about what they feared most evaporated.

"Can I see some of those reports?" Father Damian asked quietly.

Samuel nodded, looking him in the eye.

E Butte Av.

36

ARIZONA STATE PRISON
1305 EAST BUTTE AVENUE
FLORENCE, ARIZONA

Samuel got to the prison very early in the morning to see Thomas.

He was bitterly surprised when the guard informed him that they were under strict orders: no one could come into physical contact with the prisoner.

Explaining that the prisoner was his client had no effect, nor did his rising fury. One of the military guards showed him a document: an order signed by Judge Fieldmore...

Indignant, Samuel had to concede that there was no use arguing. He would just have to talk to Thomas through a thick layer of Plexiglas.

"Don't worry... I'll talk to the judge tomorrow, and we'll get this straightened out..."

Thomas nodded, but his expression was sad and hopeless.

Samuel smiled, trying to cheer him up: "Tomorrow the trial will begin, and I came by to tell you about several things that you should know before it starts. The District Attorney is going to call witnesses who will say horrible things about you; you're going to hear a lot of lies, but you can't let it have any effect on you..."

Thomas lowered his head and started to cry.

"Come on now, Thomas, you're going to have to control yourself. We can't let your emotions influence the jury, they will be paying very close attention to your body language... They are very observant, and they'll take every little detail into consideration."

"What the hell do I have to do?" Thomas wiped away his tears with the back of his hand.

"Look... precisely this right here is something you should not do. You have to control yourself. It doesn't matter what they say about you, you cannot get angry. They will try to make you lose your temper and provoke you into doing something stupid... What? I don't know... Just try to stay in your seat and look innocent..."

Thomas stood up impulsively and shouted angrily, "Innocent! What the hell are you talking about?"

Reacting automatically, the guards standing watch outside the cell pointed their automatic weapons at him and put on the masks that were hanging around their necks. Terrified that Thomas might somehow escape again at any moment right in front of their eyes, they ordered, "Sit down! Sit down!"

One of them activated an alarm, and a deafeningly loud siren echoed throughout the whole building.

Samuel said immediately, "Everything's okay, it's okay, don't shoot!"

Thomas took a few steps back and forth, while Samuel tried to get him to calm down so the soldiers would lower their guns. The air crackled with tension.

"I'm *not* innocent! Did you forget that I killed a ten-year-old boy? What do you mean, 'innocent'?"

Thomas picked up the chair that was inside the cell and threw it against the wall. More guards rushed into the passageway just outside of his cell in response to the alarm, and lined up. Samuel pounded against the glass with his fist, trying to get Thomas's attention:

"Listen to me, damn it! You are innocent and I know it, I have proof... Please, you gotta believe me!"

Thomas looked out at him: his eyes were filled with anger and pain, and he saw how the soldiers and guards all had their guns trained on him.

The firm tone of Samuel's voice and the resolve in his eyes helped Thomas start to calm down. His breathing gradually returned to normal, and when he slowly sat down on the floor, the guards warily lowered their weapons, one by one.

Samuel collapsed into the chair outside the cell and loosened his tie. "Thank God!" he murmured, exhausted by the ordeal.

37

M. J. A. ATTORNEYS AT LAW
BANK OF AMERICA TOWER
201 EAST WASHINGTON STREET
PHOENIX, ARIZONA

The next morning, Samuel was in his office getting ready to go to the courthouse. His secretary let him know that Oliver was there.

"Tell him to come down to my office, please," he said into the speaker-phone.

Oliver walked into his office smiling broadly, carrying several books. But one look at Samuel's face let him know how nervous he was and his smile faded away.

Samuel looked at him, not knowing what to say. He was clearly very worried. Oliver walked over to him and clapped him on the shoulder, trying to cheer him up.

"Everything's going to be alright."

Samuel looked him in the eye. "You were right when you said that there must be more to this case than we could even imagine... According to Father Damian, what's going on with Thomas is totally extraordinary... But we don't have anything that can help us prove it..."

"And what does he think's going on?" Oliver sat down in the chair in front of the desk.

"Basically he said that you're right, that Thomas is possessed, and some kind of angel is giving him these powers. That's why he killed all those people. Somehow, Thomas, or the angel, knew that all the victims had committed those crimes or offenses, and that's why he wrote the word "Demon" next to all of them." He paused, and added, "You know the law better than I do, and you know that this is something that can't be proved in a court of law..." Samuel leaned against his desk. "That's what I've always hated about this business, you often know that you client is innocent, but it's not what you know, it's what you can prove..."

Oliver was pensive, rubbing the back of his neck. "In all of my years of studying and practicing law, I've learned that, sometimes, it's the cases that choose us, and not the other way around. For reasons we can't understand, we get wrapped up in cases that, at the end of the day, we find out that God has assigned to us, to teach us something, or to serve as an example for all people... Maybe, this is one of those cases..."

He stood and looked proudly at his former student. He stroked his beard and remembered the young man who had walked into his classroom for the first time fifteen years ago, wanting to save the world... He added, "There's something you should know, when it comes to criminal law. The jury is never swayed by a defendant, whether he's guilty or innocent. They're more likely to decide in favor of the best lawyer, that's why I always say that lawyers have to be very, very good storytellers..."

Oliver approached Samuel and gave him a hug. "There are many stories in the world that are just waiting to be told, and maybe this is your chance..." he let out a long sigh. "Get in there and tell them the best story they've ever heard in their lives."

E Butte Av.

38

ARIZONA STATE PRISON
1305 EAST BUTTE AVENUE
FLORENCE, ARIZONA

Thomas was escorted to an armored truck that would take him to court. Several of the prison's inmates, who were working on a maintenance crew outside the building, watched in wonder as the tightly coordinated transport took place under the strictest security measures they had ever seen. Thomas's hands were shackled at his waist, he had shackles around his ankles, and he was closely surrounded by four heavily armed Marines.

The boy struggled to walk as the other prisoners murmured,

"Isn't that incredible?"

"They say he's the most dangerous killer ever..."

"Even worse than Ted Bundy or Jack the Ripper?"

"That's what they say..."

"Nobody has access to the TB unit where he's being held, only the guards..."

The inmates stood watching as Thomas was moved into the armored truck.

"No matter what they say, he just looks like a harmless kid..."

The truck drove off into the distance, down the long, straight highway, and was eventually lost in a cloud of red dust.

One of the inmates shook his head and sighed, "You can never judge how evil or how good a man is by his size, I heard somebody say that once..."

S 1st Avenue

S 3rd Avenue

W. Jefferson St.

39

MARICOPA COUNTY SUPERIOR COURT
201 WEST JEFFERSON STREET
PHOENIX, ARIZONA

Out in front of the courthouse, Jefferson Street was jam-packed with people, nervously milling around. Vehicle access had been restricted between Third Street and Fourth Avenue, while police cars surrounded the area. Television news vans with their tall satellite dish towers lined both sides of the street.

The huge crowd awaited the start of what legal analysts predicted would be the most important trial ever in state history. Several reporters stood on the sidewalk rehearsing their remarks, preparing for live broadcasts.

As Samuel, Oliver and two assistants arrived; a group of police officers took up their positions to protect them as they entered the courthouse. Several reporters frantically rushed over, while the general public started shouting angrily.

"Mr. Escobar, is it true that the District Attorney has made an offer?" The reporter thrust her microphone in between two policemen.

"I have no comment."

They made their way inside the building and into the courtroom, overwhelmed by the multitude of people surrounding them. Samuel stopped and took a deep breath, looked at Oliver, and then kept on going.

As they reached the end of the long aisle, Morgan rose to greet Samuel, shaking his hand firmly while murmuring, "Two hundred years, with good behavior he'll be out in seventy..."

"Not a chance," was the curt reply.

They both turned and took their seats on opposite sides of the aisle.

The side door at the back of the room opened, and Thomas came in, shuffling after two policemen. He was elegantly dressed in a black suit and a tasteful red tie. Two more policemen escorted him on either side, and two more followed after them.

His grandmother smiled at him, overcome with emotion as she saw how nice he looked, even though he walked with great difficulty because of the shackles around his ankles. He sat next to Samuel, while two officers stood on either side, and two more took their places right behind him.

"You look like a million bucks, Thomas," Samuel whispered.

"Where did you get this suit?" Thomas smiled, leaning towards him.

"Since you're my most important client, I want you to dress like it..."

An officer standing near the dais announced the judge's arrival.

Everyone in the courtroom stood, and an expectant silence fell over the room as the judge took his seat:

"Good morning," he greeted them, placing the folders he had been carrying down in front of him. He took a sheet of paper out of one of them and handed it to the court officer. The officer stood in front of the judge's dais and read in a loud voice,

"Case M-1902-01. The State of Arizona vs. Thomas E. Santiago."

The trial had begun, and the judge let the District Attorney lead off with his opening statement.

Morgan stood up and unbuttoned the jacket of his navy-blue suit, with gold pinstripes. A crisp white shirt and a red silk tie completed the prosecutor's impeccable look. He walked over to the jury box and turned to look at Thomas. Resting his elbow on top of the low wooden rail in front of the jury, he started to nervously tap his hand against his thigh. The twelve members of the jury, made up of seven men and five women, three of whom were Hispanic, anxiously waited for him to begin his statement.

"Ladies and Gentlemen of the jury, I'm going to ask you to please forgive me, but I am very upset. Yes, I'm extremely upset, because, just as I'm sure many of you believe, that ever since that Sunday in 1859, February 27th, when General Daniel Sickles and his lawyer shocked the nation with their plea of temporary insanity, this type of plea has been taken to ridiculous extremes. It has been abused in the eyes of the law by many criminals, who, after committing horrendous crimes, have the nerve to go to court, and claim that they simply did not know what they were doing when they carried out those despicable murders."

Army general Daniel Sickles had fought in the Civil War for several years and had later been appointed the United States' Ambassador to Spain. County Sheriff for New York, he was reelected to Congress in 1893, and was decorated with the Medal of Honor. He is primarily remembered as the first person in U.S. history to ever use the temporary insanity defense. Daniel Sickles was charged with first-degree murder on February 27, 1859, after killing a man who he had caught trying to break into his house through a second-story window. Sickles had suspected the man had been having an affair with his wife for quite some time. The murder took place only two blocks from the White House. After chasing the man for several blocks, in front of eyewitnesses and with no provocation whatsoever, Sickles fired on him several times with his pistol, wounding him in the leg. While the man was lying on the ground, defenseless and pleading for his life, Sickles fired on him again while shouting, "You must die!" The victim was Philip Barton Key, the son of Francis Scott Key, the composer of the National Anthem. After a sensational, highly controversial trial, Sickles was acquitted of all charges, and declared innocent by reason of temporary insanity brought on by a heat of passion.

Morgan crossed over to the defense table where Thomas was sitting, and, pointing at him, he continued, "Thomas Santiago has been accused of murdering nineteen people over the last two years and five months, including children. And, what is the first thing the defense does? He claims he's innocent because he's crazy..."

He turned to face the jury. His eyes flashing anger, he declared, "The time has come to put a stop to this, once and for all!"

He looked away and took a deep breath, seemingly trying to calm down. He took two steps, and in a serene tone, he opened his arms wide, lowering his head as he said, "Defense Attorney Escobar will try to convince you that it isn't true, that Thomas is innocent of all charges since he just didn't know what he was doing; that according to Thomas's testimony, he simply doesn't remember having committed any of these murders."

Morgan turned to face the jury again, and pointing to Thomas, he exclaimed,

"Please, don't let this turn into another spectacle like the Twinkie case in San Francisco! Don't let killers like this justify their atrocious deeds by claiming they are mentally incapable of understanding their own actions; don't let them make a mockery of the law!"

The Twinkies case took place in San Francisco, California, in 1979. It was one of the most widely criticized cases in the entire history of criminal law in North America. Dan White, an ex-cop, was charged with the first-degree murders of Mayor George Moscone and Harvey Milk, a San Francisco Councilman.

Whether or not White had committed the murders was never in question, since he had shot them in broad daylight, in their own offices at City Hall. What set off the controversy was the number of psychologists who testified that White was not responsible for the killings, in spite of the prosecutor's strong allegations that he had carried an extra ammunition cartridge for his pistol with him, and that he reloaded before shooting the second victim. The psychologists alleged that he suffered from a mental disorder caused by numerous traumatic events throughout his life, which elevated his stress levels so dramatically that he had a compulsion to eat Twinkies, something he had never done before. His lawyer explained that White's deep depression and the high levels of sugar in his system from the Twinkies triggered a reaction in him that caused him to go temporarily insane. Dan White was not acquitted of all charges, but the defense's allegations and the psychologists' testimonies convinced the jury to give him a reduced sentence.

Stanley paced towards Thomas again, and while looking at him steadily, he said furiously, "Not only did he kill those nineteen people; he also made a game out of it, leaving a written message at every crime scene as his signature, using the victim's own blood!"

141

Morgan shrugged his shoulders, and opening his arms, he asked, "Are those the actions of someone who doesn't know what he's doing? Of course not..."

Thomas eyes shone with fear as he saw how angrily the prosecutor looked at him, and heard how he accused him of those horrible things, in that deep, authoritative voice. Under the table, Samuel lightly tapped his knee, reminding him to stay calm and not lose his composure.

Morgan turned to address the jury, putting his right hand in his pants pocket.

"But that's not all. After his arrest on May 21st, that very night, he escaped from the Glendale police station and killed another victim. A week later, he escaped from the Maricopa Psychiatric Hospital, where he was constantly guarded by two Marines, who had to be hospitalized. One of them is still in a state of shock. And to top it off, later that night, he murdered a ten-year-old boy..."

The prosecutor paused for a few seconds. He was clearly trying to control his rising anger. He looked at the jury again and continued, "Ladies and gentlemen of the jury, Thomas Santiago is no less guilty than Ted Bundy, or David Berkowitz, or Richard Ramirez. I believe that it is time for justice to be served, and, once and for all, to send a message that insanity cannot be used as an excuse to hide from the law. It has been said "justice without mercy is being cruelty." But I think that the time has come to decide where mercy ends and justice begins. Thank you."

Samuel looked at Oliver, who met his gaze and nodded slightly, giving him his vote of confidence. Samuel took a glass that was on the table in front of him and filled it with water from a pitcher. He stood, picking up the glass and walked over to the jury box. He set the glass down on the rail in front of them. He put his left hand in his pants pocket, and looking at each member of the jury, he pointed to the glass and began,

"Ladies and gentlemen of the jury, I would like to tell you that this case is as clear as this glass of water..."

Samuel was quiet for a second, and putting his other hand in his pocket, he paced to the center of the room and went on, "But we all know that it's not like that, since no matter how clear things might seem, I can assure you that there is much more here than meets the eye, much more than we could ever imagine."

He took a few steps towards Thomas and after glancing at him briefly, he turned back to face the jury, "Thomas Santiago, as Mr. Stanley pointed out, has been accused of the murder of nineteen persons in the state of Arizona. How many of those did he actually commit? We don't know, since logic and the laws of physics show that it would have been impossible for Thomas to have traveled from one side of the state to the other, in the middle of the night, and wake up in his bed the next morning."

He paused briefly and looked towards the back of the packed courtroom. Everyone was silent. A sketch artist captured the scene, drawing quickly with colored pencils from the third row. Samuel saw him continually look up and back down at his sketchbook again as he worked on one colored drawing after another.

"What is certain," he continued, "is that the defense will never use the allegation of insanity as an excuse to justify the events."

He deliberately walked over to the jury box again, and looking at them each in turn, he went on, "One of the foundations of the criminal justice system in the United states is the concept of the mental state, which asserts that "For a person to be found guilty in a court of law, our system requires that there must be criminal intentions or understanding of right and wrong; but if that person has a mental illness, or is unable to differentiate between right and wrong, then in our society, he is not guilty."

Samuel turned and walked to the middle of the floor. He pointed towards the ceiling, and looking out into the audience he declared, "Let me repeat: If that person is unable to differentiate between right and wrong, then he is *not guilty* according to the laws of our society." He pointed to Thomas and in a loud voice he continued, "My client was not aware of what he was doing, and evidence will be presented in this court that proves it!"

He took a deep breath and, calmer, looked out into the rows of spectators packing the courtroom, observing how all eyes carefully followed his every step. Several reporters scribbled down every word he said, while Samuel, pacing from one side of the floor to the other, could feel the tension filling the room.

"Of course the prosecutor Mr. Stanley will try any way he can to prove just the opposite; he'll do anything to make sure that Thomas spends the rest of his life behind bars. We all understand very well that his job is to defend the families of the victims, and make sure that justice is served in the interest of the state. But, what no one asks is, what is the truth behind what's really going on here? What is actually happening to Thomas Santiago?"

Samuel looked to the back of the room and saw that Father Damian had just walked in. Samuel folded his hands together and paused for a second, clearing his throat. He stroked his chin and continued, "Not long ago, someone taught me that 'In life, there are times when we have to give ourselves room to imagine that, what we had never thought possible, could actually happen. No matter how strange it may seem according to our rational mind." The truth behind what has happened is what we should be pursuing, since I believe that the most unjust thing we could do here, is conceal from the people the truth of what it's going on. Thank you very much."

Slowly, Samuel walked back to his seat at the defense table, under the heavy silence that followed his closing words.

"Mr. Stanley, are you ready to call your first witness?" the judge asked, speaking into the microphone on his dais.

Stanley stood, with his hands resting on the table he said loudly, "Your Honor, the state calls Dr. Nicholas Brushevski."

Everyone in the room turned back to look at the door. A man who looked around fifty, five feet ten inches tall, wearing a gray jacket and black pants, walked through the door and down the aisle. His bright blue eyes, thinning gray hair, and facial features coupled with his last name left no doubt as to his Polish origins. Once he was in the witness stand, the court officer who had sat next to the judge came up to him holding a Bible, and asked him to put his right hand on it, saying, "Do you swear to tell the whole truth and nothing but the truth, so help you God?"

"I do."

The doctor sat down and crossed his legs. Holding a paper in his hand, Stanley walked over to him. "Can you say your complete name and your occupation for the court, please?"

"Nicholas Brushevski, psychiatrist, Chief of the Department of Psychiatry at Maricopa County Hospital."

"How long have you worked there, doctor?"

"Nine years; I worked at the Institute of Psychiatry and Neurology at the University of Los Angeles for twelve years before that."

The prosecutor took a step closer, and handing him the sheet of paper, he asked, "Doctor, could you please read the lines that have been highlighted aloud?"

Dr. Brushevski held the paper up, and took a pair of reading glasses out of his inside jacket pocket. He put them on and read, "*Whoever commits a big crime is crazy, and the bigger the crime, the crazier they are. That's why that person is not responsible, and nothing is their fault," Peggy Norman, journalist."*

Morgan rested his elbow on the railing around the witness box and looking directly at Dr. Brushevski he questioned, "Doctor, are you familiar with that statement?"

The psychiatrist took off his glasses, returned them to his jacket pocket and replied, "Yes, it is a very famous statement in psychology..."

Stanley turned and walked toward the jury, but then stopped and faced the witness again to ask, "Do you think it's true?"

"No, definitely not. The majority of the most notorious criminals in the world, such as Ted Bundy or Al Capone for example, were people who committed terrible crimes in our society, in different ways. But no one thought of Al Capone as demented, they thought of him as a criminal. People tend to think of someone like Ted Bundy, who was accused of being a serial killer, must automatically be mentally ill, but that's not so. Psychologically, it has been proven that many of them are nothing more than criminals, the only difference between them and someone like Al Capone, for example, is that Capone committed crimes for business interests, while Ted Bundy, as he himself admitted, did it for the pure pleasure he derived from killing. But they both understood the consequences of their actions; and, legally and psychologically speaking, when you understand the consequences of your actions, you are not insane..."

Stanley turned to face the other side of the courtroom and pointed at Thomas, adding, "Doctor, you examined Thomas Santiago, correct?"

"Yes."

"And what is your expert opinion?"

The doctor looked at Thomas and answered, "He seems like a very intelligent boy. We talked for around two or three hours, each of the three times that we met."

Thomas smiled slightly and lowered his head when he heard the doctor's complimentary words.

Stanley walked back to the witness box and resting his left hand on the railing, he asked, "Do you believe that Thomas Santiago is incapable of differentiating between good and evil?"

The prosecuting attorney turned to look at the jury and in a strong tone he reiterated, "Do you believe, doctor, that Thomas Santiago suffers from some kind of mental illness?"

The doctor uncrossed his legs and rested his hands over his knees. "No, medically speaking, he seems to be a person in complete control of his mental faculties..."

Stanley interrupted, "The defense alleges that Thomas Santiago is innocent of all charges against him, because supposedly he suffers from some sort of mental illness that renders him unable to distinguish between right and wrong..."

The doctor looked at Thomas again, and after a brief pause, he replied, "From a psychological standpoint, I find him to be in perfect health..."

Morgan lifted his hand from the railing and turned to face the spectators: "Do you mean to say that you found him completely healthy?"

"Yes."

"Thank you, doctor. No more questions, your Honor."

Stanley returned to his seat while Samuel looked pointedly at the doctor from the defense table. He toyed with the blue pen his father had given him with his left hand...

"Dr. Brushevski: how many times did you say that you met with my client?" he asked, standing and approaching the witness stand.

"Three times."

"And, according to your medical experience, you claim that there is nothing wrong with Thomas?"

"Yes," the doctor said firmly.

Samuel continued, "Doctor, have you seen the video taken from the security camera at the Florence State Prison, where it shows Thomas escaping from his cell, or the one from the gas station in Glendale, which is the basis for the state's charges? What do you think of them?"

"Yes, I have seen them, and they seem remarkable..."

Samuel raised his eyebrows incredulously and repeated, *"Remarkable?"*

He turned and stepped over to the defense table.

"Your Honor, I would like to show this video to the court; it has been submitted to the court as evidence type V-332," Samuel said as he signaled to Marcos, who wheeled a stand with a television on it from a corner of the room and positioned it next to the witness box.

Samuel turned on the television and the video began to play. Gasps of amazed disbelief could be heard all around the room as they watched the bright light move right through the glass door at the gas station without breaking it.

Watching the video for the first time, Thomas was completely shocked; his eyes filled with tears.

The judge grew visibly tense as he saw how the figure's face glowed, and heard that otherworldly voice as it seemed to shake the very walls of the building.

Thomas eyes stayed glued to the television and that mysterious being. His grandmother buried her face against Juan Manuel's shoulder so she wouldn't see that horrifying episode again. The commotion from the spectators in the room grew louder, as some of them started to scream in terror, and others turned their heads away, unable to bear watching it anymore.

When the video ended, Samuel slowly walked over to the television to turn it off.

Everyone in the jury was stunned; three of the women were clearly terrified; two of the six men had taken out handkerchiefs to mop their brows, having broken out in a sweat from viewing the terrible footage.

Throughout the courtroom everyone looked at each other in disbelief as they started talking about what they had just seen, the clamor growing louder.

"Silence!" the judge yelled, pounding his gavel.

"Dr. Brushevski, did that look like the behavior of a normal person? Because if you think that is normal, you must be the only person in this entire room who thinks so," Samuel asserted, gesturing towards the television.

The doctor's expression had altered dramatically. He looked very serious and somewhat angry.

"No, that's not normal..."

"So why do you claim that there is nothing wrong with Thomas?"

The doctor let out a long breath, trying to steady his nerves. "In all of the tests that we did, we didn't find any indication that there might be something wrong with him..."

Samuel stepped toward the television and rewound the video. He pushed 'pause' just as the light went through the glass door, and, looking back at the witness stand, he asked forcefully,

"Is it normal for a person to pass through a glass door without breaking it, as you can plainly see in this video? Because that is what we see happening, isn't it, Doctor?"

The doctor was speechless, his breathing erratic.

Samuel turned to face the jury and said, "You know something? We'll come back to this in a minute..."

He went back to the defense table, and Oliver handed him a piece of paper. He handed it to the doctor: "Dr. Brushevski, can you please read the highlighted text for us?"

The doctor straightened his tie, put his glasses on again, and read:

"In recent years, psychiatrists have had a growing influence over the verdicts reached by our courts, and it is not practical to ask them to make a precise diagnosis for a person they have only seen on two or three occasions." The doctor slowly lowered the sheet of paper and looked up at Samuel.

"Does that sound familiar, Doctor?"

"No..."

"Are you sure?"

"If you are asking if I agree with that statement, Mr. Escobar, my answer is still no..."

Samuel walked back to the defense table, where Oliver handed him another paper. Then he looked back at the doctor and continued, "Those words were spoken by the attorney Bryan Mcklaine to the *Los Angeles Times* the day after the Supreme Court announced its verdict in the Anastasio Martinez case, in 1999..."

"You Honor, what does that have to do with this case?" the prosecutor asked, standing.

Samuel faced the judge and, opening his arms, he explained, "Your honor I'm just trying to establish the credibility of the witness. Anastasio Martinez was accused of crucifying and burning his wife and two daughters because he believed a demon had taken possession of their souls. Dr. Brushevski examined him and found him to be completely healthy; on appeal to the Supreme Court, Anastasio Martinez was examined by two other doctors and was found completely insane."

"Objection, your Honor, the witness is not on trial here!" Stanley protested from his seat.

The judge stroked his chin and responded, "Overruled; the witness will answer."

Samuel thanked him and Dr. Brushevski said,

"Anastasio Martinez was examined by our institution in Los Angeles and, at that time, he showed that he was in a healthy state of mind. Two months later, when they appealed to the Supreme Court, they found that he had schizophrenia, and that while in prison his condition had deteriorated to the point that he was experiencing severe hallucinations."

"That's the same institution that you were the head of, isn't that right, doctor?" Samuel asked with a hint of irony in his voice.

The witness nodded with a resentful look.

Samuel took another paper from his table and handed it to him: "Dr. Brushevski, is this your signature?"

"Yes," he said after examining it.

Samuel gave a copy to the judge and another to the prosecutor. "Your Honor, this is a statement on the mental health of Anastasio Martinez, signed by Dr. Brushevski two days before the trial started. Dr. Brushevski states that there was absolutely nothing wrong with him, just as he did with my client..."

The judge studied the document. He looked at the doctor and then at the prosecutor, whose stony expression revealed a mounting anger in the face of the defense's unanticipated revelations.

Samuel put his hands in his pockets and continued, "The same defendant who had to be hospitalized just two months later because he was completely insane."

The judge looked at Stanley, waiting for some sort of response, while he slowly set the paper Samuel had handed to him down on the table.

Samuel stood close to the witness and asked, "Isn't it true, Dr. Brushevski, that the reason you were transferred from Los Angeles to Phoenix was because of the controversy and scandal set off by your report in the Anastasio Martinez case? Didn't the Institute's board of directors ask you to take the transfer?"

"Objection, your Honor! The defense has no basis for these allegations," Stanley barked forcefully.

"Sustained. I ask you to be more careful with your questions, Counselor," the judge said to the defense attorney.

Samuel nodded, and after slowly pacing in front of the witness stand, he asked, "Doctor, is it normal for a person to have this type of supernatural powers, as we just saw in the video, where the glowing figure picked up a man who seemed to be twice his weight, effortlessly, with just one hand?"

"No, that's not normal, but there have been cases where people have exhibited superhuman strength during moments of extreme crisis, when it's a matter of life and death. Still, no; this is not a normal case."

"Then, if this is not normal, why do you state that there is nothing wrong with Thomas?"

"Mr. Escobar, you want me to testify that your client suffers from a mental illness that, according to all the psychological tests we performed, he does not have..."

Samuel stepped over to the television and rewound the video. He turned to face the witness.

"Doctor, do you understand what Thomas is saying right here?"

"No, I don't..."

Samuel stepped closer to him: "The language he is speaking is Syrian Aramaic. According to experts, it is a Biblical dialect, widely considered the oldest language in the world that very, very few people on the entire planet can still speak and write. Can you explain for us why Thomas is able to speak this rare language?"

The doctor shifted uncomfortably in his seat, and blinking nervously, he admitted, "I cannot explain it..."

Samuel walked towards Thomas and turned back to face the doctor, while he pointed at the boy: "Isn't that because you don't have the slightest idea about what's happening to my client?"

"Objection, your Honor, Mr. Escobar is not an expert in psychiatry, and he has no right to cast doubt on a professional with fifteen years of experience! Besides, Dr. Brushevski is very highly regarded in the world of mental health..."

Samuel opened his arms and, pacing towards the judge's bench, he replied, "Your Honor, the witness just admitted himself that he cannot explain why my client has the ability to speak in Aramaic, or how he could pass through that glass door... Isn't that a clear indication that he doesn't know what's going on with my client?"

The judge reflected for a moment, and then, curious, he looked at the witness and said, "Objection overruled; the witness will answer."

The doctor blinked nervously again, "I think that no one could explain how he knows that language, if he hasn't studied it... There have been some cases when people were in a church, or performing some kind of religious ritual, for example, and become spiritually possessed. They can say things in different languages, but it's almost always just a few words, or phrases, they are often not even pronounced correctly, they are just things that the person has heard or read somewhere that have been retained in the subconscious, and in a moment of spiritual ecstasy, as we refer to this state medically, they tend to recall these phrases. Are you sure that what he is saying in the video is being said correctly?"

Samuel went back over to his table and picking up another paper, he read, "According to our translator, what he is saying is 'The Lord rebukes you, the Lord rebukes you sinner, son of your father Satan...' It is in perfect Aramaic, according to the expert..."

The psychiatrist's expression and body language conveyed his nervousness; his eyes darted and his fidgeting gave the impression that he was tied up, trying to break loose from his restraints. Samuel folded his arms across his chest and looking directly at the doctor, he asked,

"Can you explain or not, Doctor, how my client can speak Aramaic, how he can pass through glass doors, and how he can emit a glowing light, as we have just seen in the video?"

The doctor was quiet for a few seconds, and swallowing hard, he said, "No."

Stanley bowed his head, extremely disappointed; his witness's testimony had been a failure.

Samuel paced slowly to the center of the floor and, his back to the witness, he asked,

"Nor can you explain how Thomas managed to lift up the victim with one hand, when that person was twice his size?"

"No." This time the doctor's tone dripped with sarcasm.

With a serious expression, Samuel turned to face the jury and concluded, "No further questions, Your Honor."

40

Santiago Family Residence
6610 North 61ˢᵗ Avenue
Glendale, Arizona

"Good morning, Nana," Samuel greeted her as she opened the door.

"Hello Samuel, what a nice surprise!" Mariela said, hugging him and lightly kissing his cheek.

"Nana, this is Father Damian," Samuel said, introducing the man at his side.

Still grasping Samuel's arm, Mariela held out her other hand:

"How are you, Father?"

"I'm very well, thank you."

Samuel asked if Juan Manuel was there, but he had gone out already.

"Can you tell him that Father Damian and I would like to talk to him?"

"I'll let him know as soon as he gets back."

Anxious, Mariela asked, "What is it?"

"Nana, we'd like to talk with you about Thomas..."

Mariela's eyes clouded with fear, and she stammered, "D-did... did something happen to him?"

"No, no... Thomas is fine," Samuel quickly reassured her. "Can we come in?"

Mariela led them into the living room and invited them to sit down. Then, her hands clasped together tightly in her lap, she asked what was going on.

"Father Damian has been helping me to investigate what exactly is happening with Thomas, and I think at this point we need to let you know what we think..."

Mariela looked to Father Damian, who continued, "Mrs. Santiago, I strongly suspect that Thomas is undergoing a very strange type of possession, something that has never been seen before, and that is the source of his supernatural powers..."

"What are you talking about, Father?"

Father Damian looked at Samuel, as if asking him with his eyes if he could really tell her the whole story. Samuel nodded, encouraging him to continue.

The priest leaned forward slightly, joining his hands together over his knees, and started to tell Mariela everything, from the beginning. Her eyes opened wider and wider, stunned by what she was hearing...

"I know that this must be very difficult to believe, but it's the only explanation that we have been able to come up with for everything that has happened to Thomas," Samuel added.

"But, if it's like you say, Father, why my grandson? He is not particularly religious, he doesn't even go to mass regularly..." Mariela asked, wiping away a tear.

"Why your Thomas? We still don't know; but all of the people that he has killed, in one way or another, were evil..."

Mariela looked at Samuel, stunned by Father Damian's words.

"Nana, Father Damian is referring to the fact that all of those people had been somehow involved in a serious crime or offense, in one way or another..."

Samuel was quiet for a minute, and concluded, "You'll remember that one of the victims was the former city councilman Dan Howard, who was accused several years ago of misappropriation of state funds and money-laundering related to drug dealing in Mexico..."

"But, what about Father Fabian Campbell, who was found dead in his church in Gilbert?" Mariela asked.

"He had been transferred from North Carolina, where he had been accused of sexual abuse on several occasions," Father Damian replied, leaning back on the couch.

Mariela lowered her head, deeply tormented by their revelations. She searched for some way to effectively discount the nightmarish explanation. When she looked up, she said,

"But some of the victims were women and children..."

"The latest victim, the boy, had been suspended from school several times for violently attacking other students; he had most recently been suspended for over a month for seriously injuring a six-year-old girl," Samuel explained.

Mariela stood and started pacing around the living room, running her hands through her hair nervously.

"This is all just so hard to believe!"

"I know, Nana, but it's the only explanation..."

Samuel stood and hugged her, saying, "I still can't even believe it myself..."

E Turquoise Av

41

ESCOBAR FAMILY RESIDENCE
6889 EAST TURQUOISE AVENUE
SCOTTSDALE, ARIZONA

When Samuel got home, he put his briefcase down on the couch while loosening his tie. Hearing the front door close, Catherine appeared in the kitchen doorway:

"We're in here, honey!"

Samuel walked into the kitchen and picked up his baby daughter from her little high chair, and gave her a kiss.

"How did it go?" Catherine asked, wiping her hands off on the front of her apron, giving him a kiss on the lips.

"It went alright, better than I expected..."

"They've been covering the trial all day on the news..."

Samuel put his daughter down in her high chair again and sat next to her at the kitchen table. He took his jacket off and draped it over the back of his chair.

"Are you hungry?" Catherine asked.

"I'm starving, I haven't eaten anything since this morning."

"They showed part of your opening statement on the news, and I'm not just saying this, I thought you were brilliant."

"Oh, you're just saying that because you love me..."

Catherine put her hands on her hips and looked at him in mock jester, "Boy you have some nerve!"

Catherine started to put dinner on the table, as the ten o'clock news began on the TV on the kitchen counter. A young man, with a light-brown complexion and a deep, strong voice announced the day's top stories. Samuel picked up the remote control and turned up the volume:

"Good evening, I'm Gabriel Ramos, and this is your ten o'clock news, bringing you all the latest from around the world. Here are tonight's top stories: today was the first day of the Thomas Santiago trial, the boy accused of a shocking series of murders that took place all over the state of Arizona over the past two years. We're going now to the courthouse in Maricopa, where our correspondent Nadia Rosado is standing by with all the latest information. Nadia, can you tell us what happened in court today?"

"Good evening, Gabriel. As you said, today was the start of the state vs. Thomas Santiago, known as "the Devil Boy." A great number of people came down here today to see where this horrifying story was likely to go. Both lawyers gave their opening statements, both the defense attorney, Samuel Escobar, and the prosecutor, Morgan Stanley, were very specific about the challenges and delicate nature of this case, and they cautioned the jury to be very careful throughout the entire process. We had a chance to talk with Mr. Stanley before he went into the courtroom this morning, and this is what he had to say: "It is time for justice to be served. Thomas Santiago is not insane. The state has sufficient evidence to prove it, and we hope that the jury will send a clear message and put a stop to these kinds of criminals, once and for all."

42

Saint Mary's Basilica
231 North Third Street
Phoenix, Arizona

The next morning, Samuel decided to drop by St. Mary's to see Father Damian. When he stepped into the office, he was surprised to find Juan Manuel there, too, along with Father Steven. Father Damian asked him to take a seat, and Samuel observed that Juan Manuel seemed nervous and avoided meeting his eye. Something was wrong.

"What's going on?" he asked apprehensively.

Father Damian stepped over to Juan Manuel and, placing a hand on his shoulder, he encouraged him to speak.

"Tell him what you told us..."

Juan Manuel rubbed his forehead, his hand trembled slightly. He took a deep breath, his eyes wide.

"When I started at the seminary, three years ago, Thomas came to visit me in Los Angeles. One night, we decided to get together with some friends of mine and read through a book about exorcism. Kevin had taken it from Monsignor Noriega's study, who was away on a trip to the Vatican. We met at the chapel and started to read. Kevin stood up, in the middle of all of us, and started to try to invoke spirits..." Juan clasped his hands together interlacing his fingers, and went on,

"Thomas was there with us, we formed a circle around Kevin. We were all on our knees when Kevin started reading a passage about invoking the presence of the saints. Thomas lay down on top of the altar, pretending to be possessed, and we gathered around him, reading out loud from the book."

Juan Manuel stood up and took a few steps: "We were only playing!"

Samuel looked at Father Damian, frightened; Father Steven crossed his arms and looked at Samuel, worry etched on his face.

"We never thought that we were doing anything bad, we were just fooling around," Juan Manuel exclaimed, turning to face them, his arms open.

"What happened then?" Samuel asked.

"Thomas started to feel really bad, for a second we thought he had fainted. It was really, really... weird."

Juan Manuel paused for a minute. He seemed to be searching the floor for some kind of clue that would solve the eerie puzzle in his mind.

"There's something that I haven't told you, Father Damian... Something incredible happened when we thought Thomas had fainted. Kevin and I stood over him and, all of a sudden, there was a really strong gust of wind, strong enough to blow open one of the windows in the chapel..."

Juan Manuel paused again, swallowing nervously. "The wind almost knocked us down, it seemed to hit Thomas especially hard, his clothes were fluttering, and then he opened his eyes, real slow. Then we decided to stop. I never thought that something bad had happened; Thomas laughed and said he just felt a little dizzy..."

Samuel looked at Father Damian: "Do you think this explains everything, Father?"

"There are still many things that need to be looked into, but I would like to talk to you some more later..."

S 1st Avenue

S 3rd Avenue

W. Jefferson St.

43

MARICOPA COUNTY SUPERIOR COURT
201 WEST JEFFERSON STREET
PHOENIX, ARIZONA

Morgan Stanley stood at the prosecution's table and said loudly, "Your Honor, the state calls Mrs. Marlena McKinney."

A woman of about thirty-five, with an olive complexion and brown eyes walked up to the witness stand. She was wearing a long black dress that gracefully complemented her figure, with a purple belt that draped over her hips. Her bare shoulders, long neck and dark hair swept up in a spiral bun all had the effect of tastefully highlighting her feminine charms.

She was sworn in, and sat down. Crossing her legs, she rested her hands over her knee and waited expectantly for the first question.

"Mrs. McKinney, you are the widow of Patrick McKinney, correct?" Morgan asked.

"Yes."

"When was the last time you saw your husband?"

"The night of April third, before he went to work."

Stanley stepped from behind the table and paced over to the witness box, continuing, "And you had three children with your husband? Is that correct?"

"Yes." Her face lit up in a proud smile, as she recited their names: "Kenny, Linda and Bobby."

Stanley looked at her directly and said, "I know that this must be very, very difficult for you, but I will try to make this as brief as possible."

He turned and walked towards the jury.

"When you heard that your husband had been murdered, what did you feel?"

She was quiet for a minute, lowering her gaze.

"I couldn't believe it; when the police knocked on the door and told me, I didn't know what to say, I didn't know how I was going to tell the children..." she began to weep quietly. Stanley passed her a tissue and she dabbed at the corners of her eyes. She apologized and said she would try to control herself.

"That's alright, Mrs. McKinney, we understand how hard this is for you."

The prosecutor paused to give her an opportunity to calm down. Then he resumed his questioning,

"Now that you know who the person is that was responsible for your husband's death, what do you feel?"

"Objection, Your Honor, that has not been proven in court yet!" Samuel shouted from his seat, before the witness could answer.

"Your Honor, that doesn't have to be proven; we all watched the video from the gas station clearly showing Thomas Santiago killing Mrs. McKinney's husband."

Samuel stood and looked at the judge, refuting the prosecutor's argument:

"Whether the person in the video is my client or not has not been proven. You have to admit, Your Honor, that it would be extremely difficult to make a positive identification based on the images from the video."

"That's ridiculous, Your Honor!" Stanley yelled.

The judge leaned toward the microphone and asked both lawyers to approach the bench.

"Your Honor, the defense can't try to discount the strongest evidence in the whole case," Stanley implored, as he paced towards the bench, his arms open pleadingly.

The judge covered the microphone with his hand so that no one else would hear their conversation. He asked quietly, "What is this all about, Mr. Escobar?"

"Your Honor, the photograph taken from the security camera video which the police used to determine that the defendant is the killer, is computerized. It's a reconstruction of the face, done in a lab, where they added color to the eyes and face. It's not a regular photograph, so it should not be considered essential evidence. And secondly, in the video, you can't clearly tell who the killer is..."

"Your Honor, let me remind the defense counsel that the blood of the victim was found on the defendant's pajamas," the prosecuting attorney interrupted.

The judge looked at them both and said, "Mr. Escobar, I will let you rephrase the question, but I do not want to have any more arguments like this, understood?"

Samuel nodded.

"Rephrase the question," the judge said again, uncovering the microphone.

"Thank you, Your Honor." The lawyers turned and Samuel went back to his seat.

Stanley put his right hand on his hip and looked at the witness: "Mrs. McKinney, what did you think when you realized that your husband had been murdered by the same suspect that the police had been searching for?"

She clasped her hands around her knee again, blinked, and replied, "I said to myself, how can that be... What could Patrick have done to make that guy want to kill him?"

Stanley walked over to his seat.

"Your witness, Mr. Escobar."

Samuel stood and immediately began his line of questioning.

"Mrs. McKinney, what kind of man was your husband? How would you describe him?"

"Patrick was a man of few words, he liked to work, and he was a good father to his children..."

Samuel walked over to her, and he asked evenly, "What kind of husband would you say he was?"

She looked at Stanley, and then back to Samuel and said, "Patrick wasn't perfect, he had his flaws, like we all do, but he was a good father to my children and that was what mattered most to me..."

Samuel looked at her pointedly, and she was frightened by the look in his eyes.

"Is that why you still lived with him, in spite of his abuse?"

"Objection, Your Honor!" Stanley shouted, quickly rising to his feet. "Mrs. McKinney didn't come here to defend her marriage in front of the court."

"Sustained," the judge replied. "Mr. Escobar, how is that relevant to this case?" the judge took off his glasses and set them down.

Marcos handed a folder to Samuel. Standing in the center of the room, he held it up so everyone could see it.

"Your Honor, these are police reports for Patrick McKinney's nine arrests for domestic violence, the neighbors called the police on him nine times for beating his wife; once he beat her so brutally that she had to be hospitalized for a week."

Stanley jumped up again and rushed over to the judge's bench. He said angrily,

"Your Honor, please let me remind the defense counsel that the reason this witness has been called is because her husband has been murdered, not to defend the integrity of her marriage!"

"Mr. Escobar, what does this have to do with this case?" the judge asked again, clearly perturbed by Samuel's persistence.

"I'll rephrase the question," Samuel said, looking at Mrs. McKinney.

'The jury will disregard the last statement," the judge intoned, looking sternly at the jury.

Samuel flipped through the folder and held one of the pages out to the witness. In a firm voice he asked,

"Mrs. McKinney, isn't it true that on the night of March 30, four days before your husband was killed, you talked to your sister Patricia on the phone, you were still in the hospital, and you admitted to her that, on several occasions, you had prayed to God to kill your husband?"

"Objection, Your Honor!" Stanley shouted at the top of his lungs.

"Mr. Escobar!" the judge immediately intervened. "If you continue to disregard my instructions, I will hold you in contempt."

The judge turned to Mrs. McKinney and said, "the witness does not have to answer the last question."

Mrs. McKinney was very upset; she nervously twisted the tissue that Stanley had given to her. Her face had grown pale, her eyes shone.

"Does the defense have any further questions?" the judge asked, with a hint of sarcasm.

Samuel looked solemnly at Mrs. McKinney and replied, "No, Your Honor, I think that the silence of the witness has answered my question."

Judge Fieldmore looked at both lawyers, pounded with his gavel and announced, "This court is adjourned until tomorrow morning at nine-thirty." He pounded his gavel one more time, and the court officer asked everyone to stand. The judge gathered the papers from his dais and left.

The police escorted Thomas out while Samuel put his papers and files back into his briefcase.

"What was all that?" Oliver asked, confused.

"I'm sorry, I guess I got a little out of control," Samuel answered, looking down.

"Out of control? You were about to be arrested for misconduct..."

Samuel looked up and met Oliver's gaze: "I'm sorry, it won't happen again..."

Oliver let out a long breath and, putting his hand on Samuel's shoulder, he said, "It's been a very long day for everybody, go home and get some rest. I'll see you tomorrow at nine, alright?"

"I have to stop by the office to pick up some things I'm going to need for tomorrow, and then I have to go see Father Damian..."

Oliver put his hands in his pockets and looked at him intently. "Don't worry about what happened today, we still have a long way to go. Just promise me you'll go right home after you meet with Father Damian..."

Samuel nodded sadly.

E Butte Av.

44

ARIZONA STATE PRISON
1305 EAST BUTTE AVENUE
FLORENCE, ARIZONA

That night, an unexpected visitor arrived at the Florence prison. Thomas slowly opened his eyes when he heard someone opening the cell door. Samuel had convinced Judge Fieldmore to once again allow a select list of authorized visitors to enter Thomas's cell.

"Hello, Thomas," a man's voice said, standing over him.

"Father Damian?" the boy asked, still half-asleep, stretching.

"Yes, it's me, my son."

Yawning, Thomas asked, "What time is it?"

"It's seven-twenty," the priest answered, having just seen a clock on the wall outside. "Are you tired?"

"No, I'm just taking a little nap. I'm tired of reading, and since I don't have anybody to talk to, I fell asleep..."

Thomas paused and looked at the soldiers, who watched him intently from just outside the cell. Then he added, "The guards are forbidden to talk to me at all, after what happened the last time..."

"What were you reading?"

Father Damian approached the bed and sat down at his side.

Thomas picked up a book that was on a chair and handed it to him. The priest read the title aloud: *The Fifth Mountain.*

"Juan Manuel brought it for me the other day, he says it's really good."

"Paulo Coelho is one of the greatest writers in Brazil... in all of Latin America, as a matter of fact."

"Where are you from?"

"I'm from El Salvador."

"I thought you were Brazilian," Thomas said, surprised.

"No, my child, I attended seminary in Rio de Janeiro, but I'm from El Salvador originally."

Thomas scratched his head and asked, "How long have you been a priest?"

"It will be exactly forty-three years, as of December tenth."

"Wow! How old were you when you started?"

"When I entered the seminary, I had just turned sixteen."

"So you never married, or had children?"

"No, I was always more interested in other things..."

With a puzzled look, Thomas asked, "What kinds of things?"

Father Damian stood and took a few steps. He saw how the soldiers followed his every move with their eyes. He clasped his hands behind his back and leaned against the thick bullet-proof glass at the front of the cell. Glancing over his left shoulder, he saw how a technician wearing headphones in a little room across the hall listened to every word they said.

"You know, the kinds of questions that people ask themselves when they're young," the priest continued after a brief silence. "Things like, "Where did we come from? Who made the universe?" that kind of things..."

Thomas stood and tried to walk. Father Damian observed how awkward it was for him to move. "How can you walk with those chains?"

"At first it was hard, but I guess I got used to it." He noted the deep compassion in the priest's eyes. Looking curiously at the long black robe and the white collar at his neck, Thomas paced to the far side of the cell. "You never liked girls?" he asked, still trying to understand.

The priest smiled slightly. "What is not to like? That's not the point, Thomas. Women are magnificent; they are one of the reasons why the world is still a beautiful place. As Jesus said in Mathew 19:12, *"For there are eunuchs who were born thus from their mother's womb, and there are eunuchs who were made eunuchs by men, and there are eunuchs who have made themselves eunuchs for the kingdom of heaven's sake. He, who is able to accept it, let him accept it."*

"And which category do you fall in to?"

Father Damian paused, and, smiling, replied, "I like to think that I'm in the last group..."

He stepped away from the glass and unclasped his hands. With a serious expression, he looked at Thomas and said, "This might sound a littler confusing to you because you are very young, but, the world of the spirit is something that surpasses reason, it is the sacrifice of the flesh and the crucifixion of the spirit to be able to rise up the soul, through illumination..."

Thomas looked confused, and Father Damian realized that his words had been a bit too profound for the boy to grasp. "In other words, it's like exchanging one world of complications for another..."

Stepping closer, he added, "Someone once told me that if there were no women in the world, then men would have no need for money..."

Thomas was quiet for a few seconds; it seemed as if the priest's words had touched him very deeply.

"Father, do you really believe that God exists, a Supreme Being that made the whole world, but that nobody has ever seen? And that there's really a heaven, and a hell, waiting for all of us?"

Father Damian looked at him intently as he considered his response. His eyes darkened, conveying a well of sorrow.

"There has to be a God," he replied, sitting down on the bed, "because this can't be it... this can't be all there is in life. There has to be something better, for those of us who believe in justice, in brotherhood, in love thy neighbor..." he paused, and concluded, "because if this is all there is, then life has no point..."

They were both quiet. A feeling of peace settled over them.

"Your brother wants to be a priest," Father Damian said, his expression brightening.

"Yes, but I don't think that's going to last..."

"Why not?" Father Damian asked, leaning back, clearly surprised.

"I just know it... My brother is a good man, with a really big heart, but I think being a priest, it's just so hard...I don't know, maybe I'm wrong..."

Father Damian looked at Thomas for a long time. Then he said, "Your brother told us about what happened that night in Los Angeles, when you went to visit him..."

"When?"

"That time that you and he and some of his friends were playing around in the chapel, having an exorcism..."

"Oh yeah, that night..."

The priest slowly nodded.

"Nothing happened, we were just playing. One of my brother's friends was reading those prayers out of a book, and I pretended that I was possessed. Juan Manuel and another guy were kneeling next to me. Then I started feeling kind of dizzy, and we decided to stop."

"And what else happened?"

"Nothing, that was it..."

Father Damian looked down at the floor, as he remembered Juan Manuel's version of what had happened that night.

"You don't remember a strong gust of wind that blew one of the windows open in the chapel?"

Thomas blinked nervously, looking away.

"No, I don't remember... Why?"

"When you first started waking up with blood on you, wasn't there anything strange that you can remember that happened right before that?"

Father Damian saw how Thomas thought hard, he seemed to be wrestling with something in his mind, and he urged the boy,

"There was something, wasn't there?"

"No, it's nothing..."

"It doesn't matter how unimportant it might seem, tell me what it was."

"Well, my grandmother had gotten us into the habit of reciting Psalm ninety-one before we went to bed every night. That night, when I had gotten back from visiting Juan Manuel, I recited the Psalm, as usual... But that time, after I finished, I started feeling dizzy again..."

45

Saint Mary's Basilica
231 North Third Street
Phoenix, Arizona

After leaving his office, Samuel headed over to see Father Damian. After offering him a seat in the church office, the priest asked,

"So, how's the trial going?"

"We're doing everything we can... but, for some reason, it still seems like it's not enough..."

Father Damian handed him a book with a ruby-red leather cover, with gold embossed letters on the front. Samuel read: "The Archangel Michael: His Mission and Ours."

"What is this?" Samuel asked.

"I'd like you to read it carefully," Father Damian said, putting a hand on his shoulder.

"The Archangel Michael? What does that have to do with the case?"

Father Damian paced behind Samuel. He stepped behind the desk and sat down, replying, "Maybe much more than you can imagine. After you left that morning, we talked with Juan Manuel; based on what he told us, and the symptoms Thomas has exhibited, my other suspicions were confirmed..."

"What suspicions?" Samuel asked, wide-eyed.

Damian folded his hands on top of the desk and looked at Samuel evenly. "Remember when I told you that I suspected that Thomas has been possessed by the spirit of an angel? I wasn't kidding. Ever since I found out about what was going on, I started to do as much research as I could, to figure out why this could be happening to Thomas, since he is not an especially religious person. But after hearing what Juan Manuel had to say, I understood how this could have come to pass; what I still didn't know was what spirit in particular had taken possession of him. But now, I am sure..."

Samuel was anxious to hear his theory, but at the same time he was afraid that the explanation would be too much for him to handle.

"Do you know who the Archangel Michael is?" Father Damian had noted the dread in Samuel's eyes, sensing he was too afraid to ask.

"I don't remember very much about him, just what they taught us in catechism. I know that he is an angel of God, and one of the most powerful angels in Heaven."

Father Damian stood and walked over to the tall bookshelf on his right. He took the seventh book in the third shelf out, searched for page one hundred thirty-three, and placing the book open on the desk in front of Samuel, he said, "There is more about the Archangel Michael than many people think. He is the guardian of Heaven, some even say he is the General of all the angels."

Samuel looked down at the illustration of Saint Michael on page one hundred thirty-two. The angel had a shield in his right hand, and a long, heavy chain in his left; under his left foot, writhing on the ground, his wings spread and his face in the dirt, was Lucifer, the fallen angel.

"So... What does this have to do with Thomas?" Samuel looked up at the priest.

Father Damian crossed his arms, blinked several times, and was silent. Samuel looked at him intently: he could tell from the look in his eyes that he had made an important discovery, and it wasn't good...

"Possession is a two-way street, Mr. Escobar..."

Samuel was perplexed by the enigmatic response. He leaned back in his chair and asked, "What do you mean?"

"Possession is a two-way street in the sense that it can be for good, or for evil," Father Damian explained. "Just like someone can become a demon, like what happened to the girl in the film "The Exorcist," a person can also be taken over by a force for good, and become an angel."

Samuel looked even more confused, as the priest paced across the room.

"You think that whatever has possessed Thomas is an angel, right?"

"Yes." The priest stopped pacing.

"But if it's an angel, why is it killing people? It doesn't make any sense..."

Father Damian stepped over to the window and looked out at the deserted street. The city seemed to be asleep under a heavy calm. He rested his hand on the windowsill and leaned against it. Under his frock, he reached into his pants pocket:

"Someone once asked me, in Rio de Janeiro, that if God was a good God, as we preach, then why had he killed so many people in the past?"

Father Damian turned to look at Samuel and continued, "It's hard for people to understand God's justice, and the reasons why He does many things. But, even though many people don't believe it, there are people in this world with evil in their hearts, and they will never change, and that is why God destroys them..."

He stepped away from the window, adding, "What Thomas is experiencing is beyond our ability to understand..."

Both men were quiet. The priest sat back down behind the desk, putting his hands behind his neck.

"When I asked you in your office if there was anything that all the crime scenes had in common that you hadn't mentioned, and you told me about the strange flower smell, I began to suspect that my vision had been correct."

"What do you mean?"

Father Damian went over to the bookcase again and took out the third book from the left on the top shelf. On page one-hundred ninety-one, there was a drawing of Saint Francis of Assisi, reading a book, with a dove on his shoulder. Underneath the illustration, there was a long paragraph of text, highlighted in red: "The horrible fits and torments were accompanied by a strange smell of flowers that followed St. Francis wherever he went, forming a part of his stigmata."

Samuel knew the story of St. Francis very well. Of all the stories he had learned in catechism, that one had had the strongest impact on him. Reading the highlighted words in that book, it was as if he had been struck by a bolt of lightening, and in his mind Samuel rushed back to the moment when he had first heard about the saint:

"Saint Francis of Assisi was the son of a very powerful man of that time, a wealthy cloth merchant. As a young man, tearing off his fancy clothes, Saint Francis threw them at his father's feet," the nun Sister Maria had told the story with great enthusiasm, gesturing dramatically. All the children listened with rapt attention, including little Samuel, his wide-open eyes filled with wonder. "Then, looking at his father, Saint Francis said, "From now on God will be my father," Sister Maria told her young audience. "Then after Saint Francis returned to Assisi, he had another dream, where he heard the voice of God tell him to repair his church. In one famous story, Saint Francis preached to a flock of birds about the kingdom of God and they all listened; the people said that he could talk to the birds."

"As you can see, there's much more to that flower smell than anybody thought," Father Damian's voice brought him back to the present.

With his hands clasped behind his back, the priest paced across the office and continued, "This strange smell of flowers is known as the scent of sainthood. There are many legends about it in Israel. They say that when Jesus performed his miracles, he was always surrounded by a subtle scent of wildflowers..."

Samuel turned and, sitting on the edge of the desk, he crossed his arms over his chest:

"If what you're saying is true, then how can we put a stop to it and help Thomas?"

The priest let out a long breath and responded, "That's what I still don't know..."

E Turquoise Av

46

ESCOBAR FAMILY RESIDENCE
6889 EAST TURQUOISE AVENUE
SCOTTSDALE, ARIZONA

When he got home that night, Samuel couldn't get what Father Damian had said out of his mind. He sat down on the couch in the living room, opened the book that the priest had given him and started leafing through it. After turning several pages, he came to an illustration of an angel dressed as a Roman soldier, with a large gold sash running diagonally from over his shoulder, across his chest and around his back. His sandals were laced up over his shins and tied in a knot, with rubies in the middle; underneath the picture he read: "*Archangel Michael, the incorruptible angel, his name means*

"He who is like God." Each of his hairs contains ten thousand faces who all speak a different language, and each one prays to God for all humanity."

Samuel set the open book down on the coffee table and considered what he had just read. He blinked several times, and continued reading: "His wings are the color of emeralds, and his tears change to pearls as soon as they hit the ground."

He closed the book and said to himself, "What kind of an angel is that? He sounds more like a Hollywood superhero..."

47

Saint Mary's Basilica
231 North Third Street
Phoenix, Arizona

The next day, Samuel went over to see Father Damian before going to his office.

The priest was talking with a woman who appeared to be crying. When he saw Samuel, he gestured for him to come in. Standing, he walked the woman to the front door of the church, saying to her in Spanish, "Don't worry, leave it in God's hands, and keep praying, you'll see that things are going to change."

The two men greeted each other, and Samuel asked what was wrong with the woman, as he watched her cross the street.

There's one thing in life that will never change: mothers always suffer more from their children's mistakes than the children do themselves..."

"I'm sorry to bother you, Father, but I need to talk to you," Samuel apologized, changing the subject. "I was reading the book that you gave me last night and, really, I don't know what to think..."

Father Damian's eyes lit up with a mysterious glint, and with a slight smile, like someone who has the answer to a riddle, he said, "It's impressive, isn't it?"

"Father, are you sure about all this? The book describes a being that is pretty unbelievable: an angel, with emerald wings, a thousand faces within every strand of hair, and a lot of other crazy things..." Samuel spread his arms and concluded, "I can't imagine that any of it could be even remotely possible."

They both sat down next to each other in one of the pews.

"I know that it sounds creepy, but just as the forces of evil can be terrifying, so can the forces of good."

The priest paused before continuing, "Have you ever thought about the powers that Moses demonstrated in Egypt?"

Samuel looked at him, puzzled, while he tried to remember the few details he could still recall about the stories of the Bible.

Father Damian pointed with his index finger, "Think about how terrifying it would have been to see a man part the sea in two, changing the water of a river into blood, or to see him hit a rock with a stick and make water flow out of it," he explained, straightening his frock.

"The Bible says in the book of Numbers, Chapter sixteen, verses thirty-one to thirty-three, that the powers of Moses were so strong, that one day, several Israelites confronted him to ask, if the whole nation of Israel was holy, why he had to be the intermediary between God and men. And, as the story goes, Moses said to them, "Tomorrow you will build an altar and I will build another, and we will offer sacrifices to Jehovah, and whoever's altar ignites into flames first, that will tell us who has been chosen by God." The next day, they did as they had been told. Moses ordered that water be thrown on to the firewood placed on top of his altar. Then, praying to God, a bolt of lightening came down from the sky, and Moses' altar burst into flames. Looking at the others, Moses asked God to open up the Earth and swallow them all whole, with their families and all of their belongings, and as soon as he had finished speaking, that is exactly what happened."

Samuel was speechless. He tried to picture the scene in his mind. Father Damian gestured towards an image of Saint Michael on one of the church's large stained glass windows and asked,

"Why do you think that it is easier for people to believe in evil than to believe in good?"

"I don't know, maybe because of the things we see every day," Samuel replied, staring at the figure in the window.

"People are more effected by their nightmares than by the beautiful things in life," the priest observed, and looked at Samuel before continuing, "Good is not perceived because it is silent; but for every bomb that explodes and reaps destruction, there are millions of little acts of kindness that make up life..."

He fixed his gaze on the Jesus on the cross and added, "It's amazing that people are quicker to believe in the existence of demons than in a God; it's as if they completely forgot that God was the one who created the demon..."

The priest turned to look at him, and asked with an enigmatic smile, "Did you know that the Devil takes the form of a woman?"

"What?"

Samuel wasn't sure he had heard right.

Father Damian repeated the question, but puzzled, Samuel just looked back at him, speechless.

Father Damian crossed his legs and clasping his hands together, he rested his right arm over the back of the pew.

"I'm sure you've never heard the name "Dhajamuer," he said, beginning his story.

Samuel shook his head no.

"But you have heard of the sculpture known as the Winged Victory of Samothrace?"

"The famous sculpture of the angel without a head or arms?"

"The very same," the priest responded excitedly, as if he were about to let him in on a very important secret.

"Dhajamuer was the sculptor..."

"But according to historians, the sculptor was unknown," Samuel interjected.

"That's what they want you to believe. The statue was found in 1863, on the island of Samothrace, north of Egeo. Dhajamuer hid it away there, after he rejected the work."

Samuel was surprised by this. "Rejected his own work? But it's one of the most beautiful pieces of art in history, why would he do that?"

The priest took off his glasses and replied, "Of course it is. But have you ever wondered why it wasn't found like other works of art? This one turned up without a head, with no arms, shattered into one hundred and eighteen pieces, until the Louvre in Paris put it back together again."

The priest's eyes glowed with wonder. Discovering the work's true origins had been a real revelation for him, and had given him great satisfaction. Samuel could hear the enthusiasm in his voice with every word.

"The statue was found in 1863, but in 1950, at the same place, a hand was found, which was believed to have been part of the same sculpture."

After a pause, he smiled and explained, "But what people don't know is, they concluded that the hand belonged to the statue because they also found a manuscript there, with a poem which Dhajamuer had written..."

"A poem?"

"Yes, and in that poem, Dhajamuer explained why he had destroyed the statue."

Father Damian furrowed his brow, while he looked up towards the ceiling and said,

"If I'm not mistaken, it went something like this:

> My heart and soul I curse with damnation
> for my wild flights of imagination
> that this day brought me such disappointment.
> Because, this day my profound disenchantment
> has taken on color and a silhouette.
> Although it has no head,
> and perhaps no heart,
> I have taken its arms
> to ease my regret.
> Although my fallen angel
> I sculpted with affection,
> today I was ridiculed,
> for it was beyond their comprehension.

Samuel looked down, and was quiet as he absently ran a hand through his hair. Then he looked up at the priest and asked, "Who was Dhajamuer?"

Father Damian drew in a deep breath, and let it out in a long sigh before answering,

"According to my research, he was a sculptor and poet who lived around the year 220 B.C. He was always known for his poetry, but he started studying sculpture. In those days, the great sculptures that adorned Greek temples and buildings always depicted the gods, but he wanted to do something different, something that would stand out. Then he learned about the Jews and their history, and decided to sculpt something that no one had ever dared attempt before, the most beautiful angel of them all: Lucifer." The priest paused to take a breath.

"He worked for several years, until, finally, he had done it: he had sculpted the most breathtaking work of art the world had ever seen..."

Father Damian stood and, clasping his hands behind him, silently took a few steps down the center aisle.

"After he had finished the work, he took it to show his teacher. When his teacher saw it, he howled with laughter. Dhajamuer was devastated..."

Samuel stood and leaning against a pew, he asked, "But why did his teacher laugh?"

"The statue was stunning. Her face was as beautiful as Mary Magdalene's, but in spite of her incredible beauty, her expression was angry; her arms were strong, and her hands had deadly claws, like a bear's."

Father Damian paused thoughtfully again.

"If you examine it very carefully, you'll notice that the arms were cut off fairly high, since according to the statue's positioning, the right arm had been reaching out in front. Dhajamuer cut it off in such a way that no sign of it would remain."

He took a step toward Samuel and added, "He had wanted the sculpture to illustrate the day when the beauty transformed into the beast. There is a reason for the posture of the wet body and the extension of the robe she wore behind her, if you carefully analyze it. According to the artist, Satan fell into the sea right by the shore, and, getting up, went off like a bolt of lightening to seek revenge. It would not have been possible for the robe to have lifted away from the body in the back like that, since if it was wet, it would have clung to the legs; unless, at that moment, the angel had already taken flight..."

Samuel looked at the priest solemnly, while he thought about what he had just heard. He seemed confused. Still skeptical, he scratched his head and asked, "But why did they have to hide what had happened and the sculpture's true origins from the world?"

Father Damian's eyes opened wide, he took a step back and responded, "The statue has been of great importance for the art world and for the Greeks in particular. It represents the naval victories for Greeks, and it is believed to be a tribute to Antilochus the Third's conquest of Rhodiana. It commemorates all the brave men who gave their lives on the fields of battle... Then eighty-seven years later, to come out with a new theory... Do you have any idea what kind of a scandal it would set off? Especially in terms of feminism, not to mention what kind of controversy it would spark in Christianity... That is why the authorities decided that, out of respect for the memory of the man who discovered it, the French consul and amateur archeologist Charles Champoiseau, and for what it means to the Greek people, it would be best to ignore the manuscript, and let people continue to believe what they already believed about the statue..."

After a moment, Father Damian looked at Samuel: "Haven't you ever wondered why Lucifer was cast out of Heaven? Because it isn't explained in the Bible..."

Samuel thought for a minute and replied, "I thought it was because he must have rebelled against God."

"But, why?" the priest insisted, shrugging his shoulders. "If from the beginning of all eternity, he was the most powerful angel in heaven, right after God the Father, Son, and Holy Ghost. One day, out of nowhere, he just decided to rebel against God?"

Samuel was quiet, his mind searched in vain for a plausible explanation.

"According to legend and many ancient texts that I have read, it supposedly happened after God had just finished creating the world. God said to the angels that they had to honor man, but Lucifer got angry and asked why...If the angels had been created first, and if Man was weak-willed and did not have knowledge of the truth... But God said that Man had been made in His likeness and image, and because of that, he had to be respected. Lucifer did not want to accept this, and God cast him out down to the Earth."

Father Damian sat down in a pew again, and crossed his legs before continuing, "The sculpture represents the very moment when Lucifer, picking himself up off the ground, flies off to take his vengeance against God, to destroy his divine creation, the very reason he was cast out of Heaven..."

"Man..." Samuel murmured.

"Exactly, I'm going to tell you a secret that very few people know about... Remember how I said that the statue was found broken in one hundred and eighteen pieces?"

Samuel nodded.

"If you look in the Bible, in Psalm 118 verse 18, you may not believe what it says..." the priest trailed off with a mysterious smile.

"What does that verse say?" Samuel asked, leaning towards him.

"*The Lord has chastened me sorely, but He has not given me over to death,*" the priest recited, raising an eyebrow.

Father Damian saw how his words impacted Samuel, the story he had told seemed to have had a profound effect. The priest took another deep breath and went on,

"As the story goes, after a few days, ashamed, Dhajamuer hid the statue of the Winged Victory of Samothrace, and one day, still angry over his humiliation, he cut off the angel's head and arms, and smashed the body..."

"So whatever happened to the head and arms?" Samuel asked, intrigued.

"That's a whole other mystery; as far as I could tell from my research, he hid them away in a secret place, only he himself knew the exact location..."

Both men were quiet. Samuel looked up and stared at the ceiling, his mind trying to process the incredible story. Then he looked at Father Damian and asked, "Why did Dhajamuer think that women are demons?"

"No, no no!" the priest quickly replied, gesturing with his hands. "That wasn't Dhajamuer's idea..."

"But you said..."

"No, what I said is that with the sculpture, he wanted to show that Satan has a female form."

"But where did he get that from?" Samuel sat down next to Father Damian, putting his hands on his knees.

"From Scripture... The Bible says, in Ezekiel 28:12 and in verse 15: "*You were the signet of perfection, full of wisdom and perfect in beauty,*" "*You were perfect in your ways from the day you were created, till iniquity was found in you.*"

Father Damian scratched his head and looking at Samuel, and continued, "Lucifer was the most beautiful angel in all of Heaven... beauty has always been associated with women since the dawn of history... Who do we have beauty contests for?"

"Women?" Samuel said tentatively.

"Right. Think about it." Father Damian tapped against his temple with his index finger.

"Do you think that they would have a beauty contest up in Heaven to decide who the most beautiful male angel was?"

Samuel considered this. "But the Devil in the form of a woman, it's ridiculous!"

"Why? According to Scripture, in Exodus chapter 3 verses 13 and 14, it says "*Then Moses said to God, "If I come to the people of Israel and say to them, 'The God of your fathers has sent me to you,' and they ask me, 'What is his name?' what shall I say to them?" God said to Moses, "I AM WHO I AM."* The Bible always refers to God as a masculine being, "God the Almighty Father." Even Jesus refers to Him in the same way when he says, "If you had known me, you would have known my Father also; henceforth you know him and have seen him, no one comes to the Father, but by me." And his greatest invocation, in Matthew 6:9, "*Our father in heaven...*"

The priest crossed his arms and leaned back in the pew. Then he stretched his legs out and asked, "If God Himself has never said if he has a gender or form, why should we think any differently when it comes to the Devil? The Bible tells us "Moses talked to God as one talks to a friend." And according to our Biblical history, he is the only one who had seen God. But I'm going to tell you a secret: according to the history of the Bible, the only one who ever saw the face of Satan was Jesus, when he was tempted in the desert; no one else."

"What about Eve?"

"No, she heard his voice through the snake, but she never saw Satan's face."

Father Damian uncrossed his arms and leaned forward, resting his hands over the back of the pew in front of him. "Why do you think that the Devil approached Eve, and not Adam, and told her to eat the apple?"

Samuel was quiet, trying to revive the dim memories of the stories he had heard. He lightly shook his head.

"Adam was in charge in the garden; I'm sure that if he had convinced Adam, Eve would have eaten the fruit, if Adam had asked her to... Satan knew that he didn't have anything to offer Adam, because God had already given him everything. But the Devil understood the woman's heart, and knew how to use her vanity to trap her."

The priest paused and moistened his lips. "The old saying goes, "Only a woman knows what a woman wants.""

He rose and stepped into the aisle, looking all around the church. He slowly shook his head and, crossing his arms over his chest he declared, "I don't know why the idea of the Devil having a female form is so shocking to so many people... It has been clearly depicted by Michelangelo in one of his paintings, all this time..."

"What? Michelangelo!" Samuel exclaimed, wide-eyed.

"Haven't you ever seen his painting "The Fall of Man?" the priest asked, with outstretched arms.

Samuel tried to quickly call to mind the image of the artwork; he vaguely remembered something but he wasn't sure about the details.

"Have you seen it?" Father Damian interrupted his thoughts.

"Yes," Samuel affirmed. "My wife and I went to Rome for our honeymoon..."

"If you ever go and see the painting again, notice how Satan, half-human, half-snake, offers the apple to Eve. You'll see how, apart from Satan's feminine face, underneath the left arm, you can clearly see a female breast."

"A breast?" Samuel asked, incredulous.

"Yes," Father Damian nodded. "It is one of the most tightly guarded secrets of the ancient Scriptures that only a very select group of people has come to understand."

Samuel just looked at him, his mouth agape; he couldn't believe what he was hearing.

"But... couldn't that just have been some kind of mistake that Michelangelo made? He painted over four hundred images on the chapel ceiling..."

Smiling skeptically, the priest replied, "A mistake? Never in your life. Michelangelo was well-versed in Scripture and was very, very faithful to it in his work." He scratched his forehead and continued, "When he was summoned to Rome by Pope Julius II in 1508, the Pope told him about his idea to have the twelve patriarchs painted on the ceiling of the chapel. They both shared a great love for art, so Michelangelo managed to convince him to go even further, beyond anything that had ever been attempted: to paint the entire story of the Bible, from beginning to end. Julius was fascinated by the idea, and he granted Michelangelo access to all of the Vatican's archives, so that he could research what he wanted to depict, on the condition that he would not give away the secrets that he would find there."

Father Damian paused for a second before concluding with heartfelt emotion, "Mistake? Never! Michelangelo was a perfectionist."

He clasped his hands behind him and paced towards Samuel. He went on, "When the critics asked him why he had painted Satan in female form, Michelangelo explained that in his work, he had tried to doubly blame woman for the expulsion from Paradise... in order not to reveal the secret."

He took a breath and continued,

"There was a German painter, around the year 1500, called Lucas Cranach, who had suspicions about the messages hidden in Michelangelo's work... And he painted the scene too, but in his version he left no room for doubt, and Satan is clearly depicted in the form of a woman."

He smiled mischievously and crossed his arms. "Some day, when we have more time, remind me to tell you a story that I heard once from one of the Camarlengos, about how Satan cursed Michelangelo for revealing her identity to the world... and about his strange death on one February 18th..."

"Satan cursed him?"

The priest smiled again and explained, "There are many secrets from the Scriptures revealed in the painting on the Sistine Chapel ceiling, perhaps I'll tell you about them one day..."

They were both quiet for a long time. There was a peaceful feeling in the air. Father Damian sighed, closed his eyes, and spoke again, "The numbers are very mysterious, Samuel..."

"Why do you say that?"

The priest opened his eyes and replied, "The great philosopher Plato once said: *There are no accidents or coincidences in life, since time is made up of numbers and numbers don't make mistakes...*"

"I'm not sure what you're trying to tell me, Father..."

"Remember I said the statue was found in 1863, right?"

Samuel nodded expectantly.

"If you add up each of those numbers, one by one, for example 1 + 8 + 6 + 3 is 18. The statue was smashed into 118 pieces, and you already know what Psalm 118 verse 18 says... Right?"

Samuel nodded again.

"According to a Mayan prophesy..."

"Mayan?"

"They predicted that all of humanity would be radically changed after a certain solar eclipse..."

Perplexed, Samuel stared at Father Damian with a puzzled expression.

"Remember the solar eclipse we had a few years ago? Well, the Mayans predicted that it would be the first sign, marking the beginning of the change, and during this period Man would enter into 'The time of mirrors', to find himself face to face with his destiny..."

Father Damian paused for a moment, smoothing his frock and continued,

"That eclipse took place on the 11th day of the 8th month of 1999..."

Samuel suddenly got to his feet.

"The day of the eclipse, you could see a ring of fire that moved across the sky; it was something that had never been witnessed in all of human history, since at the same time it formed a cosmic cross, with the Earth in the center, with almost all of the other planets in our solar system, except our moon and Pluto. The planets formed the sign of the cross, in the four elemental signs of the zodiac, Earth, Air, Fire, and Water, which are the four signs of the evangelists, the four custodians of Saint John's Apocalypse..."

Samuel felt as if his heart had leaped from his chest, his face was very pale. His throat dry, he swallowed, and the ground underneath his feet suddenly felt unsteady.

"The most impressive thing about the eclipse," Father Damian went on, "is that it coincided exactly with the cosmic cross, which began on the 18th of August, a phenomena that only takes place once every ten million years..."

He licked his lips again and said, "This event and the highly specific nature of the prophecy made it the most apocalyptic eclipse in all of history..."

Samuel started to pace around the church. He scratched his neck, taking deep breaths. He turned suddenly and looked Father Damian straight in the eye:

"Is there more?"

"The Mayans called it "the time of mirrors" because, according to their prediction, certain things were not as they seemed. For example, the dates and the movements of the planets; according to their mathematic calculations, it shouldn't have happened for three hundred more years..."

"But, according to historians, the Mayans were supposed to be excellent mathematicians..."

"You're right. To them, universal processes, like the motion of the galaxies, were cyclical and never changing. What changes is the level of human consciousness that goes through them, constantly evolving towards perfection. Then they concluded that it was all like seeing a mirror-image of something; man had to interpret the reflections of his conscience and actions through destiny's mirror..."

The priest paused, and then continued, as if launching his biggest weapon:

"The Devil wasn't anything to them, they didn't know anything about him. That's why they never understood the second part of the message..."

Samuel studied him, as if he held his heart in his hands, and he waited with excited trepidation to hear the story's conclusion, like someone helplessly waiting to be drawn up into a huge tornado.

"Psychologically, when a person has a vision, his subconscious sees everything in reverse, like some mentally ill people do."

"Cognitive distortion," Samuel said softly.

"Exactly. When they compared the dates and movements of the planets, they understood that they were seeing the date in reverse, since there were still three hundred years to go, according to their calculations."

Samuel covered his mouth with his hand.

Father Damian smiled: Samuel seemed to have suddenly gotten the message.

"The date in reverse," Samuel began, "is..."

"18, 8, 6661," they both said at the same time.

"6-6-6-1... Satan's first step, after his liberation from the thousand years that the Bible talks about," Father Damian explained. "Think about how perfect the numbers are in this prophecy. The number of the beast is 666, and if you add up each digit 6+6+6 is 18."

He paused again and took a deep breath, continuing, "I once asked myself, if Hitler and the Germans killed six million Jews in the Holocaust, about nine thousand people every day... then, how many days would they have been killing for? If you divide six million by nine thousand, then you get 6.6666666666."

Samuel seemed to be in shock, looking at Father Damian with unblinking, wide eyes.

"If we ask ourselves why he had to come here to Phoenix, Arizona, we must remember that this church was founded in 1881, a date in which the number 18 appears twice, forwards and backwards, and if we add up the numbers individually, 1+8+8+1, we get 18 again..."

Father Damian lowered his gaze, scratching his forehead. Then he gazed towards the front of the church and with a slight smile he went on, "Some experts argued that the year 2000 would be the end of the world; but it was only the beginning of the end. The eclipse took place on August 18, four months before the end of the millennium, in the four houses of the zodiac, signifying the four evangelists of the Apocalypse..."

Standing perfectly still, Samuel could barely comprehend the immensity of what he was hearing, as every date and every event described connected with everything else, reinforcing the whole, giving more and more credibility to Father Damian's vision.

"You are the most unusual priest I have ever met... You talk about Mayan prophesies, about Plato, about things that don't have anything to do with your religion..."

"The truth is not easily glimpsed in palaces and their golden thrones, it walks among the flowers and the innocent souls who question God's creation with a pure heart..."

The priest leaned towards Samuel, smiling, "Remember when I told you that, after doing some research, I had been able to prove that my theories were correct? This was what I had been studying. And there's something else that's quite interesting: Nostradamus talked about that very same eclipse..."

"No!"

"That's right, the only difference was that he predicted it for the month of July. He prophesied that in that time *Down from the sky would come the King of Terror to restore the great reign of Angolmois.* According to experts, Nostradamus could have been using the Jewish calendar, since the 11th of August 1999 is the last day of the seventh lunar phase in that calendar."

Father Damian smiled brightly, "The thing that's going to really twist your noodles is that, right here in Arizona, the Indians made the same prediction."

"Father, you're putting me on!" Samuel took a step backward, even more stunned.

"I'm not kidding. The Hopis predicted that, in these times, humanity was going to have the chance to choose their path: they could choose the path of love, or they could choose the path of evil... Do you want to know another important fact about the eclipse? The shadow that the moon cast over the earth reached Europe, passing over Kosovo, then through the Middle East, through Iraq, then through Pakistan and India. Many people think that the shadow was an omen, pointing out where wars and disasters would strike...and that's exactly what we have seen..."

Samuel was completely overwhelmed. He looked at Father Damian, who was silently contemplating the image of Jesus over the altar. They both stood there, silent, for a long time. That same reassuring feeling of peace seemed to permeate the church again. They both breathed deeply, as if a burden had been lifted, somehow setting their hearts at ease.

"Do you believe it's all true, Father?"

"What do you mean?"

"The stories in the Bible."

Father Damian sighed; he seemed to carefully consider how to respond.

"You have to admit, Father, that there are some things in the Bible that are very hard to imagine," Samuel added, taking a step closer to the priest.

"When I began to study the Bible as a child, I asked myself if what it said was true, or if it was really what many people have always said it was: the greatest story ever told."

They were both quiet for a moment, thinking; Father Damian looked around at the paintings and images that decorated the church, the artworks that together told the story of the Catholicism and the kingdom of faith. Smiling, his eyes seemed to caress each figure.

"You know what?" The priest said, turning to look at Samuel, "It doesn't matter that man and science try to discount the idea that there is a God, a supreme being. They can't ignore the greatest truth: that there are mysteries in life that can only be explained by accepting God's existence."

"Why are you so sure?"

"Think about it. Do you think that something as magnificent as this world, the universe, the beauty of nature, are all accidents? A simple act of panspermia? All created by mere coincidence?"

"Panspermia?" Samuel raised an eyebrow.

"It's a scientific theory, which posits that life on this planet was inseminated by meteorites that came from other planets."

Samuel just looked at him, confused. The priest saw his puzzlement and added, "It's just one more scientific theory that tries to deny God's existence. But the great truth, Samuel, is that something so perfect, so sublime, could only have been created by a force much greater than human understanding can ever conceive, and that force is what we call God..."

S 1st Avenue

S 3rd Avenue

W. Jefferson St.

48

Maricopa County Superior Court
201 West Jefferson Street
Phoenix, Arizona

Everyone in the packed courtroom turned to watch the witness who had just been called walk in. He was about forty years old, with blue eyes, a light-brown, well-trimmed beard, a prominent nose and a slim build. He stood in the witness box and raised his right hand as the court officer requested:

"Do you swear to tell the whole truth and nothing but the truth, so help you God?"

"I do," he answered firmly.

He sat down, and the prosecutor walked over to him and began, "Doctor, can you please state your full name and occupation for the court, please."

"Josh Raymond, psychiatrist and neurosurgeon at Phoenix Children's Hospital."

Stanley put his hands on his hips. "Doctor Raymond, according to the Glendale Police Department, you were the one who called to tell them that you were holding a patient who resembled the photograph that had been shown on television, correct?"

"Yes," he affirmed.

Stanley deliberately walked back to his table, leaned against it, and folding his arms across his chest, he asked, "Can you please explain why you decided to call the police?"

"When I saw the story on the news, and considering what we were treating him for, I noticed how much Thomas resembled the photograph of the killer; so I decided to call."

"Can you please tell us why you were treating the defendant?"

"Mrs. Santiago came to my office five months earlier; one of my colleagues had recommended that she come to see me." The doctor paused before continuing, "Her grandson seemed to be suffering from a strange sort of bleeding."

"What do you mean by a strange sort of bleeding?" Stanley interrupted.

"According to Mrs. Santiago, her grandson had woken up on several occasions covered in blood, for no apparent reason; we did several tests and everything turned up negative. At first, I didn't think that it was a psychological problem; I thought it was a bleeding ulcer or something like that. But, when we analyzed the bloodstains that were found on his pajamas, we realized that it had to be something else."

"What did you find out about the bloodstains?" The prosecutor asked, this time facing the jury.

"It wasn't an ordinary bloodstain. Most patients who suffer from ulcers, for example, might stain their beds or their pillow with little drops of blood at night, but the stains that Thomas had were much bigger. Two weeks later, Mrs. Santiago called again; then I decided to perform some more specific tests. The next day, the lab called me to tell me that the blood they had analyzed was different from his..."

"It was another blood type?" Stanley asked.

The doctor looked at Thomas, and saw how intently his lawyer was watching him on the witness stand, as he turned a blue pen over and over in his right hand. He looked at the prosecutor again and replied, "The first time we examined the bloodstains, they matched with his blood type, which is A positive. When Mrs. Santiago called again, and we decided to run some other tests, we found that the blood on his pajamas was A negative."

Stanley crossed his arms, with an incisive look.

"Then what did you do?"

"I called Mrs. Santiago to ask her if she knew who the blood could have come from."

"And, how did Mrs. Santiago react?"

The prosecutor took a few steps forward.

"She seemed to be just as surprised as I was..."

"Then what happened after that?"

"That same night, I saw the story on the news. Because the photograph they showed looked so much like Thomas, and because of what we had found, I decided to call the police."

Stanley paced to the center of the floor and turned to face the judge: "No more questions, Your Honor."

Samuel stood and buttoned his jacket, setting his pen down on the table. He approached the witness box.

"Doctor, when you examined Thomas, did you find anything to indicate that he was a murderer?"

"No."

"The fact that you thought Thomas bore some resemblance to the photo you saw on television does not mean that he is a killer, correct?"

"No, of course not..."

Samuel turned to look pointedly at the jury and concluded, "No further questions."

Stanley watched as Samuel walked slowly back to his chair, and his slight smile revealed a begrudging admiration for how his adversary had handled the cross-examination.

The judge leaned toward his microphone.

"Mr. Stanley, please call your next witness..."

Stanley stood and, with both hands on the table, he said, "The State calls Detective Dan McKoskie."

The detective, who had been sitting in the middle of the room observing the trial, stood up. All eyes were on him as he straightened his tie, walked up to the witness box, and was sworn in.

Standing behind the table, the prosecutor said hello and asked the witness to state his name and occupation for the record.

"Detective Dan McKoskie, Homicide Department, Glendale Police Department."

"How long have you been involved in this case, Detective?" Stanley walked towards the witness box.

"Since they found the first victim, on September 30, 2000."

"You were the officer who arrested Thomas Santiago, correct?"

"Yes."

Stanley turned to face the jury, and with his back to the witness, he asked, "Can you please describe for us what happened?"

The detective shifted in his chair, adjusting his jacket before he began, "When we got Dr. Raymond's call, we were surprised to have gotten such a quick response from the community. Since we didn't have a clue as to who the killer could be, we went to see him. The doctor told us about Thomas and the reason he had come to see him, we examined the DNA from the bloodstain on Thomas's pajamas and discovered that it was Patrick McKinney's. Then there was no doubt."

The prosecutor looked around the room with a very serious expression; his eyes had hardened, and clenching his fists he emphasized, "The blood of one of the victims was found on his pajamas..."

Then he paced over to the witness and said, "What was your reaction when you found out that a minor like Thomas was capable of this kind of crime?"

McKoskie blinked and looked around the room; he noticed that everyone in the courtroom was completely silent. Everyone's attention was intently focused on him. He swallowed nervously and replied, "We were all very surprised. Thomas did not fit the profile of the killer that we had expected. Of all the serial killers in history, there has never been a perpetrator of such a young age that has ever done anything remotely similar. The closest example would have to be William Heirens, 'The Lipstick Killer', who was seventeen."

William George Heirens had been one of the youngest killers in the history of United States. When he was just seventeen years old, in 1946, the student at the University of Chicago kept everyone in the city glued to the newspapers, devouring the latest stories on what seemed like something out of the darkest, most diabolical stories Edgar Allan Poe ever wrote. After each murder, the killer wrote a message to the police in lipstick on the wall, begging them to catch him, since he could not control his impulse to kill—so he was dubbed "The Lipstick Killer."

McKoskie was quiet for a few seconds, and looking at Thomas, he continued,

"Nine out of ten serial killers are between twenty-five and thirty-five years old, we've never seen one who's just fourteen…"

Stanley paced across the floor, he was clearly considering how to phrase his next question. He rubbed his chin and looked at the witness to ask, "Detective: according to your report, you said the killer was one of the most dangerous, most expert serial killers of all time. Can you explain why?"

"Based on what we found at the crime scenes, we were dealing with criminal methods in the same league as people like John Wayne Gacy, Dennis Nilsen, or Chikatilo, to be exact…"

Stanley stepped over to his table and picked up an enlarged photograph of the word that they had found written at each of the crime scenes. He placed it on an easel, next to the witness, and asked, "Detective McKoskie, you found this message written at each of the crime scenes. What can you tell us about it?"

McKoskie took a pen out of his inside jacket pocket and pointed at the photo.

"Many serial killers use what criminologists call a "signature". It's a way for them to identify themselves to society or to send a message, either to the world in general or specifically to the police. The message on the wall is just one word, written with the victim's blood, in a language from Biblical times called Syrian Aramaic."

The prosecutor took a few steps towards the jury and pushed his jacket open to rest his hands on his belt:

"Can you tell the court what the word means, detective?"

"It means "demon," McKoskie answered matter-of-factly.

Gasps were heard around the courtroom. The spectators started to chatter excitedly among themselves. Surprised, Thomas looked at Samuel, while the judge pounded forcefully with his gavel to bring the courtroom to order.

"What other common characteristic, besides this word, did all of the crime scenes have?" the prosecutor asked once the room had quieted down.

"There was also a strange flower smell, but we could never find where it was coming from. But it was always there, at all the crime scenes, every single one…"

Stanley rubbed his hands together. "Do you think that all of the victims were killed by the same person?"

"There's no doubt in my mind, since the killer's methods, what we call the 'MO,' were always the same."

"Finally, detective, based on your own experience, do you think that Thomas Santiago is a psychopath killer?"

"Objection, Your Honor!" Samuel yelled from his seat. "The witness is a detective, not a psychiatrist..."

"Sustained," the judge intoned.

"Let me put it this way, detective: do you believe that these crimes were the work of a disorganized person who was not aware of what he was doing?"

"Definitely not. Serial killers fall into two main categories, in terms of the evidence: organized, and disorganized. The organized ones are more intellectual, they turn it all into a big game, they deliberately leave clues or messages at the crime scenes. Like the Zodiac Killer, for example."

"Thank you, detective, no more questions, Your Honor," Stanley returned to his seat.

Along with Jack the Ripper, the Zodiac Killer was the most notorious serial killer of all time. In the mid-sixties, this ruthless criminal kept all of San Francisco, California and the surrounding bay area in a state of abject terror. After every murder, he sent a typed letter to the Riverside police department and the local papers, the Riverside Enterprise and the Times Herald, confessing to the crime, and threatening to kill again if they didn't put the story on their front page. The letters were signed with the word 'Zodiac' and with a cross inside a circle. After a few years of playing cat-and-mouse, the killer began to send three parts of a cryptogram that supposedly revealed his identity along with the typed confessions. The three cryptograms were solved in less than a week by a teacher at North Salina High School and his wife. Even though the puzzles were solved, and a fingerprint was found on one of the letters, the killer has never caught, and his identity was never revealed. According to the police reports that remain on file, the police believe they did find out who the killer was, but only after his death at the age of eighty-two.

Samuel stood and walked towards the witness without a word. He looked at him right to the eyes and rested his left hand on the wooden railing, then he asked,

"Detective, you wrote in several of your reports that you could not understand how the crime scenes could have been so neat. Can you explain what you meant by that?"

McKoskie brought his hands together, and forming a steeple with his fingers, he replied,

"Something that really surprised us was how every crime scene was in such a perfect state. With all of the technology at our disposal these days to solve crimes, we could not find even the smallest clue, not the smallest hair fiber or any type of fingerprint anywhere on the victims."

"In other words, nothing that could help to identify the killer, correct?"

"Yes," the detective nodded.

"I'm sure you've seen the video from the gas station's security camera, right?"

"Yes."

"And the one from Maricopa County Hospital?"

"Objection, Your Honor; that video has not been entered as evidence in this case yet," Stanley yelled, leaping to his feet, upset by the unwelcome surprise.

"Your Honor: that video was submitted to the court the day before yesterday," Samuel explained as he went over to his table to take a paper Marcos held out for him. He brought it to the judge to back up his argument.

"Your Honor, that video was filmed in a cell at the hospital and has not yet been analyzed to determine its authenticity," Stanley reproached.

The judge studied the document, then he took his glasses off to look at Samuel.

"Your Honor, two soldiers from the United States Marines were guarding the defendant at that time; two soldiers who are still hospitalized; one of whom will testify in this court that everything that can be seen on that video happened exactly as you see it."

The judge asked both attorneys to approach the bench. He covered the microphone with his hands and said quietly to Samuel, "You're not thinking about showing that video now, are you?"

Stanley interrupted, "Your Honor, you cannot allow that video to be viewed in this court; we already caused enough of a scene when the first one was shown..."

Samuel leaned towards the judge and pointing to the paper he had just given him, he replied, "No, at this time I just want the witness to answer whether or not he has seen it. That video speaks very clearly about the defendant's mental state and about this case."

The judge studied the paper again and, looking at Samuel, he concluded, "I will allow it. Objection overruled; the witness will answer the question."

Both lawyers returned to their places.

"Yes, I have seen that one, too," McKoskie answered, crossing his arms over his chest.

"What do you have to say about it?"

McKoskie's expression hardened. His eyes narrowed as he asked, "What do you mean?"

Samuel faced the jury and reiterated, "What do you think happened there, according to what you saw on the video?"

"Really, I was just as surprised as you were..."

"Surprised?" Hmmm..." Samuel turned back to look at the detective. "Let me be honest with you, detective, to me, what was on that video was more than just 'surprising.' I have never seen anything like it in my whole life. I've watched these videos, over and over, and in all honesty, I simply cannot believe that what attacked Mr. McKinney is a human being..."

McKoskie looked at him coldly.

"Like I said to you at the police headquarters, Mr. Escobar, the state pays me to catch the bad guys; whether they're guilty or innocent is for the court to decide, not me..."

Samuel paced back and forth and scratched his neck before asking, "Detective, the prosecutor asked you a little while ago if you thought all of the victims had been killed by the same perpetrator, and you said that there was no doubt in your mind, correct?"

The witness shifted in his chair and looked at Samuel with an expression that was anything but friendly. "Yes, that's correct."

"I'm sure you must be familiar with the criminological term "copycat."

It's an expression for when one killer deliberately copies the methods of another killer..."

Samuel turned with his hands on his hips, insisting, "Isn't it possible that someone else could have killed some of those victims and made the police think that they were all killed by the same person?"

"That would be very unlikely," McKoskie replied, following him with his eyes.

"But it is possible, correct?"

"Yes."

Samuel went over to his table to pick up some papers, which he then handed to the witness.

"Detective, these are the police reports for two of the victims, Mrs. Luisa Mcbell and Billy Black Horse. Can you please read the highlighted text in Billy's report, please?"

"Objection, Your Honor. Those victims' cases do not fall under Detective McKoskie's jurisdiction," the prosecutor said loudly.

The judge looked at Samuel, who hurried to explain, "Your Honor, I just want to show that, logically, it would not have been possible for my client to have killed those two people. It would have been physically impossible for him to be in the Kayenta reservation on Wednesday, October 27, and then in the city of Phoenix within less than two hours..."

The judge blinked and rubbed his chin, then said simply, "Overruled."

McKoskie held the paper and read: "Billy Black Horse, a young man twenty-four years of age, was found dead on the morning of Wednesday October 27, 2004. Approximate time of death: 5:30 AM."

He handed the paper back to Samuel, who then gave it to the judge.

"Detective, this is a copy of the attendance records from Thomas' school, in which the administration verifies that he has not missed a single day of school over the previous two years, and that the school bus picks him up at the corner near his house at 7:30 in the morning, every day... Can you explain how it would be possible for my client to have killed Billy Black Horse and returned to the city in under two hours, if the Kayenta reservation is more than four hours away from here?"

McKoskie just looked at him, while Samuel continued,

"We'll return to that question in a minute."

Samuel began to read aloud from the other police report: "Mrs. Luisa Mcbell was murdered at 5:30, on May 2nd of last year, in the city of Globe, while she returned to her home after work; that is, over two hours away..."

Samuel crossed his arms and gave the witness a sarcastic look. "Let me guess, detective... you can't explain that, either?"

Then he turned to face the jury. "Logic dictates that it would have been impossible for Thomas to have been at the Kayenta reservation at five-thirty in the morning, and also taken the school bus at seven-thirty, when it's a four-hour trip between the two places. It also would have been impossible for him to have killed Mrs. Mcbell in Globe and gotten to school on time." Samuel slowly paced across the floor, and then turned to face the witness.

"Don't you think these facts are reason enough to consider that somebody else may have killed Billy Black Horse and Luisa Mcbell, detective?"

With a stony expression, McKoskie didn't respond. Samuel stepped closer to him:

"Detective?"

McKoskie shot him an angry look and muttered, "It's possible, but I doubt it..."

Samuel slowly walked back to his chair, putting a hand in his pocket. "No more questions, Your Honor."

E Turquoise Av

49

Escobar Family Residence
6889 East Turquoise Avenue
Scottsdale, Arizona

Samuel groped around for the ringing telephone on the night table in the dark, while Catherine got out of bed to go check on the baby.

"Hello?"

"Samuel?" a man's voice said.

"Who is this?" Samuel asked, sitting up in bed, rubbing his eyes and trying to wake up.

"It's McKoskie. I think you'd better get up and come down to the Florence prison…"

"What is it? Did something happen with Thomas?"

"Thomas escaped again, and he killed one of the prisoners…"

"One of the prisoners?"

"Yes, Dan Fellar… You'd better hurry up and get down here before the whole world hears about it and it turns into a three-ring circus…"

"I'm on my way."

Samuel jumped out of bed and started throwing his clothes on. When Catherine came back to the bedroom carrying the baby, she gave Samuel a puzzled look.

Samuel said quietly, "Thomas escaped again…"

"Oh my God!"

Samuel quickly kissed her on the cheek, as he always did, and as he ran out of the house he called back to her, "I have to go to the prison, I'll call you as soon as I can…"

E Butte Av.

50

ARIZONA STATE PRISON
1305 EAST BUTTE AVENUE
FLORENCE, ARIZONA

Samuel slowly drove up to the prison entrance. Several helicopters were circling in the sky above it. He looked all around: news vans already lined the street on both sides of the gate, their parabolic satellite dishes high in the air. *Shit! They're already here...* he said to himself.

As the crowd outside saw his car approach, several reporters scrambled toward it, like a swarm of flies.

Observing the commotion from the other side of the gate, McKoskie ordered a police officer at his side, "Get that pack of parasites out of here and tell Brown to let that car that just drove up in."

"Yes, sir," the officer replied and rushed off.

They opened the gate and Samuel drove through, then he parked in the visitor's parking lot. McKoskie shook his hand after he got out of the car.

"How the hell did they get here so fast?" Samuel asked, incredulous.

"I've asked myself that question many, many times," McKoskie said, leading the way inside the building.

"And where's Morrison?"

"He's meeting with the director of the prison."

Three police officers were standing in front of the cell, and as they saw Samuel, they stepped back and let him pass by.

Samuel noticed that the strange flower scent that all the police reports mentioned could be clearly detected from several yards away. He stopped in front of the cell and saw the forensic examiner was there, crouched over the body. A photographer was busily snapping pictures of every inch of the cell.

Dan Fellar's body was lying on the floor with his legs bent, his feet under his buttocks; his head facing north. A large pool of blood covered most of the floor, and his eyes were filled with blood. The expression frozen on his face captured the horrible terror he had experienced in his final moments on earth.

"What can you tell us, Doc?" McKoskie asked the small, balding man wearing wire-rimmed glasses.

"I'd say that he's been dead for an hour, maybe two..."

He took off his rubber gloves and, pushing his glasses back on his nose, he added, "Like the other victims: he presents death by strangulation, severe fractures of the skull and neck..."

He wiped his brow and gestured towards the body: "If you look closely at the bruises on his neck, you can see that he was strangled with just one hand..."

Samuel looked up and saw the word in Syrian Aramaic written on the wall, just above the body.

"Were there any witnesses?" he asked.

"The two prisoners in the cell across from him, they were the only ones that could have seen anything," a voice at Samuel's back responded.

Samuel and McKoskie turned to see Mr. Whitefield, the director of the prison walking down the hall, flanked by two guards. Samuel shook his hand while the director apologized, "Sorry I'm late, we were just finishing up questioning the guards that were on duty at the time."

"Where's agent Morrison?" McKoskie asked.

"He's calling Washington…"

"Can we talk with the witnesses?" McKoskie asked quickly.

"Of course."

"When can we talk to them?" Samuel spoke up.

"As soon as the doctor is finished examining him."

"Examining him? But you said there were two witnesses," McKoskie asked.

"One of them can't talk…"

The detective crossed his arms and looked at the director skeptically.

"What do you mean, can't talk?"

"Just that—he's in a catatonic state, he doesn't move, he doesn't even blink."

McKoskie looked at Samuel, his doubtful expression indicated that he didn't believe the director at all.

Samuel looked down at Dan Fellar's body again. He had been a short man, maybe 5' 8", he seemed to be partly Asian. A great deal of blood had streamed out of his eyes and nose, and was pooled around his head.

McKoskie stared at Samuel, concerned, and asked,

"Are you alright, Escobar?"

Samuel kept staring at the body. He put his right hand in his pocket, and scratched his neck with the other. He drew in a deep breath and, slowly exhaling, he murmured,

"This was the famous Dan Fellar… I remember the newspaper headlines very well, and the rumors that were flying around the courthouse when his trial was going on…" Samuel paused thoughtfully, and then went on, "His was the most talked-about case in the whole state at the time, because of its complexity. I never thought I'd ever actually meet him, and certainly not like this…"

Whitefield led them to the prison infirmary, where they found a tall, muscular man lying on a gurney in a little room. He was young, about twenty-eight years old, his blue eyes were open wide, and his body was pale and rigid. McKoskie stood next to him, and since he seemed to be staring up at the ceiling, he waved his hand quickly right above his face, to see if he would react.

"Oh, this guy's a lost cause!" exclaimed the detective, since he didn't react in the slightest.

"Where's the other one?" Samuel asked the director, after observing the young man's tense body and clenched fists.

Whitefield gestured for them to follow him.

They went into another room that looked like it was used for interrogations. There was a black man sitting at a table, with curly hair, who looked to be about fifty years old. He was nervously clutching some rosary beads in his hands, as he prayed desperately.

Whitefield went up to the prisoner, whose head was bowed as he prayed.

"Johnny, this is Detective McKoskie, from the Homicide Department in Glendale, and this is Mr. Escobar, he's a lawyer," Whitefield said. He rested his hands on the table and said, "Can you tell them what you saw?"

The prisoner looked up, his eyes were moist and his voice broke as he said, "I already told you, Mr. Whitefield, God has served His justice. Dan would never listen to me, I always told him that divine justice was much harsher than man's, but he just laughed at me..."

"Can you please tell us exactly what you saw?" McKoskie interjected.

The man swallowed and replied, "It was about two hours after they had turned the lights off. I was tossing and turning in my bed, trying to fall asleep, when all of a sudden I saw this really bright light shining in from the other side of the cell. I turned to see what was going on..."

He wiped away a tear rolling down his cheek, and nervously tugged at the hair at the back of his neck before continuing,

"Dan was up against the wall, terrified, while that thing went up to him and grabbed him by the neck. Then it picked him up with one hand... That thing had these huge wings, that practically took up the whole cell. Then it started banging his head against the wall, that... that... voice seemed to shake the prison walls. Then I started to scream for help," he sobbed.

Samuel and McKoskie exchanged a look.

Then what happened?" McKoskie prodded.

"I just kept screaming, everybody woke up, Texas started screaming too..."

"Who's Texas?" Samuel asked.

"He's the prisoner you just saw," Whitefield explained.

"So, what happened next?" McKoskie asked.

The man took a deep breath and continued, "Then, that thing... it turned around, and looked at us..." tears started streaming down his cheeks, and his hands shook as he grasped the rosary even tighter.

"Everything's alright, Johnny," the prison director said, placing a comforting hand on his shoulder.

"Its eyes... Oh my God, its eyes! I thought my heart stopped when it looked at me... Texas screamed, then that thing dropped Dan, and dipped a finger in his blood, and wrote something on the wall, and right there, it just went right through it, then disappeared into thin air..."

"And the guards?" Samuel asked.

"The guards didn't get there until it was all over... It all happened so fast..."

51

SANTIAGO FAMILY RESIDENCE
6610 NORTH 61ST AVENUE
GLENDALE, ARIZONA

Samuel stepped over to the window and pulled the curtain aside to look out: more and more people were gathering outside in front of the house.

McKoskie looked out the window from the other side, and seeing the size of the crowd gathering, he used his radio transmitter to communicate with an officer stationed outside: "Mike, move the barricades back. Tell Rick to keep his eyes open, somebody could be armed..."

McKoskie glanced at his watch and said to Samuel, "It's five in the morning, why don't they all go home? They'd rather be hanging around here, waiting to see what's going to happen, instead of at home with their families..."

Juan Manuel and Father Damian were sitting on the couch, while Mariela sat dozing in a chair, her head resting against the wall.

Suddenly, a terrifying cry was heard coming from upstairs:

"Mommmyyy!!"

Mariela jumped out of the chair and ran upstairs, the others following close behind.

She burst into the bedroom. Thomas was floating in the air, just above his bed, with his arms spread open in a cross, his hands covered in blood. A strong wind came in through the open windows, making it hard to see. His eyes were a ghostly white, like salt, and a very intense light glowed around his head, lighting up the room. A huge pair of white wings sprouted from his back.

"Oh, mother of God!" Mariela wailed, falling to her knees.

When McKoskie rushed into the room and saw what was happening, he fell back against the wall, screaming in terror, "What the hell is...?!"

"Holy Father!" Juan Manuel made the sign of the cross and knelt beside his grandmother.

Father Damian slowly approached the bed and stood next to Thomas. He brought his hands together in prayer and, kneeling down over one knee, he began to speak in Aramaic: "Messenger from God, Avenger of Blood, have mercy on this boy and his family..."

The others looked at each other in shock and horror, trying to understand what was going on, as father Damian remained kneeling, talking with the angel.

Suddenly, the angel spoke. His eyes were filled with anger as he said to the priest in the ancient language, "There is much evil in the world, and the Lord has sent me to destroy the bad seed..."

"But please have mercy on those who fear God," Father Damian begged.

"The prayers of the oppressed have been heard in heaven, they pray for vengeance..."

"But look at this mother's pain; please don't close your eyes to her pain..."

"The time has come for the weed to be pulled from the ground and thrown into the fire..."

After uttering these words, tears of blood ran from the angel's eyes. Terrified, Mariela began to sob helplessly.

Thomas let out an agonized scream, his head fell forward as if he had passed out, still floating in mid-air. A very bright light enveloped his entire body, and the wings at his back suddenly disappeared.

Father Damian stood and held his arms under his chest. He felt the weight of the boy's slender body collapse into his arms, and he gently laid him on the bed.

52

Judge Fieldmore's Office
Maricopa County Superior Court
201 West Jefferson Street
Phoenix, Arizona

Two days later, Samuel went to the see the judge in his office. The prosecutor Morgan Stanley, officers Morrison and McKoskie, and the governor of Arizona, a woman in her mid-fifties with dark hair, were also there, along with another man in his forties, with brown eyes and dark hair. When Samuel got there, they all stood up.

"Mr. Escobar, I'd like you to meet Gary Owens," the judge said.

Samuel nodded slightly and said, "Pleased to meet you."

"Samuel, Mr. Owens is here representing the White House..."

"I'll take it from here, Judge Fieldmore. The reason for my visit, Mr. Escobar, is that this case is taking on international proportions..."

Samuel crossed his arms and, wary, waited for him to come to the point.

"The White House is deeply concerned about how this case has been portrayed by the media. Ever since started, things have gone from bad to worse, and we believe that the time has come for us to bring this matter under control..."

With a skeptical look, his arms still crossed, Samuel replied, "I'm sure that you've watched the videos that show what is going on with my client, Mr. Owens. And you must know that the last two prisons where he has been held are the most secure in the state, equipped with all the latest technology, and, still, it has not been possible to control the situation... So what do you suggest we do?"

Owens stepped towards Samuel, looking very stern. His thick eyebrows almost joined as he frowned. He stood right in front of Samuel and said severely,

"I am here representing the White House to ensure that all of this is kept as quiet as possible, whether you like it or not..."

A shadow quickly darkened Samuel's expression. His eyes shone with fury, and holding Owens' gaze, he shouted, "I don't give a damn why you're here! My job is to ensure that Thomas is found innocent, and that is what I'm going to do..."

"Gentlemen, gentlemen!" The governor interrupted. "We're here to find a solution to a problem, not to attack each other."

Owens paced across the office and turned to look at them. "This afternoon, a group of special government envoys will arrive here from Washington, to help get this situation under control."

"Your Honor, that's illegal!" Samuel blurted out. "According to the law, Thomas must be under the state of Arizona's custody until he is tried..."

The judge stood and slowly walked over to Samuel, putting a hand lightly on his shoulder. He said, "We have to admit, Mr. Escobar, that this situation is beyond our understanding... We have been in court for over two weeks and we still don't have any sort of plausible explanation for what is going on with this boy. From a medical or scientific standpoint, no one has the faintest idea of what's going on..."

They were all quiet as the judge began to slowly walk back to his desk.

"The defense might have an explanation, Your Honor..."

The judge turned to look at Samuel, surprised.

"Remember when I asked for permission so a priest could go visit Thomas?"

The judge brought his hands together thoughtfully and nodded.

"This might sound crazy, but that priest has been working with me, trying to figure out what's going on. He's talked with Thomas about what happens to him, and now we're sure that he is possessed..."

"Your Honor, please!" Morgan interrupted, jumping to his feet.

"Hold on, Stanley," the judge held up a hand. "Let him finish."

"We've studied the videos, and according to the symptoms that he exhibits in each one, Father Damian is very sure that it is a strange form of possession. Besides, the priest is the only one who has been able to approach him when he is actually being possessed..."

Samuel turned to his left and, looking at Detective McKoskie, he finished, "If you don't believe me, ask him..."

All eyes turned to the detective, as he stood.

"He is absolutely right about that... When we went to look for Thomas the last time, we saw something we didn't expect... We heard a scream coming from his bedroom, and we all ran up there to find him, like the time before, but this time, the spirit was still in his body..."

McKoskie paced slowly across the floor, running a hand over his head as he continued, "Thomas was floating, like he was crucified, in midair, talking in that weird language. We all just fell on the floor when we saw it. The priest went up to him, he started to speak, and then after a few seconds, the priest put his hands on him, on his chest and shoulders, and the spirit disappeared..."

The judge looked at Owens and Stanley, who were both quiet, and sat down slowly behind his desk. He exhaled slowly and asked, "Governor?"

"What time will the special envoys from Washington get here, Mr. Owens?" she turned to face him.

"At six."

"We will meet here again at eight-thirty, and bring that priest with you, Mr. Escobar, and we'll see what he has to say. Is that okay with you, Mr. Owens?"

He nodded.

The judge turned to Stanley, who blinked and finally nodded his assent.

E Turquoise Av

53

Escobar Family Residence
6889 East Turquoise Avenue
Scottsdale, Arizona

Samuel took one of his law books from on top of his desk and put it back in the bookcase. He looked at the spines of all the other law books, tracing them with his index finger, searching for something more...

"Honey, how about inviting my parents to come over for dinner this Sunday, what do you think?" Catherine asked.

"Sure, that's fine," he said absently, still looking at his books. After he had gone through the whole bookcase, exasperated, he turned and asked his wife, "Baby, have you seen my book on forensic psychology anywhere?"

"If it's not there, it must be in the box of books in the attic..."

"In the attic?"

"Don't you remember that you put a box of books up there two weeks ago?"

"Oh, yeah!"

Samuel slowly sat down in the desk chair and sighed, "I must be losing my mind..."

"It's just all the stress, and you're not alone, the whole city is going through the same nightmare right now," Catherine said, standing beside him, tenderly stroking his cheek.

Samuel said, "This is all just so hard to believe, sometimes I ask myself if it's even real..."

Catherine sat down on his lap, hugging him and kissing his hair. Samuel rested his head against her chest and took a deep breath. "You have no idea how much I appreciate all the support you've given me."

Catherine kissed his hair again and hugged him even more tightly. "I've always admired your dedication and even your stubbornness when it comes to justice, and there's one thing I know for sure, and it's that you are a man of principles, and a man of honor, and that comforts me."

Samuel looked up and rubbed his face, adding, "The day when justice is truly exalted by men, then we'll all find the truth held in our hands..."

Catherine cradled his face in her hands and looked deeply into his eyes. "That is what I love about you more and more each day that the man I met all those years ago is still alive. And, if I remember correctly, I think I promised you once that I'd be by your side in the good times, and bad..."

Samuel smiled and asked, "Until death do us part?"

"Uh-huh," she nodded slightly.

"I don't know, I think you might want to reconsider, since I'm not planning on dying for a very, very long time..."

She laughed out loud. "Oh, in that case, I'd better think it over..."

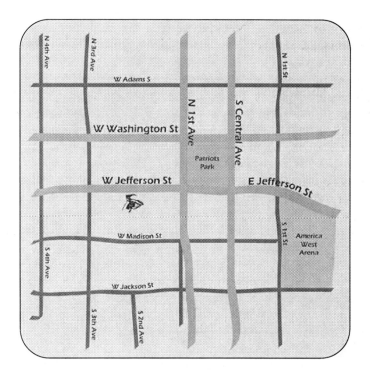

54

JUDGE FIELDMORE'S OFFICE
MARICOPA SUPERIOR COURT
201 WEST JEFFERSON STREET
PHOENIX, ARIZONA

The secretary opened the door, gesturing for Samuel and the two men with him to come in. Samuel noticed how everyone stared at the priests.

"Come in, please," the judge said, standing.

Samuel introduced them to the judge, who shook both men's hands and began introducing the others.

"This is Gary Owens, the White House representative."

Owens nodded politely.

"I think you already know the governor," he turned to the other side.

"Pleased to meet you," she said, offering her hand.

Owens began introducing the rest of the group. "This is Dr. Robert Marcus, Director of the FBI's Scientific Institute for Criminal Behavior and a forensic psychology professor at Boston University."

Father Damian shook his hand heartily and said,

"It's such a pleasure to meet you, Dr. Marcus. I read your book *The Thin Line between Insanity and Intellect*. It was really fascinating..."

"I didn't know that priests read about that kind of thing," the doctor replied with a smile, impressed.

"You'd be surprised if you knew all the things we religious read about..."

Owens introduced the man to his right: "This is Dr. Dan Phillips, Neuropsychiatrist, and this is Jim Myrick, security engineer," he gestured towards a tall, lean man with long, slender arms at the back of the office.

"Engineer?" Samuel said, curious, looking at the judge.

"Mr. Myrick helped us to design a cell that would be able to successfully hold the prisoner," Owens cut in, trying to assert his authority so there would be no mistake about who was in charge.

The governor gestured with her hand towards the back of the office, where a few rows of chairs had been set up.

"What do you say we get started?"

They sat down and watched a video on a flat screen mounted on the wall at the back of the room, as Dr. Marcus began his presentation. He was an obese man, at only 5' 9" he weighed almost two hundred and ninety pounds. His thinning gray hair was cut short, and he had dark brown eyes. His straight nose stood out between his very round cheeks.

A picture of Thomas in which he appeared to be possessed by that strange force flashed onto the screen.

"As you can see, Thomas undergoes a physical as well as a mental transformation, that, medically speaking, has no explanation," the doctor began. "The light surrounding his body is the strongest manifestation of the human aura that has ever been seen. His behavior cannot be compared with any other case of mental disturbance on record."

He traced a circle around the paused picture on the screen with a ruler as he talked. Pausing for a moment, the doctor lowered his head, then continued, "This is the first time a patient has demonstrated supernatural powers of this extreme magnitude, ever. This could be categorized as multiple personality disorder, but the presence of these powers completely undercuts that theory. Mental disturbances themselves never give a patient the ability to do those kinds of things..."

The doctor took a few steps forward and crossed his arms before going on, "However, what is completely compatible with mental illness is, his desire to kill..."

A new image appeared on the screen: it was a complete list of all of the victims, with the dates when their bodies had been found.

"As you can see, the period of time between each killing is growing progressively shorter." He looked up at everyone and emphasized, "There is no doubt, ladies and gentlemen, that what we have on our hands is a serial killer; and, unfortunately for us, because of his awesome powers, perhaps the most dangerous killer of all time. Mr. Myrick has designed a special cell to help us to keep him in custody, until we discover a way to control him..."

The engineer stood, walked over to the screen and took over the presentation, his eyes shining with pride.

When it came to designing maximum-security prison cells, Myrick had a global reputation as one of the best there was. His slim build and long arms always made a striking impression when people met him for the first time. People would typically remark that he looked more like a player in the NBA than an engineer.

"This is not your run-of-the-mill prison cell, ladies and gentlemen; if you think you may have seen something like this before, think again..."

Myrick pressed a button on the remote control. A picture appeared on the screen of a huge transparent cube covered on all sides with cement bars, resting on an iron platform. Eight aluminum columns, about two-and-a-half feet thick, ran across the ceiling, and were connected to a large machine.

Everyone stared at the screen, slack-jawed; they had definitely never seen anything like it.

Surprised, Father Steven looked at Father Damian, who, even more overwhelmed, kept his gaze fixed on the screen. Samuel turned to see Father Damian's reaction too, and the priest gave him a slight smile.

"As you can see, the cell has a metal floor, covered with a system of electromagnetic sensors."

The next photograph showed a pair of metal boots with locks on them. Myrick picked up the ruler that Dr. Marcus had left on the table and, pointing to the boots in the picture, he continued, "The prisoner will have to wear these boots at all times; in case of an emergency, the prisoner can be immobilized from the control booth by simply pressing a button..."

"What do you mean 'immobilized'?" Samuel asked.

"Just what it sounds like, Mr. Escobar," Owens interjected from his seat, "it means that if your client tries to escape, he will be stuck to the floor like a magnet, and he will receive an electric shock of five hundred volts."

"What?! Your Honor, you can't allow this..."

The governor turned to look at Samuel behind her:

"Mr. Escobar, the three times that your client has escaped from jail, he has left three police officers, two Marines, and a prison inmate in intensive care, and of the last four marines who guarded him, three were temporarily blinded, and the other was so traumatized that he has quit the military. If you don't think that's justification enough, well, I'm sorry, but I do..."

Samuel turned to look at the judge, surprised by what he was hearing, and opening his arms plaintively he said,

"Thomas is only a boy, that electrical charge could kill him..."

"He has killed twenty people, and he has hurt many others; we have to keep him in custody however we can, or the body count here is just going to go up," the judge said firmly, meeting his eye.

"Mr. Escobar, you must understand that our greatest responsibility at this moment is to protect the public," the governor added.

"As long as he doesn't try to escape again, nothing will happen," Owen said, with a hint of sarcasm.

Samuel looked at him angrily, "You'd better hope that nothing happens to him because if it does, I can promise you that I will hold you completely responsible and you'll pay for it!"

"What are the tubes in the ceiling for?" Father Damian asked calmly, breaking the tension of the moment.

Everyone looked at the screen again while Myrick used the ruler as a pointer: "The metal tubes built into the ceiling are connected to a gas compressor..."

"Gas?" Judge Fieldmore repeated.

"That's right, Your Honor, you'll see..."

Myrick signaled to the secretary to start a video. On the screen, they watched a sheep enter the cell, and then, in a matter of seconds, the cell filled completely with smoke.

Samuel stared at the screen, trying to understand what he was seeing. Then he watched as the gas was suctioned out through the metal tubes that ran along the ceiling of the cell.

"Holy Heavens!" Father Steven exclaimed, not believing his own eyes.

The sheep looked like a shiny statue made of salt, it had completely frozen in just a few seconds. Father Damian stood and, taking off his glasses, he studied the screen, a smile playing on his lips.

"As I said, gentlemen, this is no ordinary cell."

Myrick sat at the table and folded his arms over his chest, flush with pride.

"The cell has several tanks of liquid helium: it freezes instantly at minus 459.7 degrees Fahrenheit."

Samuel stood and asked, "What does all this mean?"

"The cell is capable of freezing any person in less than ten seconds," Owen replied, also getting to his feet. "We will not allow him to escape again, no matter what."

Samuel looked to the judge, who stared down at the table, embarrassed. Samuel could see that his hands were tied, he looked around and understood what their real mission was.

"That cell will not hold him." Father Damian's calm words astounded everyone.

"What did you say?" Owen asked.

"I said, that cell will not hold him..."

"How can you be so sure?" Myrick wanted to know.

Father Damian smoothed his long robe and crossed his legs. He replied serenely, "You are trying to control something that you don't understand. We know very well what your job is, Mr. Owens..." the priest turned to look at him. "You will do everything possible to make sure Thomas doesn't escape, even if you have to kill him..."

Everyone was quiet while the priest got to his feet, and placed a hand on Father Steven's shoulder. Then he went on,

"You think that with all your sophisticated technology you can hold him, but I assure you that you can't, and all of your efforts will be in vain..."

Myrick stood, and putting his hands in his pockets, he asked, "But, why are you so sure that he'll escape? Our cells have held the most dangerous criminals of our time, and we've never had a problem..."

Father Damian took two steps to his left: "of the criminals that you have held, how many of them have shown supernatural powers like this boy has? Which of them has been seen passing through a wall as if he were a ghost, or stopping bullets by simply raising his hand?"

No one answered, because they all knew that the priest was right.

Dr. Marcus walked over to Father Damian and looked at him closely, asking sincerely, "Why don't you tell us your theory on what is happening to Thomas, Father?"

The priest was quiet. He looked at Samuel, who looked back at him expectantly.

"You are men of science, while I am a man of faith... I'm not going to waste my time talking about things that you consider absurd; but I can assure you that you will not be able to hold him."

"Why are you so sure?" the judge asked.

"Like Dr. Marcus said, his desire to kill is growing, and that will compel him to escape again."

Father Damian looked around the room at each of them, pausing thoughtfully.

"You are forgetting the most important thing of all."

"What?" Myrick asked.

"That when it takes possession of his body, he is no longer human, and although his patterns may seem like a serial killer's, that is not his true nature..."

Father Damian looked at Dr. Marcus and said,

"What you have failed to understand, doctor, is that when the body grows accustomed to the possession, it becomes easier for the spirit to take control of his body, since it starts to become a habit, and if a way to stop the possession isn't found, there will be bodies piling up everywhere. Eventually the spirit will take possession of the body permanently, and there will be no way to stop it..."

Father Damian turned and concluded,

"When you realize that what I have said is true, you know where to find me."

W Van Buren St

N 3rd Street

E Monroe St

55

SAINT MARY'S BASILICA
231 NORTH THIRD STREET
PHOENIX, ARIZONA

Samuel gave Father Damian and Father Steven a ride back to St. Mary's. No one said a word during the whole drive. Samuel looked at Father Damian out of the corner of his eye and wondered why he hadn't told everyone the whole story.

When they got to the church, both priests stepped out of the car. Father Damian walked around the car, leaned down to the driver's side window to look at Samuel and said with complete confidence, "Everything is going to be alright, we don't have anything to worry about..."

"How can you be so sure, Father? Those people are willing to kill Thomas if they have to..."

"Can we go inside and talk? This desert heat is killing me," the priest said, tugging uncomfortably at his collar.

Once inside the church office, he gestured for Samuel to sit next to him: "I'm telling you, Samuel, there's nothing to worry about."

"What makes you think so?"

Father Damian folded his hands together thoughtfully and asked, "Have you ever heard of an angel in prison? Or do you know anybody who's ever seen a dead angel?"

Samuel was quiet, considering the priest's words.

"All things in this world have a reason for being, even if we never understand what it is. It's just that, very often, the spiritual reasons are beyond our ability to grasp. Up to this point, everything that has happened has had a clear reason to me..."

Samuel studied him quietly, trying to understand. Father Damian got up and, standing close to him he said, "Understanding the world requires patience, and wisdom, but to understand God, even more than wisdom, you must have faith... I am positive that they will not be able to stop him."

"But, what about that cell?" Samuel asked, following him with his gaze as he paced slowly across the room.

"That cell they want to put Thomas in is an advanced replica of an experiment that was done in 1974, in Culver City, California, with a woman name Carla Moran, who had supposedly been raped and beaten by a ghost."

"A ghost?!"

"Yes, that's what they said—at first no one would believe her, even though they did detect physical signs of rape on her body. They thought it was just her imagination, until one day, the ghost attacked her in front of her family..."

Samuel's mouth hung open, he was totally stunned by what he was hearing.

Father Damian remembered the bizarre case very well. He could clearly recall how, one morning in October 1996, the owner of a small newspaper had shown him a magazine article about Carla Moran with a photograph, which had been published in Omni Magazine, years earlier, with the heading The hunting of Culver City.

Father Damian had been frightened by what he saw. The photograph had been taken by a thirty-five millimeter camera by a team of scientists, working under the supervision of Dr. Thelma Moss, and it showed Mrs. Moran sitting underneath a clear arc of light. The article described in detail the case of a single mother in Culver

City, California, who had been brutally beaten and raped by an invisible demon.
The case became known as "The Entity," and it would become one of the most-
studied cases of paranormal activity of all time. In 1992, the popular television
show "Sightings" produced a special episode on the case, and showed the photograph.
And in 1996, the magazine Fate published on article on the famous case.

"And what happened with the ghost? Did they manage to capture it?"

"No, they didn't. In the same way that they froze that sheep in the film they showed us, they froze the ghost for three seconds, just long enough to see what they were dealing with. The team of scientists could see a huge figure in human form, surrounded by a green and white glowing light."

"Only three seconds?"

"Yes, because the ghost's vibrations broke the ice shield as it tried to escape."

Father Damian took a deep breath, shifting his weight before continuing, "Suddenly the figure disappeared. Two of the assistants helping the team of researchers fainted, and had to be hospitalized."

Samuel was still slack-jawed; this was too much. The priest said with a smile, "If you don't believe me, you can watch a movie that was made about it, it's called "The Entity.""

Father Damian thought for a moment and then asked,

"Do you want to know something interesting? The attacks that Carla Moran endured only happened late at night, just like with Thomas. One night, Carla's son, who I think was about sixteen at the time, heard his mother scream. He ran into her room and found her being violently pushed and pulled over the bed in all directions. He tried to help her, but something hit him and sent him flying across the room. One of his arms was broken in the attack."

Father Damian smiled enigmatically at Samuel: "And want to know something else? When they were making the movie "The Entity," the actor who played Carla Moran's son actually broke his arm while they were filming that particular scene..."

Samuel looked at him curiously. "How do you know all this?"

"It was one of the cases that I researched when I was studying possession, several years ago..."

With his hands clasped behind his back, the priest walked toward the window. "If they couldn't capture a simple ghost, I'm sure that they won't be able to capture the angel that possesses Thomas..."

Samuel lowered his head, rubbing his face with both hands. "Are you sure Thomas is going to escape again? Really sure?"

Father Damian pushed the curtain aside slightly to look outside, and replied,

"There's no doubt in my mind."

"Will we ever figure out some way to make sure he can't escape?"

Father Damian let go of the curtain and turned to meet Samuel's gaze. Behind the priest's glasses, Samuel could see the intensity reflected in his eyes:

"Honestly, that I don't know..."

S 1st Avenue

S 3rd Avenue

W. Jefferson St.

56

MARICOPA COUNTY SUPERIOR COURT
201 WEST JEFFERSON STREET
PHOENIX, ARIZONA

"Mr. Stanley, call your first witness," the judge instructed, settling into his chair.

"Your Honor, the state calls Detective Mckoskie."

"Objection, Your Honor!" Samuel yelled, putting his hands on the table and quickly standing.

"Detective McKoskie already told the Court his version of events in this case."

Stanley approached the judge's bench, and Samuel quickly followed him.

"Your Honor, this case was suspended for several days because the defendant escaped again and another victim was found who, according to the police report, was killed in the same manner as the others. Detective McKoskie was in charge of part of the investigation, and therefore the State has every right to call him as a witness at this time."

"Objection overruled," the judge said, addressing Samuel. "The court will allow a brief recess, if you like, to allow you to prepare."

Samuel turned around so he could look at McKoskie in the eye, who was seated a few rows back. Then he faced the judge and said, "That will not be necessary, Your Honor."

"The court will allow the witness," the judge said to the jury, while both lawyers returned to their places.

McKoskie stood and slowly walked up to the witness box, and was reminded that he was still under oath. He sat down, folded his arms across his chest, and waited for the first question.

The prosecutor began, "Detective, you supervised part of the investigation that was done at the Florence prison last Tuesday, correct?"

"Yes, that's right."

"Can you please tell the court what was the nature of that investigation?"

"We were investigating the death of one of the prisoners, and the escape of Thomas Santiago."

"Can you tell the court the victim's name?"

"Dan Fellar."

"According to your report, and the medical examiner's report, Dan Fellar seems to have been a victim of the same killer who murdered the others that Thomas Santiago has been accused of in this case."

"Everything seems to indicate that it is the work of the same killer. The medical report explains that Dan Fellar's body had the same wounds as the other victims. And, the same signature from the killer was found in his cell."

Stanley turned to look out at the public, and said in an ironic tone, "One more victim, and another person who has died by Thomas Santiago's hand."

"Objection, Your Honor," Samuel said calmly from his seat. "The prosecutor is conjecturing."

"Conjecturing? Your Honor, the medical report as well as the police report both assert that it was the same killer."

"Your Honor, neither report gives any indication of the killer's identity," Samuel insisted from his table, while he focused on his blue pen, turning it over in his fingers.

"There's another damned body! How much more of an indication do you need?"

The judge pounded firmly with his gavel and shot the prosecutor an angry look. "Mr. Stanley, I will not allow you to disrespect my court with that kind of language!"

Stanley took a deep breath, trying to calm down. He tugged at the sleeves of his jacket and replied, "I apologize, Your Honor..."

"The jury will discount that last remark," the judge instructed.

Stanley sighed heavily, and scratching his chin, he walked over to the witness. "Two other prisoners witnessed the murder, isn't that right?"

"Yes."

"And one of them described a figure very similar to what we saw in the video from the gas station at 59th and Cactus Streets, as Dan Fellar's killer, correct?"

"Yes, that's correct."

"Detective McKoskie, according to your own experience as a police officer, would you conclude that Dan Fellar's killer and the killer in the gas station video are one and the same?"

"Yes, I would."

"No further questions, Your Honor."

Samuel stood and asked, "Detective, did you find any evidence at all that would give the slightest indication of the killer's identity?"

"No."

"Did you find any fingerprints, or any hair fibers?"

"No."

"Did you find any blood that was not the victim's at the crime scene?"

"No."

Samuel paced towards the jury and, turning to face the witness, he asked, "Detective McKoskie, did you find any evidence whatsoever that would support a claim that my client could have killed Dan Fellar?"

McKoskie was quiet for a few seconds, then he swallowed and answered, "No."

"No further questions."

E Butte Av.

57

ARIZONA STATE PRISON
1305 EAST BUTTE AVENUE
FLORENCE, ARIZONA

"Hey, champ!"

"Samuel!" Thomas yelled, his face lighting up.

"I haven't seen you look so happy since you were little..."

Samuel pulled a chair over and sat in front of him.

"How do you like this new cell?"

"Well, at first, the idea of being somehow magnetized to the floor was really scary, but the boots are really light, and at least I don't have to have those stupid chains..."

"Are they treating you okay?"

"I guess, I can't complain..."

Samuel set his briefcase down on the floor and leaned forward. "How is it going with Father Damian?"

Thomas sat down on the floor, crossed his legs, and answered with a smile, "Good, at first I felt a little uncomfortable, but now I really like talking with him."

"Next week, we'll start your defense..."

Samuel noted that Thomas's expression quickly changed.

"What is it?" Samuel asked, alarmed by the dramatic switch.

"I just never thought I'd ever hear people say such horrible things about me," he said gloomily.

"Look, I told you before the trial even started, you just can't pay any attention to what people say."

Thomas looked up, and clasping his hands together he said, "Yeah, I know, but it's hard to listen to so many people talking about you like you're some kind of demon and not feel anything." He lowered his head, and added sadly, "I know there's something wrong with me, but I never wanted to hurt anybody..."

Samuel saw that he was on the verge of tears.

"Did Father Damian explain what's happening to you?"

"He just said that I had some really weird kind of possession..."

"Is that all he said?"

Thomas sighed, and looking away he replied, "And he said that later, when he was sure, he would tell me more."

Samuel blinked, wondering to himself why Father Damian hadn't told the boy everything.

"Is there anything else I should know?"

Samuel detected a note of suspicion in his voice and replied quickly, "No, no... I was just wondering what he must have meant when he said he would tell you more later..."

58

Saint Mary's Basilica
231 North Third Street
Phoenix, Arizona

"Hello?" Father Damian answered the phone sleepily.

"Father, get up, please, we have a serious problem..."

"Samuel?"

"Yes, Father, it's me... Thomas escaped again."

"Oh, God help us!"

"According to Morrison and McKoskie, it happened about an hour ago..."

"Is there a new victim?"

"We don't know yet, but the whole state is on red alert, the police and the National Guard troops are looking for him."

Father Damian sat up in bed and rubbed his neck. "What are we going to do?"

"Right now, the governor and the others are heading over to Thomas's house to wait to see if he shows up."

"I'll be there in half an hour..."

59

Santiago Family Residence
6610 North Avenue
Glendale, Arizona

It was an unusual, mysterious night. A giant red moon lit up the sky. A breeze blowing from the north carried the light scent of desert sand.

Father Damian looked up at the moon and thought, *Revelation 6:12: And the whole moon became like blood.* He took a deep breath and lowered his gaze, murmuring "Blessed be thy name, Holy Father!"

The taxi he was in came to a stop two blocks away from the house. Soldiers had blocked the street with barricades so no vehicles could get through. Father Damian got out, paid the driver, and walked the rest of the way.

The soldiers that were standing guard on the front porch were startled, for a moment they could scarcely believe their eyes. Father Damian made quite a dramatic entrance: reflections from the spotlights that had been positioned at both corners at either end of the block gave the priest clad all in black a magical appearance. Lit from behind, he seemed to be emerging from a luminescent tunnel. The enormous shadow he cast filled the street. The soldiers let him through.

"Come in, Father," Samuel said, holding open the door.

The house was full of officials. Owens was talking with the governor and the doctors, McKoskie was smoking a cigarette, while he talked with Morrison and Juan Manuel.

"Where's Mariela?" Father Damian asked.

"She's asleep. We had to give her a sedative, she was hysterical," Juan Manuel explained.

"Has there been any news of Thomas?"

"No," Samuel said.

Then Morrison's cell phone rang, and everyone turned to look at him expectantly.

"Morrison," the FBI agent answered the phone curtly. "We're on our way, tell them to come here and pick us up," he said before closing the phone.

"What's up?" Owens asked.

"They found a body in Yuma. Two helicopters will pick us up at the end of the street in twenty minutes..."

A small crowd had already started to gather outside the house where the latest victim had been reportedly found. Several police officers hurried to secure the area and keep the curious onlookers at bay. Two police cars with lights flashing were stationed at both ends of the block, while two large black SUVs with tinted windows came screeching to a halt in front of the house.

The growing crowd was surprised by the sudden arrival by the group of men that emerged from the vehicles and accompanied the governor. They all were quickly escorted inside the house.

They went into the room where the victim had been found. A woman of about forty years of age was lying on the bathroom floor, her body partially nude. Her left arm rested over the bathtub's edge, while her legs were soaking in a large pool of blood.

"Where is that flower smell coming from?" Dr. Marcus asked, breathing in deeply as he approached the victim.

"It is the scent of the saints," Father Damian answered, as he kneeled down on one knee, and made the sign of the cross over the dead woman.

"God have mercy on your soul," he said as he shut the victim's eyes.

"Don't touch the victim," Dr. Marcus said, putting a hand on the priest's shoulder. "The body needs to be examined for evidence."

Father Damian stood and turned to face the doctor, "Your efforts will be in vain, doctor, the same as with all the other victims, you will not find the slightest trace of evidence." He took a handkerchief from his pocket and, taking off his spectacles, he dabbed at the sweat on his brow. "I hope by now you have come to realize that I know much more about what is going on with the boy Thomas than any of you even conceive of..."

"You've got our attention," Owens said.

Samuel looked around and noticed that the Aramaic word was written on the wall above the tub. He remembered Nathaniel Brown's apartment, and said, "All of the crime scenes are almost identical; except for a few minor variations, they all look the same."

Morrison's cell phone rang, and he left the bathroom to answer it.

"What!" they heard him shout out in the hall.

Everyone stared at him, dreading whatever bad news he was about to deliver.

"Where?... We'll be there within the hour," he said quickly, and closing his phone, he faced the group.

"What now?" the governor asked.

"They found another body at the Phoenix Children's Hospital."

"Oh my God!" she said, leaning against the wall, suddenly unsteady.

"Two victims in one night... it seems that his compulsion to kill is getting harder and harder to control..." Dr. Marcus mused, looking at Father Damian.

"Just as I said," Father Damian remarked, "When the body becomes accustomed to the possession over time, it becomes much easier for the spirit to take control. It can stay within the body for longer periods of time, until, eventually, it is possible for the possession to become permanent... and then it will be impossible to stop him."

60

"Where are we going?" Father Damian shouted to McKoskie over the helicopter's roaring engine as they flew over the city.

McKoskie leaned closer to answer, "to the children's hospital in Phoenix..."

"Who was the victim?"

"A doctor..."

Samuel looked at Father Damian, surprised by this news. The priest detected in his expression how terrified he was; he clapped Samuel on the knee and smiled reassuringly, as was his habit, letting him know that everything would be alright in the end.

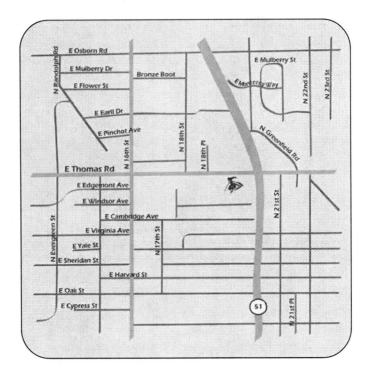

61

Phoenix Children's Hospital
1919 East Thomas Road
Phoenix, Arizona

When they arrived they were greeted by an Army sergeant and immediately taken up to the third floor.

"The whole floor has been evacuated," he said as they stepped into the elevator.

"What department did the victim work in?" Father Damian asked.

"Pediatrics."

The elevator door opened. The hallway was filled with heavily armed policemen. The doorway of the room where the body had been found had a line of police tape across it. As they ducked under the tape and went inside, they were struck by all the indications of savage violence.

"Jesus Christ!" Dr. Marcus blurted, looking at all the blood around the room.

"It looks like this one made him angry," McKoskie said a little sarcastically, seeing the blood spattered on all four walls.

The victim was a Caucasian man, around thirty-five years old, with a full head of hair that had gone completely gray. His body was lying across one of the beds, face-up, his white doctor's coat soaked in blood. Dr. Phillips went over to the body for a closer look:

"Were there any witnesses?"

"Yes, sir, a patient," the Sergeant replied.

"Did anything happen to the patient?" the governor asked.

"No, ma'am."

"Who was the patient?" Owens wanted to know.

"A five-year-old boy."

"Can I see him?" Father Damian asked.

"Yes, sir, he's on the second floor," the sergeant said, gesturing for the priest to follow him.

Father Damian left, but the others stayed in the room, looking around.

"This scene is totally different from the others," Dr. Phillips observed. "None of the others had signs of such extreme violence like we can see here."

"I agree. What do you think happened?" Dr. Marcus asked.

"I don't know, it seems that this one wasn't as easy as the others..."

After a few minutes, Father Damian reappeared in the doorway, and said, "I think you'd all better come and hear this for yourselves..."

"What is it, Father?" Samuel asked.

"You won't believe it unless you hear it with your own ears..."

They all filed out of the room and went down to the little boy's hospital room. He seemed very calm, he was playing with a little plastic soldier he held in his hands. The boy was Native American, barely five years old, and he was wearing a white hospital robe with little blue Mickey Mouse's all over. His long black hair, rosy cheeks and large, round brown eyes all accentuated his pure innocence.

Father Damian sat down next to him on the edge of the bed, while the others gathered around. The boy stopped playing with the toy soldier and looked at them.

"Rampsey, these men are from the FBI, and they're here doing an investigation into what happened. Can you tell them what you just told me?" the priest asked gently.

The boy was quiet and just looked at them. Father Damian ruffled his hair: "Don't be afraid, they're here to help you."

The boy put an arm around Father Damian's waist and nestled against him. Finally he said sweetly,

"The angel killed Dr. Golden."

"What angel?" Dr. Marcus cut in.

"The angel," the boy said simply.

Dr. Marcus and Dr. Phillips exchanged looks, intrigued by the boy's response.

"Can you tell us exactly what happened?" Dr. Phillips asked.

The boy looked up at Father Damian, who stroked his hair and said kindly, "Don't be afraid, my child. Everything's alright."

"Dr. Golden brought me some jello, we were talking and then the angel came and grabbed him on his neck and then he started squeezing..."

McKoskie looked at Samuel, who crossed his arms over his chest, focusing closely on the boy's words.

"What happened next?" Dr. Marcus asked, sitting at the foot of the bed.

"They started fighting; the angel smashed him against the wall and screamed really loud."

"What did the angel scream?" Owens asked.

"I dunno, I didn't understand..."

"Can you tell us what the angel looked like?" Dr. Phillips asked.

"He had long hair and big wings on his back, his eyes were really shiny..."

"And did he try to touch you, or to hurt you?" the governor asked.

"No ma'am..."

Samuel glanced at his watch, it would be dawn soon. He said, "It's five in the morning, we should probably get back to Thomas's house and wait there for him..."

While they started to leave the room, Samuel heard the little boy say, "He told me something."

"Who?" Samuel asked.

"The angel."

"The angel spoke to you?" the governor sounded alarmed.

"Yes," he turned his head to look at her.

"What did he say?" Dr. Marcus asked anxiously.

The boy looked up at Father Damian before responding,

"He said nobody would never hurt me again..."

Dr. Marcus looked at Dr. Phillips, and as they walked out of the room he asked quietly, "How did the angel talk to him? I thought it only spoke in Aramaic..."

Father Damian followed behind them into the hallway and said, "No, Mr. Marcus, angels speak every language, since their minds are like God's..."

He looked to his left and right, blinked, and said, "It looks like things are starting to get interesting, doesn't it?"

62

Santiago Family Residence
6610 North 61st Avenue
Glendale, Arizona

They all waited patiently in the living room, as the ritual had become almost routine. Everyone was tired and sleepy. Dr. Marcus and Dr. Phillips talked to try and keep themselves awake.

"I'm going to make some coffee, would anyone like some?" Mariela asked.

Everyone laughed at how quickly Father Damian's hand shot up.

"By now you all know I'm not the kind of priest you see everyday," Father Damian joked.

"How do you take it, Father?"

"Black and very sweet, please."

"Anyone else?"

"I'd like a cup, with a little cream, if you have it, please," Dr. Marcus said.

Samuel yawned and looked at his watch again. It was seven-thirty in the morning. He stood and went over to Juan Manuel, and asked if he could turn on the television.

"Good Morning, Arizona," said an attractive woman with blond hair and brown eyes on the television screen. "I'm Johanna Hints, and here's the latest news this hour..."

One by one, they all stood and gathered around the TV.

"The state of Arizona awoke on high alert again this morning, after news of Thomas Santiago's latest escape from the Florence State Prison. Police in the cities of Glendale, Mesa and Phoenix are pursuing the fugitive. Reporting live from Florence is our correspondent Cynthia Vega. Good morning, Cynthia."

"Good morning, Johanna."

"Tell us what's going on?"

"As you said, Johanna, the state of Arizona woke up to the horrible news that Thomas Santiago has escaped again. You can feel the terror on the streets of Phoenix, knowing that this deadly killer is on the loose again. Our news team tried to interview Mr. Jim Whitefield, the director of the prison, but he could not be reached for comment..."

"Cynthia, can anyone explain how has he been able to escape from prison, again and again?"

"No one has been able to explain it. Most of the schools in the area have cancelled classes for the day, and will remain closed until the police can inform the community that the fugitive has been captured and is once again behind bars."

McKoskie stood in front of the television, and, looking around, he said to everyone, "I think we'd better be prepared for the worst..."

"Why do you say that?" Juan Manuel asked nervously.

"There's a lot of people out there who are not going to take this news very calmly..."

Owens turned to face Morrison: "I want a platoon of Marines stationed out in front of this house as soon as possible. I don't want any surprises, understood?"

"Yes, sir."

Just then Owens' cell phone rang. He answered right away, and his suddenly pale expression conveyed how important the call was.

"Yes, sir. We're doing everything we can to find him, sir..."

Three hours had passed, and still there had been no sign of Thomas. The group waited...

"What time does he usually show up?" Dr. Marcus asked.

"He's never taken this long, has he?" Samuel replied, looking to Juan Manuel.

"It's almost always between five and seven in the morning," Juan Manuel added.

"Why is it taking so long this time?" Dr. Phillips asked.

"Because each time he is possessed, his spirit grows weaker, and the force that takes over his body has a little more control over him than the time before," Father Damian explained.

Out of nowhere, a rock smashed through a window. Everyone hit the floor. Samuel covered Mariela, shielding her from the shattering glass.

"Gregg! What the hell's going on out there?!" Mckoskie shouted to another police officer through his radio transmitter.

"There's a group a protestors out here, with torches and homemade explosives, sir..."

"Arrest them, set the barricades up a block further away from the house, and don't let anyone through without permission! Understood?"

"Yes, sir."

Then a bloodcurdling shriek shook the house.

"Mommmmmyyyy!!"

Still lying on the floor, Mariela uncovered her face and looked towards the stairs.

Samuel, still partly covering Mariela, looked at Father Damian, and they both leapt to their feet and ran up the stairs, followed by the rest of the group. Samuel pushed open the door to Thomas's bedroom, and, shocked by what he saw, he fell to his knees, his eyes shining with terror.

Dr. Marcus burst into the room and collapsed against the wall, his knees buckling, blurting "What the hell..."

"No one moves," Father Damian commanded, slowly stepping forward.

Thomas's face had changed dramatically: his skin was alabaster white, two immense white wings sprouted from his shoulder blades, and extended outward, almost touching both walls on either side. His body floated about three feet above the floor, and seemed to be encased in a sphere of bright light. His hands were covered in blood, his hair fanned out behind him from the strong gust of wind that blew in from the window.

Father Damian knelt down before him. Training his gaze on Owens and Dr. Phillips, the angel said in a loud, deep voice, in Aramaic:

"Wicked souls, repent, before it is too late!"

They both fell to their knees, awestruck and terrified, while Father Damian raised his arms and prayed in Aramaic,

"Angel of God, abandon the body of this boy, and let us save his innocent soul."

"The priest speaks that language?" Dr. Marcus murmured close to Samuel's ear, and he simply nodded slightly.

"Angel of God, The avenger of blood, plead to the Lord Almighty for humanity," Father Damian said, clasping his hands together under his chin and bowing his head. "Tell Him that there is still room for repentance, please have mercy."

Thomas let out a horrifying wail that echoed all through the house, and remained floating in the air, unconscious. Father Damian stood and held out his arms in front of Thomas's chest, until he collapsed into his embrace. Suddenly, a flash of light enveloped them both; a blast of wind blew in through the window, like a sudden hurricane. Then, the light around them was compressed into a single ray, a lightening bolt that left through the window, and as the wind suddenly stopped blowing, there was only deafening silence.

Samuel and Juan Manuel rushed to help Father Damian with Thomas, who was still unconscious. They laid him on the bed. Then suddenly Father Damian collapsed on the floor, as he, too, lost consciousness.

"Father, Father!" Samuel shouted frantically, while he lightly slapped his cheek, trying to revive him.

Dr. Marcus bent over him and put his folded jacket under his head. He took his pulse and instructed McKoskie, "Call an ambulance."

Father Damian slowly opened his eyes and looked at Samuel. In a weak, barely audible voice, he rasped, "We're running out of time..."

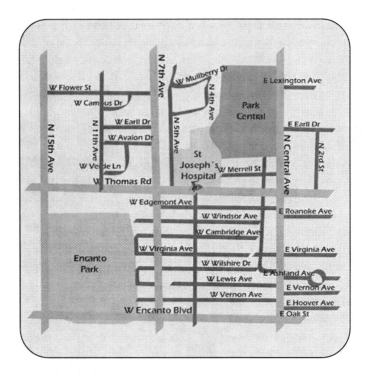

63

St. Joseph's Hospital
350 West Thomas Road
Phoenix, Arizona

"You need to have a complete physical as soon as possible," the doctor said to Father Damian, as she took the stethoscope out of her ears and left it around her neck. "Try to get some rest, you have to get some sleep."

The priest couldn't help smiling as she said this.

"Do you have problems sleeping, Father?" She asked, noting his reaction.

"I often stay up all night," he replied, buttoning his black robe.

"And why do you think that is?"

"I've never been a big sleeper. Ever since I entered the Seminary, I've gotten used to sleeping very little, with my studies, mass, and prayers, I don't have much time left over for anything else..."

The doctor looked at him with a certain tenderness in her eyes. "You seem to be a troubled man, Father..."

He stood and put on his glasses. "When one learns the things that I have learned, and sees the things that I have seen, it's like the old saying..."

"What saying?" she asked, crossing her arms.

"That to many people, faith is like coffee."

She smiled, leaning against the wall. "How's that?"

The priest stepped over to a mirror on his right, and after straightening his clerical collar, he looked at her and finished,

"Faith, just like coffee, is black and bitter and the only thing that sweetens it is hope. When we learn how to take it so it won't do us any harm, it will keep us awake..."

The doctor looked at him quietly, while she pondered his words. She lowered her gaze and, smiling, added, "That's not the sort of thing you usually hear a priest say."

"I am a priest, it's true; but underneath this frock there is a man with many questions, doctor, questions that still have no answers..."

Father Damian took a step toward her and looking her straight in the eye, he said,

"I'm not somebody who thinks by reciting an Our Father and a few Hail Marys, a killer can be absolved of a murder, as the old song goes..."

"So what do you tell people that confess to you?"

"To look inside their hearts for forgiveness and repentance, and if they know that they have done something bad, ask to be forgiven, because without true repentance, there is no point in asking for forgiveness."

E Butte Av.

64

ARIZONA STATE PRISON
1305 EAST BUTTE AVENUE
FLORENCE, ARIZONA

Two days later Father Damian went to visit Thomas, who jumped off the bed and went over to the glass window to ask,

"Father, how are you? You have no idea how bad I felt..."

"Everything's fine, my son," he said, smiling, as he stepped into the cell.

"I never wanted to hurt you, Father..."

"I know, child, I know... what happened was not your fault."

Thomas sat down on the ground, bowed his head and covered his face with his hands. "What are we going to do, Father? Things just keep getting worse and worse... you said that we'd find the way to stop all this."

"I know, child, but the people who are in charge of your security have got to give me complete freedom to work with you."

Thomas let out a long breath, looking up. His eyes welled with tears, and hugging his knees, he said, "The only way to stop this is to kill me, isn't it?"

Father Damian stood beside him and ruffled his hair. "No, of course not. I have an idea that I think will work, but first I have to discuss it with a friend of mine in Sinaloa, Mexico."

They were both quiet. Thomas wiped away his tears and Father Damian stroked his hair soothingly as he spoke. "Samuel called me this morning to tell me that we would meet with the judge tonight, to talk over what's going to happen to you. If everything goes well, I think we can start to put my plan into motion..."

65

THE GOVERNOR'S OFFICE
1700 WEST WASHINGTON STREET
PHOENIX, ARIZONA

Sitting calmly, they waited for the governor and Owens, who were on a conference call with Washington.

"How much longer do you think they're going to be?" Father Damian asked Samuel.

"I don't know, we've been waiting for over an hour already..."

"What is it? Why are you looking at me like that?"

"Are you going to tell them everything this time?"

"Yes, of course, now that I have evidence to support my theory, and they won't be able to deny the fact that I'm right."

The door opened and Owens and the governor came into the room, and judging by their expressions, Samuel could see that things were not going well. They sat down around a round table and Owens said, "Gentlemen, Washington is extremely concerned about this case," he tapped on the table nervously and continued, "This is the forth time that the boy has escaped. The whole state is furious about our total helplessness here."

Everyone was quiet. Owens looked at Dr. Marcus and the engineer Myrick and asked, "Do you have anything to say?"

"I think the first thing, as Father Damian has said, is to figure out exactly what it is that we're up against." Dr. Marcus took off his glasses and set them down on the table, and continued, "Yesterday, you saw with your own eyes that what is happening to that boy is more than just unbe- lievable."

Owens looked at Father Damian and asked, "Can you explain for us what the hell is going on?"

The priest opened the briefcase he had brought with him, took a folder out of it and put it on the table. He looked around at everyone and began, "Ladies and gentlemen: perhaps what I am about to tell you will seem hard to believe, but, ultimately, you will have to accept that it is the truth."

He opened the folder and took some photographs from it, which he passed to Dr. Phillips, so they could all look at them.

"Each of these photographs was taken by security cameras at places where Thomas has escaped from, except for the first, which is from the gas station. As you can see in these pictures, and as I'm sure you already suspected, Thomas suffers from a kind of possession that has never been seen before..."

The priest stood and began pacing around the table, his hands clasped behind his back.

"In the first photograph, you will observe that Thomas Santiago's features are still faintly recognizable, but, in the others, his body undergoes a transformation that is more and more extreme..."

He stopped to look at them and continued, "That is what I was referring to when I said that we were running out of time... With each instance of possession, Thomas's physical body grows more vulnerable, while the strength of the possessing spirit grows much stronger. As you can see in the last photo, by then he has wings growing out of his back."

He paused for a moment, gathering his thoughts.

"I can tell you in all sincerity that if we let this happen again, then we will no longer be able to stop him, since the spirit will take over his body completely, and will never leave."

He was quiet for a few seconds, and rested his hand on the back of Dr. Marcus's chair.

"According to the studies that I have done, I am convinced that Thomas is possessed by a strange force, something never seen before... a kind of possession that I believe our religion has never faced in its entire history..."

"What kind of possession, Father?" the governor asked.

The priest was quiet, and turned to look at Samuel-He had a frightened expression, and hoped that this time Father Damian would tell the whole story and reveal everything.

"What is it that takes control of him, Father?" Owens prodded, as the silence lengthened.

"According to the symptoms he exhibits, I think it is some kind of angel, or something similar. I'm still not completely sure—I need to spend a little more time with Thomas, and try to talk directly to the spirit..."

"Spirit of an angel?" Dr. Marcus, said, startled.

"What kind of angel? What do you mean?" the governor asked.

"The Archangel Michael..."

"What? That's ridiculous!" Dr. Phillips exclaimed disdainfully.

"Ridiculous?" Father Damian repeated, turning to look at him. "Of all the patients you've ever treated, Dr. Phillips, have you ever had one who has sprouted wings from his back, or who has shown the kind of powers that Thomas has?"

"But, what kind of evidence are you using as the grounds for this conclusion, Father?" Judge Fieldmore asked.

"Can you explain the wings on Thomas's back, Dr. Phillips?"

Father Damian picked up a photograph that clearly showed the wings fully extended, coming out of Thomas's back, and placing it on the table in front of Dr. Phillips, he pointed to it:

"You saw this with your own eyes, didn't you, Doctor?"

The doctor looked at the picture, but didn't reply. Father Damian looked carefully at each person around the table, and taking a breath, he added, "I'll tell you what my conclusion is based on," he paced around the table. "There are many things involved in this case which you are not aware of. Almost three years ago, Thomas went to visit his older brother at the seminary..." Father Damian told them the whole story. After he was finished, there was a stunned silence. Samuel looked around with a slight smile, happy that finally everyone had heard it all.

"What makes you think that it's Archangel Michael, instead of a demon, or some sort of evil spirit?" the governor asked.

"The first victim was killed on September 29th, right? In the Catholic Church, that is the day honoring Saint Michael, who is considered the protector of the innocents, and the avenger of blood. According to Thomas's grandmother, the next day was the first time the boy awoke in his bed covered in blood..."

"But if it's really an angel, why does he have to kill?" Owens interjected.

"This is another point that needs to be explained—he is a killer, there's no doubt about that, but he doesn't kill for pleasure..."

Father Damian turned to Dr. Marcus: "Doctor, when you said that all the victims had something in common, you weren't mistaken."

Samuel passed around a copy of a list to everyone at the table, with the names of all of the victims on it and brief descriptions.

"As you can see, each of these individuals had been accused or convicted of a serious offense, at one time or another..."

"The fact that these people committed some kind of crime doesn't give anybody the right to murder them," Morgan observed.

"That is according to the laws of man, Mr. Stanley. But God does as He wants, without being troubled by what people might think," Father Damian pointed out, turning to face him.

Everyone was quiet, since no one dared to contradict the priest. Owens looked around the table, trying to detect what the others thought of all this; then he looked to the middle of the table at a photo that showed Thomas completely transformed, his otherworldly expression one of heated fury; his immense wings fully extended. He looked around the table at everyone and asked,

"Does anyone have something they'd like to say?"

"I think that this is just an absurd strategy that Samuel has cooked up with Father Damian to absolve his client of any guilt," Stanley said, defiant.

Samuel jumped to his feet and pointed at Stanley, shouting, "What the hell are you talking about? You know even better than I do that Father Damian's theory is the only explanation for what's going on!"

Samuel was infuriated. He looked at Owens and warned, "Don't let any harm come to that poor boy—you know as well as I do that Thomas is innocent, he was not acting according to his own free will—"

"Gentlemen, gentlemen please!" the governor asked, standing.

"I don't know why you stand up for him so much... since you know full well that he's a threat to us all," Stanley said icily.

Samuel tried to calm down. He looked the prosecutor in the eye and replied, "I've always believed that a man has the right to a fair trial, no matter the circumstances, and if he cannot be proven guilty, according to the law, than he must be set free, even if that will open the doors of hell..."

The room was quiet, and Stanley bowed his head, embarrassed. Judge Fieldmore gave Samuel an approving nod, showing his respect.

"Father, what can we do about this case?" Owens asked, worried. "Could you do some kind of exorcism, or something like that?"

Father Damian looked at him, thinking; he bowed his head and studied one of the pictures of Thomas, totally transformed into that awesome being. Finally he spoke:

"As religious men, we have studied methods for extracting evil from the human heart and spirit, but what's taking control of this boy seems to be something good..."

Everyone paid close attention, while Father Damian looked at the judge and continued, "How to extract an angel from a person's soul?- I don't think anybody knows how to do that... we would have to study the particular symptoms of this sort of possession, from a religious standpoint..."

"But that's going to take some time," Dr. Marcus spoke up.

"Yes, maybe more than we'd like," the priest acknowledged warily.

"How much time?" Owens asked.

"I'm not sure, I would have to have full access to Thomas, to be able to interview him freely. Also, I will have to consult with some friends of mine in the Vatican and Mexico, and examine the case very carefully..."

"Mr. Whitefield, grant Father Damian all the access he requires," Owen said firmly, turning to his right.

"And one more thing, Mr. Owens," Father Damian interjected, "Starting tomorrow, I would like to spend the nights at the prison with Thomas..."

"You're crazy! He could kill you!" The governor blurted out.

"That's a risk I am willing to take. If everything starts when he is asleep, then I want to be there when it happens."

"I will not be responsible," the judge quickly added, looking to the governor.

The room was suddenly silent. Owens looked at Father Damian as he said,

"Mr. Whitefield, we cannot allow Thomas to escape again, and if the only way to keep that from happening is to make sure that no possession takes place, then give Father Damian permission; I will accept responsibility."

Owens paused for a few seconds before concluding, "I don't even want to think about what could happen if that boy escapes again..."

E Turquoise Av

66

Escobar Family Residence
6889 East Turquoise Avenue
Scottsdale, Arizona

"What are you doing, baby?" Catherine asked, stepping over to Samuel to give him a kiss on the forehead.

"I'm watching the news. Marcos called me a little while ago... It looks like there are some big protests going on over the case, and there have been several arrests, in Mesa and Glendale..."

Catherine sat down next to him on the couch. "What will they do with Thomas now, since he escaped again?"

"I don't know, sweetheart. All I know is those doctors and scientists that came from Washington would rather kill him than risk another mistake..."

Samuel looked at the television, the news was starting and he picked up the remote to turn up the volume.

"The State of Arizona is still on high alert today, due to the numerous protests that have broken out in response to the latest escape from the State Prison in Florence of Thomas Santiago, 'The Devil Boy', said the commentator on the screen, a dark-skinned black man with a deep voice and wearing wire-rimmed glasses. "Large groups of protestors, some armed with guns and carrying torches, have been arrested by the police. An area encompassing a half-mile radius all around the Florence prison has been declared a militarized zone. Heavily armed soldiers have erected barricades, and only authorized personnel are granted entry. Several incidents have been reported on the Ship Rock reservation and in the cities of Mesa and Glendale, and burning tires have been reported in Tucson and Yuma."

Samuel turned off the television and sighed wearily, he hung his head, looking dejected. Catherine rubbed his back tenderly.

"I just can't see an end to this nightmare," he said, hugging her around her waist, resting his head against her stomach.

Catherine stroked his hair and hugged him.

"Every day, we get threatening phone calls and letters at the office, saying all kinds of horrible things..."

Catherine stood and walked across the room, staring at the floor.

"What is it?" Samuel asked, surprised by her reaction.

She was still quiet, running a hand through her hair nervously. Samuel got up and approached her, putting his hands on her shoulders: "Catherine, what's going on?"

She looked up at him and said sadly, "I didn't want to say anything, so you wouldn't worry, but we've been getting letters here at the house too, for a few days now..."

"What!?" Samuel yelled, looking closely at her. "Why the hell didn't you tell me?"

"I just didn't want to worry you, and anyway I'm not afraid..."

Samuel picked up the phone and started dialing. "First thing tomorrow, you and the baby are going to Guadalajara to stay with my uncle!"

Catherine gently took the telephone from his hands: "We're not going anywhere..."

"Are you crazy?"

"My place is here, at my husband's side; so don't even think for one second that we're going anywhere!"

"But Catherine, those people could hurt you, and our daughter..."

"I'm not afraid."

Samuel grabbed her arm. "Catherine, please, you have to understand, these people aren't kidding around."

"I don't care, I'm not going to leave you to face this all by yourself."

Samuel let go of her arm and rubbed his forehead in frustration. "Catherine, you must realize how serious the situation is." He grabbed her by the shoulders again and said, "I could never forgive myself if something happened to you or the baby."

She held his gaze, her beautiful blue eyes locked intensely with his; Samuel was quiet as he watched her eyes fill with tears.

"I can't leave you now; you know as well as I do that without you, Thomas hasn't got a chance of getting out of this alive..."

"But you and the baby are all that matters to me..."

"I promise nothing will happen."

"How can you be so sure?"

"Because nothing and no one is going to separate me from you, except God..."

Samuel stared into her eyes and smiled, "You're a brave woman, but I still think you're nuts."

They both laughed. She put her arms around him and hugged him, resting her head against his chest.

"Remember when you asked me to marry you? That day, I promised that I would always be at your side, in good times and bad, for better or worse, as long as you let me be your wife." She paused, and kissing his chest, she finished, "I wasn't kidding then, I meant what I said."

He kissed her hair while his mind flooded with memories. He happily looked back on that beautiful, playfully suspenseful moment when, along with some police officer buddies of his, he played the most wonderful prank on Catherine:

Samuel remembered that day as if it were yesterday. He and some of his friends played a trick on the poor waitress at the coffee shop that she would never forget. Two police officers came in at lunchtime and handcuffed the girl in front of everyone. They accused her of murder in the first degree, the girl's eyes filled with tears as, scared and embarrassed, she hung her head. Then, one of the police officers looked at the customer she had been waiting on, and asked him to read the accused her rights. The waitress was stunned; just then, Samuel took a little box from his pants pocket, he kneeled down before her, and taking her hand, he said, "You have the right to be my wife, my best friend, my partner and the mother of my children." The coffee shop erupted in hoots and whistles, some of the girls who were there were moved to tears by the incredibly romantic display. Catherine threw herself into Samuel's arms and started to cry, while several onlookers started clapping. The next day, a headline of the front page of the university newspaper read: "A Cinderella Story for the Nineties: A Prominent Law Student Proposes to Waitress."

"At least let me talk to the judge about getting you protection," Samuel pleaded, closing his eyes and embracing her tenderly.

She nodded, her head pressed against his heart.

67

Saint Mary's Basilica
231 North Third Street
Phoenix, Arizona

"Hello? The priest answered the phone.
"Hello, Father Steven."
"Samuel? How are you?"
"I'm fine, thanks; forgive me for calling so late..."
"Don't worry about it, we were just watching the news."
"Can I speak to Father Damian, please?"
Father Damian got on the line, and Samuel said,
"I've been doing some research into what you asked, and you were right."
"What did you find out?"

"The woman who was killed in Yuma had been accused of murdering her husband in a suspicious accident, she may have planned it with a friend of his who may have been her lover, to collect on an insurance policy worth over a million dollars..."

"Good Lord!"

"The police could never prove that it wasn't an accident though..."

"And what did you find out about the doctor?"

"He was under investigation for over a year."

"Investigation? What for?"

"A year and a half ago, five children who were under his care died mysteriously..."

"What do you mean, 'mysteriously'?"

"From what I was able to find out, the children were all admitted to the hospital for minor ailments, and they got much worse overnight. After several months, with no signs of improvement, they all died. They couldn't find any explanation for it, so that's why the doctor was under investigation. The little boy that we talked to, Rampsey Collard, was admitted a week earlier with a mild case of gastroenteritis, and the night before they were going to release him from the hospital, he took a dramatic turn for the worse."

"Hmmm... that explains the signs of extreme violence that we detected in the room where he was killed..."

"What do you mean?"

"Jesus said that "*whoever brings harm to an innocent child would be best off to tie a rock around his neck and throw himself into the sea...*"

Samuel was quiet, and took a deep breath.

"Samuel...?"

"I'm still here, Father."

"Are you alright?"

"Yes...yes, I'm just so worried about Thomas... Do you think there's any way for us to stop what's happening to him?"

"I don't know, my son, but we'll pray to God to find the answer, and ask for His help and guidance..."

"You have to do something for him, Father, because if we don't figure out how to stop it, they'll kill him..."

"I have an idea that might work..."

Excited, Samuel asked quickly, "What is it?"

"I don't want to talk about it until I'm completely sure, that's why I didn't mention it earlier. I want to be totally confident that it's going to work..."

S 1st Avenue

S 3rd Avenue

W. Jefferson St.

68

Maricopa County Superior Court
201 West Jefferson Street
Phoenix, Arizona

The judge entered the courtroom in a hushed silence. The pressroom was packed with cameras and reporters that were broadcasting live across the whole country. Police officers were interspersed throughout the courtroom keeping a tight watch; after the defendant's most recent escape from prison and in the wake of violent protests that had broken out across the state, Judge Fieldmore had requested that security measures at the courthouse be doubled. The reporters and camera crews had to pass through two extremely thorough security checks, and all the cameras and microphones had to go through X-ray machines.

Security precautions had been tripled at every window and doorway in the courtroom. The police officers all wore bulletproof vests, and many were armed with submachine guns.

Judge Fieldmore took his place and looked to the back of the room, making sure that everything was in order. He brought a hand to his mouth and coughed lightly to clear his throat. He leaned towards the microphone and said,

"Mr. Escobar, you may call your first witness."

"Your Honor, the defense calls Dr. Dwain Rogers."

A man, who looked to be around sixty years old, with a thick gray moustache, fair skin and a kind-looking face, stepped into the witness box. After the court officer swore him in, Samuel approached him and began,

"Doctor, you work at the Jackson Memorial Hospital in New York City, correct?"

"Yes, that's correct."

"What is the nature of your work there?"

The witness looked directly at the jury, and in a firm, self-assured tone, he replied, "I have been the director of the department of psychiatry and neurology at the hospital for the past thirty-five years."

Samuel picked up the remote control for the television monitor and pointed it towards the screen:

"Your Honor, the defense would like to show this video, which was taken this past Friday, and has been admitted into evidence in this court as number V. I-22."

Then he turned to the witness, "Doctor, this is the last video which was taken four days ago at the prison in Florence by the security cameras in the defendant's cell. I would like you to give the court your professional opinion of what you see."

The video began, as low murmurings were heard around the courtroom. Samuel noted the doctor's reaction of disbelief, as he rubbed his eyes after he saw how Thomas slowly levitated off the ground as his body was enveloped in a sphere of dazzling light. Then, Thomas transformed into the angel. His outstretched wings seemed to touch either side of the cell, as it rapidly filled with smoke, and seconds later, the fog was sucked out through holes in the ceiling.

The cell was completely empty, the angel had simply disappeared. Samuel stopped the video and paused it on the image of Thomas just after he was completely transformed. He looked at the witness and said,

"Dr. Rogers, the state called Dr. Brushevski as a witness to this courtroom, who, after having examined my client and after watching another video similar to this one, declared that he had not detected anything wrong with the defendant, and that, based on his extensive professional experience, he concluded that he was, in fact, completely normal..."

"That is totally illogical," the doctor responded, as he took off the glasses he had worn to view the video. "It's blatantly obvious that something very strange is happening with this boy. You can only conclude that, whatever it is that is happening at that moment, it is definitely not normal. Human beings do not have wings growing out of their backs... And I have never seen or heard of a human being that glowed with that kind of light."

Samuel paced in front of the prosecution table, and fixing his gaze on Stanley, he asked,

"In other words, you are completely sure that something is very wrong with my client, even though so far it has not been possible to substantiate it medically?"

"Yes, of course, the evidence is undeniable. How could you medically prove what is happening? I'm not sure, but if there is a scientific way to explain it, I would be very interested to know what that is..."

"Doctor, with all of your experience, do you believe that a person could undergo a transformation like that and still be in his right mind?"

"I don't believe so. If you observe closely, at the beginning of the video, it seems as if the transformation begins when he is asleep. Just like people who walk in their sleep, and are not responsible for their actions while they are in that involuntary state, it's an automatic muscular response that makes the body react without the mind's intervention—that seems to be what is happening here."

After pausing for a moment, considering his next words, he continued, "It seems that he is suffering from a loss of neurological control that only arises while he is sleeping, and that, in a way, provokes those strange supernatural powers. But this looks more like some sort of spiritual possession than a mental disturbance..."

"Objection, Your Honor, the witness is a psychiatrist, not a priest," Stanley said loudly, as he scribbled something down on his legal pad.

"Sustained," the judge said.

Samuel walked over to the jury and curled his right hand into a tight fist, and forcefully hit his left palm with it: "According to the law, no action is a punishable offense if it was committed involuntarily! In the penal code of 1984, page 319, it states "a person cannot be found guilty if his actions were a product of a mental illness or a related defect."

He looked seriously at each member of the jury, and concluded, "There isn't a person in the world who could voluntarily provoke those supernatural powers within himself, much less when he is asleep..."

Samuel turned and addressed the witness, "Isn't that true, doctor?"

"Yes, that's correct."

He turned to Stanley and said, "Your witness."

"Doctor, have you examined the accused yourself?" the prosecutor asked, still seated.

"No, not yet."

"So, how do you know there's something wrong with him?"

"It's plainly obvious, Mr. Morgan. The videos that have been shown in this court and the other evidence, the strange feats that we have seen him perform, do not allow for any other reasonable conclusion..."

Stanley stood and approached the witness to ask with exaggerated skepticism, "Are you saying that just by watching the videos and examining the evidence, you can determine if the patient suffers from some kind of mental disturbance, without ever actually talking to him?"

The doctor crossed his arms and gave Stanley a stony look. He considered his words before speaking, and then replied, "That is what we call a 'criminal profile' in psychology, Mr. Morgan. The FBI has used this method for the past thirty years to catch the worst killers in modern history... I don't know why it would come as such a surprise to you..."

Stanley looked at him quietly, blinking; he realized that question had backfired.

"Have you ever interviewed a serial killer?"

"Yes. One of the first ones I interviewed was Ted Bundy, when he decided to talk, and Jeffrey Dahmer, Patrick McKay, and some other lesser-known ones..."

Standing right next to the witness box, with a hand at his belt and the other leaning against the rail, Stanley asked,

"Doctor, according to the law, "for a person to be considered insane, he must be devoid of understanding and conscious awareness at the moment of the crime, and be unaware of the consequences of his actions."

He stepped over to the television that was set off to the side. He held up a videotape and addressed the judge,

"Your Honor, the State presents to the Court the video from the gas station on 59th Avenue."

After putting the video into the VHS, he turned to the witness:

"I am sure that you've seen this video that shows Thomas Santiago killing one of his victims..."

Stanley paused the video right when the victim fell onto the floor. He placed the remote control down and said,

"Here you can see exactly how he grabs the victim by the neck, and while he is strangling him, he is telling the victim the reason why he's killing him. Isn't that a sign that the killer is consciously aware of his actions?"

"Not exactly," the doctor answered, leaning to his left to get a better view of the television. "Just the opposite, actually; many serial killers show their sadism in this way, since they enjoy seeing the terror reflected in the eyes of their victims."

He cleared his throat, and continued, "One of the most disturbing factors in serial murders is that the killers are rational and calculating, as we saw in Dennis Nilsen and Jeffrey Dahmer, who were both cannibals, preying on the innocent. They both affirmed that their greatest satisfaction was derived from imagining what they would do to their next victims."

Stanley stroked his chin while he paced back and forth:

"Doctor, correct me if I'm wrong, but when Dennis Nilsen was being questioned by the police, didn't he say "the human mind can act diabolically without being sick." Is that true?"

"Yes, he did say that."

"Somebody who walks into a supermarket, for example, takes out a gun and starts shooting at anything that moves, seems crazier to me than a person who chooses his victim, as we saw in the video, Thomas Santiago moves right for Patrick McKinney. He didn't even look at the woman working behind the counter, he went right to his victim, and that is premeditation. Or am I wrong?"

"This is typical behavior of disorganized killers, since their dementia is so extreme. Forgetting that the woman behind the counter could be an eye-witness is clear evidence of his dementia..."

The doctor scratched his head, exhaled heavily and went on, "The reason that they are called predators in psychology is because, just like a lion or tiger that picks its victim out of a herd and runs it down, ignoring all the others, the killer chooses his victims in public places, for example

Andrei Chikatilo at the train stations in Germany, or Dahmer, who chose his victims at the mall in Milwaukee. The only difference is that an animal kills out of hunger, and the killer is driven by criminal impulses, to feed his fantasies, or his hate..."

69

Saint Mary's Basilica
231 North Third Street
Phoenix, Arizona

Father Damian was surprised to find Samuel sitting in a pew in the middle of the church. He looked deep in thought, staring at an image of Jesus painted on one of the windows, which showed the king of the Jews carrying the cross up to Calvary, while the Roman soldiers whipped him.

"Samuel!" the priest exclaimed happily as he hurried towards him. "Why didn't you let me know you were here?"

"I was feeling a little down, and I decided to just sit here for a while by myself..."

Father Damian sat next to him and put his arm around Samuel's shoulder. "Can I help?"

Samuel looked at him, as his eyes grew moist.

"Samuel, you're scaring me... What's going on?" the priest pulled his arm back and looked at him attentively.

"I'm afraid that something's going to happen to my family, Father... I get at least ten calls a day, at the office and at home, from people threatening to kill my wife and daughter, so that I can see what it feels like to lose a loved one..."

Father Damian put a consoling hand on Samuel's shoulder again and sighed deeply.

"This kind of thing is to be expected. All the great men in history who have fought for truth and justice were threatened with death at one time or another, or thrown in jail, even unjustly killed..."

He looked up towards the altar:

"I'm not saying this to scare you, but look at Jesus, for example. They crucified him, and killed him, just for saying the truth, and declaring that he was the son of God."

Samuel lifted his head and fixed his gaze on the statue of Jesus on the cross. He noted how the sun's rays, filtering in through the window to the side, illuminated his face, imbuing it with a feeling of tragedy and mystery. He saw the figures of Mary Magdalene and the Virgin Mary at His feet, kneeling under the cross, crying bitter tears.

"I know that I am fighting for a just cause, I know very well that Thomas is innocent, and that's what keeps me going every day, it's just that all this..."

"It seems like a nightmare that just won't end... I know, sometimes I feel the same way," the priest interjected, and leaning back in the pew he went on, "The injustices of life can only be fought through faith, and the satisfaction of knowing that you are doing what is right—and that, in some way, the force that makes this world a magical place will someday bring peace to your soul..."

Hearing these words, it was as if Samuel had been doused with a bucket of ice water. With a slight smile he asked,

"How have you managed to keep your faith all these years?"

"My faith is incredulous, Samuel."

"Incredulous?"

Father Damian looked Samuel in the eye: "I believe in what I see and what I feel, and there are some things I see, and some things I feel, that feed my doubts..."

"What doubts?"

"That this is it, you're born and then you die. Seeing that the evil of humanity will bring about our own destruction."

Father Damian let his gaze wander around the church, while he smoothed his robe. He folded his hands in his lap.

"Many of the questions that I ask myself have just one answer, and that is that there must be a God, somewhere, who created all of this; in a place that we call heaven, because nothing comes from nothing. I cannot believe that, for no logical reason, a big explosion happened in the universe and thousands of years later the animals and all the other wonders of the world were formed. I believe that whoever was here at the beginning knew the truth, knew where all this came from, whether it was Adam and Eve, or whoever it may have been. I believe that the truth of creation has been greatly distorted with the passage of time..."

Both men were quiet, enjoying the complete silence. Samuel detected a warm, tender glow in the priest's eyes, the glow that grows out of the satisfaction of wisdom in the human soul.

"Father, if you had the chance to talk to God, and to ask him just one question, what would it be?"

Father Damian smiled and replied, "Of what we know about You, what is the truth, Lord?"

Then he turned to face Samuel and concluded, "I know the answer to that question would also give me the answer to so many others..."

"Do you think that it was easier for the apostles to believe?"

"To believe in God?"

"Yes, that's something I've been asking myself ever since I was a kid. I think it was easier, since they had Jesus there with them, they saw him perform miracles, and they listened to him talk about the kingdom of heaven..."

"In a way it was like you say, but just like us, they had to be convinced. I consider myself a modern-day Abraham..."

"I don't understand..." Samuel said, curious.

"Why do you think that God chose Abraham to be the father of the faith?"

"Because he was a good man..."

"There have always been plenty of good men in the world; the Bible says in Genesis 5:24 that *Enoch walked with God three hundred years and God was so pleased that he said "come with me"*, and made him the first man in history that never died."

Incredulous, Samuel pulled back.

Father Damian turned to face him. He crossed his arms over his chest and went on,

"Abraham was a man who was searching for the one true God, since he didn't believe in the gods of his ancestors. Son of an idol maker, one day he saw how a sculpture of one the gods that his father had made shattered, after falling off from a donkey that was carrying it. He thought about what he had seen and concluded that it couldn't be the image of a god: something so fragile, that could break so easily..."

"But where is that in the Bible?" Samuel asked.

"It's not in the Bible, it's one of the many, many stories that is not told there."

"Do you believe those stories?"

"Many of them are much more than isolated stories: they are manuscripts that were discovered in excavations, some more than three thousand years old. I translated many of them myself for the Catholic Church. Others are legends that were passed down from generation to generation in Israel. For example, many people don't know why Peter was the disciple that believed in Jesus the most..."

Samuel looked at him quietly, but he realized that if he didn't ask, he would never hear the explanation.

"So why was Peter the one who believed in Jesus the most?"

The priest smiled as he began his story. Samuel recognized that smile right away, the expression conveyed the deep sense of satisfaction he derived from telling stories like that one, that few people had ever heard.

"According to an old legend from Israel, when Jesus was walking with his disciples to Cesarea, Peter, who always walked at his side, stopped for a moment to tie his sandals. Looking at the ground, he noticed that the feet of Jesus did not leave footprints in the sand. Peter covered his mouth with his hand, he was so stunned, and it was at that moment that he began to believe that Jesus really was the Son of God. So when Jesus asked his disciples *"Who do the people say I am?"* and they answered, *"Some say you are John the Baptist, others say Elijah, or one of the prophets."* And Jesus asked, *"Who do you believe I am?"* Peter, based on what he had seen, responded, *"You are the Christ, the living son of God."*

Samuel tried to remember the old Bible stories, but he couldn't remember anything like what Father Damian had just told him.

"All of this scares me—just thinking about God, about religion, it makes my hair stand on end," Samuel admitted, leaning forward on the bench.

"Don't be fooled by the thick clouds of ignorance; religion, just like love, is shown through one's actions. There are countless people in the world who are preaching a message of victory, while their own lives are a disaster. People go to church, kneel down and pray to a statue of a saint to protect them and free them from evil, ignoring the truth of the words of Jesus when he said *"The kingdom of God is inside you and all around you."*

"But, do you really believe that Jesus did everything that it says in the Bible?"

"Jesus was the greatest teacher humanity has ever had; his lessons, his alleged miracles, have not been equaled by any other leader. But, if you're asking me if I believe that he actually cured the sick, gave sight to the blind and came back from the dead, I would answer 'yes.'"

"Why?"

"Because if that wasn't true, then we would not divide our history as we have: before and after Christ."

Samuel looked at him, a little disappointed; the priest's answer hadn't been exactly what he had hoped to hear.

"Why are you looking at me like that?" Father Damian asked, noting his companion's strange expression.

"You believe, just because of that?"

Father Damian stood. He stepped into the aisle and gazed at the statue of the crucifixion again over the altar. He blinked, considering his response.

"That is the basis of faith, Samuel: to believe. You either believe, or you don't, it's that simple..." He paused, took in a deep breath and sighed heavily. "Even though I am a believer and accept that Jesus paid the price for our sins, there are many things about his life that people have manipulated..."

"Like what?" Samuel asked, getting to his feet, following Father Damian into the aisle.

"According to the gospels, Jesus walked all around the Holy Land, teaching about the kingdom of God, and preaching to love thy neighbor, for three years. During those three years, people bombarded him with questions—about divorce, taxes, forgiveness, fasting, praying, and thousands of other things. I still don't understand why it didn't occur to anybody to ask him, "Maestro, do you believe that it is fair for one man to be another man's slave, when, according to your teachings, we are all equal under the eyes of God?"

Samuel felt a sudden tightening in his chest. Father Damian's words were having a real impact on him, changing something deep within him. He blinked rapidly, looking intently at the priest.

Father Damian licked his lips and continued, "That is what my doubts about the truth as we know it are based on. The Bible tells us that the apostle Paul said in his letter to the Colossians 3:22, "*Slaves, obey in everything those who are your earthly masters, not with eye service, as men-pleasers, but in singleness of heart, fearing the Lord.*"

Underneath his robe, the priest put his hands in his pockets and continued, "Jesus himself never even mentioned slavery, but his apostles did. Don't you think that's odd?"

Samuel paced slowly up the aisle behind him in silence, pensively stroking his chin, waiting for the priest to explain. Then he crossed his arms and asked, "How much of what the agnostics say is true, about Jesus being married to Mary Magdalene, and they had kids and all that stuff?"

"Let me ask you something," Father Damian countered, "would that degrade the teachings of Jesus in any way? If he had married, would that fact discredit him as a great teacher? Because, if that's the case, then we would also need to discount Gandhi, Moses, Abraham, Martin Luther King..."

Father Damian smiled and stretching his arms out he added, "And not to mention Solomon, who married about seven hundred times..."

Then he lowered his gaze and said wearily, "I don't know why just the mere suggestion that Jesus might have married provokes people so, when God Himself said that man should not be alone. Many people forget, as I told you when I first met you, Samuel, that Jesus was one-hundred percent God, and also one-hundred percent man."

Father Damian sat down in a pew at the front of the church and, bowing his head, he said, "Haven't you ever thought that maybe what terrifies people isn't so much the thought of Jesus being married to a prostitute, as some believe, but if they did in fact have children, and in accordance with the laws of Israel, they would have the right to inherit His throne..."

They were both quiet. The far-off sound of a car driving into the distance was all they could hear. The priest looked at an image of Saint Peter painted on one of the windows and finished, "God is not a creation of man; religion is. Have you ever heard it said that religion is the only thing that has kept the poor from killing the rich?"

70

MARICOPA COUNTY SUPERIOR COURT
201 WEST JEFFERSON STREET
PHOENIX, ARIZONA

"Your Honor, the defense calls David Flanagan."

The engineer, about fifty years old, with dark hair and deep-set eyes, stepped into the witness box, and slowly sat down once he was sworn in. Samuel walked over to him, putting his hands in his pockets. He began,

"Mr. Flanagan, can you tell the court what your occupation is?"

The witness turned to address the jury and said, "I work for the FBI as an engineer, I analyze audio and video recordings."

"Can you describe your work in a bit more detail, please?"

"I analyze the videos and recordings that come into our laboratory as evidence."

Samuel went over to his table and picked up a photograph that Oliver held out to him, and the remote control for the television monitor: "Mr. Flanagan, I would like you to watch this video..."

The courtroom was quiet as the video played. Then Samuel turned off the television and turned to the witness, who was clearly stunned by what he had just seen.

"It's hard to believe, isn't it?" Samuel affirmed. He walked over to the witness box holding the photo and went on, "Mr. Flanagan, this photograph was taken from the video which we have just seen, and was made available to the community by the Glendale police department, as evidence. According to them, it shows the killer who is responsible for eighteen murders that have been committed throughout the state, including the one we saw take place in the video... Do you believe that the person in this photo could be the defendant?"

Flanagan looked at Thomas, then back at the photograph, and replied, "It's not completely exact, but there is a certain resemblance..."

"Can you explain for us the process that was used to create this photo?"

The witness handed the photo back to Samuel and explained,

"First, the image of the face is converted to digital format on the computer. Then it is blown-up and made as high-resolution as possible. Often, if initially there is only a partial image of the suspect, we create a three-dimensional model, using the features that are visible to project what the rest would look like. This method was developed during the John List investigation in 1998. Sixteen years after his family was murdered, they managed to create what we call a "3-D suspect." It is called that because an imaginary figure is made projecting what the suspect might look like, according to his personal habits, if he smokes or drinks, and according to his genetic make-up. We even try to see what drastic changes his face might have undergone, if he had plastic surgery..."

Samuel walked over to the jury and, taking his hands from his pockets, he continued, "How precise are the photographs taken from a typical video tape? And by 'typical,' I mean where the suspect doesn't brightly glow with light, as in this case..."

"It would be about eighty to ninety percent," Flanagan replied.

Samuel picked up the remote control again and rewound the video to pause it exactly when the suspect's face was most clearly visible.

"Mr. Flanagan, would you be willing to swear that this face is my client's face?"

The witness paused for a moment. "You have to take into account that what the video shows is not normal, it's not the sort of thing you see every day—so I wouldn't swear to it, no."

Samuel turned and said to Stanley, "Your witness."

Stanley stood, took some sheets of paper from a folder on his table, and brought them over to the witness. "Mr. Flanagan, these are the results of a DNA test that was performed on the blood found on Thomas Santiago's pajamas, the morning after the killing we saw in the video. According to the laboratory analysis, the blood belongs to Patrick McKinney, the victim. Can you explain that?"

"Of course not."

"In your opinion, what would be the only reasonable explanation?"

Flanagan considered his response. "The only reasonable explanation would be that he killed him, or that he had been present at the time of the murder."

"Objection, Your Honor, the prosecutor is leading the witness."

"Sustained. The jury will discount the last remark."

"One more question, Mr. Flanagan. You said that the computer-generated photographs were about eighty to ninety percent accurate, correct?"

"Yes."

Stanley took a few steps towards the witness and added, "It's almost perfect, right?"

"Yes."

Stanley returned to his seat behind the table, and concluded, "No more questions, Your Honor."

Samuel quickly stood and said, "Permission to redirect, Your Honor."

"Go ahead."

"Mr. Flanagan, in a video of a normal person, one in which the person's face is not shining brightly like in the video we just watched, the computer-generated photo would be almost perfect. Isn't that right?"

"Yes, that's right."

"But the photo generated from this video, precisely because of the bright light on the face, presented special challenges..."

"It seems like in this photo, they took the suspect's face, they edited out the light all around it, and they filled in color on the face, and in the eyes. It's all done by the computer."

Samuel paced towards the jury and looked at them pointedly: "On the video, it is impossible to distinguish skin color, or eye color, since his

eyes look like two small balls of flame. That is, the killer could be anybody...
he could be a white man, a black man, an Arab, an Indian... Right, Mr.
Flanagan?"

"In effect, it is possible..."

E 2nd Street

E Washington St

71

M. J. A. ATTORNEYS AT LAW
BANK OF AMERICA TOWER
201 EAST WASHINGTON STREET
PHOENIX, ARIZONA

Samuel set his briefcase down on the table in his office and abruptly sat down, breathing heavily. He turned to Oliver, looking him in the eye. "What do you think we should do?"

Actually, I think we should stick to our strongest argument: temporary insanity due to somnambulism; Dr. Rogers' testimony was very convincing..."

Samuel folded his hands behind his neck and leaned back, thinking. Anticipating his response, Oliver said, "I know that temporary insanity is the hardest thing to prove in our judicial system, especially if you're dealing with a neurological disorder, but in this case, we have more than just medical diagnoses..."

Oliver sat down right next to Samuel and continued, "you can clearly see in the video from the prison how that presence takes control of him while he's sleeping; and the jury is aware of this."

"Do you know anybody who knows anything about this?"

"I have a friend who owes me a favor. He's retired, but in his day, he was the best in the whole country."

Samuel dropped his hands, taking a deep breath and slowly exhaling. "To be honest with you, I don't know how this is all going to end... Even if we can prove Thomas is innocent in a strictly legal sense, they will never let him go free... And it would be useless to keep him in prison, since he'd only escape again, over and over, according to Father Damian..."

Oliver rested his hands on the table and leaned forward, "We better pray that Father Damian will figure out a way to stop this possession, because if Thomas escapes again, we'll all be burned alive in court..."

"I never thought the day would come when justice would prove to be useless."

Oliver put a hand on his shoulder and said, "Don't give up; we have a good argument going for us."

Samuel looked around the room, his vision clouded over with nostalgia: "When it comes to the law, I've always believed in three things: justice, preparation, and dedication..."

He stood up and gestured to the statue of the Goddess of Justice.

"Justice, as this statue represents it, should be blind, so that even the poorest man on the fringes of society can be sure that he will have the same rights under the law as anyone else..."

His expression abruptly changed. His eyes filled with rage, his heart raced.

"See this?" he asked Oliver, pointing to the statue of David. "Every time I look at it, I think about the perfection of the human hand; it doesn't matter how hard or challenging the situation is, with a little imagination and a lot of dedication, you can do what no one thought possible. But when I see things like this case, I realize that there are some dark shadows, even in justice..."

He suddenly went over to the table, grabbed his briefcase and threw it against the wall as hard as he could, screaming, "Things they don't teach you in law school or in any damned books!"

Samuel fell to his knees and started to cry. Oliver slowly walked over to him, knelt beside him, and hugged him tightly.

E Butte Av.

72

Arizona State Prison
1305 East Butte Avenue
Florence, Arizona

Father Damian arrived with two military guards, carrying a little suitcase.

"Father Damian, it's so good to see you!" Thomas smiled, excited.

"How are you, my child?" the priest asked, as he stepped inside the cell and set his suitcase down on the floor.

"What's the suitcase for?"

"From now on I'm going to spend the night here with you."

Thomas looked at him sadly. "I guess they're really worried about what could happen next time..."

Father Damian stood next to him, and putting both hands firmly on his shoulders, looking intently into his eyes he said, "Thomas, you have to understand the situation we're in; we can't let it happen again."

Thomas shrugged him off and paced to the other side of the cell. "All the time, I ask myself, why me... Why did this have to happen to me?"

"We might never know the answer to that question, but there is one thing I do know, that you are a fine young man."

Thomas whirled around to face him, and asked angrily, "Is that why he chose me to be his serial killer?"

Father Damian could see how frustrated and sad the boy was. He took a step toward him: "Sit down next to me for a minute; there's something I should tell you, something you don't know... Thirty years ago, when I was a seminary student, I had a vision..."

He told Thomas the story. He could hardly believe what he was hearing, his eyes grew wider and wider.

"Are you sure about this, Father?"

"As sure as I'm talking to you right now."

Thomas stood and paced around the cell, not saying anything. Father Damian guessed that he was trying to figure out how to discount the story. The priest felt as if the loud clanging of the metal boots Thomas wore against the metal floor rattled his very bones.

Finally, Thomas scratched his head and asked, "But what about all those people I killed?"

"Just like I said, Thomas, they were not good people; not the priest you killed in Glendale, not even the little boy in Mesa..."

Thomas brushed a lock of hair away from his face. Looking over his shoulder, he saw how the soldiers watched his every move; they looked completely terrified.

"So you really think that what comes over me is some kind of angel of God, right?"

Father Damian slowly nodded.

"So, why do they have to be killed? Why can't those people just go to jail, or get punished some other way?"

"Why those people deserved to die is something I can't explain, but the Bible says in Numbers 35:19: *"The Avenger of Blood shall himself put the murderer to death; when he meets him, he shall put him to death."*

Thomas held his arms out plaintively and said, "But that boy was only ten years old, he could have changed, he could have grown up to be a good man..."

"Thomas, you need to understand that there are evil people in this world, from the moment they are born, and their only destiny is to sow the seeds of evil wherever they go…"

Thomas sat on the edge of the bed and, shaking his head, he sighed, "I don't get it… If it's an angel of God, why does he have to kill?"

"Many people ask the same thing when they read the Old Testament," Father Damian commented, sitting next to him. "Even I asked myself how could God command David to wipe out whole cities, burning them down, killing children and even the animals, if He is supposedly a loving God…"

They were both quiet, lost in thought. Father Damian stood and clasped his hands behind his back. He let out a long breath and said, "When I first entered the seminary to study for the priesthood, and I started studying the Old Testament, I wondered how David could have had the heart to spill so much blood. And when I analyzed it in more detail, I didn't understand how David could have gone home again, with no remorse, after having killed men, women and children of all ages, burning them alive along with all their belongings. Over time, and after studying so many stories and texts very carefully in Greek, Latin and Aramaic, I found out some things that the outside world doesn't know."

Thomas stared down at the floor, and in a shaky voice asked, "But why do things have to be like that? Why does it have to be so much bloodshed?"

The priest looked at him with a slight smile, and remembered an old story he had heard when he was just a boy. Then he started to tell it:

"You know something? There's an old story about three Indian chiefs, who each made a wish. And, by sheer coincidence, the three chiefs had the same wish: they all wanted to go to the sacred mountain and talk with the Great Spirit.

"One of them had a small child that he couldn't leave, so he decided to bring him along. When they reached the top of the mountain, one chief said,

'I come from a land much further away than either of yours, and my trip home will be very long; so, please, let me go first'. And the other two chiefs said okay.

"Then he approached the Great Spirit and said, 'Oh Great Spirit of the Sacred Mountain, I want to ask you a question.'

"And God said, 'Ask.'

'I want to know when my people will live in peace… We are always fighting with the white man and with other Indian tribes, our history is awash in blood, and I want to know… When can my people live in peace?'

"As the story goes, God looked down at the Indian chief and said, 'Your people will live in peace twenty-five years after your death.'

"And the chief wept, because he understood that his people would still continue to fight for a long time.

"Then one chief looked at the other who had the child with him, and said, 'I don't have anyone with me, but I'm from a far-away land too; please allow me to go next.' And the other assented.

"The Indian approached the Great Spirit and said, 'God Almighty, Creator of all that is, I would like to ask you a question too.'

"And God said, 'Ask.'

'I want to know when my people will have their own homeland. The white man has taken our land, and we have lived as nomads for several years, and I'd like to know, when can we have our own land?'

"As the old story goes, God looked down at the chief and answered, 'Your people will have their own land fifty years after your death.'

"And the Indian chief cried, since he understood that his people would have to keep on wandering for many years.

"The last chief approached the Great Spirit and said, 'Oh all-powerful God, creator of the Universe, I would also like to ask you a question.'

"And God said, 'Ask.'

'I want to know when my people will be free. We are slaves of the white man, they abuse us, they beat us and they even kill us with no mercy. Please, tell me: when will my people be free?'

"As the old story goes, God looked down at the Indian chief and said, 'Your people will be free seventy-five years after your death.'

"And this chief also cried, since he understood that his people would continue to be abused and mistreated for many years.

"Then, the little boy approached the Great Spirit and said, 'God Almighty, can I ask you a question?'

"And God said, 'Ask.'

'Why are there so many people in the world who are blind to the suffering of others? While on one side of the street, people cry, on the other, people are laughing. Some have too much, while others die of hunger. Many kill, rob and abuse their neighbor, out of pure evil. Why does all of this happen, oh powerful God? Why is there so much evil?'

"And, as the story goes, then God cried, because it was so hard to explain to someone so sweet and innocent why certain things like that had to happen in the world..."

Thomas was quiet for a moment, thinking about the story.

"How many languages do you speak, Father?" he asked, leaning back.

"Twelve. My main motivation for learning the languages of our ancestors was to learn the truth, to know what was true and what a lie in all of human history..."

Thomas looked up and asked, "And what did you find out?"

The priest's eyes clouded over, revealing a deep sadness.

"For example," he answered, looking out at the soldiers guarding the cell, "the irony and the evil that is found behind the walls of the houses of power. The truths that have been kept hidden from the world, simply in order to preserve an empire, and the great business of the faith..."

"And what did you find out about David?"

"Several things. Did you know that many of his psalms were songs and prayers that he recited to God right before going to war? Through them, he asked to be given the strength to keep going..."

"Really?" Thomas perked up.

"There's an old legend in Israel that the old-timers tell. It says: *"Before going into battle, David sang and prayed to Jehovah. And when he finished, his face wasn't the same: he looked like something more than a mere man. It was as if the angel of death shined in his eyes, the angel of Revelations. The one who walks over a sea of blood on the day of the final battle between good and evil."*

Father Damian was quiet, and smiled when he noticed the soldiers and security engineer listening attentively.

"That is why I am sure that the same thing is happening to you right now. You have become a tool of divine justice. David is the only man that God himself called his servant..."

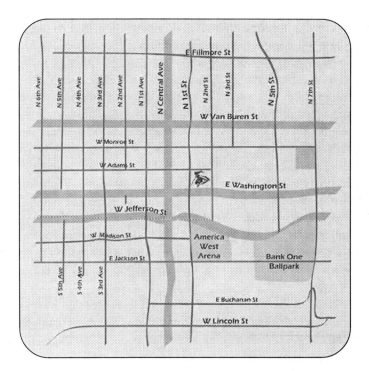

73

Morning Watch Restaurant
0 North First Street
Phoenix, Arizona

"Thanks for accepting my invitation, Father Damian," Dr. Marcus said as he shook his hand.

"You'll see why I said this is the best place to have breakfast in the whole city of Phoenix," Father Damian remarked, holding the door open for Dr. Marcus.

"What do you call this place?"

"Morning Watch. What I like about it, aside from the food, is that it's only two and a half blocks from the church, and three and a half blocks from the courthouse."

"What can I get you to drink?" the waitress asked, with an adorable smile, setting the menus down on the table.

"Iced tea, please," the doctor said.

"And for you, Father?"

"Black coffee for me, my child; but can you bring me honey instead of sugar?"

"Father, I wanted to meet with you because I'm fascinated by the theory you have about Thomas. I've always personally believed that the day when psychology and religion unite in the interest of human health, we'd start to get much better results."

"Men of science believe that the human body is a machine, Dr. Marcus. A machine that can be controlled or manipulated, ignoring that man is a miracle of God, his master work..."

"I totally agree with you, Father. But, if we knew where to draw the line between possession and insanity, everything would be much easier, don't you think?"

Dr. Marcus took a sip of his iced tea, and looking out the window, he watched as an old man helped his wife get out of their car, and settled her into a wheelchair. He thought for a minute and then said,

"Science is based on evidence, Father; we can't base everything only on faith."

"*Blessed are those who believed without seeing, as their faith was the strongest.*" Weren't those the words of Jesus?" the priest commented, stirring his coffee with a spoon. "Possession has existed from the beginning of time, Doctor. Jesus cast demons out of many people who had been medically diagnosed as epileptic. But to a man of science like yourself, those are just religious tall tales..."

He took a sip of coffee and continued, "Let's try to analyze the events from a logical, rational standpoint; if we say that what those people were suffering from weren't demons, but some kind of epilepsy or other disease. The mere fact that Jesus cured them by just using his hands and saying a word is the strongest proof that there is no better medicine for the human body than faith itself..."

S 1st Avenue

S 3rd Avenue

W. Jefferson St.

74

MARICOPA COUNTY SUPERIOR COURT
201 WEST JEFFERSON STREET
PHOENIX, ARIZONA

Samuel stood and walked towards the witness: "Dr. Cooper, you worked for the state of California as a criminal psychologist for over thirty years, correct?"

"Yes, that's right."

With a hand in his pocket, Samuel asked, "According to our records, you were consulted in the case of the State of California versus Josh Matthews, and in the state of Florida versus Jean Benedict..."

"Yes," Dr. Cooper said, folding his hands.

Samuel took a step backward and gestured towards Thomas. "Doctor, my client, Thomas Santiago, suffers from a neurological disorder that makes him walk in his sleep... at least that's what it seems like..."

"Objection, Your Honor! Counsel is leading the witness," Stanley shouted forcefully from his seat.

"Sustained," the judge intoned.

Samuel took a deep breath and tried again, "Alright, let's put it this way... Doctor, my client, Thomas Santiago, suffers from a strange phenomenon, which somehow gives him supernatural powers while he sleeps. You have seen the videos and the evidence that has been entered into this trial. What is your opinion?"

"There is no doubt that something very bizarre is going on with him. The symptoms he exhibits are very strange. I have never seen someone who appears to be able to walk through walls, or make his face glow in that way..."

Samuel walked back to his table, leaning against it as he looked at Thomas:

"What do you think the explanation is?"

"It would be logical to infer that his problem originates in his dreams, since this only happens when he's asleep, and never when he is awake. Somnambulism, as the condition is commonly called, is a loss of control in the sleep state that is most often seen in children, and in some adults who have had the condition since childhood. It is an automatic response in which the muscles of the body act without any input from the mind, like a convulsion or a muscular reflex, for example."

"Doctor, is a person who sleepwalks conscious of their actions?"

"Of course not. Many people who suffer from somnambulism have done things that, once they are awake, when they are told about what they have done, they simply can't believe it."

"No further questions, Your Honor."

"Doctor, how many different types of somnambulism are there?" the prosecutor asked from his seat.

"Two: organic, and hysteric."

"Can you explain how they are different?"

"Organic somnambulism arises out of a dysfunctional sleep cycle. It doesn't have anything to do with psychological problems; it's just a harmless lack of control that makes the muscles react in a way that the person doesn't intend." The doctor shifted in his chair, folded his hands over his chest again and went on, "The hysterical type, as its name would suggest, provokes a violent reaction. People who suffer from it almost always are trying to call attention to their emotional problems. It is very common in children and adolescents, but it should be noted that violence in these somnambulists is very rare."

Stanley stood and walked towards the witness. "You said a moment ago that somnambulism was nothing more than a muscular reaction which the mind has no effect on, correct?"

"Yes, that's right."

"And you also said that violence in these somnambulists is very rare. What percentage is violent?"

"About three or four percent of the cases."

"But they do exist?"

"Yes."

Stanley, who had paced to the center of the floor, walked back towards the witness: "Doctor, would it be easy for a person to fake somnambulism?"

The doctor smiled. "Anybody can pretend to sleepwalk. What's striking about this case, Mr. Stanley, isn't that he walks in his sleep, but the incredible powers that he has. Up until now, as far as I know, nothing like it has ever been seen before."

"Doctor, can a person plan a murder while he is awake, and then carry it out when he's asleep?"

"No."

"Why not?"

"One of the most surprising, amazing things about somnambulism is that it doesn't matter what's going on in the person's mind while they're asleep. It never has anything to do with the person's desires and thoughts when they are awake. When a person sleeps, the subconscious takes control: the mind is neutralized."

"So you allege that a person who thinks about something when they're awake cannot carry out that action when they are asleep?"

"That's right."

"But, doctor, for example, I have a friend who dreamed that he was fighting, and then, suddenly he was woken up by his wife striking him on the head, because he was strangling her..."

A few chuckles were heard from the spectators in the courtroom.

"There have been some cases, like the one you just described, when something the person dreams about is partially executed while he is asleep.

But I'm sure that your friend didn't go to bed thinking about how he would like to kill his wife..."

"I hope not," Stanley said, grinning. He stroked his chin, and turning serious, he asked, "Doctor, I think it's easier to believe, like in my friend's case, that someone who is dreaming suddenly starts to walk and to act out according to what he's dreaming about, then to believe that, as you say, he walks without wanting to, or without thinking about it..."

"No one knows for sure what goes on in the human mind during sleep. No one can explain, for example, how some people can dream about something that will actually happen in the future, in their own life or in general."

Stanley went over to his table and picked up a book.

"Doctor, do you recognize this?"

"Yes, of course, that is my book on criminal psychology."

"It's a very good book, by the way," the prosecutor commented, as he paced back towards the doctor.

"Thank you."

"I'm sure that you're familiar with the terms popularized by Dr. J. Dickinson, one of the greatest criminal psychologists in the country, since you cite him on page 133."

Stanley handed the witness the book, "Can you read the section that has been highlighted, please?"

"*In 1991, Dr. Dickinson stated in court that what was considered a mental disturbance today could be considered something else tomorrow. So the court must establish what exactly is meant by mental disturbance on an ongoing basis, according to the scientific evidence as it comes to light day by day.*"

The doctor lowered the book and rested it in his lap. Stanley paced towards the jury, and with his back to the witness, he asked, "Didn't you write that because you had noticed that many criminals were escaping punishment under the law, as a result of juries being convinced by the psychiatrists' diagnoses?"

The doctor was quiet for a moment, considering how to respond.

"The more we study human behavior, and as we expand our knowledge, we develop a better understand of what the real psychological state of the perpetrator was at the moment the crime is committed."

Stanley turned quickly and his tone dripping with sarcasm he said, "Isn't it true that at a conference you attended in Washington, D.C. this past 10th of March, you said "*It's a shame that in our judicial system, you can find people like David Berkowitz (the Son of Sam) insane, while someone like Jeffrey Dahmer, who admitted that he had sex with cadavers, was a cannibal and sadist, can be found to be perfectly healthy?"*

He stood next to the jury box and rested his hand on the rail. After adjusting his jacket, he asked,

"Doctor, do you believe in temporary insanity?"

The doctor looked at Oliver, who, knowing what the response would be, lowered his head, evading his gaze.

"Doctor?" Stanley prodded.

The witness blinked nervously, and swallowed before replying,

"If you are asking if I believe that a person can claim that, in a moment of anger, he simply lost his head and killed someone, of course not. The fact that anger may have affected his judgment is not the same as saying that a person was insane. We are all responsible for our actions, whether we're angry or not." The doctor's expression grew more belligerent, as his voice rose. "And I don't think that eating a certain amount of sugar, coupled with stress, is going to make anybody lose their mind, either!"

Stanley turned and shot Samuel a defiant look as he said, "No further questions, Your Honor."

Samuel quickly stood. He knew that Stanley had gotten the witness to say what he had wanted.

"Permission to redirect, Your Honor."

"Go ahead."

"One more question, please, Doctor. Based on all of your experience as a criminal psychologist, do you believe that a person who commits a crime while he is sleepwalking is responsible for his actions?"

"No, when a person is asleep, he is unconscious and does not know what he is doing."

E Turquoise Av

75

ESCOBAR FAMILY RESIDENCE
6889 EAST TURQUOISE AVENUE
SCOTTSDALE, ARIZONA

Catherine came running into the room looking for Samuel. She stood in the doorway, catching her breath.

"Sweetheart, Detective Morrison's on the phone, I think something happened to Father Damian!"

Samuel grabbed the phone. "Hello!"

"Samuel?"

"What happened?"

"Thomas tried to escape again, Father Damian tried to stop him and now he's in the hospital..."

"Did Thomas attack him?"

"I don't know. Whitefield called me from the prison and just said that they had to take him to the hospital."

"And Thomas?"

"He's alright, at least Father Damian did manage to keep him from escaping again."

"What hospital did they take him to?"

"Scottsdale Memorial, I'm on my way over there now."

"I'll see you there in about twenty minutes."

Samuel rushed into Father Damian's hospital room. Father Steven was sitting by the bed.

Whitefield and Morrison were standing at the foot of the bed. They looked at Samuel, as he stood in the doorway and asked breathlessly, "How is he?"

Father Damian had not regained consciousness. A monitor was attached to his chest, and a machine by the bed showed his slow heartbeat on a screen. Two thin tubes ran out of his nostrils and were connected to a respirator, helping him to breathe.

"His heart is very weak; the doctor said that he didn't understand how he had even survived the encounter," Father Steven said.

Samuel looked at Whitefield. "Do they know what happened yet?"

"The guards couldn't see anything. Just like the last time, a brilliant light blinded them for a few minutes, and suddenly the light disappeared and they saw Father Damian lying on the floor, unconscious."

"What did the security cameras get?"

"Exactly what the guards said, basically."

"And what about the cameras that the technicians from NASA installed?"

"We don't know yet, I haven't been able to talk to Myrick."

76

THE GOVERNOR'S OFFICE
1700 WASHINGTON STREET
PHOENIX, ARIZONA

In the governor's office, they were in the middle of a heated discussion about what their next step should be, now that Father Damian was in the hospital.

Just then, there was a light knock on the door, and both priests came in. Everyone stood up when they saw them.

"Father Damian!" Samuel exclaimed happily.

Dr. Marcus walked over to him, put a hand on his shoulder, and asked with a grin, "How are you feeling, Father?"

"I'm fine..."

"The doctor told him that he has to take it easy and shouldn't get out of bed, but he doesn't want to listen," Father Steven added with a hint of disapproval.

"I already told you we have too much to do right now and we can't waste time," Father Damian said briskly, as he went over to greet the rest of the group.

"It's great to have you here, Father," Owens said," "because we were just trying to figure out what to do next."

The priests walked over to the table and sat down. Father Damian looked around at everyone and began,

"The reason I am here, gentlemen, is to tell you what we must do to control what is happening to Thomas."

Everyone was speechless. Clearly surprised, Owens found his voice to ask, "You found a way to control this?"

Father Damian smiled at Samuel, who was facing him from the other side of the table. He went on, "During the last encounter I had with the angel that possesses the boy, I was able to ask him several questions that explained some things I had been unsure about..."

"You can actually talk to that thing?" Judge Fieldmore blurted, stunned.

"He is not a thing, Your Honor, he is an angel of the Lord."

"Tell us, what did he say?" the governor interrupted.

"Since all of this started, I've been wondering what it was really about, and after talking to the angel, I was able to confirm what I had always suspected..."

"What?" McKoskie prompted.

"It's a curse."

"A curse? That's ridiculous!", the judge bellowed.

"What makes you think it's a curse, Father?" Owens asked seriously.

"When I first entered the priesthood, I had a vision..."

Father Damian told them the entire story he hadn't yet shared with them. The judge leaned back in his chair and murmured, "This is too much..."

"You can think I'm crazy if you want, but it's true..."

"The angel told you that this was a curse?" Dr. Marcus asked.

"Yes."

"But, why a curse?" the governor wanted to know.

The priest folded his hands on the table. "If you read the Bible carefully, you'll see that God cursed many cities, like Sodom and Gomorrah, and

Egypt, and he sent his angels to each one, to destroy them and punish the wicked."

Everyone listened very intently to his words, as he explained his theory for what was really behind the murders. But they just couldn't wrap their minds around it; they looked at each other around the table, completely bewildered.

"The angel told me that he had come to get revenge for the blood of the innocent, and that, just like in the times of Egypt, he had been sent to fill the desert with blood."

Petrified by the thought that things could actually get worse, everyone had a sick feeling in the pit of their stomachs.

"I know that you are men of science," Father Damian continued after a brief pause, sensing their growing alarm. "But this is a problem based in religion, and it must be dealt with as such."

Owens leaned back and rubbed his neck, letting out a long breath. "What do you think we should do?"

"I talked to a friend of mine in Mexico, and after doing some intensive research, we both agree on what has to be done..."

"What's your plan?" the governor asked anxiously.

"We have to handle this situation just as if it were one of the plagues of Egypt..."

Everyone was even more perplexed; they had no idea what he was talking about.

"I don't know how familiar you are with your Bibles, gentlemen," Father Damian remarked, noting their growing confusion, "but one of the seven plagues was the death of the firstborn, and for this, the Angel of Jehovah was sent to fill the desert with blood."

"Can you tell us what that has to do with this case?" Dr. Phillips asked.

"If you'll remember, the death of the firstborn was the seventh and final plague. It was Jehovah's worst punishment for the Egyptians, for having mistreated his people..."

"I still don't understand any of this, Father," Owens said, frustrated.

"The angel told me that, just like in Egypt, the cries of the oppressed had reached Jehovah's ears, and that's why he was sent to avenge the blood of the innocent."

"What 'oppressed'?" Stanley asked.

"I spoke with family members of some of the victims, and some other people who were affected by the murders one way or another, and they were all very religious people, with very strong faith in God. For example, McKinney's wife told me that a week before the angel killed her husband, he had brutally beaten her one night when he came home drunk. She prayed to God every day after that to take that man out of her life, since she was afraid that one day he would kill her..."

Father Damian turned to look at the judge. "Remember the little boy who was killed in Mesa? I talked to Tania Baez, the little girl that he had attacked, and her mother. She told me that she had made a promise to Jesus, that she would light a candle for him every Sunday at mass, if He would give that little boy the punishment he deserved."

Father Damian got up from the table and started slowly pacing around it. Everyone followed him with their eyes.

"These things may sound foolish to you... but in the world of religion, miracles are not the works of saints, they are the works of faith..."

A heavy silence filled the room while everyone considered Father Damian's words, trying to make sense of it all.

Owens blinked, and stared down at his hands on the table as he spoke. "Let me see if I understand... You're saying that those people's prayers are what caused all of this?"

The priest clasped his hands behind his back, as was his habit, and kept slowly walking around the table as he answered,

"It's just like the old saying, Mr. Owens, *faith can move mountains...*"

"This is ridiculous!" Stanley shouted, banging his fist on the table.

"You can believe what you want, Mr. Stanley, but I would suggest that you take recent events into account... or, go spend every night with Thomas in his cell yourself, and see if you can try to keep him from escaping..."

Stanley didn't respond, and lowered his gaze.

"What's your plan, Father?" Owens persisted.

"In order for us to be free of him once and for all, we need to do two things—and we're going to need the community's help for one of them."

"What do you mean?" asked Judge Fieldmore.

Father Damian stood next to the table, and resting his hands on it for support he replied, "We have to do what the people of Israel did to free themselves of the angel of death, and what the Egyptians did to break Jehovah's curse."

"You're not suggesting that we make the sign of the cross in blood?" Father Steven cut in, his eyes shining with fear.

"Blood? What are you talking about?" The governor blurted, clearly alarmed.

Father Damian looked at her, "When Jehovah told Moses that he would kill all the firstborn in Egypt, Moses asked the people of Israel to have every family kill an animal, and, with the blood, to make the sign of the cross on the door of every house. When the Angel of Death passed by, he would see that sign, and would not cause any harm."

The judge stood, and looking intently at Father Damian he yelled, "Are you crazy?! We can't ask people to do something like that! With all the lunatics running loose out there, all over the country, it would be a bloodbath! It would be madness..."

Samuel looked at Father Damian, "Father, we can't ask people to do something similar to that; it would be too chaotic, and impossible to keep it under control..."

"I know. I was thinking that we could ask the bishop to make a public appeal to the community, and ask that everyone take communion every day for one week, and in every house, they light a candle, symbolizing their faith in God..."

The room was quiet again, as they all considered this idea.

"You said we had to do two things, what was the other one?" Owens asked.

The priest slowly sat down at the table again. "Remove Thomas from this place, take him away somewhere, as far away as possible," he said calmly, looking around the table.

"If we're going to get him out of here, why should we ask everybody to take communion?" Dr. Marcus asked.

"Because we will remove him bodily, but the curse will still be here... that is, every time the angel possesses him, he would come back and kill again. And you'll always have to go after him again, because his mission is here, in this place..."

"But, what good is the communion and candles going to do?" the governor wanted to know.

"With the act of praying and lighting the candles, we are beseeching God to lift the curse; it is a religious act that has been performed ever since Biblical times..."

"How are we going to take him away from here?" Dr. Marcus asked.

"That is for you to decide," Father Damian replied, looking at Judge Fieldmore and Owens.

"I'll call Washington, and I'll tell them about your plan. Let's meet back here again tomorrow, before court," Owens concluded.

E Butte Av.

77

ARIZONA STATE PRISON
1305 EAST BUTTE AVENUE
FLORENCE, ARIZONA

Samuel went to visit Thomas, who ran up to greet him when he saw him in the corridor. With both hands flattened against the Plexiglas, he asked frantically, "How's Father Damian?"

"He's just fine, don't worry, "Samuel said, as he pulled a chair over and sat facing his client, just outside the cell.

"Don't lie to me, Samuel, tell me the truth. Is he really okay?"

"I'm not lying, Thomas, he's really okay."

"So why haven't I seen him in three days?"

Samuel crossed his arms. "He was very weak at first, but he's going to come see you very soon. It's just that he has some urgent business to attend to."

Thomas sat on the bed and murmured sadly, "Poor Father Damian! This is the second time that he's almost gotten killed, just because he tried to help me..."

"But you must understand that he is the only one that can talk to the being that possesses you, and keep it under control."

Thomas ran a hand through his hair and sighing heavily he said,

"Can you believe this? No matter how hard I try to understand, I just can't believe it." Thomas looked up and turned to face Samuel. "After Father Damian told me everything, a lot of things started to make sense to me, but still, I just can't totally believe it."

Samuel saw how upset he was. He took a deep breath and leaned forward, resting his elbows on his knees, and asked,

"Are you alright?"

"Yes."

"Do you remember what happened?"

"No, it was like all the other times. I was really tired, and I was talking with Father Damian. I fell asleep at around ten, and when I woke up, the soldiers were pointing their guns at me. I asked them where Father Damian was, and they wouldn't tell me anything. So, I figured that something bad must have happened to him..."

Thomas stood and walked across the cell. His back to Samuel, he asked,

"What's going to happen now that Father Damian can't stay with me?"

"Honestly, I don't know... but something's got to be done..."

78

THE GOVERNOR'S OFFICE
1700 WEST WASHINGTON STREET
PHOENIX, ARIZONA

Owens was still talking on his cell phone as he breezed into the governor's office. Everyone was there, seated around the table waiting for him.

"Father Damian," Owens held out the phone to him.

The others exchanged surprised looks as the priest took the phone and raised it to his ear.

"Hello?" he said tentatively.

"Father Damian?" A woman's voice said on the other end of the line.

"Yes."

"One moment, please."

"Father, this is the President of the United States..."

"How are you, Mr. President?"

"I'm fine, Father. Is what I've been hearing about that boy really true?"

"I'm afraid so, Mr. President..."

"I've been told that you have a plan that could work."

"Yes, that's right."

Everyone in the office was completely still, waiting in suspense.

"How sure can we be that your plan will actually work?"

"Look at it this way, Mr. President... it's our only hope..."

After a brief silence, Father Damian heard a sigh.

"We'll pray to God that everything will turn out for the best," the President said at last. "Can you put Owens back on the line, please?"

Father Damian handed him back the phone. Owens quickly took it and paced to the far side of the office. The others heard him say, "Yes, sir... yessir... yessir... that's what I'll do, sir... goodbye."

Owens closed the phone and put it back in his jacket pocket. With a plainly worried expression he said,

"Gentlemen, we have the President's support to do whatever is necessary to solve this problem." He looked at Father Damian and continued, "Tell us about the rest of your plan, Father."

"Well, as I said, we need to ask the bishop to make an appeal to the community, in cooperation with the governor. After the jury reaches a verdict in the trial, he will ask the people to light a candle and display it in front of every home, and he will ask everyone to pray, for seven days. The second part is to get Thomas out of here."

"Where do you think he should be taken?" Dr. Marcus asked.

"I would like him to be taken out of the country."

"What?" Dr. Phillips asked, perplexed.

"What about the families of the victims? They're going to demand justice," Stanley said.

"Father, what about his mother and brother? Thomas is only fourteen," Samuel wanted to know.

"If the only solution is to take him far away from here, then that's what we'll do," Owens interjected.

Samuel looked at the judge and commented, "Legally, no one can deny a citizen the right to live where he wants, no one can force him to abandon the state. Don't forget that, although he wasn't born in this country, Thomas is an American citizen like any other, and what you're thinking of doing is illegal..."

Father Damian was absently scribbling on a piece of paper with a pen he had picked up from the table. Without looking up he said,

"As you can see, physically I can't handle any more meetings with the angel. That's why I want to take him some place where he can get help. Also, he has to be removed from this place, where all the trouble started. But the final decision is up to all of you. If you want to run the risk of having him escape again, there's really nothing else that I can do..."

There was a charged silence, their collective fear was palpable. No one wanted to face the possibility that Thomas might escape again.

"Just suppose we decide to get him out of the country, as you'd like, Father Damian," Stanley said, his fingers tapping nervously on the table. "How can he be absolved of guilt? You can't expect that the families will drop the charges against him? he said cynically.

Samuel shot back angrily, "Anyone who has the slightest notion of the law knows that Thomas is innocent, that there is no basis for a guilty verdict."

Looking at Judge Fieldmore he went on, "We are men of law, and the law has always served to resolve differences between people. We know that this is a very special case because of the danger he represents for everyone, but no one can deny the greatest truth here: that according to the law, he is completely innocent. One thing is to try to solve this for him, but we can't close our eyes to the facts. You've seen the videos, along with everyone else who's been at court observing the trial, and it's very clear that none of what's happening is his fault."

S 2nd Street

E Washington St

79

M. J. A. Attorneys at Law
Bank of America Tower
201 East Washington Street
Phoenix, Arizona

Oliver handed Samuel a cup of tea and sat down next to him. They were both studying Father Damian's proposal.

"I don't know how you feel about it, Oliver, but it seems very risky to me."

"But you have to bear in mind that, risky or not, he's the only one that's been able to control the situation and prevent him from escaping again."

"But, take him out of the country? You know as well as I do that Stanley would never go for it."

"If the priest can manage it, it would be the smartest thing to do..."

Through the intercom, Samuel's secretary said, "Excuse me, but Judge Fieldmore's on line one."

Samuel thanked her and turned to Oliver, "What do you suppose he wants?" he said, warily.

"Talk to him, and find out..."

Samuel pressed the button for line one on the speakerphone. "Yes, sir?" he said.

"Mr. Escobar, I'm calling to let you know that the government is going to handle this case."

"What do you mean?"

"Just what I said: the government will take over. You and Morgan just have to go along with it, and everything will be resolved in short order."

"What's going to happen to Thomas?"

"I don't know."

"But, how can this be?"

"I'm sorry, Mr. Escobar, but it's out of my hands."

"I'm warning you, if I don't agree with the verdict, I'm going to appeal to the Supreme Court."

"I would advise you against it, for your own good. You're a fine lawyer, Mr. Escobar. Don't risk jeopardizing your career, or it could turn out very badly for you in the end..."

"Did Morgan say he'd go along with this?"

"He doesn't have a choice. I'll see you Wednesday in court..."

The judge hung up. Samuel asked Oliver, "What do you think?"

"Don't get upset about it yet. Let's wait and see what they're planning on doing first."

Samuel sat down and, leaning back, added, "I'm not going to let them ruin that boy's life..."

"His life's already ruined," Oliver wryly observed.

"I wonder what they're going to do now..."

"Don't worry. You know a lot of people think the government was responsible for JFK's assassination, and the truth still hasn't come out even to this day. I'm sure they won't have any problem handling this..."

1st Avenue

3rd Avenue

W. Jefferson St.

80

Maricopa County Superior Court
201 West Jefferson Street
Phoenix, Arizona

The judge sat down just as the television cameras began filming.

"Mr. Escobar, please call your first witness."

"Your Honor, the Defense calls Father Damian Santos."

The priest seemed surprised to be called as a witness. He looked to his left at Owens, who was seated a few feet away. Owens nodded, to indicate that he was in favor of having him testify.

Having a priest called as a witness seemed to perplex the spectators in the courtroom.

Father Damian stood and slowly walked up to the witness box. The court officer swore him in, "Do you swear to tell the truth, the whole truth and nothing but the truth, so help you God?"

"I do," he said firmly, and sat down.

"Father Damian: you have been the only person who has been allowed to be in the defendant's presence over the past four weeks," Samuel said, walking over to him. "And not only that; you have actually slept in his cell with him at night, correct?"

Gasps were heard throughout the room, and quiet murmurings broke out. The judge demanded silence, and Father Damian replied, "Yes, that is correct."

Samuel took two steps forward, took his hands out of his pockets and said, "You've studied Thomas from a different perspective, in a different way than the doctors and scientists. Can you describe what condition he is suffering from, in your opinion?"

Father Damian looked down for a moment, considering his response.

"Thomas suffers from a very rare form of spiritual possession that has never been seen before, and that is the source of his supernatural powers."

Samuel stepped closer to him, but looked at the jury as he asked, "*Possession*, Father?"

"Yes... his body is taken over by a supernatural force which takes complete control of him."

"Can you explain this in more detail, please?"

"When a person is possessed, a supernatural force, or to put it in simpler terms, another spirit takes control of their body. The person's consciousness disappears, and the force that possesses him takes control. The human form continues to be basically the same, but the person is different."

"In other words, Father, it's as if we emptied out a bottle, and filled it with different liquid. The bottle would still be the same, but its contents would be different."

"Yes, that's one way to put it..."

"Father, do you believe that a person who is possessed should be considered responsible for his actions?"

"Objection, Your Honor, the witness is a priest, not a psychiatrist," Stanley said calmly from his seat.

Samuel said to the judge, "Your Honor, the witness is an expert in exorcisms. Who better than him would know if the defendant is faking a temporary insanity defense, or if he's actually possessed?"

"Your Honor, the witness is way out of his area of expertise," Stanley said, rising to his feet.

"Your Honor, the witness's area of expertise is exorcism, he has examined the defendant and stayed with him for several nights, and he has been the only person who has been able to keep him from escaping; I think his opinion is of the utmost relevance."

"Objection overruled, the witness will answer the question," the judge said flatly.

"Thank you, Your Honor," Samuel said.

Father Damian paused, putting his thoughts in order, and then replied, "Of course not. A person who is possessed goes through a radical transformation, in a spiritual as well as a psychological sense. We have seen the videos, and I am sure that all of you, just like me, know that when this force takes control of Thomas, he is no longer a normal person. Whoever denies it, simply doesn't want to see the truth..."

Samuel paced to the center of the floor, and said in an even tone, "One more question, Father Damian. Do you believe that Thomas is capable of killing a person in such a brutal, sadistic manner, as the state alleges?"

"No, Thomas is a good boy," the priest responded, looking over to the defense table with a smile.

Thomas blinked, looking up to gratefully meet his gaze.

"Thomas wouldn't hurt anybody," Father Damian concluded, as Samuel turned to face the prosecutor, "Your witness."

Morgan stood up. Father Damian watched him slowly approach the witness box.

"Father, in all of your years as a priest, have you ever been involved in a case remotely like this one?"

"What are you really asking, Mr. Stanley?"

Morgan paced back and forth across the floor, setting his trap. "I mean, Father Damian, have you ever been involved in a case in which a person supposedly suffers from some kind of possession, and the person has been accused of having committed a series of murders."

"No, I have never been involved in a similar case."

"That is, you are trying to treat something that you have absolutely no prior experience treating."

Father Damian looked at him gravely, understanding exactly where this line of questioning was supposed to lead. Showing his annoyance, he responded, "If you want to put it that way, Mr. Stanley, you and I are in the same boat..."

The prosecutor shot him an angry look and continued, "Doesn't it strike you as odd, Father, that Patrick McKinney's blood was found on Thomas's pajamas, if he is supposedly innocent, as you maintain?"

"What about this case *isn't* odd, Mr. Stanley? But if you want me to answer your question, I would say that it isn't that strange to me, since we all know what happened. What we're trying to establish here is whether or not Thomas was aware of what he was doing."

The prosecutor was quiet for a moment, putting his hands in his pockets, considering his next move.

"A moment ago you said that he is possessed by some strange force, correct?"

"Yes, that's right."

"Can you explain for the court how a possessed person could be a serial killer?" Stanley turned to face the rows of spectators. In a loud, sarcastic tone he said, "What, or who, possesses him, Father? Could it be John Wayne Gacy, Richard Ramirez, or Ted Bundy, perhaps?"

Father Damian was angry. Stanley's sarcasm was pushing him to his limits. Observing the priest closely, Judge Fieldmore was afraid that he was going to tell everything, and catching his eye, he subtly shook his head, warning him against this. Father Damian looked at Samuel and saw that he, too, seemed to implore him with his gaze not to say too much.

"What's affecting Thomas is..." he began, taking a deep breath to calm down. "It's more than a supernatural phenomenon; it's a sort of possession never seen before in the history of the Catholic Church. His extraordinary powers, and the way he kills his victims, are totally unprecedented."

Stanley paced across the floor as Father Damian spoke. He waited for the right moment to interject, "If he really is possessed, Father, this whole problem could be cleared up with a simple exorcism, right?" Stanley asked, standing still.

"It's not that simple."

Stanley held out his arms. "Why not? As far as I understand, possessing spirits are always cast out by exorcism. But, you allege that in this particular case that method would not work. So, what kind of possession are we dealing with here, Father?"

"Like I said, Mr. Stanley, this is a totally unique case, and it must be treated as such. A course of action must be carefully studied first, and the person who is possessed must be closely observed also. In order to successfully break the possession's curse, first you must have religious faith, and then there must be a clear understanding of what you're up against."

"Have *faith?*" Stanley paced towards the jury and then whirled around quickly to face the witness, "Thomas Santiago has brutally murdered twenty people over the past two-and-a-half years, including women and children! And you're asking us to leave it all up to faith? Doesn't that sound ridiculous to you? Do you hear what you're saying?"

Father Damian couldn't hold in his anger for another second. His eyes shone and his breathing sped up.

"You ask people to sit up here to be interrogated, you ask them to put their hand on a Bible and to swear to tell the truth and nothing but the truth... so help you God?; whose very existence, of course, cannot be proven in a court of law!"

Father Damian looked at the judge and the jury. He took a deep breath and continued,

"You don't believe in God; we, religious people believe in Him, because we live according to His laws. You only use God to enforce your earthly laws."

Then he fixed his gaze on Stanley. "And don't you dare have the nerve to ask me if I actually believe what I'm saying!"

The entire courtroom was silent. Stanley was momentarily speechless, and just stared back at Father Damian, as everyone waited to hear what his next question would be.

"Let me ask you a question, Mr. Stanley," Father Damian continued. "Two thousand years ago, a man who dared to call himself the Son of God was called before the court and sentenced to death, like the lowest kind of criminal. They beat him, they whipped him, and they crucified him in front of everyone. Two thousand years later, a man could commit the same "crime" and everybody would put a hand on his shoulder and just say, yeah, you're right, sure you are, and that would be the end of it... What is it that we've lost over the past two thousand years, Mr. Stanley? Our guilt in the eyes of the law, or our own ignorance?"

Stanley was still speechless. Father Damian crossed his legs and went on, "What about this other case? Thousands of years ago, a man came into town saying that he had seen a burning bush on a mountaintop, and that he had heard the voice of God. The voice told him to go liberate his people, who were enslaved by the most powerful army of that time. And do you know what God gave him to defend himself against that army? A stick..."

Stanley crossed his arms in silence, and let the priest continue.

"I'm sure that if I walked into any psychiatrist's office today and told him the same story, he would say I was suffering from schizophrenia or some kind of paranoid delusion. But, thousands of years ago, these were the great miracles of God..."

Father Damian sighed and leaned forward, clasping his hands over the wooden railing of the witness box. He looked out into the crowd for Dr. Marcus, and concluded, "The bridge between faith and madness is quite short, Mr. Stanley. There have been many men in the past who have had visions and heard voices in their heads. Some lost their way and descended into madness, while others had faith and became some of the greatest men in history."

The courtroom was silent, everyone was totally still. Father Damian's words had resonated powerfully in the hearts of everyone present.

"The foundations of faith rest on psychological and emotional factors, which have little or nothing to do with logic, probability, or evidence. This is, no doubt, faith's greatest weakness, while at the same time, undoubtedly, its greatest strength."

Father Damian turned to look at the judge.

"Your Honor, if you'll allow me, I would like to leave now..."

"Does the prosecution have any further questions for this witness?"

Stanley simply shook his head. Father Damian stood, and with all astonished eyes on him, he slowly walked up the aisle and out of the courtroom. The judge banged his gavel and broke the heavy silence in the air.

"Court will recess until the day after tomorrow, when both sides will present their closing statements. This court is adjourned."

E Butte Av.

81

ARIZONA STATE PRISON
1305 EAST BUTTE AVENUE
FLORENCE, ARIZONA

"Father Damian!" Thomas exclaimed, clearly thrilled to see him.

"How are you, my son?" the priest asked, smiling broadly, as one of the soldiers patted him down.

"I'm good... How are you feeling?"

"Very well," he said, stepping into the cell as Thomas threw himself into his arms.

Thomas rested his head on Father Damian's shoulder, and squeezing him tightly, he said, "I'm so sorry, Father. You have to know that I would never, ever hurt you on purpose..."

"I already told you not to worry about it, it's not your fault." Father Damian tenderly stroked his hair. He observed that they had put a television in his cell, and grinning, he said, "I see they're treating you a little better these days..."

"Oh, that! The TV... Samuel convinced them that it was bad to leave me alone all the time with nothing to do, because I would just end up sleeping more, and since the soldiers aren't allowed to talk to me, they decided to give me a TV so that I could entertain myself..."

Father Damian studied the boy, and could tell that he was worrying about something. He gently lifted his chin to make eye contact, and said,

"What's troubling you?"

"What's going to happen to me now, Father?"

"I don't know, child. They just had a meeting about it, and they're supposed to let me know what they decided later today... But don't worry: everything seems to be going well, they have to listen to me, they don't have any other choice..."

1st Avenue

3rd Avenue

W. Jefferson St.

82

MARICOPA COUNTY SUPERIOR COURT
201 WEST JEFFERSON STREET
PHOENIX, ARIZONA

"All rise!" the court officer said loudly.

Judge Fieldmore entered through the door at the back of the courtroom behind the bench and as soon as he had taken his seat he said, "Mr. Stanley, you may begin your closing statement."

Stanley stood. He was wearing a well-tailored, expensive black suit with a bright red tie with little stars on it. He walked to the center of the floor and began, "Ladies and gentlemen of the jury: we are dealing with one of the most extraordinary court cases ever seen in this country's entire history..." He stepped closer to the jury box, and took a moment to look at each one of them in turn.

"And the outcome of this incredible story will be in your hands."

He turned and pointed to Thomas:

"Thomas Santiago killed seventeen people before he was captured, and four more after the start of this trial. And what is the defense's argument? 'Temporary insanity'. My God! According to our legal system, "*In order for a person to be declared innocent by reason of temporary insanity, it must be proven beyond a doubt that he was not aware of his actions at the moment of the crime.*"

He quickly strode towards Thomas and said, raising his voice, "Do you believe that someone who killed more than twenty people, and who deliberately wrote on the walls in his victims' own blood, in a shockingly heinous act, did not know what he was doing?"

He took a few steps back and looked out at the spectators in the packed courtroom. He saw how everyone's eyes followed him around the room, and the television cameras focused on his face. This was his shining moment: the time had come to fire off everything in his arsenal against Thomas. He drew in a deep breath and continued, "Of course he was. There is one thing that I am completely, absolutely sure of, ladies and gentlemen, and that is that Thomas Santiago meets all of the requirements of a serial killer; his methodology of murder clearly demonstrates his sadism and shocking cruelty."

Stanley turned to face the jury:

"Don't be fooled by his childlike, innocent-looking face. We all saw with our own eyes how he can transform himself into a wild beast, with no compassion whatsoever, ruthlessly killing his victims."

He looked down and let out a long breath.

"In our society, there are certain things that can completely outrage the public, to the point where people behave erratically and decide to take the law into their own hands. Unfortunately, one of those things is when a killer manages to avoid punishment. When that occurs, the people feel mocked and abused by our justice system..."

He held a hand out toward the audience and concluded, "Don't give the people such a bitter pill to swallow, don't let this killer make a mockery of our courts. Give our citizens the peace of mind that comes from knowing that there is at least one thing in this country that they can trust, that will not let them down: the good common sense of our justice system. Thank you."

"Ladies and gentlemen, I think that for the first time since this trial began, I actually agree with Mr. Morgan," Samuel said, standing.

"Without doubt, this is the biggest trial in United States' history. I believe that the whole country hasn't been so wrapped up in a trial since the slaves from onboard the ship Amistad set foot on our beaches in 1844." Samuel paced to the center of the floor, and looking out at the hundreds of spectators, he held his hand out and continued, "America is a country with an ideology. Through good and bad times, at times of war and times of peace, the dream upon which this country was founded on has remained intact. America is a place where justice rules, where the people are born with inalienable rights that not even a king can take away."

Samuel put his right hand in his pocket and faced the jury:

"In 1954, when the state of Maryland confronted Durhan and the doors of our courthouses were thrown open to psychologists and psychiatrists, the court ruled *"a person cannot be found guilty if it can be proven that his actions were the product of a mental illness or disturbance."*

He turned and gestured towards Thomas, adding,

"We've all seen the videos which clearly show how that mysterious presence takes control of Thomas Santiago, transforming him into a very different being."

Samuel took a few steps towards the jury and, resting his hands on the railing of the jury box, he said, "If that is not a mental disturbance, then I don't know what you'd call it... And what's more, I would even swear that you all agree with me. We listened to all the expert doctors and psychiatrists who were called to testify in this courtroom, and not even one of them could explain what is happening to Thomas."

Samuel opened his arms and looking closely at the jury members asked, "Isn't that a clear indication that what he is experiencing is anything but normal?"

He took a deep breath, and he calmly explained, "You also heard from Father Damian Santos, who offered his own opinion of what is happening to my client, as a man of the cloth. No one can deny that he is the only person who has presented a logical explanation. But even though it's all very hard to believe, and even though this nightmare seems to have no end in sight, we can't forget that justice is based on evidence, and facts. And we have had all the evidence we need and more to convince ourselves that, from a strictly rational standpoint, Thomas Santiago simply could not have killed some of the victims. It is not possible that in such a short time frame, according to the medical examiner's report on the times of death, Thomas could have traveled from the reservations in Ship Rock or Kayenta and still gotten on the bus to go to school the following morning."

Samuel went back to his table and picked up a packet of folders, so that everyone could see them. He turned to the jury and said, "These are the police reports on each of the victims, and not one of them contains the slightest clue on who the actual killer could be..."

He set the folders back down on the table and walked back toward the jury:

"If we were to base this case on the videos from the surveillance cameras, no reasonable person would conclude that the thing we saw kill Patrick McKinney was a human being."

He paced back to the center of the floor, and putting a hand in his pocket, he pointed with the other towards Thomas. He passionately declared, "Don't condemn this poor boy to a life spent behind bars! Give him the opportunity to get the help that he needs to get well! No one is guilty of acting against his own will, and much less when the force that is compelling him is something beyond human."

The courtroom was silent, as Samuel walked back to his table and sat down. Several of the jury members seemed deep in thought. Some of the spectators bowed their heads, trying to find within themselves the faith to accept the truth behind everything that had happened.

"Now the members of the jury will begin deliberations and will reach a verdict," the judge announced, leaning over the microphone.

The members of the jury stood and filed out of the room in an orderly line. The court officer ordered everyone to rise, and they remained standing as the judge left the courtroom. Then all the journalists dashed out of the room to file their reports, and Thomas was escorted out of the courtroom by six guards, as usual, who took him to the holding cell.

83

Several hours had passed, and the jury had still not come out.

"How much longer will it be until they have a verdict?" Thomas asked.

"It could take an hour, a day, or two... who knows?" Samuel replied, leaning against the cell bars.

"We just need to be patient, and pray that everything turns out alright," Father Damian added.

"What do you think's gonna happen?" Thomas asked Samuel, looking deeply worried.

"I honestly don't know; we've done everything we could to try and prove your innocence. Owens told us not to worry, that he would take care of everything."

"What's going to happen to me if they say I'm guilty?"

"I don't know; we'd have to appeal the verdict, and ask the Supreme Court to have another trial..."

"That wouldn't do any good, Samuel," Father Damian said, "The reason they want to keep him in jail isn't a matter of whether he's guilty or innocent; it's simply because they understand the danger he represents for everyone; but they absolutely know that Thomas is innocent..."

84

M. J. A. ATTORNEYS AT LAW
BANK OF AMERICA TOWER
201 EAST WASHINGTON STREET
PHOENIX, ARIZONA

The next day Samuel was in his office with Oliver and Father Damian. Twenty hours had passed, and the jury still had not reached a verdict.

"This is unbearable," Samuel said, staring out the window. "Each minute that goes by without knowing anything is like an hour of torture."

"The more time they take, the better it is for us. That means they still disagree," Oliver observed calmly from his chair, as he casually turned a newspaper's pages.

"How did Thomas seem when he got up this morning, Father?" Samuel asked.

"Not very well. He couldn't sleep, he was so worried about what might happen..."

"Just like the rest of us," Oliver added.

Suddenly, Marcos burst into the office and said excitedly, "Samuel, the courthouse called—they've reached a verdict!"

They all started to rush out. Samuel grabbed his briefcase as Marcos added, "The judge wants to see you in his chambers first..."

Samuel looked at Oliver and Father Damian, surprised. Oliver could see the fear in his eyes and said, "Don't jump to conclusions, let's wait and see what he has to say..."

S 1st Avenue

S 3rd Avenue

W. Jefferson St.

85

MARICOPA COUNTY SUPERIOR COURT
JUDGE FIELDMORE'S CHAMBERS
201 WEST JEFFERSON STREET
PHOENIX, ARIZONA

The secretary opened the door and showed them in.

Samuel noted right away that the judge looked very worried. Now there was a newcomer in the group: the bishop was sitting next to the governor. Both priests walked over to him and leaned over to kiss his ring. Owens was standing, waiting for the others to sit down.

"Come on in," Owens said, waiting for Samuel and the others to get settled. Then he began, "Now that we're all here, I'll tell you what the plan is. The verdict will not be announced until tomorrow, which should give us enough time to prepare..."

"Prepare for what?" Judge Fieldmore said.

"At this moment, five hundred soldiers are on their way here. The police and the National Guard will patrol the streets in case any violent protests break out. The entire state will be under very tight security by six o'clock tomorrow morning."

Owens leaned over the table and finished, "Once the verdict has been announced, Thomas will be transported to a secret location, along with Father Damian and Dr. Marcus. I will inform you of the rest of the plan after that..."

"And what about His Excellency, and the message of prayer to the community?" Father Damian asked.

The Bishop looked up, startled, and said, "What can I say about all this?"

"We'll think of something, Monsignor," Father Damian assured him.

"At eight o'clock tonight, there will be a press conference, and the governor will address the people. We will also have the Bishop deliver a message at that time. As for the rest of you, we'll see you in court tomorrow," Owens abruptly concluded.

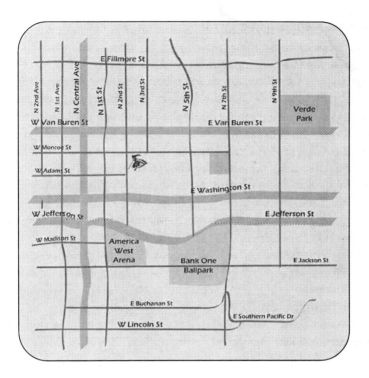

86

THE HYATT HOTEL
122 NORTH SECOND STREET
PHOENIX, ARIZONA

At 7:45 that evening, Dr. Marcus and Dr. Phillips got together to watch the governor's speech on television in the hotel bar.

"Did you talk to Owens yet?" Phillips asked.

"No, he said he would call me later."

Dr. Marcus stirred the ice around in his drink with his finger, lost in thought.

"Are you okay?" Dr. Phillips asked, concerned.

"You know something? When I started med school, I thought human behavior was predictable, or at least it could be diagnosed. But this case has made me change my mind... I have to tell you, it's been quite a shock to me..." Marcus finished, as he took a long sip of his drink. "But I still believe that psychiatry is a great science."

Dr. Marcus looked through the window to the street, and it seemed as if everything was moving in slow motion. He felt as if his rational mind and his intuition were battling it out about what course of action to take.

"I've always been impressed by the faith people have in certain things, by the physical effects it can have on their bodies that some studies have shown, but this is way beyond any scientific study..."

"Marcus, what we have here is nothing more than a mental disturbance that is somehow tied to religious beliefs. Just because we haven't found the precise explanation for what is happening to that boy yet, doesn't mean that there isn't one..."

"No, Phillips. This is something more—this case is totally unique, there's never been anything like it, ever..."

Dr. Phillips looked at him intently and then smiled, "You're not going to tell me that now all of a sudden you've found religion?"

Dr. Marcus looked at him seriously, "Wasn't it you who told me that Plato had said "*It is impossible to prove or disprove the existence of the gods?*"

"Yes, but that doesn't mean that this whole situation is some kind of Apocalypse..."

Dr. Phillips looked up at one of the televisions high on the wall behind the bar, and saw that the governor was about to start her speech. He said to the bartender, "Can you turn it up, please?"

"I know that these last few months have been very tense for us all," he heard the governor say into the microphone at the podium. "But we must believe that the authorities are doing everything within their power to manage the situation as professionally as possible."

The governor looked down at the podium to read from the paper in front of her. Her anxious expression and the dark circles under her eyes, visible despite her make-up, indicated the enormous amount of stress she was under.

"Let me assure you that we are reaching the end of what has been a very dark chapter in our state's history. We must not lose our heads: we must behave in a civilized manner, and tomorrow, when the verdict is announced, we can all go home with nothing to fear.

This is an extremely delicate situation, and we need your help."

She paused and took a deep breath.

"Our armed forces have been mobilized, to ensure that everything goes smoothly and to prevent any unforeseen disturbances."

She made a great effort to maintain her normally unflappable composure, but it was no use. She was obviously at her wit's end.

"Now I will leave you with His Excellency the Bishop, who has an extremely important message for us all."

She rushed from the podium right out of the room, in spite of a barrage of questions from the reporters.

The bishop slowly stepped behind the podium, and set his speech down in front of him. He put on his reading glasses and began,

"This is a pivotal moment in time when the brotherhood of all peoples must prevail, and we must stand together, united, no matter what our religion. The time has come for us to raise up our voices as one, and pray to God to help us, to free us from this grave threat."

He looked directly into the camera and continued, "The time has come for us to face this problem as God's children, to pray together, to find the right path to follow, together. Those of you who are faithful Catholics, please follow our instructions. For those who are not, please, do what you feel is right in your heart."

The bishop paused and turned the page of his speech.

"Tomorrow evening at seven, before sunset, every believer must light a candle in a window of their home, as a signal before God that we seek His enlightenment. Every family will pray together, for God's help at this terrible time. We will do this for the next seven nights, as a penitence, and as supplication. All of the churches of all faiths will be open until very late at night, for those who would like to pray there.

"We ask our brothers and sisters, the Buddhists, the Protestants, Evangelicals, Mormons, Hindus, Muslims, Jews, Sikhs, people of all faiths to join our fight against this curse that is here amongst us..."

1st Avenue · 3rd Avenue · W. Jefferson St.

87

MARICOPA COUNTY SUPERIOR COURT
201 WEST JEFFERSON STREET
PHOENIX, ARIZONA

The streets were overflowing with people. Barricades had been erected from First Street all the way to Fifth Avenue to prevent any vehicles from getting through. There were armed soldiers stationed at every corner.

A huge crowd had gathered outside the courthouse, since only authorized personnel were permitted inside the courtroom for security reasons.

At nine o'clock in the morning, Judge Fieldmore stepped into the courtroom.

"All rise!" the court officer intoned.

The judge took his seat and, looking out at those present, he said, "You may be seated."

Father Damian was sitting directly behind Thomas and Samuel, along with Mariela and Juan Manuel. On the other side, Dr. Marcus, Dr. Phillips, and Owens were behind the prosecutor's table.

"Show the members of the jury in, please," the judge said to the officer.

The jury filed in, in reverse order from when they had last exited the courtroom. After taking their seats, Judge Fieldmore looked at them sternly and asked, "Has the jury reached a verdict?"

"Yes, Your Honor," said a man at the far left of the jury box, standing.

The officer stepped over to the jury foreman and took a piece of paper from him, and handed it to the judge.

Judge Fieldmore put on his reading glasses, read the paper to himself, and looked up at the defendant. Thomas and Samuel stood.

The courtroom was charged with suspense, everyone seemed to hold their breath.

"Thomas Santiago," the judge said in a firm, sonorous tone, "For the count of murder in the first degree, the state of Arizona finds you..."

He paused and swallowed quickly before pronouncing, "Not Guilty."

The courtroom erupted, most everyone seemed shocked and infuriated by the verdict. Sensing the commotion, the soldiers readied their weapons. Stanley looked down, shaking his head in protest.

Samuel felt as if he had been punched in the chest: his eyes filled with tears, he hugged Thomas and waited for the rest of the verdict.

The judge took off his glasses and rested them on the podium. Then he picked up his gavel and pounded it several times, demanding order.

He looked at Thomas again and continued, "But because of your condition and the danger that you represent to the community, you are hereby ordered to remain in State custody, in a location that has been specially prepared, until a way to control your condition has been found."

The judge banged with his gavel one more time and said,

"Court adjourned."

The reporters started to rush out of the room, they all wanted to be the first to report the story.

Father Damian hugged Thomas:

"Don't be afraid. From now on, everything is in God's hands."

The soldiers that had escorted Thomas into the courtroom now surrounded him, and once he was securely handcuffed and shackled, they ordered him to walk out.

"What's going on?" Mariela frantically asked Samuel, as she watched him being taken from the room.

"Samuel!" Thomas shouted, frightened and beginning to cry.

"Don't be afraid, I'll see you in one minute!" Samuel yelled back, as his client disappeared through the door.

"Samuel! What's going on? They just said that he was innocent... Why are they taking him?" Mariela cried hysterically.

"Yes, he is innocent, I know, but the judge said that he has to remain in the State's custody until a solution to this problem is found..."

"What does that mean? They found him innocent, but he still has to stay in jail?" Juan Manuel asked.

"You have to understand they can't just release Thomas, when the whole world knows what's going on with him," Samuel replied, giving Mariela a hug.

"Nana, you know that I love you just like my own mother, I know this is very, very hard for you—but you have to trust me..."

Father Damian said, "Don't worry, ma'am, from now on your grandson will be in very good hands..."

"Now we'll see what they tell us at the next meeting..." Samuel sighed wearily.

88

Samuel and father Damian went to the holding cell, and found Thomas sitting there staring down at the floor, deeply sad.

"Come on, don't be like that, everything's going to be alright now," Father Damian said, trying to cheer the boy up.

"You have to remain in custody for just a little while longer, but after that, everything will be fine," Samuel added, seeing that Thomas wasn't reacting at all and seemed not to even have heard them.

Father Damian sat next to him and ruffled his hair, saying, "Things are going to change. They have promised me that they will do as I say, and when that happens, you'll see how different things will be."

Thomas rested his head against Father Damian's chest and began to sob uncontrollably. The priest looked at Samuel, who crossed his arms and shook his head sadly as he looked on.

89

Santiago Family Residence
6610 North 61st Avenue
Glendale, Arizona

"Hello! Come on in," Mariela opened the door and greeted Samuel and Father Damian.

"Nana, we have to talk to you," Samuel said as soon as he had sat down in the living room.

"Who is it, Mom?" Juan Manuel asked, coming into the room.

"It's Father Damian and Samuel..."

"What's going on?" Juan Manuel sensed that they had bad news.

"I got a call from the governor and the people from Washington who are overseeing Thomas's case, and they have a proposal for us..."

"What kind of proposal?" Mariela asked nervously.

"We don't know yet..."

Seething, Juan Manuel looked at them both and said, "What more do they want with him? They've got him locked up even though he's innocent; his life has already been destroyed... What do they want now, our permission to kill him?"

"Of course not, my son," Father Damian said, "but we have to listen to what they have to say. I don't think you really want to spend the rest of your lives like this, with guards outside your house, afraid that a mob is going to burn your house down with you in it, every time Thomas escapes and someone else is killed..."

Mariela looked at Juan Manuel, and then both bowed their heads and were silent. They knew that Father Damian was right.

"Nana, we have to keep in mind the danger Thomas poses, and as long as he suffers from this condition they'll never let him go free."

She kept staring down at the floor, her eyes welling with tears.

"What do you think we should do, Father Damian?" Juan Manuel asked, with an arm around his grandmother.

"Like Samuel said, first of all, we have to hear what they propose, and we can decide what to do from there."

"Nana, you know that I wouldn't let anybody hurt Thomas," Samuel said, stepping over to her and kissing her forehead.

She hugged him tightly and started to cry.

90

The Governor's Office
1700 West Washington Street
Phoenix, Arizona

They anxiously waited for Owens to arrive at the governor's office. The governor nervously paced across the floor, trying to calm down. She looked at the clock on the wall and asked her assistant, "What the hell is taking him so long?"

"I don't know, he asked me to tell everyone to be sure to be on time," he said, looking out the window to see if his car was coming.

"It's six o'clock already, soon the sun will start to set," Father Damian observed, crossing his arms.

"Sorry I'm late," Owens apologized as he quickly walked into the office, along with a group of doctors and technicians from Washington. "There were several last-minute changes."

Owens turned to Samuel and Father Damian and said, "This is our proposal: get Thomas out of the country; Father Damian and Dr. Marcus will be responsible for taking care of him and studying methods for controlling him..."

"Where will you take him? What about his family?" Samuel asked, holding his arms out.

"The President has offered them a new life in Puerto Rico, with new identities. His grandmother can have a job at the post office in a little town, and there is a position at the church for his older brother, as an assistant of the local priest."

Samuel looked at Father Damian to try and gauge his reaction, but he just blinked a few times and didn't say anything.

"Puerto Rico is the only place that we can send him; all the other countries have refused to assist us in this matter."

Samuel was quiet, as a jumble of thoughts ran through his mind all at once.

"You have to decide tonight," Owens pressed.

"Why so fast?" Samuel said quickly.

"Because I think Father Damian's right, we need to get him out of here as soon as we possibly can."

"We have to do something, the entire city is about to blow up. We've already had a few protests break out, and several people have been injured," the governor added.

"We will increase security in those areas and we will put a curfew into effect for eight o'clock tonight," Owens said.

"I'll go talk to Thomas's grandmother and I'll have an answer for you later today," Samuel said, as he hurried out of the office.

N 61st Avenue

W Maryland Av

91

SANTIAGO FAMILY RESIDENCE
6610 NORTH 61ST AVENUE
GLENDALE, ARIZONA

It was eight o'clock at night; Samuel had gone to see Mariela and Juan Manuel. The streets were totally deserted. The only vehicles driving around were slow-moving military patrols.

"Puerto Rico?" Juan Manuel repeated after Samuel had told them the plan.

"I haven't been on the island in over fourteen years," Mariela murmured, surprised, bowing her head.

"You are from Puerto Rico; it would be like going home," Samuel said, looking at them both.

Mariela stood and started to pace around the room. She crossed her arms and said, "I haven't been back to the island since my daughter died. My whole life is here now, that's why I brought the boys here, to get as far away from all that as possible... And now they want me to go back?"

"We have to give them an answer tonight," Samuel said, stepping toward her.

"What?" exclaimed Juan Manuel.

"I know they're trying to pressure us into taking their offer, but that doesn't mean that we have to accept it," Samuel explained.

E Turquoise Av

92

ESCOBAR FAMILY RESIDENCE
6889 EAST TURQUOISE AVENUE
SCOTTSDALE, ARIZONA

It was eleven-thirty at night. Samuel watched the news as he held his baby daughter in his arms. The reporter on TV was in a helicopter, and pointed down: "As you can see, the streets are completely empty, and lights from candles can be seen at the front doors of many homes across the city. All of the churches are packed with people who have gathered there, following the Bishop's instructions. From here, it looks like a blanket of stars has covered the whole city, it's just beautiful..."

Just then Samuel's cell phone rang. Startled, he picked it up.
"Hello?"

"Samuel, it's Whitefield."

"What's up?"

"I think you'd better come down to the prison."

"What happened, did Thomas escape again?"

"No, but even if you see it with your own eyes, you're not going to believe what's going on..."

E Butte Av.

93

Arizona State Prison
1305 East Butte Avenue
Florence, Arizona

Samuel got to the prison as fast as he could.

He felt like his heart would burst out of his chest when he saw what was happening: Father Damian was kneeling down before the angel, floating above the bed in the cell, within a huge sphere of radiant light.

"Oh my God! It's happening again," Samuel exclaimed, as he pressed against the glass to see.

"Father Damian has been on his knees, praying, for almost two solid hours," Dr. Marcus said, standing behind Samuel.

Myrick, the security engineer, approached the group watching through the Plexiglas. Crossing his arms he explained, "We installed a sensor in his cell to detect any changes in temperature or light. At ten forty-three, we heard the alarm go off. We ran to see what was going on, and we found Father Damian just like this. Since then we've just been waiting..."

Everyone was quiet as they looked through the glass at Father Damian, who was praying fervently.

"Did you speak to the boy's family?" said Owens, stepping next to Samuel.

"Yes, but we haven't decided yet..."

"Come on, Mr. Escobar! Aren't you seeing what's going on here?" Owens exploded, furious.

Dr. Marcus put his hand on Samuel's shoulder, and gesturing toward Thomas he said, "Please, convince them, Mr. Escobar; we can't go on living in this state of terror. How long do you think Father Damian can really hold him back?"

Samuel looked at the priest, kneeling on the floor, praying intently, and up at Thomas, floating in the air, unconscious. Then he reached into his jacket pocket and took out his cell phone. He dialed a number and waited:

"Nana, we have to talk..."

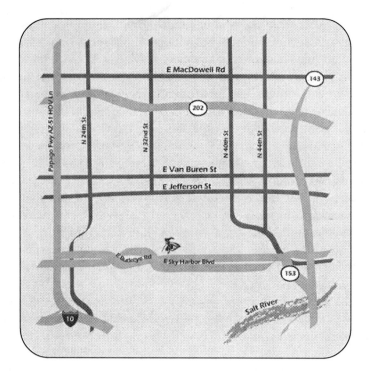

94

PHOENIX AIRPORT
3400 EAST SKYHARBOR BOULEVARD
PHOENIX, ARIZONA

The next night at nine o'clock, a private jet touched down at the Phoenix airport. A black Chevrolet SUV drove up and parked next to it, and Samuel, Mariela, and Juan Manuel got out of the vehicle.

"Samuel, promise me you'll have all our things sent," Mariela said as she stepped out of the car.

"Yes, Nana, don't worry, I'll take care of it," he said, giving her a hug.

"Tell them to be very careful with the statue of the Virgin in the living room, it's very fragile..."

Samuel turned to Juan Manuel and hugged him tightly, "Take good care of her, please..."

"Don't forget she's my mom too," Juan Manuel smiled.

Just then a police escort arrived. Two officers on motorcycles and four police cars surrounded a black Lincoln Navigator. The officers on motorcycle stopped beside the plane, and two cars drove up close to either side of the portable stairway.

Owens got out first, followed by Dr. Phillips. Samuel stepped toward them, expecting to see Thomas get out next, but Owens gestured to the other car.

Father Damian and Dr. Marcus got out of the second car, accompanying Thomas, with his hands handcuffed behind his back. Owens walked up to Thomas and took a set of keys out of his pocket. He unlocked the handcuffs and took them off.

Thomas felt as if the ground had suddenly opened up underneath his feet. The feeling of freedom coursed through his veins like a rushing river. He opened his eyes wide in wonder. He looked at Owens, who smiled and, nodding toward Mariela, said simply, "Go ahead."

Thomas took a few tentative steps, and as Mariela held out her arms he ran to rush into them.

"Thank you for everything, Father," Owens said, shaking the priest's hand. "Everything has been prepared just as you requested: your friend from Mexico will get there about an hour after you..."

"Thank you, Mr. Owens. We'll keep you informed about everything."

Father Damian turned and smiled sweetly at Samuel, who gave him a hug, his eyes welling with tears. He thanked him for all he had done, and asked that he look after Thomas and Mariela.

"Can I ask you something, Mr. Owens?" They both watched the plane taxi down the runway.

"What?"

"I'd like to know how you were able to tamper with the jury's verdict..."

Owens smiled slyly as the plane took off. He replied, "There's something you should remember, Mr. Escobar: we're all criminals, for something really small, or something serious—the only difference is that many of us just haven't been caught yet..."

As they walked back to their cars, he added, "There are some verdicts that are extremely important for the country's development or future. Those outcomes should be controlled by government officials; they can't be left in the hands of ordinary citizens..."

Owens opened his car door and turned to look at Samuel, "We discovered that several members of the jury had some dirty little secrets in their lives, or close relatives that were in some trouble with the law. Many of them had lied on their tax returns, so with a little bit of dramatic exaggeration, it wasn't that hard to convince them to do things our way..."

Samuel smiled wryly, noting how easy it was for the government to exert absolute control over so many things.

"Once my boss told me," Owens continued, climbing into the car and rolling down the window, "before sending me on a mission that didn't seem fair to me, that, often the fair path is not always the best path... because if God were one-hundred-percent fair, he would not have let the Devil torment Job, simply to prove to Satan that Job was faithful to Him. But it had to happen that way, so that the rest of us would learn the lesson."

Owens shook Samuel's hand through the car window and said goodbye.

Samuel looked up and saw the plane vanishing in the darkening night sky. He put his hands in his pockets and chuckled, shaking his head.

95

CHURCH SAN CARLOS DE BORROMERO AGUADILLA, PUERTO RICO

Two years later, in a small village in Puerto Rico, a group of people gathered around a television set in a bar to watch the news.

They listened intently as the reporter on the screen said, "Today's events here in Aguadilla, on the island of Puerto Rico, have been truly shocking. The discovery made by the police this morning at the church San Carlos de Borromeo in front of the town square has stunned and terrified the whole country. The priest of this small parish was found crucified on the wall, his body completely nude, right next to the statue of the crucified Jesus.

"Right above his head, a message was written on the wall, in his own blood, which read:

"In the name of the Father, the Son..."

About the author

Miguel Batista

"Dominican by birth, pitcher by profession, poet by vocation" sums up Miguel Batista's life in a nutshell. To really understand who he is, you have to dig a little deeper than his fame as a major-league baseball player, and get to know his human values. You have to immerse yourself in the thousands of pages he has penned as a poet and novelist, revealing his heartfelt passion for the written word.

Born on February 19, 1971 in Santo Domingo, Dominican Republic, in 1992 he made his major-league debut. He has been one of the greatest players in world baseball ever since.

In spite of his hectic schedule and precious little free time, Miguel wrote on scraps of paper and notebooks, in the dugout, on airplanes, wherever he happened to be. He wrote about his dreams, his doubts, his fears, his loves. It was 1999, and he never imagined that any of his writings might be published one day.

His first novel, *Two Hearts, One Destiny*, a love story he finished when he was only sixteen, has yet to be published, along with many other of his writings.

In 2000, Miguel joined the Arizona Diamondbacks, a team which would go on to win the World Series the following year. Then, he decided to publish his first book of poetry: *Feelings in Black and White*, a collection of impressions, photographs, and passions; a simple, yet complex volume, like life... With this book, Miguel became the first baseball player to ever have published a book of poetry. Critics and fans alike gave him the nickname "The Poet." A poet whose book is on sale at baseball stadiums, with profits going to the foundation that bears his name and helps children and elderly people in his native country. A poet on the page, and in life.

Besides playing in the Major Leagues, which implies a busy training and game schedule, Miguel set aside time to write, carry out radial campaigns and be a baseball analyst for ESPN World Series coverage, besides writing for ESPN's website, about the day-to-day experiences and routine of major-league baseball players. And he also devotes time to managing his charitable foundation and other personal pursuits.

Somehow in the middle of all of his other activities and challenges, he wrote *The Avenger of Blood*. After five years of intensive research, Miguel spent any free time he had over three years to write the novel. On its face, it is the story of a fourteen-year-old serial killer, but at its heart it explores the relationship of sin and justice, raising provocative questions about faith and religion, searching for hard answers.

This thriller includes elements of truth, but the author skillfully blurs the lines between reality and imagination.

As an athlete, Miguel Batista is at the top of his game. As a writer, his readers will show him the way on a journey that unfolds day by day for the pitcher-poet, a path he follows through his pen.

Printed in the United States
209865BV00001B/120/A